WAVE HUNTER

THE BOOK OF WATER

ALSO IN THIS SERIES

STAR DANCER

FIRE DREAMER

AND

STONE KEEPER (2012)

D1147554

1

Praise for Star Dancer

Daily Telegraph Family Book Club choice

Carousel: (Editor's Choice) An absorbing tale

Achuke: A book with genuine buzz

Books for Keeps: A many layered and satisfying tale

Praise for Fire Dreamer

Undercover: Rarely do sequels come as good as this

Teen Titles: A fantastically good read

Love Reading: Thrilling and crackling with magic

*

WAVE

HUNTER

The Book of Water

*

BETH WEBB

*

book three in the

Star Dancer Quartet

MHM
March Hamilton Media

www.marchhamilton.com

First published 2011 by
March Hamilton Media
28 Hamilton Road, Taunton, Somerset TA1 2ER UK
www.marchhamilton.com
ISBN 978-0-9568673-0-8

Printed and bound in the UK
by the MPG Books Group, Bodmin and King's Lynn

*

For John, my own Wave Hunter
who follows his magical dreams,

and for Hannah and Neil,
who like to cry over a book.

Acknowledgements

*Andy and Chloë for keeping me on track, and Bruce and Jenny for
helping me climb Cadair Idris – in the fog!*
also
*Anwen Williams and author Michael Slavin for their expertise on
Welsh and Irish history, culture and language, and Dr Alison Brookes of
Cirencester Museum. Jane McNulty for her wonderful editing, and all
the Kilvites for their creative input.*
*Thanks too to my wonderful friends, family and correspondents who
have all contributed time, knowledge and wisdom.*

*

* CONTENTS *

FINDING

LOOSING

GLOSSARY

*

* THE STORY SO FAR *

It is the end of the Iron Age and the Romans are sweeping across Britain, destroying and subduing all who stand against them. Tegen is the Star Dancer, a young druid girl with exceptional powers, born to turn aside an unknown evil.

However, the druid elders were looking for a warrior prince rather than a girl. Tegen battled with a cave demon to earn their trust and respect. Afterwards, she left her home on the Mendip hills to fulfill her destiny on Mona, the island of the Druids.

On the way she met Owein, a young ovate travelling in the opposite direction. He had a past he was trying to hide, and an uncle, Admidios, who was hell-bent on vengeance and power. Against her will, Tegen became entangled in Admidios's dark plots that began with the murder of Owein's foster father and ended with betrayal and the destruction of the stronghold at Sinodun.

Tegen has learned one important thing from Admidios: that she has the power to summon fire, and in those flames to divine the future.

As Sinodun burned, Tegen fled, once more determined to reach Mona. She had with her Epona – a white mare, Wolf – her dog, and Kieran – a boy she helped to rescue from slavery.

But Tegen has not left everything behind.

She is being watched. The demon is still alive... And it's following her.

*

SEARCHING

1   * THE HOWLING *

It was the morning after Samhain, in the valley of the river Tamesis. The dead had come from Tir na nÓg to visit the living the night before, leaving the bright autumn world crisscrossed with a multitude of spirit footprints.

To the east, beyond the hills and forests, the demon ached for its lost prey. Without the eyes, hands and feet of a human host, its non-corporeal shadow spread like a lost wave across the bare, frosted earth: sniffing, licking and groping for its quarry. But those tracks had faded with the morning dew.

The demon searched as light and dark came and went. The full moon waned to a nail pairing. Then, on the first winds of winter, the demon caught the faintest scent of *her*… But it was smothered by the dreaded stench of iron: earth-blood that had been heated and smelted, forged and turned to the will of the accursed smith-god. The ground still faintly trembled with a thudding, rhythmic beat, long gone. An image of a white horse formed in the demon's thoughts. Its prey had been riding.

The demon's emptiness and hatred tangled into a knot that swelled and grew, then burst into a low howl that keened across the land.

As the cry spread, it mingled with the ashy heart-wrenching sobs of those who had lost loved ones in fire and fighting.

Feeding on their anger and pain, the demon gathered strength. Its howl swelled and was answered, again and again...

*

Tegen shuddered as the eerie cries echoed across the chilly sweep of bare-topped hills. Her mud-coloured hound ran to her side, the wiry hairs bristling along his spine, his tail curled tightly between his legs. 'What's out there, eh Wolf?' she whispered, rubbing the back of his neck and trying not to shudder. She must not be afraid. The Goddess would defend her, whatever was coming.

The dog looked up at her with dark, soulful eyes, pulled back his lips and whimpered.

Tegen stood and sniffed the chilly air. No snow yet, so what were wolves doing in the open? She closed her fingers around her iron ring of protection. It was hot, warning of danger. She closed her eyes and listened for the wisdom of the Goddess in her mind. There were no words spoken, but she understood the Lady's warning.

It was not hungry animals keening in the wind. Something evil was on her trail. She hoped it wasn't the ghost of Admidios – Shadow Walker, worker of dark magic and servant of the demon that loathed her.

Tegen knew she could neither out-run nor hide from a spirit, but come nightfall, she'd sleep better with solid walls at her back and a roaring hearth-fire by her feet.

'Come, Epona,' she said, tugging at her horse's reins. 'Let's get over this ridge.' Quickening her pace she trudged up the chalky grass slope towards the top, where silhouetted against the skyline, a lanky boy was waiting for her.

'What's that noise?' he called out nervously.

Tegen hurried in his direction. She was unsure of what was after her, and didn't want to scare the boy. Kieran was in no danger; he wasn't the quarry. *She* was.

'Someone's hunting with dogs, I'd guess,' she lied cheerfully as she puffed up the last of the climb. 'How far is it to your Da's house?'

'Not far.' He waved his arm towards a bare-branched beech wood. 'Beyond them trees the track meets the drover's road, then it'll be downhill all the way to the Roman town of Corinium. Two more days, then we cross the Rearing River, then it's the same again to my Da's home in Y Fenni.'

The thought of a proper bed cheered Tegen, and the afternoon sun warmed her back, dispelling the memory of the howl. But she knew she hadn't dreamed it. It was a warning to hurry. For a quarter of a moon she and Kieran had been trudging westwards and a little north as Goban the smith had instructed her. Now the demon had found her trail, her need to get to the druids' island was even more urgent. 'Then how much further to Mona?' she asked.

Kieran shrugged his bag higher up his shoulder. 'Depends on the weather – and the Romans, of course.' He spat and pulled his cloak tighter. 'Take my advice and winter with Da and me.'

'Thank you, but I can't.'

Kieran tossed his head irritably. 'So we ain't good enough for you?'

'Don't be like that. You know I must help Mona's druids raise the Great Spell to oust the invaders.'

Kieran made the sign against the evil eye. 'Magic's dangerous stuff. Don't like it.'

'Without it, you'd still be a slave to Admidios, or your ghastly aunt Caja,' Tegen retorted. 'Or maybe burned to a cinder at Sinodun? Anyway, what if your Da doesn't want a hearth-guest?'

'Only trying to be friendly,' the boy grumbled as he strode along. 'You've got to stay somewhere. You've got no chance of getting through before the snows, see. Even with a horse.'

Tegen patted Epona's withers. 'She's not an ordinary horse. She'd take me to the Otherworld and back. If I press on, I'll get to Mona before the solstice.'

Kieran sneered. 'Believe me, I know what I'm talking about. After fourteen years of trailing up and down them roads after Ma and aunt on their salt cart, I've met all the flood-spirits and snow-ghasts that lurk along the way. You want to keep going north? Do what you like – but *I* ain't taking you. Not till spring, anyway.' Then he strode on in silence.

A loud honking overhead made Tegen look up. It was a skein of geese flying due west. Was it a warning not to go north? Or were they simply on their way somewhere? Not every bird is a portent, she reminded herself. I wish I could make wooden wings like the king in the story and soar away. If only! If we druids don't succeed, then our stories will soon be replaced with Roman lies.

As Kieran promised, the countryside beyond the trees was spread out before them like a tumbled blanket. Tegen paused to catch her breath and take in the view. To left and right, the chalky hills were steeply curved and wooded valleys opened to wide, fertile uplands, rich in pasture. From the arrow-straight roads and square, tiled-roof buildings along the way, she could tell the swaggering invaders had made themselves very comfortable.

'Do you know why the Romans hate us druids?' Tegen asked.

The boy shrugged disinterestedly.

'Because we inspire warriors to keep fighting.' She spread her hands wide. 'Without us, Britain would have fallen years ago.'

'Oh yeah?' Kieran sneered. 'My Da can wipe out a whole platoon of Romans just by sneezing.'

Tegen laughed, and the boy glowered at her. 'Don't mock. You never met him.'

Bowing her head contritely, she replied, 'It'll be an honour I'm looking forward to, but I really cannot stay.'

'Suit yourself,' Kieran shrugged. 'You'll be on your own.'

*

As night fell, they chose an empty sheepfold for their campsite. While Kieran was fetching water, Tegen groomed Epona and Wolf with teasels. As she worked, she whispered into their ears: 'Am I just being edgy, or is something following me? You both heard the howl, didn't you?'

Epona snorted through her nostrils and stamped.

'I thought so. I've got to know for certain whether it's that awful demon, or just some mischievous goblin.' Tegen turned Epona loose to graze while Wolf bounded after a rabbit in the dusk, then she searched the hedges for a heap of carefully chosen woods. 'Holly, bring me brightness and truth,' she prayed as she stacked the branches into a mound. 'Rowan, defend us from evil, but show me what is out there...' As she stretched out her hands, bright flames leaped and spat, and the bonfire roared.

At that moment, Kieran returned with a duck he had pinched from a farm that had refused them hospitality. He averted his gaze from the magical flames and sat a little too far away for comfort while he plucked, gutted and skewered the bird. Wolf was less worried Fire was fire and food was food. He swallowed the offal Kieran tossed to him, lay down in the warmth, and snored.

Tegen ignored her own rumbling stomach and the smell of cooking. She threw dried herbs onto the hot ashes and breathed their smoke until her head swam. She watched the flames dance and spit as the dripping duck fat sizzled. Deep in the red and gold embers, an image was forming, something that shifted and shimmered, but wouldn't quite take form...

It was ghastly. It was familiar. Tegen flinched and turned away. Fighting the chills that crept across her skin, she thought of Goban the smith who, now she came to think of it, had taught her more about fire magic than Admidios had done.

'*If you ever need an answer, look for it in fire,*' Goban had said. '*Remember, fire protects from magic, but it also leads you into the deepest part of the mysteries. Fire will lead you to your innermost soul, and bring you out into the world again... Be careful. Always use fire to drive shadows away, never to summon them.*'

Tegen hesitated. She was summoning shadows now. But I have to understand my enemy to know how to fight it, she told herself firmly.

She glanced under her lashes towards Kieran, his face red and black in the flickering firelight.

With a small gesture she wove a spirit shield around them both. Kieran shivered.

Concentrating on the flames, Tegen lowered her head and whispered:

Show me your form, dark or bright,
Spirit of hope, or shadow of blight!

The fire crackled and spat, sending sparks everywhere. Wolf jumped up howling. The roasting duck crashed into the ashes, and Kieran swore.

2   * THE ANSWER *

Then Tegen heard a faint *sniffing* coming from the darkness.
Brushing the embers from her skirt, she yelled at Kieran to wipe his nose.

'What for? I ain't got no cold,' he retorted, pulling the greasy, half-cooked meat from the ashes.

The faint *sniff-snuff* came closer.

With shaking legs, Tegen stood and called, 'Who's there?'

There was no reply. She pulled a rowan stick with a glowing tip from the remains of the fire and stepped into the darkness behind their bivouac. Nothing moved. Fog was beginning to close in. Not a twig cracked, not a dead leaf rustled.

Snuff-Sniff…

*

The demon had heard her summons… and had answered.

It could smell her: it was near enough to reach out and enfold her. But frustration and fury welled – it had no power to speak or touch or kill. Without a physical host, it was as ephemeral as the mist.

Once more it gathered raw anger and hopelessness out of the air and released it in a moan that made the earth shudder.

Tegen trembled. Now she knew for certain what was there.

'What's happening?' Kieran asked, his voice tight with fear.

She didn't reply.

'Get the flames going again, will you?' he demanded nervously. 'If there's wolves around we'll need a good burning to keep 'em away!'

Cold fog dripped as the greyness closed in.

The iron ring that warned of danger was burning Tegen's finger. Unmoving, she listened to the night.

'You all right?' Kieran asked nervously.

Tegen nodded and turned back to the crimson glow that had been their hearth. This time she dragged on every piece of wood she could find. Spreading her hands once more, she invoked the Goddess to bless the fire. 'Burn until it's light!' she commanded. Then, tugging her cloak around her, she lay down, closed her eyes and tried to ignore the chilling, misty fingers that stroked the back of her neck.

Her spirit had recognised the demon she had summoned. It had first come to her from the depths of the funeral caves by the Winter Seas when she was little more than a child. It was the ominous presence that had almost penetrated the fire circle when she had walked in Tir na nÓg. It had been the driving force in Admidios's black heart. She suspected it had forced Derowen's witch soul into a raven form.

Goban was right. Fire must never summon shadows, for although Tegen now knew what was pursuing her – she had also revealed where she was.

But what did it want?

3   *VISIONS*

That night, Tegen dreamed that a handsome woman was watching her through a silver circle edged by darkness.

'Star Dancer! *Star Dancer!*' she whispered urgently.

Tegen sat up and rubbed her eyes. The fire at her feet was low and crackling gently. Wolf was stretched out by Kieran's back, and they were both snoring. Everything seemed perfectly normal, yet she could see the speaker's face as clearly as if she were truly present. 'Are you a dream?' Tegen demanded.

From beyond the circle, the woman's knuckles whitened on a handle of twisted serpents with gleaming ruby eyes. 'I am not. I am quite real and you will soon come to me, Star Dancer – to my home over the waves. The Land of Heroes has need of you.'

'I can't. I am needed here,' Tegen replied. 'Who are you?'

The woman raised her chin. 'I am the High Queen of a great land. You must come when I command.'

Tegen shook her head. 'No. You are only a dream – one sent to distract me. The only place I am going is to the druids of Mona, to raise a spell to protect Britain.'

The image of the woman tightened her lips. 'It is too late. Your country is defeated. There is nothing more you can do. Now it is your destiny to help us.'

'You're wrong,' Tegen murmured, still unsure whether she was waking or sleeping. 'I was born to turn aside a great evil.'

'One that threatens us too…'

'That's why I must stay here and fight – so it spreads no further.'

The queen's face softened. 'But you are so young... Do you truly want a life of fighting, day after day?'

'I want...' Tegen began, but a sudden roar and stench of burning overwhelmed her. Heat and flames stung her skin. She was back at Sinodun, helplessly watching the stronghold burn. Then she shivered, as icy black water rushed around her in the flooding caves. People fleeing. Griff wading through the surge, a child in his arms. Darkness. Death. Romans. Blood.

...A demon.

Gasping, Tegen opened her eyes and stared into the night sky. The Watching Woman's stars sparkled in the frosty air. 'I am the Star Dancer, I want to save my people. That is who I am. It is all I want.'

In her heart she added, and I also want to be free of heart-ache and to dance for joy. But that will be another day.

As if she had spoken aloud, the woman's eyes crinkled. 'And so you shall. Our finest musicians will play for you. I will make you the happiest princess in my country.'

But Tegen was asleep once more.

The serpents' rubies winked accusingly. High Queen Étain of Tara in Ériu scowled back. 'I have done nothing wrong. I must help my people.'

As she passed her hand over the mirror's blackened surface, Étain memorised what she had scried: a young druid-girl with raven hair, but not an ordinary student of the arts who stuck rigidly to spells and potions; this one worked instinctively with raw magic plucked from the elements. She understood how to inhale the breath of inspiration, she could dream in the fires of Tir na nÓg and wield them without fear. She would not dread the spirits of Water as she trod the waves to come to her land.

But where *was* she? To see her was one thing, but to *find* her was another altogether. Étain needed a tangible thread to draw her home.

Placing her dark mirror in its box by her side, the queen tapped the clasp with a spell so none but she could open it. She would resist the urge to look into the darkness again, for she had also glimpsed spirits of Stone and Winter lurking in the conjured shadows. Such portents promised the death of someone close to her. 'Better not to know such things,' she sighed and raised her chin. 'I must be strong – for my Land. I will go to Tir na nÓg and find someone who knew her in life.'

A faint curtain of spiders' webs crackled on the queen's shoulders as she stepped from her little stone sanctuary into the sunlit autumn woods. Crouching on the warm stone step, she shivered. The journey she was about to make was perilous. She must go to the Otherworld in spirit alone, leaving her body behind. Étain shook her plait into corn-coloured waves, cut a fine strand and wound it tightly around the hilt of her dagger. Pricking her thumb, she let three drops of blood fall on the ground, then pierced the spot with her blade. 'Bring me back to this place,' she whispered.

4 * THE SHADOW OF TIR NA NÓG *

With a yawn and a stretch, she took the appearance of a brown tabby cat. As it spread its whiskers, the queen's soul slipped to Tir na nÓg, leaving the animal apparently dozing in the sun. Étain dared not leave her human form behind, for if it was found and touched or moved, her soul might never find its way home.

A cat would be left in peace – she hoped.

On the threshold of Tir na nÓg, Étain's spirit looked up and watched the real world shimmering like images on water above the head of a swimmer. The cloying dampness of death seeped into her mind. Dare she go on? This was the home of Gwynn ap Nudd, Lord and Gatekeeper of the Beyond, where souls awaited rebirth. If she could not find her way back, this would be where she must stay. Maybe forever.

Étain swallowed hard as she stepped into the hollow gloom.

Here there was neither heat nor cold, although what seemed to be a pale fire flickered to her left. Étain dared not look into the wan flames – that magic was too strong even for her.

She hovered, a mere flicker of light amongst the insubstantial, shifting hints and memories that beckoned her with ashy fingers, whispering, reminding her of love and regret. Étain pulled away from them all. It would be too easy to become lost and forget… I must concentrate, she told herself firmly. I must find someone who knew the Star Dancer in life – someone who will give me a spirit link to summon her.

Time did not exist as Étain wandered amongst the dead, looking into their soul-eyes, searching for a true memory of the one she sought. At last, in the furthest depths, amongst those cursed never to be reborn, she found a shrivelled hag, full of bitterness and resentment. This soul had known the Star Dancer since birth. Étain shuddered as tendrils of the old woman's spirit reached out and touched her. The crone's knowledge was suffused with fear and hatred, but the link was a true one and she could now bring the girl to Ériu's shore, like a fish on a line.

At that moment, a hopeless chill froze her to the spot. An even more malevolent presence was approaching. Étain shook herself free from the hag. She must flee, but she could not remember the way back.

Nothing pressed all around her, squeezing her soul with empty fingers. Unraveling her spirit.

Gasping for life, Étain leaped into the void. 'Save me Lugh!' she cried.

Darkness.

Then sunlight and the warm, soft body of the cat.

*

But as Étain slipped between the worlds, the old witch nudged a spell into the gap, keeping it ever so slightly ajar.

*

Drifting in the emptiness between life and death, the demon smelled the queen's spirit pass by and sensed her quest. Why, it

24

asked itself, had the Gatekeeper of the Otherworld allowed a living being to enter? His task was to keep the two worlds apart! And why was the intruder seeking the one it also hunted?

Deep magic must be at work...

The demon sniffed along the trail of footsteps until it came to the old crone's shade.

Sneering, the demon grabbed the remains of her heart.

'Tell me,' it whispered, 'Who was that woman? What did she want? Why was she asking about that girl?'

'I do not know, my Lord.'

'Useless vermin!' the demon roared. 'You let her go! Get out of my sight!'

'But look,' the spirit snivelled, pointing at the crack between the worlds, 'I, your servant Derowen, have made a gateway for you!'

Spitting icy fire, the demon stared into the hazy world beyond the gates of death. 'It's in the wrong place, imbecile! How am I going to find her *there*? That's another country altogether.' And it tossed the witch aside.

The demon didn't bother to follow the intruder. She tasted of power-lust well enough, but mixed with *integrity*. She was of no interest. It needed more than an unreliable slave to trap this prey.

The human girl was unnaturally canny: she had destroyed the stupid witch twice, once as a human, once as a raven. The Shadow Walker had been a better tool but a mere *boy* had killed him!

The demon sweated venom. It must make a move soon, but how? 'I will catch her myself. My soul can neither walk nor see in the living world without a body, so I will find a mindless creature that will allow me to possess it completely – one strong enough to withstand a few spells and a little poison.'

Ignoring the gateway, the demon oozed out of the earth near to where it had last seen its quarry. 'This girl holds the greatest magical power in the daylight world. Once she is captured, I will destroy her heart. She will serve me and bring to birth the chaos I crave!'

5 * BAGENDUN *

All the next day, Tegen and Kieran followed the ancient road that dropped down from the hills to lush pastures where fat cattle and sheep grazed. The people seemed well fed and wealthy, and spoke cheerily of the invaders' need for grain and meat.

Am I in Britain at all? Tegen wondered. Are these Romans that bring so much prosperity the same who rape and burn and murder? It doesn't make sense. I cannot, *will* not, trust the invaders. With that she increased her pace.

As the sun rose to its zenith, Kieran pointed out a range of tree-clad hills a little to the north. 'That's Bagendun, the old king's stronghold,' he announced.

'What? You didn't say our road took us that way.'

'You never asked.'

Tegen sighed with exasperation. 'I've got to go there. I need to find my old friend Owein, that's his foster-father's stronghold.'

'Thought you was in a hurry to get on?' Kieran cocked an eyebrow at her. 'Make your mind up.'

'I am in a hurry, but this is important too.'

He shrugged and chose the next turning to their right. 'Whatever you say. We'll be there by dark.' The lane followed a green valley with a snaking silver stream, but as evening fell, they found themselves in a gloomy wood, and the path slid into a rancid bog.

Tegen held back. This place was all wrong. The oily water lay undisturbed by traveller's feet. 'I don't like this,' she whispered, looking back over her shoulder. She drew Epona to a halt. 'Look, there's no smoke from the stronghold.'

Kieran sniffed the damp air. 'Wind's in the wrong direction?' he suggested.

Tegen shook her head. Epona shifted nervously and Wolf slunk to his mistress's side. The sun had almost set and purple shadows mingled with the mist between the trees. Tegen studied the silent road that led to the hilltop above. 'Let's find somewhere else to stay tonight,' she suggested. 'Leave Bagendun until daylight.'

'There's only Corinium, and the gates'll be locked before we get there.' Kieran squared his shoulders and stepped into the squelching mire. 'Come on, we're almost there.'

Tegen climbed into Epona's saddle and urged her forward slowly. Mud sucked at the horse's hocks as she picked her way between submerged roots and loose boulders. At last, with a cheerful snort, her hooves clattered on stone and she trotted up the opposite bank, closely followed by Wolf and Kieran, both thick with green, greasy mud.

'Hooray! We'll soon be feasting on ale and roast boar!' Kieran laughed.

Without a word, Tegen dismounted and led them warily up Bagendun's hill.

Her foreboding was getting stronger by the heartbeat. At the top, the great wooden gates stood drunkenly ajar in the twilight. There was no warning challenge. No fires. No one there at all.

Tegen's heart pounded as she clutched Epona's reins with sweating fingers. Wolf's hackles raised, as he sniffed the ground nervously. Kieran ran ahead, calling, 'Hello! Hello!' into the shadows.

'Be careful!' Tegen warned, following him into the enclosure. The place was deserted with only a faint acrid tang of wet charcoal in the air. Every building had been burned. Caer Bagendun, the pride of Dobunni tribe, was no more.

Kieran stared around him, his eyes wide with despair.

Tegen searched the darkening silence with all her senses and shook her head. 'There's no one here, so we find somewhere to sleep, I guess. How about in there?' She pointed to a lone hut that had been spared, forlorn under its sagging thatch. Then, unsaddling Epona, Tegen turned her loose to graze.

'Anyone home?' Tegen called as she pushed open the woven door panels. Rats and mice scurried from around her feet. In the musty darkness, she could just make out a few sticks of broken furniture and some straw.

'Aren't you going to light a fire?' Kieran asked as he squatted down by the cold hearthstone.

'Too tired. Here, help yourself,' she yawned and pulled half a loaf and some cheese from her bag. 'Give Wolf some. I can't face food. Something smells foul in here, I wonder what it is?' And with that she rolled up in her cloak and fell deeply asleep.

Her dreams were of an old woman in a threadbare cloak, muttering as she rocked, holding her bony fingers to a fire's last embers.

'Who are you?' Tegen asked.

The crone watched Tegen with rheumy eyes, set deep in a cadaverous face. 'Listen,' she said, 'what's following you ain't got no legs. Helpless, see? But it won't give up. It wants you as its slave… It'll grow legs an' then it'll come after yer! Old Gwen knows.'

In her dream Tegen sat up. 'What *is* it? Why does it want *me*?' she asked.

'Cos it don't make no sense, see?'

'What doesn't?'

'*It* don't.' The apparition stared into the fire. Tears glinted on her cheeks. 'Nothing to do with *that* makes *any* sense…'

'Please,' Tegen whispered urgently, 'what do you mean?'

Ignoring her, the old woman went on, 'and *she's* calling you from across the seas. You'll have to go.'

'Who's calling me? What seas?'

The old woman just nodded, then faded away. Tegen woke with a start. Early light was seeping through the mouldy thatch around the door. From outside she could hear a blackbird's warning scold and the heavy tread and snort of Epona somewhere nearby.

Tegen opened the door and stood in the cold drizzle of morning and sleepily tried to make sense of her dream. Wolf came bounding across the abandoned enclosure, a half-eaten rabbit in his mouth. He dropped it lovingly at her feet, but the sight of blood and torn fur, combined with the hut's foul smell, turned her stomach. She scratched Wolf's head. 'No thanks, you eat it.'

Kieran yawned and turned over. 'Who're you talking to?'

'Just Wolf.' She sighed and shook her head. 'Where do you think Owein might have gone?'

'Corinium?' Kieran volunteered.

'Maybe. He'd feel at home there – he was raised in Rome although he is British. Let's try.'

Yawning, Kieran struggled to his feet. 'You definitely won't make Mona before the solstice if you hang around here.'

'I can spare one day. Owein and I didn't part on good terms. I want to say sorry. But most importantly he needs to know King Eiser is dead. He took a vow to make Princess Sabrina queen. The tribes of Britain need leaders *and* magic to free our Land – and the sooner the better.' Tegen waved her hand across Bagendun's blackened hilltop. 'Look at this. How can people be so fickle? The Romans build decent roads and make a few farmers rich, then all the burning and destruction is forgiven!' And she spat.

'I wish I was rich. Da gave me a whole silver piece once, but Caja took it off me.' Kieran considered the meagre crust of dry bread left over from the night before. 'Can we stay in Corinium for two days? If we get some work we can buy food. Right now, I'd kill for a chunk of smoked ham and a horn of beer…'

Tegen's stomach rumbled as she picked up her things. 'Me too. Very well, but no longer, I have to…'

'Get to Mona before the snow comes, I know!' Kieran finished in a singsong voice as he followed her out of the door.

Tegen saddled Epona and whistled for Wolf who was still gnawing the remains of his breakfast. Returning to check they'd not left anything, Tegen noticed a heap of rags on the far side of the hearth. Stepping closer, she held her breath. Sightless eyes stared up at her from a shrivelled face. It was Gwen, the old woman she'd dreamed of, dead for half a moon at least. 'That's where the rotten smell came from. Was it out of compassion or fear of your curses that you were left in your home?' Tegen wondered. 'Well, you shall go to Tir na nÓg with my prayers.'

Then going outside, she held up her hands and summoned fire to the thatch.

'What you doing that for?' Kieran demanded. 'You're as bad as them bloody Romans, burning for the sake of it.'

Tegen glared at him. 'Not at all. It has always been our way to burn what is old and broken to make way for new growth. This place will become green and fertile again one day. I have seen it.' Then with a twist of her wrist, she commanded the flames higher and hotter.

Kieran stepped back, shielding his face from the raging heat.

'Take the animals and go on, I'll join you,' Tegen said.

'What you gonna do? More of that magicking?' Kieran growled nervously.

'Something like that. Now *go!*' When she was certain she was alone, she turned to scry patterns in the dancing flames. Tegen whispered aloud: 'Blessing on your spirit, Old Gwen. You came from Tir na nÓg to warn me, but what of? I didn't understand. How can the demon "grow legs"?' The more she looked into the flickering red and gold, the less she could divine. There was only fire...

Until a shape began to form – a tall man with a hooked nose and a scarred cheek. 'No, not him, *please!*' Tegen prayed fervently.

But the man's face glared back at her with seething hatred. Suetonius Paulinus, the Roman Governor of Britain. She had hoped never to see him again.

Tegen clapped her hands at the vision. 'Be gone!' she commanded. With all her strength, she willed the flames to die, but they climbed higher, forcing Tegen back. There was a creaking sound, then a spark-filled crash as the burning roundhouse collapsed in flames.

Sorrow and anger gnawed at her. 'I was born to avert evil,' she told the smoke-filled air. 'The Romans have bought Britain with blood and gold. Was Admidios right? Am I too late? *Is* there a magic strong enough to purge the rot?' She turned to leave. 'When we get to Corinium, we will work for one day, then search for Owein for one more, then I will set off for Mona.'

At the thought of the Great Spell, Tegen straightened her back. 'All *must* be well!' she yelled. 'Gilda promised it, so did Goban, whose ring protects me.' But as she trudged down the road, her head was full of all the dreams and visions of the past few days.

Most of all, Old Gwen's prophecy disturbed her: why was the demon intent on its pursuit? Was Suetonius Paulinus part of the demon's plans? Would she ever find the island of the druids in time to turn aside the Romans' evil?

Tegen sighed as she thought once more of the strange queen who had tried to summon her. She couldn't go, of course, but the woman was right, there always did seem to be something more to do, some other obstacle, some new trial to overcome. Tegen felt tired and lonely. The thought of stopping and simply dancing for joy was wonderful – but she knew it was impossible.

'When the Great Spell is cast,' she promised herself, 'I will find Tara and happiness. But not yet.'

A shrill whistle brought her back to reality. She had marched right past Kieran and Epona.

'Wake up!' Kieran chided. 'Or are you walking by yourself now?'

'Sorry.' Tegen smiled, taking the horse's reins. 'I was thinking. Let's go.'

Behind them, Old Gwen's funerary flames roared, spinning ashes into the morning sky.

6   * CORINIUM *

The Roman town was the biggest settlement Tegen had ever seen. A high palisade swept its wooden arms around a vast array of terracotta roofs and whitewashed walls. A tall gatehouse straddled the entryway, with red-kilted soldiers in metal breastplates, standing to attention on either side. Occasionally they barked challenges as carts and packhorses came and went. People yelled out greetings, curses and news in equal measure. Everywhere was bustle and shove.

Tegen's heart thudded in her chest. What would she say if they stopped her? Don't be silly, she told herself, no one will know who you are – you're just a girl with a white horse. But Epona stood two hands taller than any British mount and they were too close to turn back without looking suspicious. Tegen pulled off her cloak and draped it over Epona's Roman saddle, at the same time weaving a spell that made the horse appear weary and old.

'Come on,' Kieran urged. 'Act as if you live here. No one'll give a pig's snout whether you're Roman or British as long as you ain't armed.'

Tegen loosened her hair and hung her head. Few would understand the meaning of the tattoo on her cheek, but she had to be careful – just in case. Momentarily the sky darkened as they passed beneath the wooden gatehouse. Tegen stared at the feet of a sentry to her left. The sight of the man's leather boots planted firmly on the cobbles bought bile to her throat as she remembered being captured in the stone forest.

'Right! We're in!' Kieran interrupted her thoughts with a sharp prod in her ribs. 'Food first. I'm hungry!'

The air was heavy with the smells of cooking and Tegen's stomach growled in unison with Kieran's. When had she last eaten? 'But we've got no money,' she began.

'Then we'll barter!'

'What with?' Tegen rested her head on Epona's withers. 'I get the feeling that a travelling druid won't be welcomed and feasted like in the old days.' She gestured towards a British man ladling stew from a cauldron into a bowl held by a Roman soldier. Behind him stood a tall black man swathed in a flowing gown, selling golden-brown loaves from a basket. A beer-seller slowed her cart and offered a dripping tankard for bread.

Tegen sighed. The old ways might be gone, but the smell of food was almost painful. It was all right for Wolf, nosing his way between the crowds for scraps. 'Kieran,' she shouted above the hubbub, 'where can I set myself up as a healer?'

But he was gone. Apart from Epona, she was alone. 'Kieran?' she yelled, looking around anxiously.

Just then, he reappeared jiggling a hot loaf between his fingers. Tearing it in half, he gave a chunk to Tegen who bit into it ravenously. It was soft and nutty.

'How did you get it?' she mumbled.

'Nicked!' Kieran announced proudly. 'So were these!' And he produced two apples from his pocket.

Too famished to feel guilty, Tegen let the sweet juices trickle down her throat. 'We've got to *earn* food,' she scolded. 'And then I've got to find Owein.'

'Don't bother to say thanks!' Kieran scowled as he munched.

'I am grateful, but we can't risk getting into trouble.'

Kieran shrugged. 'How about dancing for money? There's usually jugglers and musicians somewhere about.'

'It's better than stealing.' Tegen wiped her mouth on her sleeve. 'And if Owein's here, there's a chance he'll see us.'

'Follow me.' Kieran whistled for Wolf, and together they elbowed a path through the bustle until they came to a square where the crowds were less packed. All around, stone and brick open-fronted shops jostled for space with wattle and daub houses. Tegen stared wide-eyed and open-mouthed at the size and grandeur of the dwellings.

Then she heard music. Outside an inn, four men were playing drums and whistles. On an impulse, Tegen handed Kieran Epona's reins, kicked off her shoes and danced on the smooth flag pavement. Soon a crowd gathered and coins fell thick and fast into the men's basket.

At last she leaned against a wall to rest, quite out of breath. The musicians stopped, picked up the money and walked away. 'Hey!' she yelled, 'What about my share?'

A thin man, who'd played the whistle badly, raised an eyebrow. 'We didn't ask you to dance!' he snarled, sliding between the crowds, leaving Tegen fuming.

Kieran cracked his knuckles. 'Shall I go and thump them? Eh?'

Tegen stared at the usually passive Kieran.

There was real fury in his eyes.

Just then, the innkeeper who'd been watching from his door waddled across the road, narrowly missing being mown down by a dung cart.

'Hey, miss,' he called in a heavy foreign accent, 'My name Aten! You dance in my alehouse. You and your little brother get meal and bed. Yes?' He didn't wait for a reply. 'We got deal!' He slapped Tegen jovially on the back.

Kieran seized the moment. 'If I help in the kitchens, will you feed the horse and the dog too?'

'Why not, eh? Why not?' The man laughed, setting his belly wobbling as he beckoned them to follow.

*

The innkeeper's wife was as round as her man, with the same dark skin and black hair. She came bustling from the kitchen at Aten's call, wiping her hands on a rag as she wove between the press of drinkers. Her man explained about Tegen and Kieran as he tried to pour wine and ale at the same time – spilling both.

'What mess!' the woman chided, dabbing at the spills with her cloth. 'I am Phenice,' she said. 'Now, show me you dance, eh?' Tegen obeyed, but she'd scarcely taken a dozen steps when Phenice slapped the table.

'Wait!' she ordered, then waddled away. When she returned, she was struggling to tie a blue shawl sewn with small silver and bronze coins around her ample waist. Phenice flapped her hands and hissed, making everyone move back, clearing a space between the tables and stools. Everyone fell silent. Holding her head high, the innkeeper's wife raised the backs of her hands to her forehead.

At first, it seemed as though nothing was happening, but slowly Tegen could hear a tiny jingling that grew, almost imperceptibly, until it was a merry sound that filled the room.

She looked around to find the source, but then laughed as she realised it was the coins that were shaking musically around Phenice's hips. Yet that was *all* that was moving, somehow she kept the rest of her huge body absolutely still.

'This called shimmy!' the older woman shouted, then suddenly she sprang into movement.

Aten struck the end of a bench with a wooden spoon, tapping out a complicated five beat dance rhythm.

Spreading her arms, Phenice wove intricate patterns with her fingers, rolling her thighs and shivering her shoulders. Then Aten began to sing strange, wailing hypnotic words in a throaty voice. Phenice joined in, until she collapsed on a bench, puffing, panting and glistening with sweat.

Aten clapped and hooted gleefully. 'There my snaky-girl, *yes!*'

Still gasping for air, Phenice untied her shawl and wrapped it twice around Tegen's waist. 'Ooh,' she squealed, 'When I was girl in Egypt, I dance like Isis-Goddess with this!' She giggled and pinched Tegen's cheek. 'That's when I catched Aten's eye! He was charioteer tall, dark, handsome as pharaoh himself!' She winked playfully.

Tegen had no idea where or what Egypt was, but she tried not to smile at the thought of this huge woman as a 'snaky-girl'.

Phenice pushed Tegen gently, 'Now you try, yes?'

Tegen made a few experimental moves, swaying by using her

knees and hips as she'd been shown. Wide-eyed with delight, she added little flicks and swivels to make the coins jingle and shimmer in the firelight.

'Well done! Well done!' Aten and Phenice cheered, and behind them, the inn's customers clapped and yelled for more.

Tentatively, Tegen touched the shawl. Her fingers tingled. It was made of *silk*… I wonder, might Phenice lend it to me when I've finished work? If only I could go outside and dance for *my* Goddess under the stars, like I used to at home. She closed her eyes and remembered her own precious green silk shawl. Once she'd believed it was the source of her magic… Until it was stolen.

Silk was rare and precious. Dare she ask?

But Phenice had already returned to the kitchen. As more customers poured in to the sweaty, smoky room, Tegen stood alone in a small space, her heart pounding with excitement.

'I found musician,' Aten shouted across the room. Between the tables stumbled a stooped old man with a whistle. Aten smiled. 'I've told him keep lively!'

Tegen glared at the whistle-player. 'Oh, it's *you*. This time you're working for *me*, and I didn't ask *you* to play!' He blasted a dud note at her as he crouched by the hearth. Behind him, Kieran picked up the innkeeper's spoon and suddenly began a strong rhythm the old man was forced to follow.

I didn't know Kieran could play! Tegen smiled as she began to sway. The music dispelled any thoughts of fear and loneliness. Tegen leaped across the small space, stamping and flicking her fingers, quite lost in the music.

When the dance ended, the applause was deafening. Tegen's

heart thudded and her face glowed as she caught her breath. She drank water and then nodded to Kieran for more. *This* was what she really wanted – just to have fun and dance all night!

Once more the music began and Kieran kicked the whistle player in the backside. 'Keep up this time!'

*

At the end of the evening, the tables and benches were stacked and the floor was swept. 'A good night!' Aten roared as he poured Roman wine for all. He raised his terracotta cup. 'Well done!'

Tegen and Kieran sat down to bowls of boar stew. Hungrily they chewed on slabs of bread dipped in the salty juices. Kieran had never tried wine before and was soon giggling and telling silly jokes.

Phenice leaned across the trestle and patted Tegen's cheeks. 'The Lady Isis proud of yous dancing. You keep shawl – I'll never dance again! No breath enough no more!' And she laughed until all her chins shook.

'You mean it?' Tegen asked, wide-eyed, 'I can really keep this?' Then she pushed it back. 'I can't t. It's too beautiful and valuable!'

Phenice pulled herself upright and scowled. 'And why shouldn't I give?' She demanded. 'My shawl, so there!'

Blushing, Tegen leaned over and kissed Phenice's warm, dark cheek. 'I'm sorry, thank you,' she said. 'But tell me, who is the Lady Isis?'

Phenice smiled. 'You not know Lady Goddess of River Nile?'

'No, I'm sorry.'

'She in Egypt, where me and Aten come to here from.'

This time, Tegen had to ask, 'Where *is* Egypt?'

'Oh! Long, long way from here. It always hot. There are gods in water with killing-teeth and mighty tails. Oh, and great stones pyramids that point to sky and take pharaohs to stars. There lotus blossoms so pure and white, they give birth to Lord Horus. And oh, the scent…!' She closed her eyes and inhaled.

'It sounds wonderful, why did you leave?'

'My man was soldier for Romans army, but he got discharge papers! Now he's innkeeper. We no like last town. Too many fightings! Heard they build this place, so here come we. Where there soldiers is…' She rubbed her fingers together gleefully. 'There *money* is! Have more wine.' And she filled Tegen's cup to the brim.

'Did the Romans take Egypt too?'

'Oh yes, but that long times ago.'

'But didn't you *fight*?'

Aten's face became drawn and angry. 'Oh yes, we fight! Our armies were *great!*' He thumped the table, making the cups dance. 'The best armies in world! But Divine Ones willed the birthplace of gods fall to strangers.' He spat.

A grunting noise made everyone jump. Kieran had fallen asleep and was snoring on his arm.

'Time for bed,' Phenice laughed, hugging Tegen. 'Leave him. You, upstairs. Be wrapped in best rug all night.'

This was not the time for Tegen to excuse herself to go outside and dance under the stars, much as she longed to. Reluctantly she obeyed, and allowed Phenice to swathe her in a soft blanket woven in brilliant colours. As she drifted off to sleep, she was excited and happy for the first time since… She couldn't remember when! Was this what life in Ériu might be like? Might the Goddess allow her to have a life like this one day? Working, laughing, dancing and earning a living?

Since she had arrived in Corinium, the sense of being followed had faded. Perhaps there were too many people around, confusing the demon? Perhaps the hubbub drove her own dark fears away and there was nothing pursuing her at all?

But in a corner of her mind, Tegen knew that the demon was real and it would not give up. If she didn't move on soon, it would find her, and it would have no mercy on these good people who had taken her in. She dared not stay long. If she found no trace of Owein tomorrow, she must leave for Mona.

She must never forget that she was the Star Dancer. Reaching out, Tegen fingered the precious shawl. Two coins clinked together in the darkness.

7 * DANCING FOR THE ROMANS *

The following night, there was hardly enough room for Tegen to dance. At the back of the inn, a Roman in a short red cloak whispered with Aten, then money changed hands.

When everyone had gone, Aten gave Tegen a bowl of stew. 'We have job. A *good-money* job…!' He jingled the silver pieces in his pouch. 'Here come big games for new Governor-Britain.'

Tegen's throat tightened. *Suetonius*? Not *him*? Not *here*? 'What sort of games?' she managed to ask.

'The gladiators and *glad-ia-trix-es*!' he enunciated carefully.

'Huh?' Tegen mumbled through a chunk of gravy-soaked bread.

'Armed girls fighting to death! Most excellent sport! Anyway, gentleman from Rome wants you dance while people in-coming. You know, keep crowd merry while waiting for blood-action!'

'*Big* honour to dance in arena. Yes, much!' Phenice laughed and shimmied.

Kieran was nodding wildly. 'Say yes, Tegen! We need the money.'

Tegen's mind raced. The idea of performing for the Romans was appalling, and what if Suetonius recognized her? But if Owein was in Corinium, he might come to the games. She took a deep breath. 'We'll do it,' she said.

*

To the west of the town, an earth bank had been thrown up to form an amphitheatre between two small hills. A high palisade kept the ordinary people out, but undaunted ale and pasty sellers teemed around the entryway, jostling with pickpockets and children trying to sneak in for free.

Inside, benches had been built on hillside platforms above a wooden perimeter wall. There, people jostled and argued over the best seats and lost cushions. Most were men and Roman citizens, well wrapped against the bitter north wind by layers of toga covered by thick scarlet cloaks pinned over their right shoulders. Behind them were soldiers and servants, and at one end in a separate area, the women gossiped, giggling as they hugged hot stones wrapped in cloth.

Aten led Tegen and Kieran past it all, and left them in a compound by a high wooden gate. 'Dance good you twos!' he smiled. 'I watch!'

An elderly woman shooed him away, then opened the door of a hut. She pointed to a heap of sour-smelling costumes. 'Choose something bright to wear, you both look like slaves. Pah!' She slammed the door, leaving Tegen and Kieran in semi-dark.

Kieran spotted a small drum under a bench and dragged it out, tapped it lightly and tightened the skin as Tegen pulled through the clothes, holding up shreds of coloured cloth. At last she chose a red dress. 'I didn't know you were a musician till last night. You're really good.'

Kieran shrugged. 'Da taught me a bit, but Ma and Aunt wouldn't let me play. Said I was making a bloody noise.'

'You never told me,' Tegen said, as she tied the precious

jingling shawl twice around her hips.

'You never asked. No one ever asks me nuffin' about me.'

Tegen tried to give him a hug but he wriggled away and began to work on a few rhythm patterns. 'That's just right,' she said, doing a few practice twirls.

The door flung open and six tall, helmeted women barged in, all shouting and swearing loudly, filling the hut to bursting.

'Let's get outside,' Tegen suggested, tossing Kieran a bright green cloak. 'We'll see what's happening in the arena.'

From behind the wooden wall came loud cheers mingled with pained yapping. Peering between the slats of the gates, they watched as a pack of brindled hounds baited a badger chained to a stake. The captive ripped viciously at the dogs until, bleeding and howling, they threw themselves at the wooden barriers, desperate to escape.

At last, a man stepped forward and threw a large net over the badger, then hauled it away. A huge black slave with one eye beckoned to a boy who struggled into the arena with a sack. He opened it and sprinkled sand over the blood.

Standing just beyond the southern gate, Tegen watched and waited.

What will happen if Suetonius Paulinus recognizes me? she wondered as fear gnawed her stomach. She steadied her breathing and wove a spell to disguise her face, but she had scarcely begun when the one-eyed slave glared at her and clicked his fingers. It was her turn to dance for the pleasure of the hated invaders.

She and Kieran exchanged glances. 'A jig?' he asked.

'Yes please – nice and fast before my feet freeze to the ground.'

The sky was dark and a shower of icy rain was spitting as Kieran ran ahead striking the drum tucked under his arm. Tegen skipped behind with the beat tingling up her spine. She shivered as the bitter wind slapped her face, then clapped her hands and stamped her feet in the blood-soaked sand. Swinging her hips her blue coin-spangled shawl tinkled and shimmered. She lifted her arms to the biting winds, then risked a glance up to the canopied seat of honour.

It was empty. So her enemy hadn't arrived yet. She smiled and felt lighter. Now she could *really* dance! If only she could be certain that Owein was there…

From the corner of her eye, Tegen could see Kieran. She smiled, and he speeded the tempo. Tegen moved faster and faster, whirling, stepping, leaping and twisting. In her mind she became a gleaming bird filled with sunshine and freedom. Her dance was in honour of the Goddess. It didn't matter what she was called: Sul, Bera, the Lady… Isis even, as long as the life she brought was celebrated.

The ground beneath Tegen's feet was slippery and sticky. Carefully, she moved to a different part of the field. She didn't dare fall. This dance was her way of telling these invaders that Britons would *never* be defeated. Theirs was a spirit of summer fire, fanned by free winds, made thoughtful and wise by rain and rivers, then rooted, solid and firm in the rock beneath their feet.

Kieran brought his music to a crescendo, then stopped with a thundering roll on the drum. Tegen held a pose, then bowed to the four quarters, 'Thank you spirits of this Land, who gave me dance,' she whispered. The applause was good, but not rapturous. Tegen didn't care. The spectators were here for the fight, after all. She'd done her bit and she was shivering now she'd stopped. She beckoned to Kieran and together they ran through the tall wooden gates towards the hut where they had changed.

As she was about to step inside to fetch her cloak, someone yelled at her. Tegen glanced over her shoulder at a figure swathed in thick woollen bandages and a heavy helmet. She ignored it.

Then the shout came again – '*TEGEN!*'

She swung around and the figure waved awkwardly. 'It's me,' a muffled voice called again. 'It's *Sabrina*.'

Tegen stared in disbelief.

As the Dobunni princess struggled with her visor, strands of her wild black hair crept around her shoulders and her dark eyes peered from the metal shadows.

'What are you doing here?' Tegen gasped, hugging her old friend.

Before Sabrina could answer, the one-eyed slave slapped her across the shoulders. '*YOU*! *IN*! *Get fighting!*'

As Sabrina pushed her helmet back into place, an ivory hair-pin fell to the ground. Tegen picked it up. It was carved with the face of a woman. 'As beautiful as the Goddess,' Tegen whispered. She went to hand it back, but Sabrina was striding away, so she slipped it into her pouch, changed into her own clothes and looked around for Kieran. She would wait and watch the fight, then try and speak to Sabrina afterwards. The princess needed to know that Bagendun was sacked, her father was dead and that Owein would make her queen. Tegen also longed to tell Sabrina about the Great Spell and the tribes rising to rid Britain of the tyrants.

Just then Kieran shouted across the muddy courtyard. 'There's food at that kiosk over there. C'mon!'

Tegen shook her head. 'I know one of the warriors. I need to talk to her.'

Trumpets sounded.

Squeezing between slaves and soldiers, Tegen managed to peer through a gap in the wooden gates once more. Sabrina was marching behind the one-eyed slave into the oval arena. She held her head high and put a swing in her gait. Three other women followed. They lined up at the far end, removed their helmets and drew their swords. A man shivering in several cloaks climbed over the wall and ran his finger along the blades. Then he raised his arms and yelled, 'All well sharpened! Let the fight begin!'

The crowd cheered and the gladiatrixes moved into pairs across the field. They planted their feet firmly, readied their weapons and waited.

Then the trumpets blew again. Governor Suetonius Paulinus, who had been watching from the back for some time, took his seat. He raised his hand, and the games began.

8 * THE FIGHT *

At the far end of the arena, the two other gladiatrixes burst into immediate action, shouting and screeching as they swung vicious cuts at hips and legs.

Sabrina waited while her opponent adjusted her helmet, but without warning the girl swung her sword, forcing Sabrina towards the churned blood and sand.

Tegen bit her lip. What a nasty trick!

Despite Roman-issue hobnail boots, Sabrina was struggling not to slip.

Tegen groped in her mind for a spell to help. What was best? Drying the mud, or strengthening her ankles?

Sabrina's blade flashed at her opponent's neck. The other girl ducked, then sprung forward with a stabbing thrust. Sabrina turned the blow with her shield and stepped aside, letting the girl's own momentum throw her forwards.

'Stop dancing!' Sabrina sneered, slapping her opponent's thigh with the flat of her sword.

The crowd laughed, and Sabrina cursed them loudly. 'Combat is a noble art, not *entertainment*!' she yelled. But the other gladiatrix had found her balance and was ready for the next onslaught; spitting and stamping like a bad-tempered mule.

Sabrina raised her shield, peered over the crescent cut-away, and watched for the girl's next move.

Tegen held her breath.

'Fight, damn you!' yelled the one-eyed slave as he prodded Sabrina in the buttocks with a long pole.

Furious, she span around and rapped his knuckles with the iron boss of her shield. Cursing wildly, he staggered back. Before he could regain his balance, Sabrina slashed her sword down hard on the inside of his unprotected arm. A long wound seeped purple blood over his peat-coloured skin. The slave looked from the dripping mess to Sabrina. His lips and eye narrowed. Grabbing his pole in his left hand, he sprang forwards with relentless swipes and harsh curses.

Ignoring her real opponent, Sabrina faced the slave and raised her shield. His reach was longer than hers. The odds were against her…

Undaunted, she sliced at the slave's staff hoping to break it. But her blade caught in the wood.

Snarling with rage, the slave wrenched his pole free and cracked it hard against Sabrina's wrist, almost knocking the sword hilt from her grasp, but she managed to hold on.

With his enormous power and height, the slave's relentless left-right rhythmic blows were wearing Sabrina out. She couldn't get a thrust between them and he was too fast and skilled to let her sidestep.

Tegen watched breathlessly from behind the gate and tried not to think of fire. To bring such obvious magic into the fight would be seen as a foul. Her friend's life would be forfeit. Tegen held her breath, there *must* be something she could do…

The slave's right arm was shaking with pain and loss of blood.

His hold on the slimy, reddened staff was slipping, but grinding his jaw, he pushed forwards.

Sabrina slammed her shield's lower edge onto his weapon and at last, it slid from his grasp.

Furious, the slave jumped back. He reached out his good arm towards Sabrina's first opponent. '*Sword*!' he roared. She tossed hers across. It looked like a toy in his huge fist.

With white knuckles, Tegen tried to force the loose planks a little further apart. She *had* to get a better view.

The fight began again. Tegen guessed the slave had been a gladiator far too long to be defeated by a mere woman. He would win this, even without a shield. Blow by blow, he was driving Sabrina back, and further back until her shoulder jarred against the wooden wall.

There was nowhere left for her to go.

The slave leaned over his prey and his lips curled into a leer.

Sabrina's eyes widened as she gasped for breath.

The slave lowered his head and lunged.

In that instant, Tegen murmured a spell: *Be quick, be strong*!

Sabrina slammed her shield boss up and under his jaw. She dropped her sword, sprang to his blind side and ripped open his armpit with her dagger. Twisting the blade, it came free, gleaming sticky-red.

The slave howled and staggered, slipped on his own blood, then crashed on to his back.

The crowd roared approval as, with one foot, Sabrina pinned his right elbow, and, with the other, drove a hob-nailed heel into his throat.

Gurgling and convulsing, the slave grabbed her ankle. Rocking his shoulders, he tried to dislodge her, but she ground the iron studs into his neck. At last he let go and glared up at Sabrina with his one, hate-filled eye. Bloodied foam boiled in the corner of his mouth and his nostrils flared.

A chant swelled from the spectators, 'Let him have it!'

Sabrina didn't wait for the order from the guest of honour. She dropped to one knee and sliced her victim's throat. Hot blood sprayed thickly.

The crowd roared in delight.

The slave's body twitched. His single eye rolled, then he lay still.

Sabrina hacked off her victim's head. His blood puddled and thickened on the muddy ground. Grabbing her prize by its black, oily hair, she held it high.

A long moment of silence lay heavy in the air, then the crowd erupted into ecstatic applause. 'Give her the wooden sword!' someone hollered.

'Wood-en sword, wood-en sword!' The spectators chanted, stamping and clapping as the demand for Sabrina's freedom echoed between the hills.

The princess tossed the head to one side. The applause became frenzied. She wiped her dagger on the slave's leggings, then, retrieving her shield, raised her bloodied weapons high. 'That's what happens when you insult the Dobunni Tribe,' she yelled, and without waiting for dismissal, she stormed out of the arena through the Gate of Life.

'*Sabrina!*' Tegen yelled, but she was shoved aside as slaves and soldiers pounced on the princess. They dragged her into the hut and slammed the door.

*

Two men hauled the dead slave away by his feet. A pale man with a whip ran into the arena and chased the other gladiatrixes off the field.

Tegen could just make out their hushed conversation as they hurried through the gate.

'Fancy daring to take on the training master!'

'I didn't think anyone could kill *him*!'

'What's worse, the new Governor of Britain was watching, did you know?'

The first woman looked nervously over her shoulder towards the seat of honour. 'Suetonius Paulinus…' she whispered. 'Vicious bastard! Poor old Sabrina, I don't hold out much hope…'

At the mention of the new governor's name, Tegen ran back to the gap in the gates. She'd forgotten all about him. Where was he? Only a short distance away she could see a scrawny figure wringing his hands as he knelt shaking before a dark-haired man on a canopied throne.

Tegen's heart missed a beat as she recognised Suetonius's hooked nose and cold eyes. She'd been warned of his presence in the spirit dream in Bagendun, but she had dreaded its meaning! Now her enemy was scarcely the length of five men away.

Tegen could hear the small man whining, 'My lord, she is new… Just a *tiro,* she doesn't understand all the rules of the arena…'

Suetonius rubbed his scarred cheek thoughtfully. At last, he kicked the supplicant. 'Oh do stop snivelling man! Tell me, how much do you want for her?'

9   * QUEEN OF THE DOBUNNI *

The crowd calmed as the next act entered the arena. Tegen crept stealthily behind the wooden hut that had become Sabrina's prison. It was badly built with gaps between the planks. By standing on tiptoe, she could just see her friend sitting on a bench, panting and shivering. The other gladiatrixes huddled around her, whispering.

'They'll flog her,' one woman said.

'Na, death for sure!' a second replied. 'Seen it before! If you even scratch the *primus palus* you're on your pyre! What was she thinking of? He never beat her very hard!'

Sabrina glared through her wet curls. '*Beatings*? You think I was worried by that slug's attempts at *hurting* me?' She laughed bitterly.

'So why…?' the first woman asked.

Sabrina winced as she straightened her back. 'That bastard wouldn't leave me alone at night. Amongst my people, rape is a matter of honour. It demands…'

Just then, the door of the hut swung open and two soldiers marched in. They grabbed Sabrina and dragged her outside.

'*Kneel!*' one yelled in coarse British, kicking the back of her knees. Sabrina had no choice but to crumple in the mud before a tall figure. Gaius Suetonius Paulinus, Governor of all Britain.

Her enemy.

Suetonius considered her for a moment, then nodded and strode away, pulling his red cloak tightly against the wind.

The first soldier yanked Sabrina upright while another clipped iron chains on her neck and feet. Gripping the heavy links, Sabrina slammed the nearest man in his teeth, sending him howling. The other man twisted her arms behind her back. 'You bin sold, all right? Suit your majesty? You're goin' with the boss.' He sniggered as he hauled her back towards the hut and threw her inside.

Behind the back wall, Tegen crouched out of sight, waiting until the games were finished and the crowds had wandered into the night. All was quiet and the guards were warming themselves by the brazier.

At last, she risked whispering, 'Sabrina!'

There was a shuffling and rustling inside. Tegen called again. Chains rattled and Sabrina's voice answered, 'Who's there?'

'It's me, Tegen!'

A couple of fingers wriggled between the planks. 'You're still here! Are you well? Are you free?'

Taking Sabrina's hand as best she could, Tegen replied, 'I'm fine. I'm on my way to Mona to meet with the other druids to weave a spell to free our people. How did you end up here?'

'It's my own stupid fault!'

'What happened?'

'You remember I was called to fight alongside the Brigantes, and you divined it was a trap? You were right. I should've listened. We reached the marshlands in the east then we were attacked by night. I never saw my warriors again. I was trussed up and thrown into a prison pit. After a couple of moons – I'd guess it was about Samhain, I was handed over to the Romans.' She thumbed her nose in contempt. 'I was kept in a prison pit for several moons, then taken to market and sold like a goose. Now I'm a slave, forced to fight as *entertainment*!' She spat. 'I use my own weapons, but that's the only blessing!'

On her side of the wall, Tegen glanced around to see if she was being watched. 'Listen,' she whispered, 'I have a friend nearby. We'll get you out. My magic is much stronger these days.'

'Don't risk it! A whole clan of the Old Ones couldn't get past this lot.'

'But I can't leave you *here*…'

'Is Owein with you?' Sabrina asked.

'No. I've been searching for him, but I haven't seen him since I left Sinodun.' Tegen hesitated, then added, 'Your father was murdered – and we had to surrender. The village was burned.'

'I'd heard father was dead,' Sabrina whispered. 'I didn't know if it was true.'

There was a long silence.

At last Tegen ventured, 'Owein's sworn to proclaim you queen of the Dobunni.'

Sabrina hesitated, then said, 'Forget rescuing me. It's too dangerous. I swear that as long as I live I'll bite and gnaw at these invaders' bones until they're only fit for dog meat! The important thing is that *you* are free, but you'll be crucified if you're caught helping me. It is your destiny to make magic to force these demons from our shores.

'I know Owein,' she went on. 'Wherever he is, he will keep fighting in his own way.'

'But you must unite the tribes. They must be ready with a strong leader when the spell is made.'

Sabrina pressed her mouth close to the planks and barely murmured, *'There are revolts brewing.'*

Tegen's eyes widened. 'Where?'

'All across the land... Listen, I daren't talk now. Just put faith in that Goddess of yours.'

Tegen hung her head. 'But I miss you, and with your sword arm I would get to Mona more quickly.'

'Ask the spirits. You were right about me, don't be wrong about yourself.'

Tegen closed her eyes and, for a moment, she had a fleeting image of Kieran and herself vainly wrestling Roman guards. Even with the full force of her fire magic, they were losing!

'Very well,' she conceded. 'But I swear I'll tell the Dobunni warriors about you – they'll rescue you.'

Sabrina shook her head. 'They won't find me. Now I've been sold to Suetonius – who knows where I'll be sent?' Then she leaned closer to the crack and whispered: 'But don't let *anyone* know who I really am or I'll be sent to Rome and put to death. Now *go* and may the Goddess light your path!'

'And yours,' Tegen replied, touching Sabrina's fingers and sending a blessing between the gaps in the wall. Then wrapping her cloak around her head, she sped back to the warmth of the inn, where Kieran was waiting.

That night, Tegen could not sleep. Staring into the remnants of the fire, she saw Sabrina was right. Here and there, discontented rebels were re-arming. Tegen sighed. Maybe the great spell would help them forget their differences and bring them together at last? It was unlikely, but not impossible.

Tegen was glad she had come to Corinium, for, according to the old law, simply telling Sabrina she was the queen of the Dobunni made it so.

She tossed and turned all night, then in the pale light of dawn she felt the spirits whispering to her to hurry. As Tegen dressed and folded the Egyptian rug, she wished she could at least explain to dear Aten and Phenice why they were going. But there was no time. Waking Kieran, who was sleeping downstairs by the hearth, they slipped out to the back yard where Epona and Wolf were both tethered.

Tegen prayed that Wolf would not bark as they crept out of the courtyard and shut the gate behind them.

'How much did Aten pay us?' Kieran asked as they crossed the market place.

Tegen's heart sank. 'Oh no, he was going to pay me this morning…' She turned back. The latch had fallen and they were locked out.

'Never mind,' she sighed as she thought of her beautiful dancing shawl. 'I have money.'

She led the way towards the market, which was just setting up. Stallholders with trestle tables jostled for pitches with traders spreading goods on blankets. Tegen soon found what she wanted;

a man selling strong British-style boots studded with Roman hobnails. As Owein would say, the best of both worlds! Tegen chose a pair each for herself and Kieran.

They haggled over the price, then she cut six pieces of silver from her dancing shawl and handed them over.

The man bit the coins, nodded and the boots were theirs.

*

By the time Tegen and Kieran reached the westerly edge of Corinium, the sun had risen at their backs and the great gates stood wide. No one challenged them. The soldiers weren't concerned with who left the town, only who was coming in.

As they strode past the high, silent walls of the arena, Tegen sent a spell to strengthen Sabrina's fighting arm and to keep her feet steady.

For a heartbeat, her mind's eye saw Sabrina wounded at the bottom of a prison pit – but was it the one she had already suffered in, or one that was yet to come? Tegen wasn't sure.

10 * THE REARING RIVER *

An icy wind tossed the last bedraggled leaves as Tegen and Kieran followed a stony track through the valley's desolate marshlands. At last they stood on the clay shore of a vast stretch of raging yellow water.

Tegen dismounted and stared in amazement. 'Is this the sea Gwen was talking about?'

Kieran laughed. 'It's the Rearing River, haven't you heard of it?'

'I have,' she replied, 'but I thought it'd – well, rear like a horse. That's how Owein used to describe it.'

'It does when the river goddess makes it happen. Spring and autumn mostly, and it's deadly. Not many folk know how to cross even when the river's calm like this...' He leaned over and whispered in Tegen's ear, 'But the ferryman's got *water magic*!'

Tegen stared at the swirling eddies. Her mind reeled at the thought of this torrent being 'calm'. In midstream a rough streak of water raked backwards, like the ridge along a wild cat's back. 'I hope his magic's strong,' she said.

Suddenly she realised she was alone. 'Kieran?' she called, 'Where are you?'

'Oi! Over here!' His voice called from a stand of bare trees that encircled a few ramshackle buildings. He emerged from the dark doorway of a decaying roundhouse.

'The ferryman's gone!' he shouted. 'Now we're in trouble!'

Tegen considered the river. 'I wish *I* knew water magic,' she sighed.

Kieran's face brightened. 'We could wait until low tide and walk across. It's muddy here at the edges and there's quicksand further out, but if we're careful we can do it. Especially with Epona to hold onto.'

Tegen walked to the end of the slippery jetty. Below, the sludgy river margins crumbled like rotten cheese. Gulls, oystercatchers and sandpipers fished in the foaming wavelets that lapped on glistening mud-banks. Walking looked impossible. 'Are you *sure*?' she asked.

Kieran shrugged. 'I did it last summer when the water was low. I guess it'd be more difficult now. We've had lots of rain…' He jerked his thumb over his shoulder. 'Or there's a coracle in the shed. It looks sound.'

'Have you paddled across before?' Tegen eyed him doubtfully.

'The ferryman let me help,' Kieran hesitated. 'Once… I got us caught in a whirlpool.'

Tegen winced.

'Or we could stay here a while?' he suggested.

'How far upstream before we can ford safely?' Tegen asked with a sinking heart.

Kieran rubbed his chin thoughtfully. 'The Romans are building a bridge a day's walk to the north, after that… Not sure really.'

Exasperated, Tegen sighed. 'You'd better show me this coracle.'

The little boat was almost circular, made of thick hides stretched over a frame of woven withies. It looked sturdy enough.

Together they hauled it to the water's edge. The tide was high and only a narrow strip of mud separated the reedy margins from the deadly waters. Kieran didn't hesitate; he jumped into the little boat and whistled. Wolf bounded out from the reeds, but drew back when he saw the boat. Tegen pushed the huge hound forwards, and Kieran dragged him on board by his fur. Shuddering in the bottom of the craft with his thin tail curled tightly between his legs, Wolf whimpered.

Tegen led Epona to the river and spoke to her gently. The horse lowered her head and flared her nostrils as her hooves slithered; then she lurched and splashed into the water. Tegen leaped and landed on top of Wolf. He whimpered. The boat rocked and shipped water, but didn't sink. Kieran shoved against the jetty with a paddle, spinning the boat onto the yellow tide.

Epona swam alongside, tugging the coracle after her. She tossed her head and snorted, but kept going with steady strokes, startling a flock of ducks into the sky as they passed. Slowly the bank receded until both shores seemed to be too far away. Tegen wished she had brought an offering for the River Goddess. 'What's the river lady's name?' she asked Kieran.

'Sabrina,' he answered as he pulled the oar against the noisy, rushing waters.

'Then she'll have a temper,' Tegen whispered nervously. 'My blessing on your waters. Spirits of the West, give us safe passage.'

Her prayer was answered with rough waves that slapped and

sucked at the little boat. Tegen stretched her hands over the swells. 'Be at peace!' she commanded, adding *please,* inside her head.

'Is the river going to rear?' Tegen yelled at Kieran over the roaring flood.

'Dunno,' he shouted back.

Epona's swimming became frantic as the waters combed her mane into ragged strands. She flung her head back and rolled her eyes, then a rising surge smashed the coracle against her shoulder. Dark blood seeped from a cut as the horse whinnied and thrashed in panic. Tegen wrapped Epona's reins twice around her wrist and leaned across to calm her.

Kieran paddled with all his strength, but a thundering wave wrenched Tegen's arms as she struggled to keep the boat and the horse together. 'The Goddess is angry!' Kieran squealed, working furiously to counter the deadly tug. 'We're doomed!'

Tegen clasped Epona's neck and held on. 'Come on girl!' she said. 'You can do it! We've always honoured the spirits of water. Think of dry land and grass!'

But Epona's struggles almost dragged Tegen overboard, just as another swirl crashed against the boat. Wolf whimpered in the bottom.

'We've got to hurry!' Kieran yelled. 'Beat the horse can't you?'

'I will *not!*' Tegen closed her eyes and imagined solid rock ahead and Epona striding up the shore.

I am a druid-ovate, she told herself firmly. I *can* magic us to the other side!

But before she could weave a spell, another heavy, yellow wave slammed the coracle into Epona's flanks once more. The horse screamed. Kieran was tossed overboard. With one hand he grabbed the rim of the boat, with the other he caught Wolf's tail.

Tegen stretched out her free arm. 'Catch hold!' she yelled, her mouth filling with water.

Kieran reached... And slipped. He screamed as the water dragged them apart.

'*Try again!*'

Splashing frantically, Kieran reached the sinking coracle.

'Get on Epona's back!' Tegen ordered.

Panting and struggling, Kieran clambered up. Wolf jumped out too, and swam in Epona's lee. Light and free, the little boat twisted away in the current.

Tegen was so numb, she could no longer feel the reins in her fingers, but she managed to climb onto Epona's back behind Kieran.

Clinging to the horse's neck, Tegen screeched at the river goddess: 'You have our boat as your offering Lady! Now bring us to shore, unless you want the Land to lose its spirit... Then you'll have no more worshippers... *Ever!*'

In that instant, Epona's hooves did find rock. Clambering and slipping, she hauled herself up onto dark oozing mud. Tegen and Kieran slithered down and the exhausted travelers dragged themselves across the rocks, up the steep bank and between the trees.

Wolf shook himself, but seemed none the worse for his ordeal. Muddy water streamed from Epona's coat as she spread her legs, then standing foursquare, she stretched her neck out and down, then gave a long, loud snort.

Tegen wrung water from her hair and clothes. 'Remind me to learn water magic before I get on a boat again!'

Kieran's teeth wouldn't stop chattering. 'Damn you! I th...thought d...druids did magic. I could have d...drowned back there.'

'I haven't had all my training yet,' Tegen snapped back. 'If you could be bothered to take me to Mona, I'd learn magic like this.'

'I ain't taking you till spring, and that's final!' Kieran glowered.

Tegen rolled her eyes in exasperation. 'Only to your Da's in Y Fenni. I know. Now, it's getting cold and dark. Let's get a fire going.' She looked around; there was a hollow with a rocky outcrop to their right. 'There'll do.'

Kieran twisted as much water as he could from his clothes, then stamped away to look for fuel, leaving Tegen tugging at a rotten holly bough. 'This should burn bright enough to keep even *demons* away!' she said, snapping it into pieces.

But at that moment, she pierced her hand on one of the prickly leaves. 'Ow!' she squealed, sucking at the dripping blood.

Kieran dumped an armful of branches. 'You all right?'

'Just a scratch. Let's get this fire going. We'll freeze if we don't get ourselves dry.' She held her hands over the pile of sticks. 'Burn!' she commanded. Nothing happened. Tegen held her breath. Had the jealousy of the river goddess taken her fire magic in return for her safety? How *dare* she!

Seething with anger, Tegen closed her eyes. 'I said *burn!*' With a *woomph* a sheet of flame engulfed their wood and half the nearby hedgerow.

At last they were settled, shivering as their cloaks and tunics steamed, and sucking on sodden bread as they huddled together. Beyond the edges of the firelight, the night creatures shuffled and scratched around them. A little further off in the forest, something howled and was answered by more hungry cries. Wolf pricked up his ears and raised his hackles.

Tegen pulled her damp blanket tighter. 'Whose territory are we in?'

'The Silures, my father's people.' Kieran puffed out his chest. 'They're warlike, but you've nothing to worry about as long as you're with me.'

Tegen hoped she could believe him, for she was sure she could hear the tread of human feet nearby, but sleep soon overcame her.

And in the gleam of the fire, a few drops of dark blood fell from the cut on her hand to the cold ground.

*

Far away, deep in the Otherworld, the demon caught the scent. The raven body it had shared had tasted that blood once. The memory filled the demon with horror and delight, loathing, and an unquenchable desire for more.

Wrapped in a dark, chilling fog the demon swirled westwards. As it rolled, it gathered momentum. The river was no obstacle, neither was the night. Evil smiled in its ancient bitterness, summoned by the hateful longing for its prey. The one that danced with Star Magic was bleeding and all the Smith's iron could not disguise that smell.

11 * MEN OF SILURIA *

In the morning, Tegen and Kieran's clothes were still damp. They woke to the dripping silence of a fog-bound world, and a path that wound between looming ghosts of larch and oak. Their stomachs raged with hunger as they climbed uphill until they met the track to the west.

'This is the way we should have taken last night,' Kieran announced. 'We'll be by my Da's hearth in Y Fenni before long, then we'll feast like kings, you'll see.'

But Tegen was on edge. The blanketing cold grey-whiteness unnerved her. All the colour and life of Corinium had shielded her from the demon's misty tendrils. Now in the midst of raw nature, she could feel its presence, and on her finger, Goban's iron ring throbbed once more with warning heat.

*

All day, the sunless fog swirled. Hungry and on edge, they walked, unsure of their direction. Tegen dismounted and led Epona through the skeletal woods and tripping roots. 'I don't like this fog, do you?' Her words felt dead.

Kieran didn't answer.

'Stay close!' Tegen warned. 'I sense danger. This is no time for moods!'

He hunched his shoulders and quickened his step. 'I'm not in a mood. I just want to get home.'

'*Kieran*!'

But he had slipped into the dank nothingness. A dark shadow amongst dark shadows.

Tegen bit her lip, but she dared not hurry her horse across the chancy forest floor. Somewhere in the nothingness she could hear sniffing, as if something was searching for a trail. She tried not to think of the demon. Her ring was painfully hot.

'Come on Epona, we can do this,' she muttered, speeding up a little. The horse flicked her ears and nickered softly. The fog became thicker. Silence wrapped the world. A few tall trees groped like hands here and there, but nothing else moved. Tegen stopped. She was alone.

'Kieran? Where are you?' she called urgently, 'I don't care if you don't want to talk, but we *must* keep together!'

A charcoal shape resolved itself from the swirling dampness. 'Over here. I got to tell you something,' Kieran's voice called back.

Tegen breathed more easily as Kieran's shape became clearer. 'I'm listening.'

'I'm sorry if I've been a bit sulky. Truth is, I'm dead worried, and now we're almost at Y Fenni, things might, well – not be quite what I've said. I should've told you before.'

After a long pause, Tegen asked, 'What about? Is there anything I can help with?'

'You might find my Da's family – well, a bit odd. You remember my aunt?'

Tegen nodded. 'Only too well.'

'You know what a cess-pit she was. She and Ma traded salt ever since they were children. Their Da did it and his Da before him. Back and forever, I guess.' He hitched his bag higher and started walking again. 'Ma was the younger sister and pretty. Aunt Caja was a looker too, but she was always angry. No one wanted to hand-fast with her. Well, Ma fell in love with my Da. He was a warrior, not one of them grand ones with a five-coloured cloak, but he did own a real sword. He was a Silure who protected traders from wolves and thieves.

'His name is Cei. He loved my Ma and she loved him. She should've gone with him, but Aunt was jealous, so she told him lies, and Da left. One morning it were, just before I was born.'

Tegen winced at the awful tale, but she wasn't surprised. Caja blighted everything she touched.

Kieran went on. 'Ma and Aunt often came this way to buy salt, so I was taken to see my Da once or twice a year and sometimes I stayed for a while. Da and me got on great. He offered to keep me, but Aunt said no. Anyway, it meant Ma working even harder if I weren't there.' He shrugged. 'I always swore I'd come back to live.'

Tegen patted Kieran on the back. 'And here you are with no Aunt or Ma to worry about. So – what's wrong?'

Kieran plodded on in silence. At last he said, 'Last year, Da took another woman. They're a funny lot, them Silures. Very proud. I don't know what she'll think of me. I only heard, see? Never met her.'

Tegen nodded. No wonder Kieran was anxious. He was scared his Da would disown him. 'What will you do if... If you don't feel welcome?' she asked at last.

'Come spring, I'll take you to the druids' island. I know most of the way, honest!' Then he strode ahead once more with Wolf trotting beside him.

Alone again, Tegen wasn't sure whether to be pleased or worried. Deep under his pain and sulks, Kieran was a good lad, and she felt sorry he'd had such a tough life. But he wasn't the best company or the most reliable guide. She couldn't afford to take chances on the road to Mona.

Tegen's unease returned. She comforted herself by putting one arm around Epona's withers, then, stretching out her free hand, she caught some of the foggy drips in her palm. It was just floating rain, what was there to be scared *of*? Silently she bowed her head to the spirits of the West and blessed them for their gift of water. The air smelled mushroomy and Tegen breathed it deeply, as she thought of Gilda, Huval, Bronnen and Dallel: all the people who had taught her the strength and beauty of nature's own magic. Tegen let go of Epona and danced a few steps along the path to celebrate the fog.

Then she stopped and looked around. Something was wrong. Nothing moved in the grey-shadowed world. Apart from the drip-drip of water droplets and the huff of Epona's breath, everything was swathed and silent.

With a thudding heart, Tegen realised it was *too* silent. 'Kieran?' she called. She gripped Epona's reins. 'I wish he'd stop rushing ahead. Kieran!' She called again.

No reply.

'This isn't the time or place to start getting the sulks again. Grow up!' Tegen took a step or two into the shrouding mist. Her boots shuffled last year's leaves. The back of her neck prickled.

72

She held her breath. Was she was being watched?

A twig snapped. She span around. 'Kieran? Where are you?'

The forest's dark shadows closed in. From somewhere ahead, Wolf barked.

She heard footsteps clearly. Several men, coming towards her. Running.

A leather-gloved hand slapped around her mouth. Harsh fingers dug into her cheeks and rammed a rag between her teeth. She thrashed and tried to spit it out. She thought she'd choke. Her arms were yanked behind her, and her wrists tied painfully.

Tegen glared up at her captor, a tall man with dark curly hair, a horseshoe moustache, and a red and black chequered cloak.

He gripped her chin, tilting her face to examine her tattooed cheek.

'Walk!' a second man commanded, prodding Tegen in the back.

A third figure slid out of the shadows and took Epona's reins. She whinnied and shifted uneasily, but followed the hand that led her.

For a long time, Tegen was pushed and shoved between the trees, then over rough moorland. When it was almost dark, they came to a camp where several tents were made from cloaks and skins spread over bent branches and pegged to the ground. Five or six more plaid-draped warriors huddled around a miserable fire that was struggling to keep alight.

Kieran was already there, his hands and feet bound.

Tegen tried to make a noise to attract his attention, but one of the men stood between them. 'Do you know that boy?' he demanded.

She nodded.

The man yanked the wad of cloth from her mouth. 'Who is he then?

Tegen tried to look past him. What was happening? Kieran had promised they'd be safe in Siluria. She swallowed hard. 'His name is Kieran, son of Cei the warrior.'

A second man joined them. 'What tribe is he from?'

Tegen took a deep breath. 'He's of the Silures,' she said.

'How can he be? His hair looks like piss!'

Tegen considered her captors. They all had fine dark curls. 'His mother is Dobunni.'

The first man stepped closer and gripped Tegen's chin once more. 'And you? What's *your* story? Why've you got a Roman horse with a military saddle?'

She stood as tall as her twisted arms would allow. 'I am Tegen, daughter of Clessek and Nessa, silver workers of the Mendip hills.' She paused, then spoke slowly and clearly: 'And I am also an ovate of the druids of the Winter Seas. I travel with the horse because all white mares belong to the Goddess. I am on my way to the island of Mona to complete my training.'

At this, the men started arguing. The one with leather gloves wanted to let her go immediately. 'Their stories match,' he growled.

'Don't be silly, Dewi. How can a slip of a girl be a druid?' the other sneered.

Tegen's arms and shoulders hurt. She didn't have time for this.

'I'll *prove* I'm a druid!' she snapped. 'Just untie my hands!'

'Do you think we're fools?'

'I couldn't run if I wanted to,' she reasoned. 'Where would I go? You'd catch me in no time.'

Dewi shoved the others aside, drew his dagger and cut the thongs that bit into her wrists. He held the knife to her throat. 'We're watching you!' he snarled.

Tegen pushed the blade aside, stepped towards the smoky campfire and held out her hands. 'Burn!' she commanded.

With a roar, golden flames leaped, devouring the logs.

Shielding their faces from the raging heat, the men gasped, then stepped back and knelt.

12 * THE ROAD TO Y FENNI *

Guarded and fed by the men of Siluria, Tegen felt safe and slept well. The following day she and Kieran set off along the road with gifts of bread and profuse apologies.

'We can't be too sure, see?' Dewi said. 'The Romans send spies in all shapes and sizes. When we saw that horse, we had to know who you were for certain.' He leaned over and whispered in Tegen's ear, 'That *magic* with the fire!' He gave a low whistle, '*Glorious*! Are you sure you don't want to stay and be our battle druid? With you beside us, we'd slaughter our enemies – like in the old days!'

He looked hopefully at Tegen, but she shook her head. 'I must leave for Mona, but the spell the druids are building will free our lands forever.'

'Then may all the gods speed you to the sacred isle,' the warrior replied. 'But when you ask the way, remember that here in Cymru, we call it *Ynys Môn*.' Then he pointed between the trees to a wide valley spread out below. 'Cross that river, and the road will take you to straight to Y Fenni where Cei the warrior has his roundhouse.'

He turned to Kieran and slapped him on the shoulder. 'You'll like your Da's new woman. A sweet girl, she is, and a little'un ready to pop out any day now. Your Da's got to protect a caravan of travellers next moon. I know he'll be glad you're home. You can look after the family. He'll be proud of you.'

A slow smiled warmed Kieran's face. He gripped his staff and held it high. 'I'm a man of Siluria. I'll guard them with my life.'

'Then you'll be fighting with us soon, eh?' Dewi laughed.

'If you'll have me?' Kieran gasped with delight.

'When your Da gets home again, we'll make your first spear together. It's a promise.'

Then the warrior knelt for Tegen's blessing.

As she raised her hands above his head, summoning the spirits of victory to his aid, her mind's eye glimpsed a woman weeping over his blood soaked corpse, a small child wailing in her arms.

Tegen finished the spell quickly. 'We must go. Farewell.'

*

Wolf trotted ahead with his tail curled, then he stopped, turned back and howled.

'What's the matter, Wolf?' Kieran asked, running after him. Then he stopped and held his nose. 'Blimey, what a stench! Rotting meat!'

Tegen saw a dark flapping movement between the trees. 'Ravens. Over there.' They stepped closer. A frenzy of cruel beaks ripped the flesh from the wounds of three corpses. At the sound of footsteps, the birds scolded with a harsh p*ruk pruk*! and deserted their meal.

Tegen shivered. Ravens were meant to be birds of wisdom, but since Derowen the witch had been re-born as one, Tegen found them sinister, and always expected to feel the demon's presence close behind.

She took a deep breath and stepped closer. The corpses' close-cropped hair and shaven faces identified them as Romans. One bloated hand still clutched a figurine of an ivory goddess. It was shaped like the hair-pin Sabrina had dropped in the arena. Tegen shed silent tears for the dead man's unanswered prayers.

Kieran swaggered up to the bodies and kicked one, sending up a swarm of flies. 'We Silures did this!' he proclaimed. 'Surprise attacks you see! We creep around in bands, pick off patrols and…' He drew a finger across his throat, then flexed his scrawny muscles. 'I was *proud* of being captured last night. You heard Dewi. By next moon I'll be a man of Siluria with my own spear. You were amazing too, mind. You really threw that fire! You could have fried this lot like a fish if you'd wanted! You'd be better than most warriors in a battle.'

These dead men prayed to the Goddess for their lives, Tegen thought. If both sides love the Lady, whom should she help?

'Tegen? You listening?'

'These corpses were human once, just like us…' she replied quietly.

'*What*?' Kieran snarled. 'You mad? They're Roman dung!'

She nodded towards the oldest man. 'That's someone's Da. He could have been yours if he'd been born here.'

'But he's not. He's one of them filthy invaders!'

'What about his little boy back at home?'

Kieran spat. 'Who cares? Anyway, it doesn't matter about dying, does it? I mean we all go to Tir na nÓg and come back for another go…'

Picking up her bag, Tegen took Epona's rein and walked on.

'You make it sound like a game. Suppose one of those Romans comes back as a Silure? Your new baby half-brother maybe?'

Kieran ran after her. 'The Lord of the Otherworld wouldn't let that happen!'

'Don't be so sure! We're all just people – born in different places.'

'Rubbish!' Kieran snorted. 'They're nothing!'

Somewhere, something laughed.

Tegen shuddered and tried to close her mind to whatever spirits might be lurking. She strode on with Wolf on one side and Epona on the other. At last she turned, cheeks blazing. 'I should never have let you come. You're moody, narrow-minded and pig-headed. I'm glad you're staying in Y Fenni. I don't need you – the Goddess'll guide me.'

Kieran made the sign against the evil eye. 'Well that's good, cos I don't want to travel with a Roman-loving *witch*!' He sprinted ahead of Tegen, spitting on the ground as he passed her, his bag bouncing on his back.

*

By the following night, Tegen and Kieran had reached an uneasy truce as they made for a narrow gap between vast, dark-breasted hills.

They stayed overnight in a stronghold that looked down the valley. In the morning light, they headed off with the rising sun warming their backs and the crisp, white sparkles of a first frost underfoot. The air smelled clean and clear, and Tegen managed to forget about demons and disagreements.

'Those slopes on the left are the Brecons and to the right are the Black Mountains,' Kieran announced. 'Y Fenni lies between them. The road north is easy for a while. You should get a good way before the snows. I... I hope your Goddess guides you well. I really am sorry I've been tetchy. I've been worried. And – death scares me.'

Tegen nodded. 'It scares me too at times. Come on, let's hurry, then we'll be curled up by a nice warm fire in Y Fenni before nightfall.'

Kieran nodded and, using his cap, he searched for the last few fungi of the year to take as a gift.

Knitting her brows, Tegen squinted up at the light-bathed road ahead. It is such a calm morning, is this a sign that all will be well? she wondered. I hope the Goddess is still talking to me. When was the last time I did a full ritual in honour of the spirits? Hanging her head, she took a deep breath. As soon as I am alone, she promised, I'll perform a full ritual. But why have I been so lax? Is it shame because I've got no incense or rush lights to offer? Or is it Kieran watching me all the time? He gets so edgy every time I do anything magical.

She kicked a stone and tried not to be glad he wasn't coming to Mona. She felt sorry for him and his difficult life, but she longed to find a loving home one day as well. She daren't let any of that get in the way of defeating the demon and saving Britain.

Lost in her thoughts, Tegen smelled, rather than saw the burning. It wasn't the welcoming hearth-smoke she'd hoped for – it was a heavy pall of black that choked the gap between the mountains.

'Kieran, look!' she gasped. 'Something's wrong!'

Rooted to the spot, the boy's eyes widened. 'Y Fenni's on *fire!*'

'Hurry! We might be able to help!' Tegen swung into Epona's saddle, pulled Kieran up behind her and kicked the horse's flanks.

As they trotted down into the valley, they heard shouting and the clash of iron on iron. Tegen's hands felt sweaty with fear and after a short way, they heard shouting, swearing and cries of agony. From out of the woods, a terrified mother ran, dragging two screaming children. 'Flee!' The woman sobbed, '*Run for your lives! Romans!*' She tore past them and darted away.

'Get off!' Kieran shoved Tegen down from Epona's back and grabbed the reins. 'You said the Romans were *human*! Stay here and think nice thoughts if you like. I'm going to *get* them for this!' And swinging into the saddle, he kicked the horse's flanks.

Epona danced nervously as Tegen picked herself up and reached for the bridle. 'Stop! Think! What are you going to do?'

'I'm going to kill them all!' He tried to turn Epona aside.

'Don't be stupid!' Tegen replied. 'This is what the evil spirits *want* you to do! You won't stand a chance. You've got to guide me to Mona *now*! It's too late for fighting. Help me find the other druids. Magic is the only answer!'

From somewhere close by, a scream rose and fell.

Kieran spat. 'Then do something useful and magic my Da and his woman somewhere safe. Why not do the same for everyone while you're at it?' He kicked Epona hard, but she refused to move, so Kieran slid to the ground and ran.

Tegen fought tears and anger as she called after him, '*Don't*!

The Romans will gut you like a fish! Even Sabrina wouldn't take on that lot alone!' Kieran slowed his pace.

Tegen added, 'And what if you don't come back from Tir na nÓg as a *British* warrior… What if you are re-born as Roman, or a slave? What then, eh?'

Kieran stared back at her, wide-eyed and furious.

Tegen turned Epona's head from the smoke and the noise. 'Do what you like, stay or go, but at least show me where to go, or my magic won't save *anybody*!'

With a face like thunder, Kieran pointed towards the Black Mountain on their right. 'There's a shepherd's path. Up there,' he snarled. He hesitated. 'Come on, I'll take you.' Then kicking at every pebble, he stamped ahead.

All morning they worked their way along the track until they came to a road churned into mud by the marks of Roman boots. Warily they crossed and crept through the forest on the lower slopes of the mountain, skirt the burning remains in the valley below, trying to block out the distant screams and shouts, mingled with the soft, silent falling of ash.

Eventually, the rocky path climbed above the line of leafless trees. Epona was edgy and Tegen had trouble keeping her calm. Wolf slunk behind, his tail between his legs.

By the prickles down her spine, Tegen knew the demon was somewhere close by. But at least they were safe from the Romans.

For now.

13 * SUETONIUS PAULINUS *

Behind them, the demon was indeed swirling through the forests, sniffing for any trace of Tegen. Since her bleeding finger had healed, the spirit had lost her trail. Using the cover of low cloud it swept this way and that, searching for a hair from her comb, a pool where she had washed, or a bone she had gnawed.

It sensed she was not far away.

Then demon heard the music of cruel warfare. Trumpets, clashing swords, and pathetic humans begging for mercy. It became distracted by the smell of a hate and vengeance as intense and bitter as its own. A man it might be able to inhabit and use. He was in the valley. He was the master of the burning and fighting.

The demon drifted to the midst of the mayhem and found him. What magnificent prey! He was strong, a leader with his own goals. It would be difficult to make him turn aside from his purpose and chase a mere girl through the mountains. But he would have his uses – one day.

Laughing, the demon oozed away, leaving its loathing to fester in Suetonius's mind, ready for another time and another place. The only mark of its visit was an unquenchable obsession for destruction of everyone and everything.

*

Suetonius Paulinus, Governor of the Britannic Isles, was too busy ensuring the complete ruin of Y Fenni to notice the *presence* that had seeped through him.

Absently, the Roman watched a few pathetic figures fleeing into the mist-laden landscape. They weren't worth following. The destruction of their homes was what mattered. Cold, hungry people would be submissive in the teeth of winter. These Silures were costing his legions dear. It was too late for the appeasement his predecessor had favoured. He was here to show these pagans that Rome was master.

But there was more.

Suetonius touched a raw scar on his face. Two moons before, a young girl with a tattooed cheek had almost killed him with fire. He thought he had seen her dancing at Corinium, but she had slipped through his net. The gods alone knew where she was hiding. Until he found her, *she* was responsible for all that happened to every man, woman and child in these damp, miserable islands.

He would find her and have vengeance.

*

The demon oozed away from Y Fenni, spreading its searching vapour as it explored the ground. There were so many human footsteps it could find no trace of her stench. Gathering malice, the demon-mist flowed northwestwards along the valley, leaving fear, war and murder in its wake.

She must have taken this road, for the druids' island was in this direction... If only it could see her with eyes, or run after her with feet, call to her with a voice... It dreaded the human world that flowed like water all around, yet was as elusive as quicksilver. Material bodies were weak and cumbersome, but they had their uses.

Like an angry serpent, the demon's miasma slithered onwards.

14 * KIERAN *

By evening, they were well beyond all sight and sound of the battle. Tegen lit a fire, then sat on a log and rubbed her face. Her mind was a turmoil of hungry flames: Sinodun, Dorcic, and the strongholds along the Ridgeway. She had seen them all burned by the Romans. By now, Y Fenni would be just like them – acrid, blackened remains.

The sound of sniffing made her gasp and look up. But it was only Kieran wiping a slime trail of yellow on his sleeve.

'Blow your nose. You're disgusting,' she snapped.

He glared at her. His eyes were red with silent crying. 'Stop getting at me. I just lost my Da, my new Ma and a little brother. You let me be or I'll sell you to them Romans you like so much. Gettit?' He waved a thin fist in her direction.

Tegen's throat tightened. 'Sorry, I didn't mean it that way. Listen, if you don't want to come, I'll understand.'

'Nowhere else to go,' he snarled, pushing his thumb against his nose and blasting the snot away.

Trying not to throw up at the performance, Tegen asked, 'I've often wondered, why did you follow me from Sinodun?'

'Don't be stupid! I didn't want to get skewered by them Romans!' Then he paused and added, 'Oh, dunno. It felt like I *had* to – and I wanted to find my Da. Too late now.' He buried his face in his arms.

'Shall I say some prayers for him?'

Kieran shrugged. 'What good would that do?'

'Your family might be reborn more quickly.'

'And get slaughtered all over again? No thanks.'

For a moment, Tegen's faith wavered. He had a point. Right now she had no time to ponder such issues. She'd discuss it next time she met a friendly druid.

His spirit's in agony, Tegen thought. I don't have time to wait while he mourns, but I can't abandon him either. Does he really know the way to Mona? He was certain about crossing the Rearing River and it almost killed us. As for his promises that the Silures would be hospitable...

She took a deep breath. 'I need to know the truth, Kieran. Can you *honestly* take me to the druids' island?'

'Sort of.' He kicked a stone.

She fought a strong urge to shake him hard. 'Look, I didn't *ask* you to flee Sinodun with me. I felt sorry for you! Now listen. Without the druids' spell everything will be lost. You wanted to fight the invaders? This is your chance – help me. But don't pretend you know the way if you don't. This is too important.'

Kieran sneered at her. 'Ah! So, you're not really my friend! You just want me for my way-finding!'

Livid, Tegen jumped to her feet. 'How *dare* you talk to me like that! I risked my life rescuing you at Sinodun! I argued against the druids when you were enslaved – and I didn't even *know* you then! I'd never have helped you flee Sinodun if I'd realised what a sulky, bad-tempered, selfish brat you are! You only want *me* for the kudos of travelling with an ovate.'

She glared down at him. 'In fact, I've decided. I'm going to turn you into a *slug*!' As she raised her hands, sparks flew from her fingertips.

Cowering, Kieran muttered, '*Don't*! I'm sorry! If I take you north, do you swear to destroy every Roman?'

'I swear to raise a great magic against them.'

'There's a place called the House of Bera. It's in the northern mountains on the salt trading route. I went a couple of times with my Da. I can find the way that far. I've heard tell that Ynys Môn ain't much further.' He looked Tegen squarely in the eye. 'We might just make it that far before the snows, but no further. And that's the truth.'

She sighed. 'Thank you. Now, are you certain you won't regret coming? Would you rather stay to look for your Da?'

Kieran scraped his heels in the mud. 'No point.'

Exasperated, Tegen put her hands on her hips. 'Look, we're *both* alone and needing friends. I won't *make* you come, but I'd *like* you to.'

Kieran's eyes narrowed. 'You need me now, but what'll happen when I'm no more use?'

'Don't be silly, of course I won't!' Tegen chided. Inside her head she groaned. She felt guilty for threatening him with magic and for not being more sympathetic for his loss. 'Come or stay, but be certain,' she added more gently.

Kieran sniffed. 'You'll go off without me one day. Me getting left behind is what always happens. You'll see.'

Tegen snapped back. 'I'll take an oath if you like. You ought to know I'm not like your aunt – I'll not hand you over to strangers!'

Kieran raised an eyebrow. 'Oh yeah? And what will an oath do? It's just words – easily broken.' He snapped a stick.

Tegen was about to reply, then lay staring into the flames. Once more, he had a point. Her spells were good for lighting wood, but they couldn't put out the fires of Sinodun, or make broken hearts mend. 'What *am* I doing here?' she whispered to the Goddess. 'What's this all for? What would happen if I simply turned around and went home – or ran away to Tara?'

Ignoring her, Kieran lay back and stared at the stars.

Fed up with arguing, Tegen rested her head on Wolf's warm belly. Stroking the dog's wiry ears Tegen listened to Epona gently cropping the turf nearby. At least she had two true friends in the world.

When at last she slept, her dreams were uneasy. A misty malevolence drew closer, summoned and fed by her fear.

15 * MOUNTAIN FOG *

All day, a smoke-laden wind pursued them along the valley. At last they left the Black Mountains behind and for three days they journeyed northwest across the fertile lowlands, staying in farms and villages. The weather was clear and the going was good, but soon the paths became rockier and steeper, and hunger set in. As they climbed, a northerly wind brought icy rain that seeped under their cloaks. Local people had little bread or meat for sale, and Epona grazed on tussocks of wiry grass. Wolf's hunting was so meager, his ribs rattled under his pelt.

Their hilly path became a mountainside. The unease Tegen had felt in Y Fenni was growing worse. She felt they were being watched. Every time they rested, she searched the rain-drenched crags and bare scrub, but they were alone.

Kieran looks exhausted and I need to listen to the spirits to know what is following us, Tegen decided. 'Let's stop and eat,' she called to Kieran who was striding ahead.

'Here's a cleft in the rocks,' he yelled back. 'It'll keep the weather off us for a bit.'

And keep us out of sight, Tegen added to herself. Then taking Epona's rein, she led her to where the boy waited by a narrow crack in the looming granite. Inside was musty and damp, but there was room for them all. Tegen flopped herself down on a boulder.

'Thank you,' she sighed. 'I just wish this rain and wind would ease up, they sap my spirit.'

'Would this help?' Kieran asked, pulling half a loaf from his bag. 'We could toast a bit of this on a fire.'

The thought of hot food made Tegen's mouth water. 'I'd love it, but there's nothing to burn and I daren't light a magical fire. I don't want to scare you, but I think something from the Otherworld is following us. A spell would attract it.'

Kieran gulped, looked over his left shoulder into the shadowy crevice. 'Then get rid of it, why don't you?'

Tegen shook her head. 'It isn't here yet, and I don't know what it wants. I can't destroy it until I have a clearer idea of what it is.'

'Don't care!' he pulled his cloak over his head. 'You know I don't like magic!'

'Sit down! You're quite safe. It's after me, not you.'

'Then let's at least make a real fire,' Kieran begged through chattering teeth. 'There's a dead tree back along. We've enough kindling to get it going, it'll burn a treat.'

'That's a good idea. I'll help,' Tegen said.

Soon their shelter was piled with half-rotted branches. Tegen smiled and berated herself for doubting Kieran as a travelling companion. It wasn't his fault he was nervous of spirits. She needed to be a bit more patient, for sometimes they got along well. Here he was, building her a fire with rowan. Its power would protect them while it burned.

But the wood was very wet and their efforts left them with a few charred twigs. Dog, horse, boy and druid were all shivering miserably. Tegen considered the rocky shelter. Perhaps, as they were out of sight of the road, a *little* magic might not be noticed…?

Taking a deep breath she spread her hands over the wood. Immediately flames curled and leaped, wrapping the travellers in golden warmth.

*

The rowan held true and protected them from harm, but not far away, the demon smelled the magic and smiled. Now it knew for certain the road they were on. The fog that carried its malice thickened and smothered the freezing mountainside. A chilling howl echoed through the rocky steeps, waking the sleeping creatures of the mountain.

Then, hungry and confused, a beast stumbled from his lair.

*

On the road once more, Tegen was beginning to wish she had never longed for the wind and rain to pass, for the fog was worse, blanketing every detail of the road. Kieran led, edging his way up the twisting, stony track. The sun was no guide, for the whole sky was the same dull grey as the rest of the world.

As the light began to fail, Kieran flopped onto a boulder. 'It's no good,' he said. 'Everything looks the same. I'm lost.'

As he spoke, Epona's hoof slipped, dislodging a stone. It tumbled over the right-hand edge of the path into the smothering nothingness, but the sounds of echoing knocks and cracks told that it was still falling… and falling.

Gingerly, Tegen dismounted. 'We're above a ravine!' she whispered.

Then her heart sank with another truth…

This fog was all *wrong*. It felt uncanny. She stood still as ice and one by one, used all her senses.

Sight was useless.

Listening hard she could discern nothing except the flat wall of rock behind her, faintly echoing Epona's steady breathing and Kieran's light, fearful panting.

The world smelled and tasted of rot and damp.

But as Tegen spread her fingers into the fine misty droplets that clung to everything, the hairs on the back of her arm rose and her skin prickled.

Lady Goddess, she whispered inside her head, show me what is hiding. Give me sight beyond sight.

As she did so, an icy, coiling tendril of hatred crept up her back.

And the *sniffing* returned.

So, the demon had found her once more. Where was it? Could it see her?

Tegen knew that using magic at a time like this would be like lighting a beacon. But *not* using magic would leave them at the demon's mercy. Closing her eyes, she raised a spirit shield around them all and tried to listen to the Goddess in her mind. If only she could dance! That always helped her to think. One thing was certain; shivering on a foggy precipice wouldn't help. 'Come on Kieran,' she said aloud, 'we'll be fine if we keep going slowly.'

Ignoring her, he crouched staring at the ground. 'I'm scared. There's nasty spirits up here. I ain't done them no harm, but they're coming to get us! I can feel them.'

He buried his face between his knees.

Tegen held out her hand. 'Then let's keep going. I've made a spell to keep us safe.'

Kieran pulled his cloak closer and shook his head.

Tegen's heart sank. Had the demon touched him or was this just one of his moods? 'Get up,' she coaxed. 'You ride Epona and I'll lead,'

'Can't. Won't. Don't like this.'

Tegen's heart sank. There was no point arguing. He needed kindness and support. 'Come on. The light's fading. There'll be a nice cottage further along, you'll see.'

But he would not budge.

All around, the gloom was thickening. Tegen sighed.

'Very well, you stay here. I'll go ahead and find out how far it is to the top. Wolf, stay.' The hound sat next to his friend and pushed his long face under Kieran's chin. Taking Epona's rein, Tegen swallowed her fear of the mist-veiled drop and shuffled forwards, one step at a time. All around, uncertain shapes loomed out of the fog, sometimes appearing as a man or a tree, then fading to a wraith that shimmered back into nothingness.

Epona's shoes struck cheering tiny sparks in the endless grey, and Tegen blessed the smith's iron that protected them. His ring burned hot on her finger – so danger was close, but where? She didn't want to stay and find out.

Just then, Wolf barked from out of the gloom. Tegen span around as he bounded past her, then sank growling to the ground, ears back and teeth bared.

Epona whinnied and reared. One of her hind hooves slipped

over the edge, sending a shower of loose pebbles rattling away.

Tegen gasped, as she grabbed her horse's bridle and a handful of mane.

More stones clattered, but this time from above. With her arms around Epona's neck, Tegen drew back under a small overhang.

Heavy footsteps shuffled closer. Looking up through the whiteness, Tegen saw the dark shape of a huge man lumbering down the rocks towards her. Was it a farmer searching for his goats? She took a deep breath and cupped her hands around her mouth. 'Hello?' she called out. 'Hello! Can you see me? We're lost! We need help!'

The heavy footsteps hesitated. There was no answering cry, but the giant's head swayed from side to side. Tegen could hear it sniffing and huffing. Wolf threw back his head and howled. The strange traveller made sharp clacking noises, then fell on all fours…

And *ran* at them!

Tegen screamed and let go of Epona. Wolf leaped forward, sinking his teeth into a thick arm. The creature shook itself, sending the dog flying over the edge.

Wolf yelped pitifully. There was a thud, then another.

Tegen raised her hands to summon fire, but heavy claws raked across her shoulder.

Gurgling, the monster opened its jaws and with a blast of acrid breath, the fangs closed.

16 * DANCING WITH THE STARS *

Epona screamed as her hind legs cracked into the beast's ribs. Bellowing, it swiped back at her, stumbled, then fell roaring over the precipice. Heavy thudding ended with a broken whimpering far below.

Snorting, Epona shook herself, trotted over to Tegen, and breathed sweetness into her face.

Just then, Kieran arrived, panting. 'You all right…? Tegen? Tegen! Gods help us! That's the biggest bear I ever seen!' He picked up a heavy stone and peered into the mist, ready to throw.

Tegen eased herself upright and wiped the blood from her shoulder. The wound was not deep, but she was bruised and her cloak was badly ripped. Shaking, she clambered to her feet. 'That was a *bear*?' she gasped. 'I've heard stories about them, but never imagined they'd be that *big*! Epona saved me.'

'Bears don't like horses.'

Tegen hesitated, a painful lump swelling in her throat as she tried not to cry. 'Wolf fought too, but he fell… Thank you Epona,' she whispered, burying her face into the horse's mane. 'Thank you Wolf,' she added. 'Fare well in Tir na nÓg.' Using her sleeve, she wiped her tears as she took Epona's reins. 'Let's go.'

But Kieran did not move. 'What about Wolf?' he demanded. 'We've got to find him, he might only be hurt.'

'We can't see to climb down,' Tegen replied.

Kieran peered over the edge into the fog. He listened. Silence. 'Wolf?' he called, but there was no sound. 'Curse that bloody demon of yours!' he screeched. 'You said we'd be safe!' and he thumped Tegen in the chest.

She staggered. 'There's nothing we can do. Come on.' She held out her hand kindly. 'We must find somewhere safe before dark or we'll be dead too.'

Ignoring her, Kieran picked up his bag and stamped miserably after her.

As the daylight faded, the fog lessened and the cliffs gave way to a grassy field. On their left, a stone hut was built at the junction of three paths. 'Thank the Lady,' Tegen sighed. 'Somewhere safe at last!'

Kieran scowled. 'How d'you know it's safe? There could be more bears in there – or wolves – anything!'

She listened to her heart, and felt no hovering demonic presence. 'My instincts tell me it's safe,' she insisted. Letting go of Epona's reins she pushed the rickety door wide. 'Hello?' she called, but it was empty: fox-musty, but dry. 'This'll do,' Tegen said. 'Maybe the fog'll have cleared in the morning.'

Kieran said nothing but slumped miserably in a corner. He was asleep before Tegen had unsaddled Epona. As the darkness settled around the hut, she summoned fire to the stone hearth. There was no wood, so it burned silently and without warmth, but the glow was cheering. It was too late to worry about hiding her magic.

Staring into the flames, Tegen felt drowsy, but there was one thing she had to do before she slept. Throwing off her heavy outer garments, she stepped outside. The bitter wind had shredded the last of the fog, and high above, the nine points of the Watching Woman burned brightly in the black sky. Tegen unbound her hair and listening for her childhood memory of a little drummer-boy. As the rhythms came, firm and thrilling, she stamped and swayed for her Goddess. 'Keep us safe,' she prayed as the starlight wrapped her in a silver cloak. 'Bring us to Mona to make your Great Spell, then may your people serve you without fear, forever.'

Tegen swept her raised arms towards the darkened landscape, bowing to the four quarters.

Bless the Land – your body,
bless the Air – your inspiration,
bless the Fire that gives life its passion,
and bless the Water that washes away painful memories.

Scarcely had she finished, when the Goddess spoke inside her head:

And bless the one who dances with the stars!
Let the boy bring you to my mountain,
from there I will lead you to the waves.

Hearing the voice she loved, Tegen's heart pounded with delight. She was no longer afraid. She had the courage to defeat the demon *and* free the sacred Land from the Romans!

Tegen danced. As she leaped into the night sky, the brilliant points of the Watching Woman's constellation slipped like quicksilver between her fingers.

Back inside the hut, the fire was burning hot, bread was baking on the hot hearthstones and a pitcher of ale stood nearby. As Tegen entered, she looked around in amazement. 'Where did all this come from?' she gasped, but Kieran was still curled up snoring in his corner. Had he found all these things? She would have seen if anyone had come. There was only one possible answer...

She poured a little of the ale into the ashes and crumbled some of the bread. 'Thank you Lady Goddess,' she whispered, certain that it was no less than she who had provided this feast.

Tegen wondered whether to wake Kieran, but he seemed so heart-sore and bone-weary she thought it better to leave him. Putting aside a share for his breakfast, she ate and drank, wiping away a tear as she wished Wolf was there to steal from her.

When at last she curled up and closed her eyes, her happiness was clouded by dreams of a great creature lumbering after her.

It was a bear, but it was not a bear.

It was dead, but it was not dead.

*

Crumpled and broken at the bottom of the ravine, the bear whimpered in agony as he lay in a rill. Starlit, ice-cold water flowed through his shaggy pelt. He struggled to roll over, opened his great jaws and tried to drink.

Drips of the demon's mist landed on the bear's hot tongue and dribbled down his throat. Deep inside the scarcely beating heart, the demon found hatred for the girl and the horse. Here at last was a host willing to lend eyes and ears, legs and cruel claws to the demon's needs. The bear's body was badly broken, but he could be kept alive long enough to hunt the demon's prey.

Slowly at first, then with a rush of wind, the fog swirled around the bear's open maw and was swallowed.

The demon had entered its new host.

*

The morning was bright and the fog had gone by the time Tegen pushed the door wide and led Epona out to graze on the wiry grass.

Tegen stretched her aching limbs and looked around. On all sides were towering mountains, precipitous and grey. To her right, the bare slate ravine fell away. Far below were meadowland, a few bare trees and a stream.

Leaning over, she called for Wolf until she was hoarse, but only echoes returned.

Miserable, she went back inside and shook Kieran. 'Wake up, time to go,' she said, offering him his share of the bread.

Kieran yawned and opened his eyes in amazement. 'This is *fresh*. Where did you get it?'

'Magic,' Tegen replied simply.

He eyed her suspiciously. 'Can't make *real* food out of magic.'

Tegen shrugged. 'The Lady can do anything.'

'Don't believe you!' he said, squeezing the loaf suspiciously. But as he did so, a long, brown shadow slipped between them, snatched the food and swallowed it.

'*Wolf!*' Tegen and Kieran cried together.

Stiffly, the huge dog rested his paws on Kieran's shoulders. With hot, bready breath and a sticky tongue, he licked the boy's face joyously. Kieran hugged Wolf until he whimpered to be free, then Tegen inspected him all over for wounds. Apart from a few scratches and small cuts, he seemed to be in excellent shape.

'What about my breakfast?' Kieran whined. 'Have you got any more?'

'Sorry,' Tegen spread her hands and laughed. 'You have to use the Lady's gifts quickly and not ask so many questions!' Tegen found a piece of smoked meat at the bottom of her bag. 'You'll have to make do with that.'

Chewing on it, Kieran picked up his cloak and followed her outside. Not far away, a stream ran fresh and bright across the rocky ledge, so they drank and filled their water-skins. Using a wad of moss, Tegen sponged her shoulder wound clean, and tossed the sodden lump into the stream.

'I'm ready,' she said, and they set off northwest.

*

Far below, in the valley, what was left of the bear awoke. Ignoring the animal's searing pain, the demon forced its host to stand, and look around. It could see through the bear-eyes. Carefully, for the demon was not yet used to this rather cumbersome form, it shifted one leg, then another. It smelled water. It knew its host would have to drink, so it steered the lumbering creature back towards the stream.

The bear's black nose twitched – he smelled a trace of blood. A wad of dark stained moss sailed past. He scooped it up and licked.

The demon-bear gurgled with delight.

It was *her* blood!

The stream tumbled from high above, but the slope was too steep to climb, especially with the bear's cracked ribs. They would have to take the long, slow way around. But the demon didn't mind. *She* was up there, of that, it was certain. And soon, it would be close behind her once more.

17 * RIVER-SONG *

Without the mist, the weather was colder, but brighter.
They were now in the territory of the Ordivices where they
were welcomed to snug roundhouses with feasts, songs and
storytelling. The Romans were just a rumour in these parts, and
Tegen longed for it to stay like that. These were good people who
deserved to be protected. She longed to stay and rest here, but the
wind was getting colder by the day. She had to press on to Mona.

As both the weather and Kieran's mood brightened, Tegen
tried to ignore the demon, although she sensed it was somewhere
close by, waiting to pounce. For now, pressing on was more
important than worrying about what may lurk behind.

As they wound through wooded valleys and along rocky
passes, which to Tegen's eyes were very similar, she became
intrigued at Kieran's certainty as he led. 'You say you've only
been here a couple of times, how can you remember the route?'

He shrugged. 'Salt traders learn paths. Got to.'

'But there are so *many* little tracks!' She pointed up at a crag
like an old man's nose, 'Some of the hill shapes must help, I
suppose?'

Kieran sniffed derisively. 'They're *mountains*! Mostly they're all
cloudy and you can't see them proper. Good thing too.'

'Why?'

He shuddered. 'Their spirits change the shapes around for fun.

Chancy, it is. You won't catch me going up there!'

Tegen craned her neck to study the white-capped ridges above. 'So, how *do* you find your way?'

Kieran shook his head. 'Secret. Can't tell, or they'll pinch me all night.'

'Who will?' Tegen laughed. 'Tell me or *I* will pinch you all night!'

He ignored her. Ahead, the path split – the wider part turned to the right, fording the river. 'We gotta cross here,' he said, jumping from boulder to boulder, trying to keep his boots dry. Tegen mounted Epona and rode her through the water.

On the far side, Kieran stopped and cocked his head. 'There's the river-song, of course. That helps.'

Tegen dismounted, for the path was steep and the trees were low. 'What's a river-song?'

'Can't you hear it?'

'I might, if I knew what I was listening to.'

The sun sparkled on the tumbling water, making the rocks gleam gold and dark blue. Wolf splashed in the shallows, spraying everyone with icy drops.

Kieran called to him. 'Here boy, sit! Quiet! Now Tegen, just listen.'

She sat on a rock and clasped her knees. The valley was filled with noise, blackbirds rustling and calling, the creaking of heavy-boughed ash trees, copses of bare hazel rods rattling together, making a woody music. But above and beneath it all was the river's endless gurgling and rushing.

Kieran sighed. 'I s'pose as you're a druid, you *need* to know the truth. It's Y Tylwyth Teg. They can hear river-song and they leave the way-signs.'

'*Who*?'

'Y Tylwyth Teg. They call themselves "Children of Rhys the Wise". They're small, with spiky hair. They don't build houses – they're always travelling, but they do stuff for people if they like them. Sometimes they play tricks, but they was always kind to Da 'cause he paid them with salt or silver.'

Tegen laughed. 'Ah. The Old Ones – some call them the Hill People. I thought they'd gone north to escape the Romans. Are there many here?'

'Oh yes, lots. Look.' Leaning over, he pointed to scratches on a boulder. 'That shape means, "The mountain with a broken back is ahead".' He brushed leaves from the other side. 'This means, "The long lake is this way".'

Tegen cut a coin from her shawl and laid it reverently on the boulder. Raising her arms she intoned a blessing on Y Tylwyth Teg, the hidden people who loved the rocks.

Kieran looked away.

'What did Y Tylwyth Teg teach you about the river-song?' Tegen asked.

'Like I said, just listening.'

Tegen put her head on one side. 'Lee-la-low…' she sang softly. 'No it's not, it's rush-rush-swoosh… Then it's glob, de-glob… Oh, there're too many sounds, where do I begin?'

Kieran lay on the bank and trailed his hands in the water. 'I know that lots of rain makes the notes low, and dry weather

105

makes them high. Each river's different: how deep, how stony – all sorts of things. And each river tastes different too.' He shrugged. 'But I just can't get the knack of it. There's too much to take in!'

Tegen closed her eyes and listened intently. Kieran was right, layer upon layer of myriad notes, some rich and rolling like underground echoing drums, others light and playful as silver coins – all rushing and swirling into a magical song.

Tegen threw off her cloak, spread her arms and began to dance along the rocks at the edge of the flow. At last she found a ledge above a pool with water-carved hollows and flood-tumbled stones. Unmoving, she perched like a heron, peering into the depths where a brown trout rested on the gravelly bottom. For a heartbeat or two, she held her breath.

Then it happened. She heard the voice of the river, not in words, but in meanings and pictures.

Her mind was so filled with stillness she *became* a rock. All around, fine strands of green stroked and tickled her. At first she was immovable, part of the earth's bones, then suddenly, she was sliding and tumbling, falling and rolling. It was exhilarating. She had *become* a pebble in the torrent.

Where are you taking me? she asked the stream.

Follow, it replied, *I will lead you where you need to go. I will take you to the sea, where you must dance with the waves.*

All around, the water rushed, roared, sang and whispered its secrets in a thousand liquid voices. The world twisted and turned about her – shadows splashed with palest green and dazzling yellow sunlight.

Without warning, Tegen became conscious that now she had *become* water. She and it were one as the little river splashed in gleeful drops or swirled in deep pools. Her hair became twisting weed and her arms swayed with the current, spreading, flowing and playing with the fish.

Then Tegen found she was stroking her speckled side against a dark rock, keeping steady in the current with the merest flick of her fins. Opening and closing her mouth, forever tasting the flow, knowing where it had come from and was going to. She could understand the language of the diving insects and the minnows. The gravel, the weed, the rocks, all took on meanings more ancient than any magic.

Then she became rock once more, washed and splashed forever.

*

'You all right?' Kieran called out behind her.

Tegen opened her eyes. She was precariously balanced on the edge of an outcrop above a tumbling waterfall. Below was a pool of icy boiling rage. Above, grew two or three leafless hazel trees. She took a deep breath and stepped back from the brink. Something cracked under her heel, a nut, round and milky. Picking it up, she tossed it into the stream as a thank you to the river.

A huge silvery fish leaped and swallowed the gift.

'Oh!' Tegen gasped.

Kieran ran to her side. 'I've never even seen Y Tylwyth Teg call one of them, not just like that.'

The Salmon of Wisdom! Tegen wondered in amazement. Was it you who were my teacher just then? Was I really shape shifting, or did I imagine it?

'Kieran,' she asked aloud, 'where does this stream lead?'

He pointed back to the marked boulder. 'To the sea, but it goes through the lake of Tal y Llyn first, and very close to Bera in the shadow of the great mountain of Cadair Idris.'

Tegen remembered the Goddess's words: *Let the boy bring you to my mountain, and from there I will lead you to the waves.* They were on the right path, travelling northwest to the sea – as Goban had said. Everything was coming together.

'We need to follow it – all the way,' she declared with a surge of happiness. 'We'll soon be at Mona, and I will fulfill my destiny!' She knelt and scooped water with cupped hands. First, she poured a little back in honour of the Goddess and the Spirits of the West, then she slaked her thirst.

Picking a rusty fern leaf, Tegen placed it on the surface and watched it sail downstream. 'Tell the sea I'm coming,' she said.

18 * THE BEAR *

Tegen and Kieran followed the river northwest until they came to a long, narrow lake. Its slate-black mirror reflected slopes of red bracken and towering mountaintops.

'That's Tal y Llyn,' Kieran announced proudly. 'We'll soon be at Bera, then it's not far to Mona, just like I promised!'

They camped on the shore in a shepherd's hut. All night there were ominous rustlings and shufflings outside. Kieran fretted and Epona stamped while Wolf howled. Around midnight, Tegen summoned fire-spirits to protect their hearth. In the darkness, something bellowed, then there was silence and they slept at last.

Dawn glowed with a fine sprinkling of snow, and around the shack's walls were huge, bloodied paw prints.

Not far away, the north wind gnawed at the bear's pain-wracked body as he cowered inside a rocky cleft, licking at the pus that oozed from his blood-matted wounds. He longed to lie down and die. But for aching days and nights, the demon in his heart had goaded him on and on.

Just get her on her own, the spirit urged. *Find a nice clear space then you can eat the male and the dog – the horse too if you like. Crack their necks, rip out their livers, and lick their hot, salty blood – just leave the female.*

Then you can please yourself. Sleep – or die.

The demon's hate had become the bear's own, and he willingly obeyed. But the valleys were narrow and overgrown – there was too little room to attack. Unrelenting, the demon-bear followed the scent-tracks it loved and dreaded, until by a long lake, its quarry sheltered in a stick and turf hut.

As the first flakes of snow began to fall, the bear raised a paw to smash down the fragile walls and pluck the travellers like nuts from a shell.

But as he spread his claws, fire-magic blazed out through the cracks. The possessed creature screamed and fled to a rocky crevice.

As dawn brightened, frost spirits sparkled in the clear air, turning the world to stone-hard ice. The prey would search for somewhere warm with others of her kind. There she would be safe. The demon knew it must cut her off before then. This was its last chance to kill the unwanted ones and drive her onto the mountainside alone.

There she will fall to her knees and despair, the demon whispered. *There she will lose her mind and her powers will serve my chaos.*

My patience is over. Terror will be my weapon now.

*

In the blue-grey morning light, Tegen saddled Epona while Kieran went to the stream to fill the water bottles. He came running back, white faced and breathing hard. 'Look, there's enormous paw-prints all around our hut,' he pointed urgently. 'I smell bear on the wind, too, plain as anything.'

Tegen tried to stay calm. 'There must be hundreds of bears in these mountains.'

Kieran's eyes widened. 'But they're all bloody.'

'Bears eat meat, don't they?'

'Not at this time of year,' he replied. 'They sleep all winter. Sometimes one'll wake up hungry, but not when it's snowing...'

Wolf sniffed at a paw-print and his hackles rose.

The early brightness had clouded over and snow was falling once more. The bear tracks were almost gone. Tegen pulled her cloak tightly around her shoulders. 'How far to the House of Bera?'

Kieran waved his arm along the lake. 'Along there, then around that mountain to our right – that's Cadair Idris.' The rising wind snatched his words. 'Lake-edges-boggy,' he shouted. 'Deadly-path.'

Tegen closed her eyes and searched in her mind for the bear's whereabouts, and more importantly, what *sort* of a creature it really was. She did not like what her senses told her. She said nothing to Kieran. She needed him to keep calm.

'We'll be fine,' she yelled back. But she wasn't sure she believed herself.

The path followed the lowest slopes of the mountain on the left, keeping the dark lake on their right. All morning they walked, heads down into the driving snow, both holding onto Epona as they slipped and struggled. Wolf padded ahead, sniffing and pushing his nose into the soft whiteness, finding solid ground between the rattling reeds and the shivering black waters.

Above, the scowling mountain gods shrouded themselves in heavy clouds.

With a sweeping gesture, Tegen commanded the spirits of the north to hold back the blizzard until they were safe. Then bowing to the south she prayed: 'Great Bel, give me sun, just today, I beg you…'

In mocking reply, the wind blasted with renewed strength and the snow flew so fast they had to huddle behind Epona, hiding their faces in her flanks.

'Can't you do no magic?' Kieran grumbled, between chattering teeth.

'I just tried,' Tegen muttered, pulling her cloak over her head. The air was too cold to breathe. Tegen tried not to swear at the spirits for throwing such foul weather at them. Why do you give us bread and shelter one day, just to kill us here? she grumbled.

'Don't worry. We'll make it!' she shouted as a squall of wind slapped her in the face.

*

The demon was also cursing the weather. Although the bear did not dread the cold, it could neither see nor smell any tracks. Its prey had escaped once more.

The great animal raised himself up and shook his snow-laden fur. He felt ill and hot and needed to eat. He now hated the hatred that drove his aching body on.

Lashing the bear with more and more pain, the demon forced him into the swirling white nothingness.

*

As Tegen and Kieran left the lake behind, the valley widened and sloped downhill. The stream became a river and sang more slowly, with dark warnings. The rage of the snowstorm lessened to a few flurries and at last, the great mountain on their right gave way to another valley.

With a whoop of delight, Kieran sprang like a goat across the icy stones that dotted the river. He laughed for the first time in days. 'This is the valley of Bera! We'll be feasting on boar tonight!'

'Be careful,' Tegen called as she hesitated on the water's brink. Wolf rushed past her, splashing into the flood. For a few heartbeats he was swept downstream, but he struggled out, shook himself and ran to Kieran's side.

Tegen dismounted and stared at the forbidding water. She hesitated.

'Ride across!' yelled Kieran from the top of the opposite bank. 'It's easy!'

But something was wrong. She stopped to listen. Was it the song of the river warning her of hidden danger in its depths?

Or was it the snuffling, gurgling noise behind her?

She turned and her knees almost gave way. The dark shape of the bear was thudding towards her across the endlessly white snow – still a long way off, but closing fast!

Kieran saw him too and shouted, 'Quick! Cross!'

Grabbing the horns of the saddle, Tegen pulled herself up and coaxed Epona into the water. The horse snorted, her ears flattened and her head went down. Tegen's boots filled with ice, but she gritted her teeth as she urged Epona gingerly forward, praying for a firm path through the swirling waters.

Too late, Tegen heard the throaty drumming of a deeper, underwater pool with loose rocks. Where was it? She pulled on the right-hand rein to steer Epona that way, but the horse stumbled and lurched. Icy splashes soaked Tegen to the knees, but Epona gained a gravel bank, then they were out and safe on the far side.

'Thank you,' Tegen said, stroking her horse's neck. But Epona did not move. She simply stood and shivered.

'What's the matter?' Kieran called down.

Slipping from the saddle, Tegen emptied the water from her boots. 'Epona's hurt!' she replied. 'How far have we got to go?'

'One hand-span of the sun, if the snow lets us through.'

Taking the reins, Tegen coaxed the horse gently up the bank. Epona's head hung low and hot air steamed from her nose in sharp snorts. But she would only move in short hobbles, holding her left fore-leg high.

Suddenly Kieran roared, 'Watch out!'

Tegen turned.

The bear was wading into the river, belching clouds of white breath as he plunged towards them.

'Come on Epona,' Tegen urged, 'Think of Mona!' Laying her hands above the leg tendons, Tegen wrapped a healing spell around the swelling joint.

With a low bellow, the bear staggered on his hind legs, then lurched forwards.

Kieran drew his knife and rushed into the water, followed by Wolf.

'Don't fight – *run*!' Tegen yelled. 'Get to the stronghold! Get help! *Quickly*!'

'I ain't gonna leave you!' Kieran yelled back.

'Fetch warriors with spears!' Tegen ordered. '*NOW!*'

The bear smelled their fear, and that gave him strength. Falling on all fours he loped and splashed towards the bank.

Closing her eyes, Tegen held her breath until the water's rolling, throaty sound became a part of her, then raising her hands, she called to the river:

Spirits of Water, true and bright,
Wash this creature from my sight.
With your waves and ripples free
Drag this bear away from me.

The river rushed. The bear roared.

The demon did not listen to Tegen's words. It simply saw its prey standing quite still. *She is coming to me at long last!* it gloated.

It made the bear lunge forwards.

In that instant, the river-song changed. Its notes deepened, stones clattered and the bear lost his footing. He staggered into a swirling pool, churning with boulders. Ice and water drenched his coat and dragged his massive body under. Round and round he twisted, then tumbled away downstream.

'Water spirits take him!' Tegen commanded. 'Demon, I send you back to Tir na nÓg,'

As the great bear's bulk rolled out of view, the demon side-stepped the spell and laughed. *You can't command me – not until you know my name!*

*

Bowing her thanks to the river spirits, Tegen took Epona's reins and led her gently away from the water. The bear might be dead, but she knew she had not won – her spirit could still hear demonic laughter.

But she and Kieran needed rest and Epona needed care. At the top of the riverbank, Tegen looked around. The whole valley was spread before her, wide and white. Right in the middle rose a high rocky outcrop topped with a stronghold. The only movement was Kieran's ungainly figure bobbing across the still, silent landscape.

Maybe they'll have a druid who can help me bind the demon, she hoped wistfully. Then she rubbed Wolf under his chin and pointed to the threads of cooking smoke that curled into the sky.

'Come on, boy. That's the House of Bera, we'll be safe there.'

19 * ATTACK! *

The demon's hatred was stronger than the water-spirits' magic.

Not far downstream, the bear's shattered body rolled in a shallow pool. He ached to die, but the demon forbade it. Easing his pain-racked bulk upright, the bear climbed the bank with trembling limbs. At the top, he squinted through blurred vision at the land spread smooth and white in all directions, then sank into the snow. There he swayed, shivering and panting, dribbling saliva and bloody pus.

The demon raged and swore at the bear's dying flesh. There were no other hosts were to hand. It had to keep this lump of rotting meat going a little longer. It could not afford to return to an insubstantial mist that could neither see nor touch.

Its fury forced the animal to stagger to his feet and follow the wind that brought smells of horse, dog – and human.

The bear bellowed, then with strength borrowed from hell he ran.

Tegen felt the ground shake. She turned.

Dark hugeness loomed overhead. A heavy paw swiped her sideways. Hot foetid breath made her choke and buckle into the freezing snow.

Somehow Tegen raised her hands. '*Die!*' she roared, sending flames crackling through the frozen air.

At the same moment, Epona's hooves lashed out. Iron cracked against bone. Claws gouged her neck.

A heavy thud. The bear fell backwards.

Tegen's heart pounded as she held her breath and waited. Wolf barked frantically.

More snow fell, blanketing the valley in white silence. Tegen dared not move. At last Wolf's hot tongue licked her face, and Epona neighed pitifully.

Shaking and weeping, Tegen stood. She put her arms around her horse's bloody neck and kissed her. Epona trembled and her flanks heaved. She held her wounded leg high.

'Oh you poor dear,' Tegen gasped. 'How did you manage such a kick? You are magic, Epona, I swear it.'

Wolf urinated on the bear's dark, blood-streaked pelt, melting a steaming path in the snow that had settled there.

Tegen stepped closer. The bear's jaw was ripped from his face, and eyes stared blankly from the smashed skull. Scarlet blood mingled with jellied brains splattered across the pristine snow.

Drawing her knife, Tegen stabbed the massive corpse again and again, screaming, 'Look what you've done to my horse!' until she could no longer breathe.

Then she stopped, looked at her blade and shook her head. 'I'm sorry. It wasn't your fault, brother bear,' she said quietly, wiping her hands and knife clean with snow. 'If I hate you, the demon will have won.' Then she laid a hand on the bear's hot shoulder. 'Go well to your new life, and next time, be more careful who you make friends with.'

The wind gusted with malicious cold, tearing at Tegen's cloak and biting into her almost-blue flesh. Wolf slunk to her side, she knelt, put her arms around him and was comforted by his damp oily fur. They were both shivering uncontrollably.

Reaching out, Tegen touched the hot swelling of Epona's leg. The horse whinnied and side-stepped. 'We must get you rest and warmth quickly,' she said. 'The demon is loose now, but probably without a form. It's still nearby.'

She turned away from her friends and lifted her face to the wind. 'Demon, go back where you belong!' she yelled into the storm. Touching the herb pouch at her waist, she wished she had dried aconite, hemlock or even hogweed to make an incense to drive the spirit far away – at least for a short while. But she only carried healing herbs, a habit she would have to change in future.

Anyway, she told herself, if the demon could have been expelled by simple exorcism, great druids like Dallel or Huval would have done it a long time ago. Once she was somewhere safe, she would have to create a binding spell to safeguard the rest of her journey. Turning to the north, she bowed to the spirits there:

Spirits of winter, ice and stone,
Bind this demon till Sun's return.

Then turning to the south, she bowed to Bera, guardian of the valley and one of the many names of the Goddess she loved and served:

Lady of summer, warmth and light,
Protect your people from this blight.

She had no offerings, and ached with cold so badly, she could hardly move. It was only the merest magic, but it would have to do – for now.

Just then, distant shouts and a horn echo filled the valley. A dozen warriors were racing their horses across the white expanse.

Rescue! Tegen waved frantically.

Barking loudly, Wolf leaped through the snow towards Kieran who was leading the rescue party astride a chestnut pony.

When the people of Bera arrived, they did not hesitate. Fresh meat was always welcome at this time of year, so baskets were sent for and the bear corpse was butchered. Much of the flesh was rotten, spoiled from infected injuries, but there was good eating on the legs and arms and the pelt was saved.

Tegen rubbed snow into Epona's swollen knee, while the horse nuzzled the back of her neck, reviving her with warm breath. Tegen jumped as a voice next to her said: 'You'll have to put your horse down.'

An elderly, white haired man was running careful hands over Epona's damaged leg. 'She's bad, she won't recover. It's a shame. She's a beauty.' He drew his knife. 'Do you want me to do it?'

'*No!*' Tegen said, knocking the blade from his hand.

The man stepped back and spread his hands. 'I didn't mean any harm,' he said quietly.

'I'm sorry.' Tegen picked up his dagger and handed it back. 'She's... not an ordinary horse. She's saved my life twice, I'd like to give her a chance.' She packed more snow on Epona's injury.

The man coughed painfully as he nodded. 'The boy says you're a druid, is that right? I suppose you do healing?'

'I'm only an ovate, but yes, I think I can help her. Anyway she's not really mine,' she added.

The man raised an eyebrow.

'She's borrowed – from a friend of mine.'

'Then you must do all you can for her.' He coughed again and wiped a smear of blood from his mouth. 'My name is Teithi. Let's get you all back to my fireside. I don't like the weather that's brewing. Looks like all the snow in the sky is about to be dumped on us.' With that, he gave a shrill whistle and beckoned to his followers.

Wheeling their horses around, they rode towards the rocky outcrop in the middle of the flat valley bottom, their richly coloured cloaks flying behind them.

Tegen followed, leading Epona gently, talking softly to her all the way.

*

All was silent where the remains of the bear lay. Then from out of the broken muzzle, a thin wisp of mist wound and spread across the ground, seeking, smelling and reaching for its prey.

The demon was free once more, but Tegen's spells had done their work. Snow was falling hard and all traces of her scent were gone. Howling with anger and frustration, the spirit drifted, leaving shreds of bitterness and fear in the wind. Some hung in crevices of the great rock of Bera, others were blown over the craggy slopes and left to twist in the mists that churned above the mountains.

It was trapped by the winter, but the demon did not despair. Its prey could not leave the valley until the thaw, and in the world of humans, more chaos was brewing. Suetonius was working well, stirring hatred and division across the lands, and in the east, other souls were ripening. Soon there would be more bloodshed to relish.

But it could not let the so-called Star Dancer slip away. When her magic was harnessed into service, she would be convinced she was serving the cause of right, but as a demon-slave, she'd become the instrument of overwhelming vengeance. Then sense would lose its meaning, and chaos would rule.

First it needed to get her alone, and then, by fear or persuasion, to teach her its ways.

20 * THE HOUSE OF BERA *

On top of the great rock that crouched in the midst of the valley, the stronghold gates were shut and barred. Inside, Tegen shivered in a cobbled courtyard as Epona was led away.

From somewhere out in the snow, a feral cry echoed around the valley.

Everyone stopped and listened as the sound faded. The wind whistled and snow fell in huge, soft-pawed flakes.

'Come inside,' called a friendly voice. 'Bring your dog. You must be frozen stiff.' A young woman, maybe ten years older than Tegen, was smiling from the doorway of a large stone and thatch roundhouse. Firelight and the smell of food spilled around her. 'I'm Enid. Welcome to the House of Bera. This stronghold is dedicated to Lugh's mother, the goddess of fruitfulness, for our valley is the best in all of the lands of the Cymry. My father is Teithi, the chieftain.'

The roundhouse was warm and welcoming, and one by one, warriors in rich coloured cloaks joined them. Kieran was already seated by the hearth, eating a bowl of stew. Cheerfully he waved a spoon at Tegen. Wolf curled up by his feet with a contented sigh.

The woman put a bundle of dry clothes into Tegen's hands. 'You can change behind the screen over there, then come and eat.'

As Tegen peeled off her wet things, Enid called out, 'What makes you travel at the dark time of the year?'

Tegen hesitated as she pulled on the clean dress and shawl. Instinctively she trusted these people, but she wanted to be sure before telling everything.

Then she heard Kieran's voice replying. 'I came here as a child with my father, the Silurian warrior Cei who helps salt traders through the mountains. His village was destroyed by the Romans and I sort of hoped that maybe he was here, or someone had news of him?'

Tegen stepped from behind the screen and sat beside Kieran who now looked pale. So, she thought, he thinks his Da might still be alive? He needs hope.

The assembled company exchanged worried glances, then Teithi replied. 'We haven't seen your father since Lughnasadh. He was heading south.' The chieftain nodded for Kieran's beaker to be refilled. 'Make yourself at home both of you. Winter's set in and you are our welcome guests.'

A serving girl squeezed between the benches and poured ale, while outside, the raging winds reinforced Teithi's words.

'But what's the young lady's story?' came a voice from beyond the hearth.

Tegen peered into the darkness. An elderly figure nodded and raised a hand. Two young men stood, lifted his chair of basketwork and carried him forwards. The old man's hair hung in strands of black and silver over his shoulders. His thin face showed pain, and he winced as he was placed next to Tegen.

'I am Gronw, druid of Cadair Idris and mentor to Enid who will be taking the druid's white come Imbolg.' He leaned forward, touched the tattoo of the Watching Woman on Tegen's cheek, then

124

whispered, 'And I will be honoured to give you any guidance you may need, *Star Dancer.*'

Then he sat up straight and clapped his hands. 'A song to welcome our guests!' he announced and someone passed him his harp.

*

That night, Kieran and Wolf were taken to the kitchen to sleep by the ovens and Enid invited Tegen to share her straw at the back of her father's roundhouse. 'Of course, I'll have my own home when I am a full druid,' she confided. 'But until then, I like sleeping by Da's hearth. Mam died three winters ago and we both miss her.'

She tossed Tegen some blankets and pulled the screen between their bed and Teithi's. As they curled up in the straw, Tegen couldn't help asking, 'I thought you had to be really old to become a full druid?'

Enid laughed. 'I'm twenty-five, but I've been training since I was a small child.' Then she squeezed Tegen's fingers. 'We're going to be great friends. You've no idea how lonely it can be, stuck here with Old Gronw. My father and brothers only think of war.'

'What about the women?'

Enid sniffed. 'They're only interested in hairstyles or how to outdo the men at swordplay. There's no one young to talk *magic* with. You're going to be a druid too, aren't you?'

'How did you know?'

'Partly your tattoo, but also Gronw welcomed you with a song. He rarely sings anymore. He's in too much pain.' Then she yawned. 'You can tell me everything in the morning.'

Tegen lay awake listening to Teithi's cough. As she stared into the smoky darkness, she chewed her fingernails and wondered whether the sprits of fire were strong enough help her travel through the snow. She dared not wait for the thaw. Out there, the demon was waiting for her. Somehow she had to slip past it. She had to get to Mona. The druids needed her. The fate of Britain hung on the spell they would make together.

Then an awful thought struck her – what if she *failed*?

Would the Goddess abandon her – or punish her somehow? Could she end up evil and twisted like the witch Derowen? What if her soul was condemned never to be re-born?

She mustn't fail, whatever the cost.

The dread of Britain being overrun by Romans was bad enough – but then a new thought struck her: if she were caught, what would Suetonius do to her?

21 * GRONW *

When Tegen awoke, she was warm and comfortable. The bright light that seeped around the door told her dawn was well past. The sleeping space next to her was empty and she was alone. Groaning, she turned over. Gronw'd think she was a poor sort of a druid, not bothering to get up to greet the spirits just because she was tired.

Crawling from under the blankets, Tegen pulled on her dress and shawl. She must tend to Epona. She was sure Teithi's people would have done their best the night before, but the horse's injuries would need her magical healing.

Stepping outside, Tegen blinked. The world lay brilliant white under a lapis blue sky. High above, two hawks circled. She took a deep, delicious breath, crunched a few steps in the snow and looked around. The House of Bera was about a dozen slate-built roundhouses and a scattering of huts encircled by jagged teeth of natural rock and stone walls. Thin wisps of blue-grey smoke drifted from the thatched roofs. Shouts and laughter echoed as villagers carried firewood or drew water from the courtyard well. A boy struggled past with a heavy basket of bread.

Tegen stopped him, took a loaf and asked where the horses were kept. He nodded towards a low barn by the outer wall.

There was no door, just a creaking ox hide. The gloom beyond was sweet with the tang of hay and animals. Tethered to the far wall were six mountain ponies, all handsome cobs with strong necks, thick chestnut coats and black manes.

For one dreadful heartbeat, Tegen could not see Epona. Once before, Goban the smith had taken her back. 'Please, not again,' she whispered, but then a soft whinny by her ear made her jump. Epona was just behind her, an old rug thrown over her shoulders and a greasy ointment covering the bear's claw marks.

Tegen ran her hands down her horse's legs. The left fore was still very bad, so she fetched more snow and rubbed it over the hot swelling. 'I won't let you die,' she promised.

The sound of heavy steps slipping on the cobbles outside made Tegen look up. A young man shouldered the skin aside. 'You're the druid-girl? Gronw wants to see you,' he said. 'Follow me.'

'I'm just coming,' she replied. Then weaving a strong blessing together with a fresh healing spell, she spread them like a soft blanket over Epona's back. The horse nickered and pushed her velvet nose under Tegen's chin, making her laugh.

The messenger smiled. 'She's a beautiful animal.'

Tegen kissed Epona's nose. 'I wish she were mine. She belongs to a smith called Goban, but I love her as a sister.'

'Ah, Goban!' He ran a kind hand down Epona's mane and she licked his fingers. 'No wonder you wanted to save her. It's an honour having the smith's mare in our stable. Come on.' Tegen followed the young man, wondering if everyone in the world knew her friend. She wasn't surprised.

*

Gronw's little house was smaller than Tegen thought a respected druid should have. It was long and narrow, built of slate against an outcrop of rock, straight sided and thatched. There was just room for a bed and a wicker chair on which the old man was sitting.

'Come in and welcome,' the druid said. He pointed to the brazier by the door, 'Build up the fire then make yourself comfortable. I'd freeze and starve if I had to rely on those idiots who are supposed to care for me.' He chuckled. 'They are my nephews and will become fine warriors one day, but uncle-sitting isn't what they imagined as their path to fame and glory. I live simply so I can look after myself. A proper roundhouse would mean having someone living in to look after me.' He rolled his eyes and sighed. 'They'd probably try and marry me to some young girl who thinks she knows everything. Might as well be dead when I get to that state!'

Tegen smiled and imagined someone her own age trying to get Gronw to do as he was told. 'How did you know I was the Star Dancer?' she asked quietly.

The old druid's eyes lit up. 'Apart from the tattoo on your face and the fact you carry magic wrapped around you like a seven coloured cloak?' He rubbed his chin thoughtfully. 'I heard you calling to the spirits in the valley when you were on your way here. Something to do with stopping the snow I believe? It took me a long time to counter *that* spell! I knew someone fairly powerful must be on the way.

Tegen sat up straight, her eyes as wide as an owl's. 'You *stopped* my magic? *Why*? We had a raging bear following us!'

Gronw shook his head. 'You wear the green of an ovate yet

you don't know the very first rule of magic – you *listen* and *watch* before you even raise a finger. A druid understands clearly what is needed before flinging spells around like snowballs!'

'I didn't have *time* to listen with a possessed bear coming for us!' Tegen snapped.

Gronw leaned back as pain racked his face. 'Pass me that leather bag from my basket. It has dried willow.'

Tegen found his pouch and handed it over. As their fingers touched she sensed his spirit was good. She knew she should trust him. 'I'm sorry,' she said, 'I shouldn't have spoken like that. You're quite right, I didn't listen then, and I wasn't listening just now. Please explain why you broke my spells.'

Gronw chewed the pain-relieving bark quietly for a few moments then asked, 'Why do you think I did it?'

Tegen shrugged. 'I don't know.'

'Think!' Gronw repeated quietly. 'Bears don't usually attack humans, especially if there are horses around. What happened? Tell me the whole story.'

'We came across a bear in the mountains. It was foggy and we met suddenly on a narrow path. We frightened each other, I suppose. He came for me, but Epona kicked him over a precipice. I thought he was dead – he should have been – but since then, a wounded bear has been following us.'

'And what do you make of that? Instead of finding a safe place to recover or die, he trails you – for how long?'

Tegen shrugged. 'Maybe half a moon. But I think I know why...'

Gronw nodded. 'Go on.'

'There's a demon that's after me. It was in the bear.'

'How long has it been after you?'

'Almost a year. A witch called Derowen summoned it in the funeral caves near my home by the Winter Seas last spring. At first I thought I'd sent it back, but it's been pursuing me, or driving its servants to do so, ever since.' She shuddered at the memories of the witch-raven, and Admidios with his hypnotic voice. They had been driven by the same spirit – she could see that now.

'If you didn't raise this demon, then why is it following you? Gronw asked.

'I don't know. I've tried banishing to Tir na nÓg, but I did it in a hurry and it didn't work. Now the bear is dead, the spirit could be anywhere. I need you to teach me how to destroy it.'

'That is something you must discover for yourself.'

'But isn't there a spell?' Tegen's green eyes were wide with dismay.

The old man shook his head sadly. 'Demons aren't subject to mere spells. They are older than magic. They may be bound for a short while, but you must discover this one's name and meaning before you have any power over it.'

Tegen stood and paced the tiny room. 'That's impossible.'

'Is it?'

She turned on her heel and spread her hands. 'Then I must leave. If it's followed me here, it'll bring evil on you all.'

Gronw raised a bushy eyebrow. 'You think my magic is too thin to protect us?'

Frustrated, Tegen clenched her fists. 'No... I'm sorry, I... There's more: I have to get to Ynys Môn, *urgently*. The other druids are gathering there to raise a spell to send the Romans away forever. I *have* to be a part of it.'

'Are you sure that's your true destiny?' Gronw asked mildly.

Tegen drew herself up. 'It's what I was born to do. The Goddess herself chose me.'

The old druid closed his eyes. 'Humph. Maybe. I need to sleep now. Come and see me soon and tell me why I blocked your spells.'

Struggling to suppress her irritation, Tegen put another log on the fire and left. He's a good man, she told herself, but he's past it. He doesn't understand. She looked up at the white mountains – more snow was falling. Her heart sank. The truth was that Kieran was right. She was trapped in Bera for the winter, and the demon was howling beyond the rocky walls.

There was no way out.

22 * THE WEB OF MAGIC *

That afternoon, Tegen and Enid sat spinning by the fire, talking about what Gronw had said. Wolf lay stretched out by their feet, snoring contentedly.

'But why did Gronw counter my spells? We could have died,' Tegen complained.

'Silly!' Enid laughed. 'If a bear was following you, it would smell and see your tracks. Snow may have slowed you a little, but it also kept you hidden. If your spells against the snow had worked, you really would be dead. Gronw saved your life.'

'I never thought of that! Gronw said I hadn't listened before throwing magic around, and he was right! When I was a child, Gilda our village midwife, said the same.' Tegen flushed red. It was *she* who was losing her grip, not the old druid. She had forgotten to listen to the Goddess' wisdom before acting.

She was *playing* with her powers.

Tegen tried to concentrate on easing the wool between her fingers. At first, the steady rhythm of the work was calming and helped her think, but the thread kept twisting and catching. 'Do you think that Gronw would mind if I went to see him again?' she asked at last.

'Not at all, but don't be long. I like having you here talking with me.'

Still clutching the spindle, Tegen made her way across the icy courtyard. Inside Gronw's hut, the brazier was burning low and the old man was snoring on his bed. Not wanting to waken him, but guessing he liked a good fire, Tegen slipped inside and piled more logs onto the embers. Gronw raised his head from his pillow. 'Oh, it's you. Have you come to bring me warmth or answers?'

'Both.'

'Fetch me some food, then we'll talk.'

When Tegen returned with a bowl of fish stew and half a loaf of bread, Gronw was sitting in his basket chair.

'You could get the carters to put wheels on that,' she suggested. 'Then people could push you around, or you could harness a pony. You'd have a chariot-chair!'

Gronw tutted as he ate. 'What frivolity! Let's discuss *real* issues. Why did I stop your spells meddling with the weather?'

'To save my life,' Tegen replied meekly. 'Thank you – I've been enjoying my magic, but I haven't been careful about *how* or *when* to use it.'

Gronw waved an ale jug at Tegen. 'Get that topped up for me.'

She obeyed, slipping and sliding across the cobbles once more. At last she was back in the warmth of Gronw's hut and filling the druid's beaker.

'Where did you get that ale?' he demanded.

'From the kitchen, why?'

'Sit down and pour yourself some. Taste it.'

Tegen did as she was told. It was rich and tasted of summer hedgerows.

'What's in it?' Gronw asked.

'Don't you like it?'

'I like it well enough, but I want you to think about the *contents*.'

Tegen longed to snap she was training to be a druid, not a brewer, but she kept quiet. The old man's methods were odd, but she wanted to learn. She sipped the dark brown liquid again and closed her eyes with pleasure. 'Malted barley, hops, honey and hazel twigs, maybe some water from peat pools?'

'Very good. Now, when the ingredients were gathered, what happened to the pools and the barley fields?'

Tegen frowned. What on earth could he mean? 'The pools remained, and the fields, well, they were harvested. Next year they'll be resown or maybe left fallow. Who knows?' She absently picked up her spinning again.

'Think again.' Gronw insisted. 'In your mind's eye, take a bucket down to the pool and scoop up some water. What happens to the pool?'

'Well, there're a few frogs and dragonflies darting around…'

'But the water Tegen, think about the *water*!'

'It's gone down, just a tiny bit.'

'Now go to the barley field in your mind. You take a scythe, swish the blade through the stalks and take an armful home to the malting kiln.'

'Yes?'

'But what is left behind?'

'If you mean is there less, then of course there is.'

Gronw leaned back in his chair and knitted his fingers across his belly. 'And is there less fish stew in the kitchen because I have eaten?'

'Of course.' She shrugged.

'And if a troupe of warriors came through the snow, could we feed them all?'

'We'd try, but it might be a struggle.'

'So the food in the pot, the water in the pool and the barley in the field aren't inexhaustible?'

'No.'

'Can you get more?'

'When the rain comes the pool will fill, if the field is manured and sown, then barley will grow again, and when the fish have spawned there'll be more to feed us next year.'

'Good!' Gronw smiled. 'And what happens to food we have eaten and drink we have swallowed?'

'It passes out the other end of course.' Tegen scratched her head. She was at a complete loss as to where this conversation was going.

'So, please be so good as to pull my slop bucket out from under my bed, call Pani the carpenter to me, then go away. Come back when you can tell me where your power comes from, and what happens when you've used some.' He waved his hand in dismissal.

Bemused, Tegen did as she'd been asked, but as she left, her spindle thread caught on the doorjamb. She was so preoccupied, she didn't notice until she was half way across the courtyard. At first, she simply tugged, but the wool was strong and didn't snap.

She ran back and hammered on the door.

'You can't come in, I'm on my bucket!' Gronw shouted back.

'It's all a web!' Tegen yelled between the planks. 'Any spell I cast has to *take* power from somewhere, and that will affect *everything*. Magic isn't something I just make "happen" with no consequences! The world is like a great piece of weaving. Every thread affects the whole. If I make a twist, the other end will pucker.'

Inside, she could hear Gronw puffing as he hauled himself back onto his bed. 'Good! Now go and think about what you are going to do about this demon – and get one of my nephews to empty my slops, unless you want to do it. I'm suffocating in here!'

23 * RHIANNON'S CHILD *

A slight thaw brought Tegen hope, but she struggled with whether to risk leaving for Ynys Môn alone. She knew no one in the stronghold would contemplate guiding her through the mountains – or even to the sea – until spring.

Will the Goddess protect me if I have faith and go alone? she wondered.

At night, she listened to the wild howling beyond the walls. Was it wolves, or the wind…? Or the demon, waiting for her? She shuddered and wondered how much faith she would need to reach the druid's island.

Then the snow fell thickly once more and Tegen resigned herself to staying. Life in the House of Bera was happy. Gronw's new chair with wheels was a huge success – all the children begged turns to push. The days were short and dark, midwinter solstice was approaching and there was much to do.

During the long evenings, Tegen sat with Enid by the fire in Teithi's house as they laughed about spells gone wrong and disastrous potions they had made.

Two nights before the solstice, they were summoned to Gronw's hut to discuss the coming ritual. Enid pushed her feet into her clogs and swung her cloak over her shoulder. Tegen sat poking a stick into the fire.

'Aren't you coming?'

Tegen didn't move. Squatting down, Enid put an arm around her. 'What's the matter?'

'Nothing. Just thinking.' She gave a pretend smile. 'Let's go.'

As their heavy shoes clopped across the icy cobbles, Tegen's mind was in turmoil once more. There's so little time before spring. If I simply sit around *listening* like a lump of dough, I'll be too late to help make the druids' spell.

Then an awful thought struck her: Gronw questioned whether that was my destiny – perhaps there's some mistake? Perhaps I'm not the Star Dancer after all? Maybe that's why the Goddess has not smoothed my path and brought me to Mona?

Just then she stumbled and Enid caught her arm. 'Careful, it's very icy here.'

'Thanks.'

That's what happens when I think nonsense, Tegen scolded herself. I must concentrate on what I know to be true! The Lady is always wise. Gronw acknowledged me as the Star Dancer, so did Witton and Huval, Dallel and even Goban. It had to be true. I have to believe…

At that moment, Enid knocked on Gronw's door.

'Come!' he called out. The choking heat and sour stench of the old man's room brought Tegen back down to earth. Both girls sat on stools by the flickering brazier.

Gronw peered at Tegen through narrowed eyes as if he could read her doubts and fears, but he only said, 'What have you done to celebrate midwinter in the past, Tegen?'

Glad to have something positive to focus on, she replied, 'The first year, when I'd been given my name but not yet proclaimed a bard, my mentor Witton was dying. I spent the dark days trying to keep him alive so he could teach me a little before he went to Tir na nÓg.'

'Did you have no ceremony with darkness and fire?'

Tegen thought for a moment. 'I had to stay awake one night and watch the flames. Then I had to make a poem about the Birth of Light.'

'Tell it to us,' Enid joined in, 'I love poems.'

'Later,' Gronw snapped. 'We must study before we play. Enid, will you please tell us the story of Rhiannon's child?'

Enid leaned back in her chair and smoothed her green robe with her hands. 'After Rhiannon married Pwyll, she gave birth to a boy she called Pryderi, the Mabon, the Bright Child, the Son of Light. She laid him between herself and the wall and slept. But that night, a huge claw reached into the chamber and snatched the child away. The serving women woke first, and fearing they'd be blamed for his disappearance, they took a new born puppy, killed it and smeared Rhiannon's face and hands with the blood. They swore their mistress had murdered and eaten her son.

'Rhiannon was condemned to wait by the mounting block at the castle gate and greet all visitors, offering to carry them on her back into the great hall while she told them of her heinous crime.'

'I always think that's so unfair!' Tegen exclaimed.

Gronw raised a bushy eyebrow. 'Do you remember what happens next?'

Tegen nodded. 'Nearby lived Lord Teyrnon whose favourite mare was pregnant. On Beltane eve, Teyrnon helped with the birth, but again, a claw reached in through the wind-eye and grabbed for the foal, but Teyrnon saved it by swinging his sword and hacking off the monstrous arm. He was about to chase the thief, but by the stable door he found a baby boy wrapped in silk. He and his wife raised him as their own, but after many years it was discovered that this was Pryderi. The young man was returned to his parents and became a great warrior.'

'We tell another ending here,' Enid put in. 'The Mabon child was put into a tiny cell and locked in the dark until the great bear-warrior Artoris rescued him – once again in time to do great deeds.'

Gronw leaned towards Tegen. 'So, Rhiannon's child is born, but taken away or hidden until he is grown. Tell me, what is the story *about*?'

Tegen thought hard. 'The birth of hope in winter?'

'Explain!' the old druid demanded.

Tegen hesitated, but Enid jumped in. 'The Goddess conceives the Child of Light when the world is darkest,' she began. 'He represents all sorts of things – especially the new plants ready to grow. But the winds and snow are deadly cruel, so she hides him as a seed in the ground until the light of Imbolg, when he begins to stir. Then by Beltane, he's almost fully-grown, ready to woo the Maid of Spring and fertilize the crops. When the harvest is ready, he is cut down and becomes the sacrifice at Lughnasadh to feed us all through the next winter. Then round it all goes again.'

Tegen's eyes were bright as she remembered how her friend Goban the smith had acted the part of the Mabon and died at

Lughnasadh. 'At first I was horrified that a human was a blood-sacrifice, but then, Goban isn't human, he's a god – isn't he? A human couldn't do it, but he can die each year, then bring the spring back. Isn't our world a wonderful story?'

Gronw grunted, and picking up a stick, he poked a hole in the earth bank around the hearth. 'That story isn't just about the world's turn. It part of the Great Spell you keep going on about Tegen. It promises hope in the face of despair.' He spat and made the sign against evil.

Tegen's head swam as she fought sudden, unbidden images of Bera's summer fields under a pall of smoke and a golden eagle tearing at a corpse...

Enid grabbed Tegen's hand. 'Are you all right?'

She nodded. 'I just felt a bit odd... Tell me about your ritual.'

Enid hugged her knees. 'There's a secret chamber in the side of this rock we live on. At midwinter, Gronw climbs inside and hides with a sacred fire that he keeps alive for three days and three nights. When the light starts to grow with Sun's Return, he comes out. We kindle new hearth fires from his flame and have a feast!'

Gronw was silent as he gouged harder into the earth, making the hole bigger and deeper. 'It's going to be done differently this year.'

Enid looked blank, but Tegen listened to the unspoken meaning behind the druid's words. 'You want one of us to go into the chamber in your stead. You aren't well enough, are you?'

'No, my dear, I'm not.'

'Of course *I'll* go,' Enid said immediately.

Gronw lifted a burning branch from the hearth and shook it,

making sparks fly. 'And will you nurse the hidden fire for three days and three nights and bring it out for all to share?' he asked quietly.

'I will!' Enid replied.

'Humph!' Gronw grunted. 'Good!'

*

Tegen found an excuse to return to Gronw's hut while Enid was eating. The wind was particularly bitter, sobbing and howling through the stronghold with promises of more snow.

The old druid was sitting in bed, casting ogham sticks over the greasy sheepskin covers. He looked up and frowned as Tegen entered. 'Well?'

Tegen shut the door, then stared at the marked sticks in Gronw's fingers. They said what she feared. 'You can't let Enid do this,' she said. 'That demon is out there wailing for my soul!'

'If it's wailing for your soul, it won't bother Enid.'

Tegen pointed to the Ogham that spelled *disaster*. 'Are you sure?' she asked.

Gronw gathered his sticks and dropped them into a basket. He fixed Tegen with his dark, glinting eyes. 'Listen – and that's something I fear you still don't do – Enid's fate is to go out there. If she is to be a druid, she must face demons every bit as bad as yours. Yes it breaks my heart to send her, but if I don't, she will never wear the white robe that is her birth-right. Neither you nor I can protect her from what must be. Good night.' Dismissing Tegen with a flick of his fingers, he rolled over to face the wall.

*

143

That night, Tegen and Enid and went to the straw-filled sleeping place behind the screen. 'Why did you volunteer?' Tegen whispered as they cocooned themselves in blankets.

'To go into the cave?' Enid asked. 'Because as the next druid, I must.'

Tegen squeezed her friend's cold fingers. 'Are you afraid?'

Enid rustled on her straw bed in the fire-lit darkness, but said nothing.

'Let me do it this year,' Tegen urged. 'Please.'

Rolling over, Enid buried her head into Tegen's shoulder. 'Thank you for offering, but it's the way it has to be. I'm certain that one day you'll be shown how to become Rhiannon – or maybe even the Mabon, who knows?'

Tegen's spine tingled at her words, but she said nothing for just then Wolf wriggled his long body between the friends. Enid turned over and slept, leaving Tegen to rub Wolf's wiry ears.

'You know what?' she whispered.

Wolf replied by pushing his cold nose under her chin.

'I think I understand why I am here, at last.'

Wolf twisted his head back, as if he were really listening.

'Enid's right. I'm a little like the Mabon. Somewhere out there the demon waits for me with its hideous claw: but I must stay hidden here in Bera. All things will come together for good in their own time. I can only pray that Enid will be safe out there on her own.'

24 * MIDWINTER'S NIGHT *

Heavy clouds made the exact calculation of midwinter's night difficult, but Gronw had cut a picture-calendar into the wall of his hut. It showed the moon in her light and dark stages hovering above images of the mountain peaks that surrounded the valley. Also carefully marked were the points where the sun rose and set at the solstices and fire festivals.

Enid and Tegen watched as the druid's thin fingers traced the patterns. 'The day you arrived, Tegen, the sun was just over this point here,' Gronw explained. 'So, even if heavy weather does keep up, we can be certain that tomorrow night, the Sun will die. All our hearths will be smothered. With spindle and kindling, Enid will give birth to a new flame which she will carry into the sacred cave. If the times ahead are good, the fire will still be burning when she comes out. If the next Sun's ride is dark and dangerous, the fire will have died.'

Back in Teithi's hut, Enid sat pale and silent by the hearth, her knees pulled up under her chin.

Tegen reached for her friend's hand and squeezed it. 'I've spent a few nights in wight-barrows, it's not so bad. The spirits were kind and gave me dreams and I danced to help me listen to the Goddess.'

Enid's voice was taut. '*Dance*? Our cave's more like a tomb.'

'But you'll have a fire…'

Enid turned and considered Tegen. 'Don't you find fire scary?'

'Yes,' she replied. 'I do.' A log shifted on the hearth. Tegen looked and turned away as an unbidden image came to her mind: of Enid lying pale and distraught on Gronw's bed.

*

Throughout the following day, Tegen had piled as much wood as Gronw would allow in the secret chamber to see Enid though the coming days. She sneaked in a little more when he wasn't looking, although he'd been adamant about the exact amount allowed. 'Enid has to stay awake and guard the fire. If it gets too warm in there, she might fall asleep. She may have a bucket, two pitchers of water – no, make that three, a sheepskin to sit on and two extra cloaks.'

As she piled everything in place, Tegen put a sprig of rowan in as well, to protect the new fire and to guard Enid. As she wriggled back out again, Tegen blessed the chamber and banished any lingering spirits.

The old druid peered in as well as he could and *humphed*. 'It'll do,' he said, 'but I didn't say you could put a blessing in there. Enid must make her own spells.'

'It's a long time to be blocked up and alone,' Tegen replied.

*

That evening, Tegen brought Enid warm honey cakes from the kitchen. 'You must build up your strength,' she coaxed. 'And I've made this for you too.' She held out a necklace of dried rowan and mistletoe berries. 'To keep evil spirits away.'

Enid sat numbly by the fire. 'It'll be like dying, won't it?' she asked. 'Three nights in a tomb, without even you to talk to.' She stared at Tegen wide-eyed. 'Would you come in with me?'

'If Gronw would allow it – but would there be room?'

'No, but it helps, knowing you would if you could. You see things in the flames, don't you?'

'Sometimes.'

'What do you see for my future?' Enid was pale and wide-eyed.

Tegen looked, then closed her eyes. 'I see a deadly struggle. You will win in the end, and you will do a great deed to save a friend.' Then she picked up a comb and tidied Enid's hair, although it was perfect already. Once more, she wished she could take Enid's place, but that could not be.

As night fell, Enid stood alone in her father's house, dressed in her long green ovate's robe. Her hair was plaited with ribbons and shells and around her neck was an ancient collar of gold, shaped like the crescent moon. Her arms jingled with silver bracelets and her ears pulled slightly under the weight of heavy pearl earrings. Over it all, she wore Tegen's necklace of rowan and mistletoe.

Outside, in the dark courtyard, someone blew a horn, long and low. Enid came to the door of her father's roundhouse and bowed to the spirits of the four quarters, then to Gronw who was seated in his wheeled chair.

Here and there, shadowy figures held flaming torches. The weak, golden lights danced and guttered in the wind, lighting the chilly faces of Bera's people, as well as the farmers and their families who had gathered from the valley.

One of Gronw's nephews pushed his chair towards Enid. The crowd followed. As they moved, the old druid played his harp and sang the story of Rhiannon and Pryderi. Snowflakes fluttered and fell, sticking to eyelashes and crusting cloaks with white – luminescent in the deepening gloom.

Enid led the clan elders back inside Teithi's home. There, Gronw was pushed widdershins around the fire, moving from right to left, undoing the Sun's natural path. As he moved, he splashed water from a bucket and doused the flames, leaving a sizzling, charcoally mess.

At the same moment, every torch was doused.

'The Sun has died,' Gronw intoned mournfully. 'Where shall we find our hope?'

Enid, her voice tight and high with fear, took a deep breath and answered, 'I, Rhiannon, am pregnant with the Child of Light. Tonight, my son, the Mabon, will be born to bring hope to you all.'

This was Tegen's cue. She stepped forward with the fire-making tools in a bronze cauldron and placed them on the floor. Enid knelt, took up the bow and spindle and worked them hard. At last smoke and then a small spark, caught in the dried grass. Tegen had wood chips ready: holly to bring brightness and truth, oak to protect the Light and ash to make a bridge to Tir na nÓg.

From somewhere out in the dark valley, there came a low, mournful cry.

Tegen shivered. The demon was very close, but she knew she'd be safe inside the House of Bera, just as the Child of Light would be safe with Enid in the Otherworld. She had to trust the Goddess, it was all she could do.

The tiny newborn fire flickered gold and uncertain within the sacred vessel. Gronw took up his song once more. Enid fed the flames with more shavings then, using the edge of her cloak, picked up the hot cauldron and carried it out into the swirling snow. The empty night was blue-black. The wind gusted. The fire flickered, looking for one awful moment as if it might die, then it strengthened into a glowing arc against the midwinter darkness.

With a steady step, Enid led the procession out of the main gate and down the steep eastern slope until she came to a narrow ledge cut into the rock. Gathering her cloak about her, she stooped and entered the Winter Chamber.

Tegen knelt at the cave mouth to give her friend one last smile and a blessing. By the red glow of the sacred flame, Enid's face looked like blood splashed in the shadows. She was wide-eyed and terrified.

Tegen remembered Goban's calmness as he was sacrificed to feed the Land at Lughnasadh. She shuddered. I hope Gronw's right and it seeks me, not her, Tegen thought. This is Enid's path. For now, she *is* Rhiannon. She must face the monstrous claw of death and winter with the power and blessing of Lugh's fire.

Maybe my demon is still waiting for me to play the part of the Mabon. But not tonight.

Tegen glanced back at the inky night then, reaching inside the cave, she touched Enid's fingers and whispered, 'All shall be well.'

'And all manner of things shall be well,' Enid replied with a quavering voice. Then the great stone was rolled across the entrance, letting only a tiny glimmer of firelight ripple gold in the snowy night.

For one instant, Tegen thought she heard a sob. 'It's just the wind,' she told herself as she followed the others back to warmth and safety.

25 * SUN'S RETURN *

Everyone in Bera was cold without fires, but the people kept busy. Women pounded fat and wheat with dried fruit and honey, then tied the puddings into linen-wrapped bundles ready to boil. Men soaked salted beef or cut berried holly and split ash logs. No thought was given to the Romans. No one fought at midwinter. The snow was too deep and the Mabon's birth, loss and reappearance had to be celebrated with great ceremony.

Nearby, the demon had neither forgotten not forgiven its latest defeat. Once more disincarnated and angry, it waited in the snow and watched the comings and goings of mere mortals with their petty spells. It could not enter the stronghold on the rocks. It had not been invited.

But that would only be a matter of time. All it had to do was wait.

Then, on the darkest night, it smelled a human presence outside the walls.

Sniffing, feeling and searching, it spread its icy mist until it pooled in warm footprints. Bitter winds had chilled the hollows, but there was no doubt. *She* had walked this way.

Then the demon heard a music it loved – fearful sobbing.

The sounds came from a glimmer of light behind a rock. Spirit shields were in place, but the maker was terrified. Their magic was unsteady. Stray wisps of mist slithered into the little cave, caressed a warm human cheek and feasted on the weeper's dread.

*

High in the stronghold, Tegen sat awake on her bed behind the screen in Teithi's house. She knew something was wrong. It wasn't just the emptiness of the sleeping space without her friend. It was more than that.

Enid was in danger.

Ought I to go to her? Tegen worried. She could not sleep.

She dressed, crept from the roundhouse and crossed the silent courtyard. The bitter cold burned through her clothes. She longed for Epona's comforting warmth, as well as the steady wisdom of Gronw. She hesitated. Which did she need more?

She chose wisdom and knocked on the druid's door. He was awake in his chilly, fireless cell. Moonlight streamed through the wind-eye onto his bed, where his ancient hands cast Ogham bones, again and again. He did not pause when Tegen entered.

'Something's wrong with Enid,' she said quietly.

'I know,' he replied. 'But we can do nothing except stay awake and protect her with love.'

'What about spells?' Tegen asked, amazed.

Gronw looked up at her, his face stark with pain in the meagre light. '*Think* child,' he said, 'cast your mind back to the finest spells you have ever known, were they made with love or magic?'

Tegen hesitated. 'Both, I suppose.'

'But without emotions, they wouldn't have worked at all. Love – or hate – is what fuels magic. Now, sit here and help me.' Side by side, they stayed awake all night, listening to wolves howling in the mountains. Together they breathed incense and wrapped

Enid in warm, safe thoughts while all the terrors of the night stalked the path outside her living tomb.

*

They were already too late.

Enid could scarcely move. With her extra cloaks and the small fire, the cold was not as intense as she had feared. But *something* was prowling nearby. Something she could neither smell nor identify from the padding of paws. But it was there all the same. In the coldest, loneliest, longest hours, she was certain she could hear a faint *sniffing*…

She clutched Tegen's necklace of dried mistletoe and rowan berries. She gripped it so hard the thread broke.

There was a low laugh and icy cold crept around her heart.

She screamed. But there was no one to hear.

By dawn, the presence slipped away. But Enid's terror remained.

*

Tegen was scarcely aware of day melting into night, then back into day again as she huddled on Gronw's stool, sending wave after wave of loving protection around her friend. It was only the ramshorn blown for dawn on the third morning that made her look up. She was freezing cold. Her head ached and her stomach was in knots.

Gronw stretched and yawned. 'The Sun has returned,' he announced. 'Help me into my chair and we will fetch the New Year's fire.'

Tegen ran on shaky legs to fetch Gronw's nephews, then

followed the druid out of the gate and down to the little rock chamber. The snow was melting and the air hung cold and damp.

The courtyard was full of sleepy, yawning people, shivering and silent in the half-light. Together, they made their way out of the gate and down the slushy slope. Tegen prayed Gronw's nephews wouldn't slip as they steered the wheeled chair down the treacherous path. At last they reached the shelf of rock that marked the entrance to the cave. 'We're here, Enid,' Tegen called out. 'Are you all right?'

'Wait a moment,' Enid replied. 'Let me shield the flame.'

But Tegen only heard muffled sounds as she and Gronw's nephews struggled to ease back the covering boulder. It fell back with a thud.

A gust of bitter wind blew into the little chamber and Enid's fire, so tenderly nurtured, spluttered and went out.

Tegen's face fell as she saw the trails of faint smoke wafting away on the icy air. Quickly she raised her hand over the ashy bowl. A small light flickered on the ashes. 'It's still alight!' she said, sprinkling woodchips into the hot embers.

As the tiny flame rekindled, Enid sprinkled tiny golden granules of incense over the hot embers. 'A blessing on the Mabon, the Son of Light,'

But Enid hid the fury in her heart. Tegen had destroyed her carefully nurtured flame and replaced it with *her* magic. That was all this half-trained girl cared about: showing that she was so much better than everyone else.

To think she'd thought of her as a *friend*! The voice had promised vengeance – but meanwhile she must be dignified.

Enid struggled out of the hole, weak and shivering. Tegen tried to hug her, but Enid shook her away.

Wrapping the bronze bowl in her cloak edges, Enid lifted it high and carried it towards her father's house. As she walked, she shouted, 'The Sun has returned, the Mabon is reborn! I, Rhiannon hid my son in a dark place until he was strong. Now he is amongst us to bring light and hope to our land. Rejoice!'

'*Rejoice!*' the people answered.

Tegen shuddered at the stony chill in Enid's voice. She's just tense and it's been a dreadful ordeal, she told herself. But she couldn't help worrying. Enid's footsteps wavered, but she refused all help. Soon they stood in the courtyard once more and the gates closed behind them.

One by one, people from every house came to light their flames from the sacred bowl. As they took the light, she blessed each one of them. But her eyes were narrow and the old sparkle was gone. Instead, there was a hard look that had never been there before.

Once all the fires had been re-kindled and food was cooking for the feast, Enid sat by her father's hearth devouring thick slices of bacon with fresh bread and stewed apples. She bathed and lay down to sleep on her bed behind the screen. Tegen brought her a hot stone wrapped in a shawl.

Instinctively, she knew she was no longer welcome as a companion in the little bed-space behind the screen, but how could she excuse herself without more offence?

She whispered, 'Epona's leg isn't healing well. I'm going to the stable.'

'As you wish,' Enid snapped, and turned over. Tegen gathered her things and slipped away.

*

At the feast that night, Enid sat next to her father. Firelight glinted on her golden jewellery and her hair shone like a raven's wing. She was a strong and beautiful druid princess at the height of her powers. Her three brothers stood proudly around her. Food was plentiful, everyone was merry. Jokes, games and songs abounded. Rhiannon was gloriously restored to her rightful place, bringing the Sun's Return.

All evening, Tegen watched silently from a stool by the door.

One by one, people drifted to their homes, or fell asleep where they were. Gronw had gone to bed hours before, so Tegen went towards her improvised bed in the stables. She longed to curl up hugging Wolf, listening to his rumbling snore under her face, but Epona's leg really did need attention before she could sleep.

Crossing the courtyard, Tegen looked for snow, but the partial thaw had done its work, and a sense of foreboding prevented her from going out of the gate to gather more. She did not want to ask Kieran to go for her. He was asleep nursing an empty mead flagon in the kitchen. Instead she went to the well in the courtyard and lowered a bucket. The water would be icy and she could make Epona stand in it. That would work just as well.

As Tegen leaned over the stone parapet, she saw the stars reflected in the black water. Shimmering above her own head were the nine silver points of the Watching Woman. So clear and bright. No one was around, so she put the bucket down, drew a sacred circle and bowed to the four quarters, greeting their spirits.

Then, untying her hair, she danced. In her mind she thanked the Goddess for a safe place to hide for the dark months, but she also prayed to be free to travel soon.

If only I could dance my way to Mona! But show me what is wrong with Enid, what happened to her in the cave? Can I help her, or is this anger part of her path?

As Tegen leaped across the cobbles, the wind blew her hair across her face, around her arms and twisted in the brooch that clasped her cloak. The tangling hurt and made her afraid. She stopped to sort herself out, but as she did so, a shadowy figure crept across the far end of the courtyard towards the stable.

Tegen pretended she had seen nothing. Her heart thudded. Why didn't the person speak? She tried to concentrate on the rest of her ritual, but she could not. So, leaving the water she had come for, she followed the figure.

Tegen pushed against the stable's hanging ox-hide. In the deep darkness, the ponies shifted uneasily. The intruder had one hand on Epona. The horse whinnied and strained against her tether, stamping in the straw.

'There, there, it's all right, don't fret my beauty,' Enid whispered, stroking Epona's thick mane.

Tegen was about to speak, but Enid began again: 'I dreamed in the dark, you know. I dreamed of you and me, riding across the valley and far, far beyond. Me a Queen, you my white mare, my prize, my sign of the Goddess's favour. The Lady's revealed to me that I really *am* Rhiannon, reincarnated to bring hope to the Land. Together we will find my Pwyll and give birth to a new Pryderi.

You too will have a foal, just as in the story. It's true! We will get rid of Tegen and you shall be mine. I saw it in the fire and in the darkness. The spirit of the Goddess whispered it to me in the night. Be patient my lovely and soon we shall both become great!'

Tegen held her breath. What's Enid talking about? she murmured. I *have* to know what happened in the winter chamber.

Enid stroked Epona's nose. The horse shifted forward nervously and trod on her foot. Doubled in pain, Enid screamed and stumbled backwards out of the doorway. Right into Tegen, who caught her.

'Are you all right?'

Enid writhed free, straightened herself and spat. 'You spying bitch! What are you doing here?'

'I sleep here now,' Tegen began, but Enid shoved her aside.

'Out of my way!' she snapped, then hobbled back to her father's roundhouse.

*

Next morning, Gronw called them both for lessons in herb lore, but although Enid behaved normally, the ice between the two girls had thickened. Afterwards, Tegen offered to make Gronw's bed so she could talk with him alone.

'Enid has changed,' Tegen whispered, shaking his blankets out.

'I know,' the old man grunted tersely.

'But how could anything have got through all that love we wrapped her in? We couldn't have prayed harder.'

Gronw shrugged. 'You can be given the finest cloak, but you have to choose to put it on.'

'But…' Tegen protested, but Gronw raised his hand. 'All will become clear by Imbolg. Now go, it is time you ate something.'

Later that day, Tegen tidied the winter chamber. She was worried. Enid's belief that she'd become Rhiannon made no sense. Maybe she'd eaten vision-food, or put seeing-herbs in the fire? Using a magical besom of dried birch and broom, Tegen cleansed the stones, then strewed the floor with chamomile, oak twigs and mistletoe to keep evil spirits away. As she worked, she searched, but there were no shreds of desiccated fungi or dried leaves and no charcoaled elder.

Only the broken remains of the rowan and mistletoe necklace.

As Tegen climbed back up to the stronghold, she bit her nails. If Enid hadn't taken hallucinogens then her strange ideas could only have come from one other source...

*

The demon did not care about Tegen's spells and cleansing rites. It had long gone from the lonely cave where it had played with its new toy – one who had not quite submitted to its will, but who at least listened.

And one day, she would invite it inside the gates of Bera.

*

After a while, Enid's old self seemed to return. She went around singing and chatted with Tegen about what she was going to do when she became a full druid at the next round moon on the night of Imbolg.

Tegen did her best to forget what she had overheard in the stable. She tried to believe Enid's ordeal had simply exhausted her, but there was always unease when they were together.

Enid refused to talk about the Winter Chamber. The nightmares lingered on: icy fingers of mist stroked her cheek and an unseen mouth whispered words that weren't words, hinting at monstrous ideas. These both thrilled and appalled her:

That girl has brought an evil spirit with her to the stronghold. She has stolen the Goddess's white horse. She has no right to the animal. The old man cannot see it – you must act! Send her to the mountains alone – and with nothing. You may keep the horse, and the boy – a thief doesn't deserve a servant. And the dog too? Why not? You are the blessed one. You are entitled to everything.

'But I can't do that, Tegen is my friend,' Enid told the shadows.

Is she? Is she? the shadows questioned back. *If you trust her, you will lose my protection against your fears.*

And Enid's fear was greater than her love.

Enid longed to talk to Gronw, but she could not frame her worries into words. She dared not allow her teacher to think she wasn't fit to take the white robe, so she kept her mouth shut. These stupid thoughts would pass.

Everything would be as it should once Tegen was gone.

Or would it? In the wakeful hours of the night, the voice persisted:

There is one other preventing you from becoming queen.

Who?

Look and see... Images of Enid's brothers drifted through her mind. It wasn't them. They were born and bred to the sword and didn't care who wore the crown. *They will lead the people of the tribe into glorious battle, which you, as their queen and chief druid, will control by your magic. You will be glorious.*

Then Enid's thoughts turned to Teithi. The people of the house of Bera adored him. Patricide was a sin Gwynn ap Nudd would never forgive, but Enid need not stoop to that, for the old man's days in this body were numbered. All she had to do was wait.

But, the voice persisted, Rhiannon *had* to have her magical white horse and surely there was none better in the whole of Cymru than Tegen's mare. If all the horse-breeders of the Silures, her own Ordovici, or even the Ceangli, put all their white mares to every white stallion for a thousand years, nothing as fine as Epona could ever be bred.

Enid daren't kill a fellow druid, the curse would follow her throughout her many lives to come.

Epona can be won, the voice in her head assured her. *Let me live inside you and I will guide you. I will make you into Rhiannon reborn. Single handed, you will chase the cursed Romans away. You will become the Star Dancer. Your story will be celebrated in song at every chieftain's hearth across the land.*

'I want that,' Enid whispered back.

The demon sighed and slithered contentedly into Enid's heart and mind, swathing them in a blanket of numbness that she took for peace and well-being.

There was one small place in her heart where the demon was denied access. Deep down, Enid knew that Tegen and Gronw loved her.

But all around that tiny sanctuary of truth, the demon's voice tormented Enid until nothing made sense.

26 * PREPARATIONS *

Two days before the great festival of Imbolg, Gronw summoned Tegen to his hut. 'Well,' he asked, 'do you have an answer for me yet?'

'An answer to what?'

Gronw smiled. 'To where your power comes from. Like the beer and the fish stew – it has to come from somewhere.'

Tegen hung her head. Since they'd discussed the web of magic, she'd racked her brains, but the answer was *too* obvious. She hesitated. 'Magic comes from the Goddess?'

'And from where does the Lady get the gift to give to you?'

'From herself.'

'And who is she?'

Tegen was irritated. Why does he *always* answer one question with another?

She resisted snapping back at him as she thought of last Samhain, when she had stood in the middle of a fire spiral, seeking answers to vital questions. Like Gronw, the spirits had only asked *more* questions in reply. These riddles had forced her to find the answers within herself.

Children required straight answers, Tegen realised. Druids need to learn to find wisdom within themselves.

She was silent for a long time, then answered, 'The Goddess is in us and we are in her – she is the fabric of all things. She is the weft and the warp – we are part of her woven pattern, and she is a part of ours. Her power is the rhythm of the loom, which is the turning year. My power comes from being able to hear that rhythm, and to be able to move with it. For me it comes best with dance, for you it comes in song and storytelling – and in questions,' she laughed. 'For Enid… I'm not sure about Enid.'

Gronw frowned as he drew himself upright in his chair. 'Enid is not being discussed at this moment. So, when you do a spell, where does the power come from?'

'Everything and everyone.'

'And what is affected by your spell?'

'Everyone and everything.'

Gronw pressed his hands together and considered Tegen over the tips of his fingers. 'Three days from now is Imbolg and Enid will take the white robe of a druid. First she must climb our great mountain, Cadair Idris. She must spend the night up there, for it is said that any who do so will either become a prophet, a poet – or go mad. Some even die. The peak is the seat of the greatest bards that our land has ever known. It is also known as the "perilous" seat because of the risk.'

'Of madness and death?' Tegen asked.

'Precisely.'

Gronw leaned forward and took Tegen's hand. 'I want you to go too, to look after Enid and be her friend. I fear her ordeal in the winter chamber was too much for her. When this is over, I give my word I will help you on your way. Will you do it?'

The thought of being in such a lonely place with Enid filled

Tegen with dread. 'I'm not sure whether she'd want me with her.'

'She asked for you. Remember I said all would be made clear at Imbolg? For Enid's safety and the success of your own quest, I believe you must both climb our mountain. By my reckoning it must be sixteen years since the night the stars danced for your birth. Cadair Idris will be auspicious for you.'

Tegen hesitated. 'My demon is out there waiting for me.'

'Are you afraid?'

Lifting her chin, she replied, 'No.'

'Then you're a fool. The Lady herself would be afraid up there.' He sighed. 'I can smell your demon on the wind. You know there is no way out of Bera without facing it. You have all the skills you need. Now, will you go?'

'Yes.'

'Good. Love sometimes makes the weave of a spell, but it also is capable of unpicking it. Sometimes it's hard to tell which way it is working, or why. As I told you before, Imbolg will resolve everything. Have faith in the Weaver.'

*

The following day, Kieran helped to pack provisions into strong bags, while Gronw ordered men's breeches for both girls. 'To wear under your robes, it'll be cold up there.' Hearing this, Kieran found Tegen's sheepskin jerkin and brushed up the pile to make it thick and fluffy once more.

'I wish I was allowed to come,' Kieran moaned. 'Wolf and me would rather be helping you than working in the kitchens. We feel so useless.'

'Making bread isn't useless,' Tegen replied.

Wolf pushed his nose into Tegen's hand and licked it warmly. Kieran stuffed a pouch of dried fruit into the rucksack and scowled. 'You don't want us to come!'

'Of course I do, it's just that…'

'I always said you'd leave me behind.'

'It's not like that. Anyway, I thought you believed mountaintops were best left to the gods? We're going to do druid things up there, and you don't like magic.'

'You need looking after. I'm not scared!'

Just then, Gronw wheeled his chair into the kitchen. 'Ah, Tegen's young friend! I think it'd be a very good idea for you to go as well. The girls'll need someone with a long knife and a sharp eye to protect them while they're meeting with the spirits. What's your name boy?' he asked.

'Kieran ap Cei.' He puffed out his chest. 'Son of the great warrior.'

Gronw nodded. 'Well, he'd be proud of you. Make sure you put in extra food for yourself – and water skins, but tie up that great hound in the stable. If he wanders off up there, Gwyn ap Nudd, Lord of the Otherworld, could steal him. He rides his wild hunt across the summit and he's always looking out for good dogs – as well as good souls,' he added under his breath.

That evening, Gronw called for the girls. 'Enid, I asked your father to have this made for you, to mark your passing into your full powers tomorrow.' He held up a cloak of cat pelts, gleaming a hundred different shades of red, gold and black in the firelight.

'How exquisite!' Enid gasped. As she draped the cloak around her shoulders, it swung almost to the ground.

'It's so soft and light!' Tegen exclaimed, jumping up and giving Enid a kiss. For a moment, she felt the touch of her old friend, happy and alive.

But then Gronw handed a heavy bundle to Tegen. 'I've nothing as pretty for you, but this should help to keep you warm and safe on the mountain.'

Tegen unfolded the cloak. It was made of ordinary sheepskin, stiff, cracked and smelly. Over her jerkin it would keep the weather out, and that was what mattered. 'Thank you, Gronw. I'll be very grateful for it in the middle of the night.'

A glance from Enid told Tegen that her resentments had once more arisen. But *why*? Tegen wondered, it's only an old cloak – not nearly as wonderful as hers.

*

The following dawn, Teithi pinned Enid's catskins over her many layers of clothing. He kissed her on the forehead as he pulled the furry hood over her tightly bound hair. 'Come back to me in the morning, my song thrush, I'll miss your music tonight.'

The old chieftain turned away with a coughing spasm. He held a piece of linen to his face and tucked the tell-tale splashes of blood out of sight.

Tegen glimpsed a malicious smile flicker across Enid's face, but she told herself she was wrong. Enid adored Teithi.

It's just trepidation, she told herself, glancing up at the fog-swathed majesty of the mountain. I'm sure the demon's up there waiting for me. But this is my path, I must walk it, even if I do look more like a sheep farmer than a druid. With that, she slung a stout leather bag full of food over her shoulder and chose a thick ash staff. She smiled at Kieran who wore so many shirts and socks he looked like a small bear. His back was stooped under a heavy bundle of firewood wrapped in a long length of linen boiled in oil.

Teithi ordered the stronghold gates to be opened and his chief warrior blew a ramshorn.

Gronw spread his arms and kissed them all.

May the Lady watch you and keep you,
and turn her face towards you.
May you learn her wisdom, her words and her ways,
and may you return to us safely,
with her favour upon you.

Then he handed Enid a white lambswool scarf. 'In earnest of the white robe that will be waiting for your return,' and he pressed an acorn into her hand for protection.

'Go,' he said to the travellers, 'and always do what is right.'

Enid bowed her head respectfully and turned away, leading the group down the rocky path through the flat meadows, then northeastward towards the mountain-seat of Cadair Idris.

As she walked, Enid let the acorn fall in the mud.

*

High in the mountain passes, the demon waited. At last its puppet and its prey were on their way together.

27 * CADAIR IDRIS *

Enid chose a track that climbed steadily out of the valley, but walking was miserable. Sleet slapped them in the face and pale clay made their boots heavy. High above, Cadair Idris towered, its head swathed in forbidding clouds.

Tegen tried not to let her heart sink at the prospect of the journey ahead.

They passed Bera's farmsteads within their high-banked enclosures where chilly cattle and sheep huddled with scolding geese. The path swung to their right and began to climb a wooded foothill, rich with the purple haze of early leaf buds. A few catkins tossed in the wind and Tegen reached up and touched them, smiling at her dusty yellow fingers.

As they walked, the hazel and ash gave way to scrubby hawthorns and silver birch dotted between furze and sharp, shattered rocks. They climbed higher and the stony pastures became patched with rusty bracken scattered like weavings of red, green and gold – royal cloaks for mountain gods. The path became slippery and treacherous as it led them high above the deeply creased valleys.

Enid stomped ahead, jumping icy streams and clambering over the grey outcrops of rock that bulged in their way. As she moved, the cat-skins shimmered, making her seem both lithe and predatory. Tegen and Kieran dragged behind with their burdens.

At last Enid sat on a boulder and waited for them. 'Fill the flasks,' she ordered, 'then we'll eat.' Kieran clung to the overhanging boughs of a silver birch and scooped at the rushing water while Tegen opened her satchel. 'What would you like? Meat? Bread? Cheese?'

Enid took a beer loaf and washed it down with water. She said nothing, locked in her own thoughts.

It's like she's built a stone wall around herself since midwinter, Tegen thought. I wish she'd let me in. I might be able to help.

As she repacked the food and shouldered her bag once more, Tegen looked around and tried to use all her senses. Was the same demon that tormented her, now destroying Enid? Where was it now? In what form was it lurking? She wished she knew what it wanted.

Far below, thick mist drew a veil across the valley's wild rusted hillsides and the tossing bare-branched trees. Above, the path became steeper and more slippery, winding ever higher between tufts of whistling rushes.

As soon as she had eaten, Enid strode ahead, quickly fading into the whiteness. Under the weight of their burdens, Tegen and Kieran struggled behind her. Cloud droplets soaked their clothes. The weight sapped their energy.

'What's that?' Kieran whispered, pointing at a grey horned shape looming out of the mist.

Tegen, whose thoughts had been on demons, stood stock still, her heart pounding.

Another apparition joined the first. It snorted, stamped, and sent a hollow thud ricocheting between the rocks.

Kieran slid alongside Tegen. 'It's not…?' he began as both figures became wreathed in white steam.

For a split second, Kieran grabbed Tegen's hand. Then he leaped away and burst out laughing. 'It's a bloomin' goat!'

Tegen shuddered. She was glad her blushes didn't show. Demons, bears, goats… The fog was too full of the unknown for her to laugh. What new demon-possessed creature might be waiting for her at the peak…?

'I wish *we* were goats,' she said. 'Then we might be able to get up this mountainside a bit more easily.'

'We can do it, but I don't think her ladyship really wants us here,' Kieran replied, shifting his baggage across his aching shoulders.

Tegen sighed as she saw how quickly the path disappeared into the gloom. 'Whether she wants us or not, we'd better hurry or we'll lose her in the fog.'

*

But Enid *did* want Tegen with her. Very much so.

The voice that had comforted her in the midwinter chamber had often spoken since – teaching her to understand things that doddery old fool Gronw had never explained. Now she could read what people were *really* thinking behind their false smiles. She understood how they were plotting to keep her from greatness. Gronw and all his chatter about the web of magic, the fabric of all things: it was just talk, preventing her from doing *real* spells.

He was going to make Tegen the new druid.

Why hadn't she seen it all before?

He'd made it clear when he fobbed Enid off with a mangy cat skin instead of his magic cloak. Cracked and smelly it may be, but it was his, and it carried all his hoarded powers.

Enid slowed her pace. 'How are you doing, Tegen? Is Kieran still with you?' The fog muffled her voice.

'We're fine!' Tegen shouted breathlessly as they struggled against the steep incline into the swallowing blankness of the cloud.

'Good, I wouldn't want to lose you. Let's rest.' Seated on a lichen-streaked rock, she shrank under her cloak and shivered as Tegen shared bread and cheese around. Enid's body was weary, but her will was not. Once more they ate and drank.

Come to me alone, the voice in Enid's head whispered. *We must speak without being heard.*

'Stay here and get your strength back,' Enid suggested as she brushed the crumbs from her clothes. 'I'll go ahead and find the best path.' Then the fog swallowed her once more.

Tegen and Kieran sat on wet boulders and waited. Tegen called out once or twice, but there was no answer. She was beginning to get worried, when suddenly Enid's dark shape appeared to their left. 'This way. Not far now!' she shouted.

Aching and exhausted, they got to their feet and trudged after her. Soon the marshy turf and tussocks of rushes gave way to a bare mass of crushed slate and broken rocks. A bitter wind began to blow, buffeting them from all sides. Staying upright became a struggle but the fog did not clear.

'How will we know when we're at the top?' Tegen panted.

Enid put her arm around Tegen's shoulders. 'It's just there, look!' Her hood fell across her face as she pointed to a steep escarpment that loomed out of the mist. 'Do you see? There was once a great giant called Idris who lived up here and the gods carved a stone chair for him to look out over the world. Now it belongs to us druids so we can see everything and know all! It's the centre point of the night sky, all the stars spin around this very spot.'

Kieran dumped his burdens. 'Is that where you're stopping?'

Enid stretched her arms and span around triumphantly. 'Yes, oh yes, this is where *everything* will happen!'

'I'll make you a shelter,' he said, 'but it can't be right at the top, or it'll get blown away.' He walked downhill until he found an outcrop of black rock that would provide a windbreak. Struggling against the gale, he tossed his bundle of wood onto the ground and spread the oiled linen between the boulders, weighing it down with large stones. Sacrificing a precious piece of firewood to make a centre pole, he erected a low tent. The linen flapped and cracked in the wind. 'It's going to be a cruel night,' he shouted to Tegen as she struggled to help. 'It won't be so bad for me, I'll be moving around keeping guard, but you'll probably freeze!'

He considered what was left of the wood. 'This won't burn all night,' he said doubtfully. 'I'll go and look for more.'

'Where?' Tegen yelled over the slamming winds.

'There's a dead tree – quite a long way back, but I think I can find it.'

Tegen looked up at the sky. The sun was completely veiled,

but she guessed it was half way through the day's course. There was plenty of time. 'Don't get lost,' she said nervously.

*

Enid was busy in the little shelter, arranging incense, beeswax candles, her silver bowl and a small sacred rock into their ritual positions. Tegen built a walled hearth with flat stones, then stacked the firewood beside it.

'What do you want me to do now?' she asked.

Enid crawled out of the tent and looked around. 'Where's Kieran?'

'Gone back down the path for more firewood.'

'He'll be ages,' Enid smiled. 'Come with me, I want to show you something.' With that, she led the way past the Seat of Idris and along a rocky track, scrambling over grey stones and slithering down the treacherous scree between broken moraines. At last, the wind parted the clouds enough to show a steep-sided crater ahead. 'Careful, the path is loose here,' she said, grabbing hold of Tegen's arm, almost unbalancing her.

'Let go!' Tegen called back. 'I have my staff, I can keep better balance on my own.'

But Enid did not let go. She held on tightly until they reached a crag above a wide, black lake, as still and polished as obsidian. 'That's Llyn Cau. It's bottomless, you know,' she said, still grasping Tegen's sleeve. It's the gate to Tir na nÓg where Gwyn ap Nudd leads his hunting dogs, the Cŵn Annwn. White they are, with red ears and red eyes, like drops of blood on snow...'

She breathed into Tegen's ear. 'Their task is to round up souls and imprison them below the lake, from where there will be no rebirth.'

Tegen stepped away, but Enid pulled her back towards the edge. 'The howling of Gwyn's dogs foretells the death of anyone who hears them. They herd that soul into the underworld. Did you see those ridges of rock that looked like smooth white flocks of sheep on the way up? They are really some of the Cŵn Annwn that stayed in our world, ready for the nightly hunt. By day they stand so still you'd think they were stone, but they're *hell hounds*, waiting for nightfall…'

Enid stared around wildly and Tegen shuddered with horror. Her friend was quite mad – and they were alone on a narrow ledge with a deadly drop below.

'I thought I heard Kieran calling,' Tegen shook herself free. 'I ought to go and help him.' Her heart was pounding. They were too near the edge.

'He doesn't matter,' Enid laughed. '*We* do.'

'Why have you brought me here?'

Enid parted her lips, blue with cold and breathed, 'Ahhh…' A tiny trickle of pale mist seeped out. Her eyes rolled back and she began to tremble.

The demon was using Enid! Tegen flattened herself against a boulder. Her head was spinning. She had to weave a fierce spell to repel the evil, but one that wouldn't destroy her friend.

This had no time to listen – she had to *act*.

In that instant, Enid lunged forwards, snarling and digging her nails into Tegen's throat.

28 * LLYN CAU *

The steep rocks echoed with the sound of Tegen's screams.

Above, the mist was clearing, but in the hollow below it rolled and boiled like a giant's cauldron, pouring over the easterly lip and down the edge of the mountain.

A few stones shifted and rattled, bouncing down the steep scree and disturbing the iron black surface of the Llyn.

'You've woken Him now,' Enid laughed with a sneer, pushing Tegen away.

'Who?'

'Gwyn ap Nudd, of course, the King of the Otherworld, the Lord of Tir na nÓg.'

'I've nothing to fear from him,' Tegen began, but at that moment, a lonely howl echoed across the lake.

Even Enid stopped. Her blank eyes found their focus, her face went white and her hands shook. 'He's come, with his hell hounds, his *Cŵn Annwn*, to hunt you down,' she whispered.

'Why should he hunt me?' Tegen asked.

'Because you won't give me your magic horse, without which I cannot be queen. You must also hand over your powers so I become chief druid of all of the tribes. You are nothing. I am the Star Dancer. I will save Britain.' Enid's unbound black hair flew as wild as a banshee's. She unclasped her cat-skin cloak and it rippled in golden folds around her feet.

Enid snarled and hissed as more mist trickled from her nose and mouth. 'Give me what I want!'

Tegen shoved her aside, but as they touched, she heard Enid's trapped soul call out in terror. *Help me*!

Tegen tried to remain calm, but a tangle of powerful magic was tightening around her, demanding to be used… Magnificent spells that would destroy her enemies, making *her* the most powerful druid in Britain *and* Cymru!

But she could not find the Goddess's patterns within the spell-weaving that shimmered in her mind. Such glory would do no good in the end. She pushed the temptations aside. 'Enid, I'll help you get through this, but you've got to *fight*!'

Enid draped her arms around Tegen and wheedled, 'I know you hate what's inside me – make a spell to destroy it, *please…*'

'I can't. That would destroy you, too.'

'Do you think I care?' a thin voice crackled from Enid's lips.

Just then, at the edge of the lake something moved. Was it hell hound or fox?

In that vital moment of lost concentration, fear overwhelmed Tegen and she intoned the words of exorcism:

Spirit of darkness, night and fear,
I banish you, come not near.
Go to the place of utter dread,
Leave this woman's heart and head.

As Tegen spoke, Enid grew stronger and stood straighter. 'Good,' she smiled, her eyes still rolling and unfocussed, but at the same time peering right into Tegen's soul. '*Very* good, do more… Send my tormentor away… Do it for me Tegen!'

Taking a deep breath, Tegen summoned all her fear and cursed the demon. The form that should have been her friend shimmered, became shadowy and *grew*.

Unutterable weariness made Tegen stagger. Then she realised the enormity of her mistake. It wasn't where her magic was coming *from* that was the problem, but where it was going *to*… Gronw had said that magic was fueled by emotions.

Spells built with fear *fed* the demon!

Enid leaned forward, her wild hair whipping at Tegen's face as she grabbed her arms and shook her. 'I need *more magic*! NOW!'

'*No!*' Tegen yelled, pushing her away.

Enid lost her balance and grabbed at Tegen's cloak with flailing arms.

Together they tumbled over the edge and onto a bed of shattered slate.

With a roar, the scree gave way as the girls slid on the rushing, cracking stones. Kicking, screaming and biting, Tegen and Enid tumbled over and over. Hair caught in stone, blood trickled in their eyes, teeth crunched on grit. Skin scraped, heads thudded. Breath slammed from chests and elbows cracked.

Sky and stone, blood and body changed places again and again.

For a brief moment, they both came to rest on a small ledge of white rock. Blood dripped and splattered as the opponents gasped for breath.

Tegen's right shoulder raged. She kicked hard with both feet. Enid flailed and struggled to balance. Screeching, Enid grabbed Tegen's hair, yanked her head forward and dragged her down with her onto the next stretch of scree.

At that moment, another mournful howl echoed from the mist that boiled in the night-black lake below. Tegen tried not to think of hell hounds. More stones shifted and fell into the edge of the water, sending slow, even ripples across the surface.

They were sliding fast. Too fast. The cauldron of Llyn Cau was ready for them. At the very edge, their clothes caught on a hummock of sharp reeds. Enid's boots kicked mud into water.

Tegen managed to sit. '*Stop it, Enid*!' she gasped, spitting sand and blood. She wiped her arm across her mouth and flicked her hair back. 'I don't want to hurt you. You're my friend. Let's go back and talk to Gronw! This isn't how it's supposed to be…!'

Enid began to yell a foul-mouthed reply, then they both saw it… *Something* was moving across the llyn.

Out of the mist, a dark shape was gliding towards them flanked by gleaming arrow-ripples.

In her own voice, Enid screamed, 'The Cŵn Annwn, they've come for me…!' With that, she convulsed and fainted. A final trickle of vapour trailed from her mouth.

Scrambling to her feet, Tegen grabbed Enid under her arms and struggled to drag her back from the water's edge, but she was a dead weight and impossible to move.

Tegen staggered, defeated by pain and lack of breath. Struggling to keep upright, she stood on the loose scree and tugged her sheepskin cloak around her. She touched Enid's face.

She could sense no evil – the demon had gone – for now at least. All she could find was Enid's soul caught in a lost, far corner of her being, fluttering like a terrified bird, unable to make sense out of anything.

The light was beginning to fade and the Cŵn Annwn were on the loose. Tegen knew that unless she chose the right path, both she and Enid would die before dawn and maybe their souls would be lost as well. Did Llyn Cau have a song like the rivers? If only she had time to listen and learn it. Maybe it was about being calm in a fearful place? Maybe the Lord of the Otherworld was not unkind if spoken to with courtesy?

Tegen stilled her breathing, tugged back her tangled hair and spread her arms towards the lake: 'Lord Gwyn ap Nudd, forgive us for trespassing in your sacred place. We ask safe passage back to our world. Show me how to help my friend.'

The only answer was the sound of claws scrabbling for purchase on the shattered slate shore.

29 * CŴN ANNWN *

Tegen closed her eyes and tried not to dread the spectral beast with red ears and eyes that was closing in on her.

'I greet you, hound of Gwyn ap Nudd,' she said aloud. 'I'm ready to come if your master has called me, but please leave my friend Enid; she is not in her right mind. Unless she faces death with clarity, she might not be born a princess in her next life. She doesn't deserve to come back as a slave.'

Light paws padded closer…

She did not dare look. She held her breath.

…And was showered with icy water.

Squealing, Tegen jumped back and stared in disbelief.

For standing in front of her, wet and shivering, was a very ordinary, mud-coloured dog. Its long pelt dripped in points and a skinny tail wagged frantically. The animal leaped at Tegen, knocked her to the ground and licked her face all over with a warm tongue.

'Wolf?' she gasped. 'How did you get here? You were tied up in the stable!' Tears of relief and joy streamed down her face as she hugged him until her shoulders hurt.

'Listen boy, I know you've only just found me, but I need to leave you here. You must stay and guard Enid. Look after her. I'll be back straight away. *Stay…*'

Then, with every joint and bone aching, she worked her way

back up the edge of the scree to the top. There she saw a glimmer of light and smelled wood-smoke. She braced her feet, took a deep breath and called out, 'Kieran! Kieran, come quickly, I need you!' But there was no answer from the thickening mist.

Tegen tried to run, but she hurt all over.

Kieran must have returned from foraging because she hadn't lit a fire before going to Llyn Cau. She called again.

'Tegen!' he yelled back. His lanky frame sprang from the fog, waving wildly. 'Where was you? I was worried!'

She told him what had happened. 'Didn't you hear shouting and screaming?'

He shrugged. 'I did, but I thought it was some weird ritual, you druids do awful strange stuff at times. I kept me distance. I know I mustn't get in the way.'

'Well you're needed now, Enid's hurt, we have to get her back up the slope. I left Wolf guarding her.'

'But Wolf's at Bera,' Kieran began.

Tegen shrugged. 'I've no idea how he got here, but I've never been so glad to see him!'

In the semi-darkness they picked their way down to the water's edge. Wolf's barking led them to where Enid lay, semi-conscious and whimpering with fear.

Together they half-dragged, half-carried her back up to the little shelter. Kieran rescued Enid's cat-skin cloak from the top of the cliff and wrapped it around her. She stopped shivering, but screamed every time she caught sight of Wolf.

Unperturbed, the dog lay down under the far edge of the tent and chewed contentedly on a piece of cold meat.

Tegen cleaned herself up a little and put her hair into a tangled plait. She shared her food with Kieran and tried to make Enid eat, but she only tossed and screamed, 'Hell hounds!' until she sobbed herself to sleep.

'What's wrong with her?' Kieran asked, keeping as far away as possible.

Tegen stroked Enid's hair tenderly. 'I think the demon that possessed the bear took over Enid for a while. It's gone now, but she's been terrified out of her mind. What's left of her can't see what's real. She thinks Wolf is a hell hound come to take her soul. I've no idea what she thinks *I* am…'

'What're we gonna do with her?' Kieran asked.

'Nothing we *can* do, except wait for morning.'

'What about me? It's cold up here,' Kieran looked at the fire longingly.

'What do you mean?'

'Well, you'll be doing druidy things all night, you won't want me around. I guess you want me to keep me distance?' he held his hands to the warmth.

Tegen laughed. 'Of course not. Enid might have sent you away, but I'd much rather have you and Wolf by my side. Now, come further in, it's warmer.'

'I'll lie here then, if that's all right?' Kieran curved his arms around the dog and was soon snoring as well.

*

While the others slept, Tegen sorted through their scarce supply of wood. It was just about enough. She sat by the fire at the tent entrance and stared into the flames. She was angry. If this was the demon that pursued her, it had no right to attack her friend. Why hadn't the Goddess protected Enid at midwinter? Why had she allowed a good soul to be bullied and beaten down?

Tegen jabbed a stick into the embers, making sparks fly into the night sky. I suppose it wants to prevent me from being the Star Dancer and expelling the Romans. But *why*? It's not a Roman demon – it came from our own funeral caves.

Then she remembered old Gwen's ghost at Bagendun saying, 'Nothing to do with *that* makes *any* sense…'

Tegen watched Enid tossing and turning. What it's done to her makes no sense! She buried her face in her hands and remembered her man Griff, Gilda the midwife and her dear friend Owein. How many more good people must suffer because of me? she groaned. Who's next? Gronw? Teithi? Not Kieran, please…

There's nothing for it, she decided. The weather's mild, so guide or no guide, in the morning, I'll leave Enid in Gronw's care and set off for Mona.

Inside the tent, Wolf grunted contentedly and Kieran rubbed his ears. What about them? she wondered. Kieran's done all he promised and more. They both deserve a home and the people of Bera will welcome them.

But I will need a friend. Now Epona's leg's healed, I'll take her.

Staring into the flames, she read the patterns that danced there. Kieran's path really did lay in Cymru.

Her own future was always difficult to read, but at the moment it seemed to be green-grey and rising and falling. Never mind, she told herself, the Goddess will show me the way. Both Goban and the river-song told me to head for the sea. So that's what I'll do.

Tegen wriggled out from under the tent and climbed up to the rocky summit. She had to think. The misty dark made her feel lonely and heart-weary. Why doesn't the wind ever blow the fog away? she wondered.

Then understanding made her shiver. It's because it's just around *me*, that's why! The demon is trying to cut me off from all that is real!

She took a deep breath and raised her arms. I've had enough of being chased, she told herself. I *have* to see the stars. I *need* to do magic. The power will come from the Lady, but I'll make a spell to bring light and hope it won't damage the fabric of all things. It will strengthen it. Here on Cadair Idris, there's a part of the weave where the thread is weak – it needs a new, stronger yarn – the Lady's work entwined with mine!

It will be a sacred spell made with love that will choke the demon, not feed it. Taking a deep breath, Tegen blew into the fog. As she did so, the mist parted like steam from a cooking pot.

In that moment, starlight from the Watching Woman twinkled through. All around, the pale vapour rolled back leaving the night sky black and crystal-bright. Above her head, stars danced in constellations that Tegen had never noticed before. Each one was intensely sharp and clear, and so close she felt she could have touched them if only her arms had been a little longer. Low in the east, the new moon was rising, as clear as a sickle of silvered ice.

She could scarcely breathe with the wonder and beauty of it. Here indeed was the centre-point of the night sky, and all the stars were swirling slowly and majestically around her.

Now was the time for magic!

*

Tegen's spell rolled the demon up in its own blanket of fog and flung it down the mountainside to ache in a lost ravine.

There it lay, oozing venomous hatred for the Star Dancer.

Once again it had failed to terrify her into submission.

No! It was the woman who had failed! Her task was bring the girl-prey to this desolate spot, feed her with dread and hatred, and then desert her. But she had hesitated over – what was that word? *Love*?

The demon had enjoyed ripping the woman's mind apart. Now nothing would ever make sense to her again.

It had left her quite mad.

The demon took an oath. It *would* control the Star Dancer and bring her power under its will. The fight was not over yet. All across the land there were others who clung to its spirit of hatred and vengeance.

It would use them.

The mist rolled away westwards towards the sea and hung there, smothering the jagged black rocks where waves crashed.

30 * DREAMING *

It was of waves that Tegen dreamed as she curled up under the stars.

Dressed in hunting breeches and tunic with her hair tightly plaited, Tegen found herself running through a thick forest, but underfoot was all water – clear and grey-green, rising and falling. Her feet stayed dry and the trees were firmly rooted: it was, and was not, the sea.

It was clearer and wilder than she'd imagined and the spray coated her lips with salt.

In her dream it was a bright day, the sun was warm and she was happy. In her hand was a small hunting bow with one arrow. From time to time, she could hear the belling cries of hell hounds in the distance. But she wasn't afraid, for they were hunting *with* her. She had no idea what she was hunting, or why, but the world was wonderful as she wandered between the rising and falling woodland, her booted feet splashing the surface of the water. Ahead, the sun was setting, turning the sky pink, yellow and cornflower blue.

Then there were no more trees. The swelling sea was rippled with purple and deep green, slashed with sunset's golden road westwards. Here and there, the white dogs of Gwyn ap Nudd danced in the waves and were gone.

Laughing for joy, Tegen ran towards the burning red of the dying sun until she came to a shore of soft, silver sand where a warm breeze stirred her hair. The sense of happiness and wellbeing swathed her.

From behind came a roar of anger. She turned. Across the beach thundered a giant in Roman armour, raging and shouting. Tegen did not understand his words, but she knew he had come to plunder the green inland hills. Horrified, she nocked her one arrow, wondering if such a little thing could destroy this creature.

Then a voice she knew and loved spoke inside her head. *No, don't waste your arrow. You must hunt for the Wave that will heal the Land.*

It was the Goddess.

'How can I hunt a *wave*?' she gasped.

The Wave will come to you.

Then she saw a tall figure of a man. She didn't know who he was, but she had to run to him, for he was the source of the happiness she felt.

Then by her side another figure appeared. Tegen held out her hand with delight. It was Sabrina, still dressed as a gladiatrix, her wonderful hair pinned up and her strong limbs bound with the thick protective bandages. Her eyes were bright with the exhilaration of the hunt.

The princess caught Tegen's hand firmly in her calloused grip. '*Together!*' she called out.

'Together!' Tegen laughed.

Then a cold trickle of fear made the hairs on the back of her neck stand on end. She wasn't frightened of the giant, even though he crashed closer, ever closer.

But far away there was a *presence* on the water.

One she did not want to meet again, but knew she must.

*

Tegen woke with a brilliant morning sun in a bluebell sky. For a moment she feared she might have fallen off the end of the world, for she could see no valleys or plains, only a vast bed of intense downy whiteness spread in all directions. Here and there stark mountain-peak islands rose up like thrones for heroes.

Tegen laughed and jumped like a child. It was Imbolg, her sixteenth birthday, and she had dreamed of wonders. 'Thank you Lady!' she called out to the Goddess. She found a flattish platform of rock and threw aside her heavy sheepskins. Shivering in the clear-wine air, she raised her arms and stamped her feet to a merry rhythm in her head.

But her celebration was broken by the sound of sobbing and screaming. Grabbing her cloak, Tegen rushed back towards the camp. There she found Enid thumping Kieran with her fists.

He looked exhausted. 'Tegen! Thank goodness! I tried to make her calm down. I only got bits of sleep all night. Every time she woke, she screamed the Cŵn Annwn were after her and she tried to throw rocks at Wolf. The moon goddess has stolen her wits!'

'You should have called me.'

'You was doing druid-things.'

Tegen took Enid by the arm. 'Everything's all right. We're taking you home, to Teithi and Gronw. Let's go and see them, shall we?' Then she turned to Kieran. 'Take Wolf, run ahead and tell Gronw what's happened. Ask someone to bring a pony as far up the track as they can. We'll meet you.'

Kieran folded the tent and gathered up as much of their gear as he could carry. Then, whistling for Wolf, he set off.

Step by step, Tegen coaxed Enid down the mountain after him. The sun was already on its journey towards the west by the time they struggled through the clumps of hazel and ash at the head of the valley. There was a sharp whinny beyond the trees, and then Kieran appeared with Epona and half a dozen of Teithi's men.

But when Enid saw the horse, she screamed and clawed at Tegen's eyes. 'The White Horse of Gwyn ap Nudd! You've betrayed me! You've led me to be swallowed up by the Otherworld, I *knew* I shouldn't trust you!' She grabbed a handful of Tegen's hair and yanked hard.

One of the warriors sprang forward, grabbed Enid's wrists, then flung her over his shoulder, ignoring her yelling and screeching.

Bloody and exhausted, Tegen took Epona's reins from Kieran and hauled herself into the saddle. 'I'll go ahead and speak with Gronw,' she said, and set off.

*

As she made her way up the narrow path cut in the rock that led to the House of Bera, Tegen's heart sank. What was she going to tell everyone? Would they blame her for what had happened?

The stronghold's courtyard was crowded with people, all facing Teithi's roundhouse. Some were weeping, others waving talismans and bundles of smouldering herbs in the air. All fell silent at Tegen's approach. Some even made the sign against the evil eye and averted their gaze.

Ignoring them, she led Epona back to the stable. From the gathered crowd, she guessed Teithi was dying and Gronw would be with him. Enid should not be brought into the enclosure for everyone to gawp at, but there was no choice.

The crowd parted as Tegen marched across the courtyard, past the well and into Teithi's roundhouse.

'A druid's blessing on this home,' Tegen intoned, peering through the semi-darkness for the old chieftain.

On the far side of the roaring fire, Teithi raised a pale hand in greeting as Tegen entered, but the effort made his chest hack and rattle. He sank back into the piles of rolled sheepskins and closed his eyes. Blood-streaked mucus stained his white tunic. The coughing sickness that had plagued him all winter was about to claim him.

Gronw nodded briefly to Tegen as he lifted a bowl to his patient's frothy lips. Sweat beaded on the chieftain's face as he tried to drink. Even his sparse silver hair weighed him down.

'How is Enid?' Gronw whispered, placing the bowl on a table. 'Kieran told me what happened,'

Tegen knelt by his side. 'Clud the warrior is bringing her home now. They shouldn't be long. She will need a strong sleeping draught.'

'Please make one up for her, Tegen. Put her to sleep in my bed, I won't be leaving here tonight. Ask Clud if he and his woman will watch over her, then you must return here straight away.'

Outside, the crowd started shouting and wailing. Tegen went to the door and saw Enid, still screaming, being brought through the gates over Clud's shoulder. Tegen gave the man Gronw's instructions and collected vervain, hops and honey from the druid's cupboard to make a sleep-inducing tisane. The hut was so narrow, she went to the stronghold kitchen to brew. While the little bronze cauldron was heating, Tegen washed her own cuts and scratches and combed her hair.

When the draught was ready, Tegen found Enid tucked up in the druid's bed, just as she had seen in the midwinter fire.

Clud's woman was bustling about, demanding Gronw's bucket to be emptied and rearranging the old man's things.

Tegen handed her the potion-filled cup. 'I will get bread and soup sent in for you both. Don't be frightened. Enid sees things in her head that aren't real, so ignore her. She may even hit out at you or try to flee. If she does, tell Clud to tie her to the bed. I will be back as soon as I can.'

In her mind, Tegen was struggling. Her plans were falling apart. Should I stay and help Gronw care for Enid and Teithi, she asked herself, or should I leave right now?

A low whistle interrupted her thoughts; Kieran was beckoning her to join him in the woodshed.

'Bad stuff's happening,' he whispered. 'They're saying that you brought Teithi's illness when you arrived, then you turned into a demon on the mountain and drove Enid mad. I keep telling them, but they won't listen.' Kieran looked nervously over his shoulder. 'Watch out Tegen. I ain't no warrior, I'll always do what I can to protect you, but these Cymry are deadly!'

'I'd rather have you by my side than any of them,' Tegen whispered. 'I need to get back to Teithi. Take food to Gronw's hut

191

then meet me in the stables as soon as you can.'

With a sinking heart, Tegen walked back through the silent, angry gathering to the chieftain's roundhouse. She bit her lip and her eyes stung. It had been like this in her childhood home by the Winter Seas, when the people she had cared for turned on her for no reason.

Nothing ever seemed to make sense.

31 * LEAVING BERA *

Tegen fought sleep as she sat with Gronw, reciting prayers. The chieftain's sweaty hair lay plastered to his face. Behind closed lids, his eyes flickered wildly.

'He's halfway into the afterlife already,' Gronw whispered.

Tegen gripped Teithi's damp hand. How could she leave him and Enid when they were both so ill? 'Can I try some magic?' she asked quietly.

'What for?' Gronw's eyes glittered in the firelight.

Tegen fought her irritation. 'So he gets better.'…And so I can leave *now*, with a clear conscience, she added to herself.

Gronw shook his head. 'If he recovers, he'll be an invalid, raging at his incapacity and tormented by Enid's madness. Tir na nÓg holds no fears for him and his son Penn is ready to rule.' Gronw placed a kindly hand on Tegen's shoulder. 'Let Teithi go. It is all part of the weave. It takes a strong love to allow what must be to happen.'

Silently, Tegen watched the hearth-fire's dance. She knew what the flames were telling her. She had to hurry and there was no reason to feel guilty going. But she couldn't leave with the people's hatred following her. 'Gronw, have you heard what's being said about me?'

'I have. I will turn their fears aside.'

'I dreamed on the mountain.'

Gronw nodded slowly. 'And Enid went mad... Did Kieran come back a poet?'

Tegen laughed quietly. '*Kieran*? I don't think so!'

The druid stroked his dark moustache as his eyes sparkled. 'Wait and see. *No-one* is beneath the Lady's bounty!' Then he became serious. 'Speaking of that, I have a confession. I always feared for Enid sleeping alone on the mountain. I'd guessed her mind was weak, but she had to face her own trial. When you turned up at midwinter, I was overjoyed. A suitable companion for her! I'll never climb to the Seat of Idris again. As you know, whoever sleeps at the top must return as a prophet, a poet or mad. I knew one of the greater gifts would be yours, which was as it should be for you are the Star Dancer. I suggested that Kieran went too, not just as a servant, but so that there would be one other to go mad – someone who didn't matter – so Enid could take the third gift.'

He hung his head and sighed. 'But I presumed to dictate to the Goddess. I didn't listen. I was wrong and now Enid's mind has unravelled.'

Tegen was livid. How *dare* he think Kieran didn't matter? She took a deep breath... Then she let her anger go. The old man had confessed, and now he was suffering. It was enough that the child he had lovingly trained to take the white robe in his place was ruined. He would have no successor.

After a moment's silence, Tegen asked, 'Why did you give *me* your cloak, not Enid?'

Gronw raised an eyebrow. 'Do you really believe the old tale that a druid's power is in his cloak?'

Tegen smiled as she remembered thinking her magic was in her silk shawl. 'No,' she replied quietly.

'Enid did, and that belief *might* have helped her, but she was also vain and wouldn't have worn it because it was old and smelly. As it happened, I *had* rubbed a few spells into the leather. I hoped the extra protection might help you to save her.' His eyes were wide with grief as he reached for Tegen's hand.

'Never doubt the Lady's love. Things don't always work out as we think they ought to. If it hadn't been for your love and spells, things might have been much worse.'

Tegen squeezed the old man's fingers and told him all that had happened on the mountain. 'We both knew Enid was in danger at midwinter. I'm certain that the demon found her then, and has been using her to get to me. Because of that, I've decided that I must leave. Now, before it does any more harm to the people of Bera.'

Just then, Teithi's chest heaved and rattled. Gronw took a cloth from a bowl of cold water, squeezed it and wiped the dying man's forehead. 'That is best,' Gronw replied. 'If you stay, I cannot guarantee how Penn will read your part in all of this. He is a man of action rather than words.

'Ride due west along the valley bottom. Keep to the path with the river on your right and you'll see a sheep fold where you can sleep tonight. In the morning, the mountains will fall away behind you and the road is marshy. Take the path to your left and you will find a fishing village by the sea. There you will be given a boat. You have my blessing.'

Then turning back to his patient he added quietly, 'There are many gods and spirits in these mountains and valleys. Some are the Lady in her various guises. She will lead you.'

Teithi's chest strained as more pink foam trickled from his lips.

'May she bless and keep you both,' Tegen replied, then she left the roundhouse.

*

Night had fallen and the crowd had dispersed. A small brazier burned outside Teithi's home, casting frantic shadows in the dark.

But the courtyard was not empty. The sound of a tapping, sliding footstep echoed in the icy air. Tegen stood still as Enid came into the firelight. Her eyes stared wildly as she laughed and wept. Her dark hair swayed like a tangled cloak down the back of her linen under-dress.

'Hello Tegen!' she giggled. 'Look, I'm dancing, I'm as powerful as you now!'

Just then, Clud and his wife came running after her, scolding and begging her to come back inside. Clud had a rope in his hand.

Tegen said nothing but walked briskly to the stables where Kieran was waiting. 'I'm in danger, I have to leave,' she said. 'You'll be safe here, do you want to stay?'

Kieran shook his head. 'Not after today!'

'Then collect your things and *hurry!*'

While he was gone, Tegen packed her belongings and saddled Epona. Leaving Gronw's sheepskin cloak near the doorway, she led the white mare into the courtyard. Hooves clopped on the cobbles, breaking the silence.

The door of the kitchen opened briefly and Kieran's shadow

slipped out with a bulging bag on his back. Behind him loped the ever-faithful Wolf.

At the great gate the two guards heaved back the oak bar. 'Can't let you back in until dawn,' one snarled. 'You could be anyone.'

'We're not coming back.' Tegen replied.

'Good riddance.' The second man spat as the gates crashed together.

Tegen ignored them, but when they were well away she slowed Epona, turned, and sent a blessing back to the House of Bera.

'They ain't worth that!' Kieran said.

She shrugged. 'They weren't evil, just frightened. Anyway, if you send a curse it'll come back to you eventually.'

'What about blessings?'

'Same thing. Come on, I'm cold. Gronw says somewhere along this road there's a sheepfold where we can sleep tonight. I smell more snow on the air. It'll be cold.'

Kieran slid the bundle from his shoulder. 'Lucky I got these then.' He tossed her a spare cloak. The folds of heavy wool smelled of lanolin and wood smoke.

Tegen felt comforted as the moonlight led them due west towards the sea.

32 * BRIGID'S FIRE *

The morning brought brilliant sunshine and a deep, sparkling frost. By noon, the mountains were behind them and they were midway across the salt marshes. Wolf ran barking in circles of delight, scaring long legged curlews into reed banks where they bubbled and hissed at him. The sky seemed huge after the narrow valley of Bera.

As the sun began to sink they came to a scattering of huts and houses, beyond which was an open, green and silver expanse that took Tegen's breath away. 'Is that the sea?' she gasped, running across the shingle to greet the waves that crashed urgently forward, then slid back, sighing.

'Course it is!' Kieran puffed out his chest with pride at knowing something Tegen didn't. 'Ain't you never seen it before?'

'Only in my dreams,' she replied. 'Then there were smudges of gold on the water... I think.'

'That's what you get when the sun sets over there in the west.' Kieran pointed.

'What's over there?'

He shrugged. 'I've heard tell it's a land called Ériu. Who knows?'

Tegen frowned. She had met men from there before, great warriors and wise druids, but something more recent nagged in her memory. Something about a queen – and a summoning?

Just then they heard the distant clang of hammer on anvil. 'I can hear a smith working!' Tegen exclaimed gleefully. She ran back up the beach, jumped onto Epona's back and followed the sound.

It wasn't a large village; there wasn't even a palisade, just a scattering of houses, each with its own high, earth-bank enclosure where a few geese grazed with a pig or two. People bustling about their business stopped and stared at the strangers. Some called out a greeting, but most seemed wary.

Epona trotted merrily towards the smithy.

Two high dry-stone walls made a corridor that led to an inner courtyard. To one side was a slate-roofed hut sheltering the glowing lights of a furnace. A couple of gossiping housewives were sitting on a bench, clutching knives that needed sharpening. Next to them was a farmer leaning on a broken plough.

They all fell silent and turned as Tegen dismounted and led Epona in. Wolf went straight to a bucket of water and lapped noisily. Kieran followed, dropped his bundle and sat on it, stretching his feet and hands to the warmth of the furnace.

Epona nickered a greeting. The smith stopped work and stood straight. She was tall, dark haired and broad shouldered. Her eyes gleamed in the flickering light, and a stout leather apron covered a blue dress.

Tegen's eyes widened. She had heard legends and stories about the Lady's daughter Brigid, more skilled in magic and iron than even Goban… Could this really be her?

The woman put down the heavy pincers she was using,

pushed back her hair and nodded to the waiting customers. 'Leave everything that needs seeing to. I have guests I must welcome. Come back in the morning. All will be ready.'

Murmuring irritably, they did as they were told and filed away, casting suspicious glances back at the newcomers.

The smith sat on a stool and poured milk for them all. She took Tegen's hand. 'We are merrily met. I think you have guessed I am Brigid. I hope your birthday has filled you with hope, Star Dancer. Did you dream?'

Tegen knew better than to be thrown by what a smith might do or say. 'I did,' she replied. 'I dreamed well, thank you.'

'Then remember it, and fear nothing as you act on it.' She turned to Kieran, 'And you, have you become a poet?'

He laughed.

'I duno 'bout that,
but a rhyme's as good as a hat
when it sits in me head
and fills me like bread!'

Then he stopped, listened to himself and laughed once more. 'Where did that come from? I like that! I bet I can't do it again…'

'I bet you can!' Brigid smiled. She rubbed the coarse hair on Wolf's head as she dropped him a tit-bit. She stood and worked her bellows until the shed was filled with swirling sparks. Then turning back to her visitors, her face was solemn.

'But what of the other one?'

Tegen sighed. 'Enid went mad.'

Brigid stared into the fire for a few moments. 'She won't live long, then she will be born again, free of the affliction. Have you any idea what might have caused the malaise?'

'It was a demon, one that has been following *me* for a very long time. I think it terrified her until her mind gave way. It grieves me that she suffered when I was the one it was after.'

'There is more to her illness than you could possibly know. There always is.' Brigid put a skillet on the flames, added a knob of butter and flopped in dollops of coarse, black and white dough that sizzled and smelled delicious. 'Lava cakes,' she said, flipping them expertly with a flat knife. 'I make them from boiled seaweed and oatmeal. Try one.'

Once they were cool enough to be handled, Tegen and Kieran ate ravenously. The salty-crispy mouthfuls melted on the tongue and filled the belly excellently.

Brigid asked them about their journey while she sharpened the village women's knives on a whetstone. Brigid's blue eyes smiled at the mention of Goban the Smith. 'He's my brother, but it's a long time since we met.'

By the time Tegen and Kieran had eaten and told their tales, it was late afternoon. Brigid put her work aside and pulled on her cloak. 'Bring your things,' she said, 'and come with me… No,' she added as Tegen reached for Epona's rein, 'you won't need her.' The smith dipped a tar-soaked torch into her fire and led them along the track between the cluster of high-walled enclosures, and down to the sea.

The sun was very low in the west, washing the sky with salmon pink and pale woad, gold and purple. It was just as Tegen remembered in her dream. The water was calm, lapping the shingle beach, like a mother soothing a child to sleep.

'It is good you wear Goban's ring,' Brigid said.

Tegen held up her hand. The incised ogham glinted slightly in the light of the torch flame. 'Keep it close.' She pointed to an upturned currach on the shore. 'Take that, and the sea will bring you where you need to go.'

Tegen's eyes sparkled. 'To Mona at last!' Then she turned and hugged Brigid. 'Thank you! I've been longing for this!'

But the smith shook her head. 'Not Ynys Môn, not yet. But you will go there one day.'

Tegen's mouth dropped open. 'But… but I *must*, I'm *needed*…'

Brigid raised an eyebrow. 'Indeed you are, but it might not be where and when you think. Have you not yet learned that things don't always work out as you think they ought to? First, you must hunt for the Wave that will heal the Land. You must learn to *listen*, Tegen. Remember the dream you were given on Cadair Idris, remember Gwen's words and the river-song? Now, are you ready?'

Tegen dared not argue with the Lady's daughter, but she still had to fight welling anger and disappointment. She helped to right the boat and drag it to the water's edge.

Brigid lashed her torch to its prow as waves slapped at the hull. 'Get in.' Then holding the gunnels firmly, she looked around. 'Where is your dog?'

Tegen whistled and Wolf abandoned the pile of seaweed he'd been playing with and leaped in beside her, eyes bright and tongue lolling with excitement.

Kieran tried to join them, but Brigid caught his shoulder. 'No.'

she said. 'Their story isn't yours.'

'Oh, so I'm not wanted now?' Kieran sneered, 'I *knew* it'd end like this!'

Brigid smiled. 'Not at all…' she began.

'Perhaps I'm not *good enough* to go?' He scowled.

Just then a thundering wave hurled itself at the boat, and the undertow dragged it out to sea. Brigid struggled to hold it steady. 'You must stay in Cymru and follow a different path.'

Kieran folded his arms and scowled.

'May he not come? Please, it's important to him,' Tegen begged.

'No.' Brigid turned the boat's prow into the next wave. 'You have a destiny here, to become a warrior-poet. If you go, you will die within three moons.'

Kieran waded after her. 'You're making it up. I don't believe you…' He made a grab for the boat. Brigid seized his arm.

'Let me go, you bitch!' Splashing and kicking, he sank his teeth into her sooty, calloused fingers, but she did not flinch.

'Tegen!' he yelled as he struggled, 'You've broken your promise not to leave me! I *knew* you would! You're just like Caja, I hate you!'

Leaning over the prow, Tegen spread her hands in a blessing over her friend. 'Don't hate!' she warned. 'Remember, it will rebound on yourself. It's time to become a man of Siluria with your own spear and sword, like you always dreamed.'

Knee-deep in the foaming water, Kieran glared after her, shaking his head in tearful disbelief.

Just then, another wave slid under the boat, dragging it afloat. Brigid let go and it drifted away. Panic washed Tegen's face. 'Brigid – Where are the paddles? How do I steer?'

'Do nothing,' the smith called back over the crashing water. 'This is my own currach and it is guided by my sacred fire. They will carry you well. There's food and drink under the seat. Now, the tide is on the turn. It is time. Farewell!' Then pushing Kieran aside, she waded up to her waist, and with a mighty heave she sent the boat on a swell that lifted it away.

Unsteadily Tegen stood, cupped her hands around her mouth and yelled, 'But what about Epona?'

'I'll look after her, I always do,' the smith called back. 'You'll see both her and Kieran again.' Then she grabbed the boy's arm and hauled him up the pebbly beach.

'Thank you and goodbye!' Tegen called. Then she made herself comfortable as the tide tugged the currach out to sea. She would have liked Kieran's company, she had learned to become fond of him. But they both had to trust Brigid.

Wolf curled up around her feet in the bottom of the boat, his nose buried under his paws. At the prow, the torch guttered but kept burning. Tegen took a deep breath. All she had to do was to find the Wave that would heal the Land; then she could go to Mona.

The wind rose. Swell after swell raised the boat high, then plunged it into a trough. Each time, Tegen's stomach turned a somersault. She tried to distract herself by rummaging around the bits and pieces stowed under the seats. 'This looks like a sail!' she said aloud as she struggled to open it up. 'There's no mast, but it'll keep me a bit dryer at night.' With difficulty she unfurled part of a huge leather sheet, spread it over the seats and crawled underneath.

But it was not long before she sprang out again and spewed her supper over the side.

*

It was then the demon smelled the presence of its prey, the one it longed to inhabit and enthrall. It was delighted. All was not lost! Here was another excellent chance to gain her submission. It only had to separate her from the magical fire that burned at the prow and she'd be alone and terrified.

Then it would whisper promises of rescue in return for her obedience… *Now* was its moment!

With petulant rage it smashed waves and wind at the little currach, swinging it around, up and down.

But Brigid's flame burned on, holding the demon's fury at bay.

*

Tegen missed Kieran more than ever. A stormy sea at night was an achingly lonely place. The thudding and sucking of the waves under the thin hull grew louder as the night became darker. Spray rushed and splashed, then the torrential rain began.

Tegen thought maybe she should eat, but the sight of the food satchel made her stomach churn and spew bile into the slopping water in the bottom of the boat. Hour after hour, she lay miserably in the freezing wet.

All this, and I'm not even going to Mona! she fumed. I wonder if I could do some magic to make the storm go away? Would that harm Brigid's plan for me? How do I do sea-magic? I know Lir is Lord of the Waves, but I have no idea how to gain his favour… Another wash of water filled her mouth with salt, making her cough and splutter. Gronw had called him *Llŷr*, but did it matter how it was pronounced?

They were all a part of the web of great magic that bound air to fire to water to earth and back to air again. One spirit of myriad names and gifts.

'Lord of the Seas,' she whispered, 'Do you see Brigid's fire burning? I'm her friend. I have no offering to bring you, but help me, please.'

The waves pounded on.

Tegen was about to rage at the god, but then she remembered Gronw had fought against her magic when she faced the bear. He had also warned her that the Lady's love came in many guises.

Goban's ring was still cool on her finger. There was no danger. Tegen closed her eyes. 'I have been launched into Lir's care by Brigid. There is nothing to fear.' Curling up as comfortably as she could, Tegen remembered the joy she had dreamed as she'd run westwards across the waves. All would be well.

This was the best sort of magic.

33 * THE SEA *

By dawn, Tegen was miserable and exhausted. Her teeth ached with chattering and she was on the edge of tears. She had not slept, despite Wolf's warmth pressing against her.

She poked her head from under the stiff leather sail. Beyond the dark waves as big as mountains, there was still no hint of land. 'How long does the sea go on for?' Tegen asked, but the dog just whimpered and wriggled closer.

Then Tegen noticed the torch in the prow was reduced to a smouldering black stump. 'Now we are lost,' she groaned. 'Brigid's magic has failed,'

She spread her fingers to reignite the flame.

But in that moment of lost faith, the demon slammed a furious breaker broadside on, followed by a second that thundered amidships.

The last, weary flicker of Brigid's fire went out.

And Goban's ring slipped from Tegen's finger.

The currach's spars creaked and shattered, ripping open the leather hull. The boat filled and Tegen tumbled backwards into the icy foam. Wave after triumphant wave smashed over her. Tegen flung her arms around Wolf's neck.

She tried to scream, but there was only water.

Tegen broke the surface as the next wave hit – heavy and cruel. She caught hold of Wolf's pelt, but they were wrenched apart.

The currach was sucked away from beneath her. She longed to call to Lir, but green and grey light swallowed her into blackness that bubbled and gurgled in her ears while water demons tugged and swirled her hair.

For one, hope-filled moment she felt her fingertips brush a spar. But it slid away.

Why have you brought me to this? she raged at Brigid. I thought you *cared* about our Land! Her lungs ached and burned for air. Coldness plucked at her clothes and dragged her deeper. She was beyond thinking of spells of protection.

She forgot to breathe.

She felt warmer.

In her ears, the sea's roaring became softer and more distant.

Comforting.

*

The demon swelled and grew, but did not pounce. Savouring the girl's suffering was good sport. More importantly, its prey now had anger and resentment within her. These needed to be nurtured.

It would wait until the very last moment before her soul slipped to the Otherworld before making its offer of help. Dread would make her a more willing slave.

34 * THE SPIRIT OF THE NORTH *

On the Hill of Tara, Queen Étain also waited. A knowledge gnawed inside her mind – the Star Dancer was in danger. The girl *had* to come safely to Tara at all costs.

Étain had sworn not to look at her mirror again until the girl trod on Ériu's soil, because of the other fate she brought with her… One that might make her turn back from her resolution.

But if she did *not* look, she would not know what danger the Star Dancer faced. Then she might never arrive at all…

The queen loosened the clasp of her box with a single word and reached for her darkened mirror. The bronze serpents writhed slightly under her touch, their ruby eyes glinting in the shadows. She lifted the blackened surface and looked. Slowly the darkness swirled and dragged the colours of midnight across the surface… And grew malicious teeth and eyes of hatred.

Holding her breath, Étain reached through the mirror and grasped the Star Dancer's hand, 'Stay alive!' But the insubstantial fingers slipped away. She couldn't hold her.

Bringing the magic mirror to her lips, Étain begged, 'Come to her aid – someone strong. *Please…*'

Then the Spirit of the North, whom the queen dreaded, breathed its chill air of death into her face, and Étain dropped the mirror.

Tegen was being pulled upwards until glassy bubbles danced above her face. A piece of wood knocked against her shoulder. She reached out and grabbed it. She tasted air. She spat and gulped, just as another wave slammed against her, rolling and pushing her under once more, but she gripped the broken plank.

Just then, someone shouted. There was another boat!

Tegen waved feebly. The sailors changed the angle of their sail and went about. A figure threw off cloak and breeches, tied a rope around his waist and jumped, striking out into the raging waves.

The last thing Tegen knew was being shoved, hauled and dragged over the side of a strange currach. Men were shouting in words she knew, but could not quite understand.

Then everything went black.

*

The demon cursed, but its hatred rebounded on itself, dragging it back down to the depths, tangled in the seaweed-weight of its own loathing.

Somehow, the Star Dancer was safe. It could do nothing.

But as Étain had reached through the mirror to save Tegen, the demon had recognized her – she was the living spirit that had walked in Tir na nÓg and talked with the soul of the old crone. It also remembered the crack in the doorway to the world of the living, which that miserable slave had managed to wedge open...

So, the demon smirked, *that* was where its prey was headed. That chink between the worlds might not be so useless after all. Slithering along ancient spirit-paths, the demon came at last to the gap behind the cobwebby door of the queen's little sanctuary.

There, it waited and watched, but it did not cross over into the land of the living. The demon was wary of Queen Étain – if her spirit was strong enough to walk in Tir na nÓg and still live, she must be a powerful magician and would notice its presence. Indeed, the sanctuary was so thickly draped with protective spells and charms it would be impossible for the demon to creep through unsummoned.

For now, that did not matter much. It could see and smell well enough from where it crouched, although sometimes a large, brown tabby cat sat guard by the gap, watching with one eye glued to the hole as if the demon was no more than a mouse.

It did not waste its energy in anger at the animal, for now it had new plots and traps to plan.

And like the queen, it too had smelled death on the northern wind.

It *would* bring the Star Dancer to her knees, and it *would* make her submit to its powers. If not now – then later. Meanwhile, the forces of war and hatred were building across the sea in Britain. When the demon had the girl's magic in its thrall, then whole nations would plunge into senseless chaos.

From the crack behind the door, the demon blew a tiny trail of mist across the sanctuary floor.

If the Star Dancer passed nearby, it would know.

*

FINDING

35 * TARA *

Étain put her mirror away. She had no more need of it now. The Star Dancer was safe, as were her own sons who'd dragged the girl from the water. She was ill with the coughing sickness, but the boys would bring her to Tara where she would be healed.

*

Tegen awoke to the sound of children laughing. Dust motes danced in the spring sunlight as it streamed through the door. She rubbed her eyes and turned over, dislodging a large, brown tabby cat that landed with soft paws on the rush-strewn floor and stalked outside.

Where was she? Her chest was on fire, she needed to cough but it hurt too much. Wheezing and spluttering, she opened her eyes. She was in a bed, a fine, carved one with a soft, woven rug that smelled comfortingly of lanolin. The walls were whitewashed and painted in curled red and yellow designs. A good fire burned in the central hearth.

She eased herself up, coughed violently and had to spit on the rush-strewn floor, which made her ashamed. On a small table next to her bed were a jug and a beaker. With a shaking hand, she poured water and drank. What was the matter with her? She collapsed back onto the rolled sheepskin pillow and gasped for air. She couldn't help shivering, despite wearing a warm shift she had never seen before. Who was looking after her?

She listened hard to the children's banter. The words were familiar, but spoken with a soft, song-like accent. It was difficult to understand, but she'd heard it before.

She must have somehow reached land after… After what? She only remembered being very cold and wet. She rubbed her face and tried to think.

A girl with a rosy face and bright red hair came in.

Tegen tried to speak, but the cough hacked at her chest once more.

The girl dropped the wooden bowl she'd been carrying and ran outside yelling. Moments later, a crowd of children peered in, wide-eyed with astonishment. 'Where am I?' Tegen wheezed.

'Doesn't she talk funny?' the children giggled, then scattered at the sound of approaching footsteps.

The sunlight was momentarily blocked by a tall figure. The floor-rushes were scuffed into the air as a woman strode across to Tegen's bed and sat on the edge. The visitor had dark gold hair in a braid tied with green ribbon, and there was a faint smell of thyme as she held a piece of dried moss under Tegen's chin.

'Spit!' she ordered. Tegen didn't understand the word, but guessed what was wanted and obeyed.

The woman looked at the result. 'Humm, still pink and frothy. You're to lie absolutely still, do you hear?'

'Pardon?' Tegen wheezed. She was certain she'd seen her visitor before, but when? Where?

The visitor felt the skin on Tegen's brow, then more slowly and carefully, she asked, 'How are you feeling?'

'My chest hurts and I'm freezing. Where am I? Who are you? How did I get here?'

Smiling, the woman replied. 'Well now, there's a great many questions in one breath! You are in the Ráth of Grainne, in Tara, the seat of the High Kings of Ériu. This is the home of the greatest heroes since the Dagda bought the people of the Danaan to this land. And me? I am Étain, a true descendant of Queen Maeve, warrior goddess and fountain of all strong drink. In my own right I am queen to high king Feradach and mother to seven fine sons and two beautiful daughters.' She spread her arms expansively as she proclaimed, 'I am mother to *all* the people of Tara!' She smiled, her round face wreathed in warmth.

Tegen's head was spinning as she struggled to understand.

'I'm… I'm…' she started to say. But she couldn't remember who she was, and before she knew it, she was asleep.

*

Days and nights melded into each other. Fever came and went. Tegen was vaguely aware that sometimes people sat with her. There was a large, mud-coloured dog with a cold, wet nose that liked to lick her face and sleep by her bed, even when the brown cat was also there. Gradually Tegen's coughing subsided, as did the shivering and the sweating. Her mind began to clear, but the chest pain dragged on.

Étain sent vegetable broths and tinctures of yarrow and garlic, rosehip tea and a tough, strong tasting dried root that Tegen had to chew. As she grew stronger, Arlene, the serving maid, helped Tegen sit in a chair and fed her buttered porridge, sweetened with

217

honey and sprinkled with flaxseed.

As she recovered, Tegen listened to the way her new friends spoke until she understood their accent. She learned she had reached Ériu – the island in the west that Kieran had mentioned, named after its Goddess.

Thinking of Kieran made her lonely but Wolf stayed by her side, his face on her lap and dribbling as he looked adoringly up at her. She scratched behind his ears as she struggled with her muddled memories of what had happened in the sea. Hands had pushed that spar into her arms and others had pulled her up from the depths – dragging her away from something awful…

In time, Tegen grew to like and respect Étain, but there was something about her that made her wary – A sense of hidden purpose.

Slowly, Tegen became convinced that this secret side concerned *her*.

And she was certain they had met before, but how, and when?

*

Tegen regained strength, but still wasn't allowed outside, so when Arlene brought her food, Tegen often begged for tales of Étain and Tara while she ate.

'Is Étain's man, still alive?' she asked one day.

'He is,' the girl replied as she straightened Tegen's bed. 'King Feradach. He doesn't live here of course, but he visits every day.'

'Why?'

The girl's blue eyes widened. 'He's an *invalid*. It's bad luck for a maimed king to live at Tara.'

Tegen's thoughts strayed to her old friend Owein, also unable to take up his kingship because of his lame leg.

I wonder if he's still alive? I miss him…

'Can't Étain heal Feradach?' she asked aloud.

Arlene rearranged Tegen's sheepskin pillows and whispered as she leaned over, 'No, it's beyond even *her* skills! It's said he's been cursed by an angry spirit. He stole a prize bull, was gored in the belly and never really recovered. The spirit was the friend of the bull's owner.'

Tegen was shocked. 'A king *stole* a bull?'

Arlene laughed. 'Well, stealing between kings and queens is more like sport than a crime. They want to see who can have one up on the other and get away with it. Everyone likes to think they have the best cattle in the land, and if they can't buy them, they help themselves.' She shrugged. 'If I had just one cow, or even a goat, I'd be over the moon without worrying about if it was the best colour or had a splodge on its nose. I must be along now, or Cook'll have the whip across my back.' Then she took Tegen's empty dishes and left.

*

The conversation with Arlene unnerved Tegen. She decided she'd rested long enough. She had to be on her way. Although these people had been so kind, she could not shake off an uneasy feeling that all was not as it seemed – or was she being silly? Either way, she could not stay in Tara.

Brigid had hinted that she might not be needed on Mona just yet, but her vision had told her she must hunt for a Wave that would heal the Land. Sitting on a hill in the middle of Ériu would not achieve *that*! She had to get to the sea at least!

How long ago was Imbolg? Tegen guessed at half a moon, but she couldn't be sure, the days and nights had become a blur.

Her journey was urgent. She had been on the road for five, maybe six moons and she'd felt the demon's malevolence pursuing her all the way from the lands of the Dobunni, through the mountains and even under the sea. But oddly, she hadn't felt its presence here. Not yet, anyway.

Perhaps it was the Goddess's will that she be free of it for a while, to give her time to think, or to gather strength for what was to come?

The sooner I'm well, Tegen told herself, the sooner I'll be able to think clearly and sort all this out. Lying in bed all day makes my head muzzy. It's time I made an effort. She pushed her feet into her shoes and stood. By the time she reached the doorpost, her body ached and her head pounded, but she had made it.

The roundhouse she was staying in accommodated guests and was built on a steep little ring-ditched mound they called a *Ráth*. Étain said this one was named after Grainne, a very beautiful princess who had fled an unsuitable wedding, married her sweetheart and had hidden in this very house. It was a tale Tegen loved, although she didn't believe the last part.

The outside air smelled good and the colour and noise of life beckoned to her. I'll try and have a walk, she decided. I won't go far.

Then gingerly, with one hand on Wolf's sturdy back, she stepped outside.

The Ráth was high enough to give Tegen an excellent view.

Spread across Tara's gently rounded hilltop there were twenty or so similar ring-ditched mounds, each with its own building, and in between the Ráths a village bustled. 'So this is Tara,' Tegen whispered. 'The seat of the High Kings of Ériu.'

Not far to Tegen's left ran a long, earth-banked walkway that lead south towards a spread of the finest Ráths. Each of these was topped with magnificent halls and roundhouses.

I expect the queen lives in one of those, she thought. I wonder which? And where does the injured King Feradach go at night?

Wolf pushed his wet nose under Tegen's arm. Absently, she rubbed his ears as she watched the people hurrying about their business. Most were blond with blue eyes, but just a few were as dark as she was. One or two like Arlene had hair the colour of fire. The merchants and servants hopped out of the way as warriors strode across the cobbled walkways: strong and fierce, with full beards and tempers to match. As she watched, Tegen could hear arguments and laughter spring up and fade away like summer lightning.

It was a place filled with colour and spirit. What was more, there wasn't a single Roman in sight!

This is what my home should be like, Tegen mused, as she leaned against the doorpost. She cast her mind back to Corinium, which had been bustling and exciting, but where warriors had to step out of the way for the invaders, and Queen Sabrina of the Dobunni tribe was a gladiatrix – a *slave*!

Tegen felt bile rise in her throat, but her thoughts were interrupted by the arrival of Étain.

'It's good you are outside, but you mustn't leave the Ráth, do you hear now?' The queen shooed Tegen inside and examined her, then presented her with another foul-tasting tisane. As she talked, Étain's long plaits uncurled themselves from the confines of a bone comb. The soft, golden waves were peppered with a little grey, but Étain's strong frame and straight back showed no signs of age.

The queen smoothed her embroidered gown and rested her hands in her lap as she considered her patient. 'Tell me now. What do you think of Tara?' she asked.

Tegen smiled. 'It's wonderful. Everyone seems so beautiful and proud.'

'That's because we are the Danaan People, the children of the Dagda, the Good God.'

Étain leaned forward and brushed her fingers lightly across the tattoo on Tegen's right cheek. 'Now you're well enough to walk, you must feel up to talking. Tell me about yourself Tegen. Why did my sons drag you from the sea like a cod?'

Pulling her hair across the sacred tattoo on her face, Tegen told the queen a little of her life and how she had been shipwrecked while on her way to Mona to train as a full druid. She said nothing about the Great Spell or the gathering on sacred isle. That and her true identity were too secret.

The queen listened carefully, sometimes asking for a word or phrase to be repeated, for she too had difficulty understanding her guest.

At last she smiled. 'So, you are *fáith*?'

'Pardon?'

'In our land, a druid is either a poet – we call those a *file*, or a law-giver – a *brehon*, or a – *fáith* that is…' she searched for a word, 'I think you might say a *prophet*, am I right?'

Tegen closed her eyes as visions she had seen in fire flashed into her mind, followed by images from her dream at the top of Cadair Idris. She guarded her words for she was still uneasy in Étain's presence. 'I don't know what I am,' she replied quietly.

The queen looked deep into her eyes and saw many, many things that Tegen herself was unaware of.

And inside Étain's mind, a certainty was growing.

36 * TONN *

One moon after she had arrived in Tara, Tegen was seated in a rush chair watching the busy settlement below. Lost in her thoughts about her dream on Cadair Idris, she didn't hear footsteps approaching.

'Good morning, would you like me to show you around?' a warm voice asked.

Tegen jumped and immediately started coughing again. At last, she breathed easily enough to look up. Standing at her side was a tall young man, a few years older than herself. His fine dark hair lifted slightly in the breeze and blue eyes twinkled above a short beard. Breeches made from a well-woven green cloth and a clean linen shirt showed he was from a wealthy family.

'I'm sorry,' she managed to say at last, 'I'd love to, but the queen has forbidden me to move.'

'She sent me,' he said simply and smiled. 'But perhaps you don't feel well enough today? I'll come back another time.' He turned to leave.

'Don't go!' Tegen stood up. 'I've been sitting here for what feels like forever. I would like to walk with you.'

The young man smiled. 'My name is Tonn,' he said. When Tegen didn't react, he added, 'I'm Étain's youngest son. She's said I'm to escort you around Tara.' He proffered his hand.

Tegen was glad of his strong arm as she made her way down

the stone-flagged path to the midst of the exciting world that, until now, she had only been allowed to observe from above. In the heart of the busy village street, the smells and sounds jostled with the vibrant colours of the people's clothes. They wandered between the steep banks of the many Ráths towards the distant fields beyond Tara's hill, planted with early beans and cereals, and lush green pastures edged with the gauzy green of ash, oak and hazel.

Now and then, Tegen rested while Tonn waited quietly by her side, sometimes offering her water from a leather bottle, sometimes just talking in his soft lilting tones, explaining the wonderfully embroidered history of the Danaan people at Tara, the seat of the High Kings.

At the centre of the complex of Ráths and buildings they came to a mound about the height of three men, but no bigger than a roundhouse across. The slopes were grassy and there was nothing on the top, but to one side stood a tall, thin stone with a rounded end. Tonn stopped and stood silently with his head bowed.

'What is this place?' Tegen asked after a few moments.

Tonn looked up proudly. 'The stone pillar is the *Lia Fail* – the Stone of Destiny. It roars when a true king of Tara touches it. None may be crowned unless it has spoken for them. Mother said it bellowed like a bull when father was proclaimed king!'

Tegen pointed to the hillock. 'Has anyone ever lived up there?' she asked.

'It's not a Ráth. Some say it's a *Lios*, a fairy fort. Our ancestors are buried under it with their treasure so they may rule in splendour in their next lives. But that's not all… When the Dagda, the Good God, gave his people this land, he also gave four great gifts, the *Lia Fail,* the Cauldron of Plenty, the Spear of Victory, and the Sword of Light that none can evade. Over time, all except the stone were stolen, but Lugh of the Long Hand fought for us and brought everything back. Since then it's all been buried here for safekeeping.

'This mound is the soul of Tara – and Tara is the heart of Ériu.'

He turned to Tegen, his face alight. 'And the Dagda's magical harp is hidden here too. When it's played, children laugh, crops grow and enemies weaken. As long as Tara remains safe, then so do we all.'

Tegen walked around the mound and examined it carefully. Then, on the south-easterly slope she found what she was looking for: two upright, flat stones that held open the small portal to the dark, internal chamber. A heavy cover-stone almost blocked the entrance. Tegen peered inside. 'We'd call this a wight-mound,' she said.

'To us, it's the Womb of Life,' Tonn replied. 'This is the one place mother and the druids both use. We put a sheaf of barley in here at Lughnasadh, so the goddess of the full moon may bless the harvest, but at dawn at Imbolg, Brigid appears from there to ensure that all our young animals are strong and have plenty of milk. Then at dawn at Samhain, Lugh fills it with sun, promising the light of rebirth to those who have died.'

'I'd like to dream in there,' Tegen said, wistfully.

'Why?' Tonn was surprised.

'To hear the wisdom of your ancestors.'

Tonn laughed, 'That entrance is protected with so many spells and charms, even mother doesn't go right inside. Come on, the sun is getting low and you must be tired.'

Taking her hand once more, he led her towards the double earthen-banked Ráths that protected the royal enclosure. Together, they wound their way between the labyrinthine twists and turns of the ditches until at last they stood in front of the queen's longhouse. Tonn brought Tegen in by the western door that stood wide open, letting the golden evening light fill the hall.

Tegen looked around in wonder. It was a huge, rectangular structure supported by whole tree trunks and thickly thatched. As they walked across the floor, the fresh rushes and dried meadowsweet rustled, stirring the scent of summer in the room.

At a table, a group of men and women sat drinking and throwing dice, while in a corner, musicians played softly on drums and whistles for a group of children who were learning to dance. Despite her weariness, Tegen's toes itched to join them, but Tonn led her towards a raised platform near the central hearth.

There, Étain sat on a carved oak chair, her glorious hair combed out over her deep green dress. Next to her, on a long wooden bed, a pale, thin, almost hairless old man in a dark blue robe was propped up on sheepskins. He smelled of aromatic oils that barely masked the stench of a rotting wound.

The queen rose as Tegen approached. 'Welcome,' she said, holding out her hands. 'This is my husband, Feradach. Sadly he is ill and unable to rise to greet his new daughter in law.'

Tegen blinked, *what* had the queen said? She'd misunderstood, surely? But before she could open her mouth to ask, Étain turned to her man. 'My lord, this is Tegen of the Winter Seas, the druid girl I told you about. Isn't she lovely?' She hugged Tegen and led her towards the king who raised an emaciated arm and smiled.

Tegen took his cool fingers and bowed. 'May the Lady strengthen your bones and heal your wounds, sir,' she said.

'Thank you, and welcome daughter.' He smiled and eased himself upright, although movement made him wince. 'I trust you like the man the gods have set aside for you?'

Tegen looked from Étain to the king, then to Tonn. She had not misunderstood this time. '*Pardon*?' she whispered, stepping back from Feradach, wide-eyed and shaking. 'It's not true – I *can't*! You don't understand…' And her knees gave way.

Tonn sprang to catch her in his arms. 'You mean she doesn't *know*?' he hissed between his teeth. 'Didn't you at least *talk* to her?'

Étain stood, her bright green eyes dancing with happiness and took Tegen's hands. 'No need to my dear: the Gods have decided. There is nothing to discuss.' The queen clapped her hands and held her arms high, so her golden bracelets gleamed in firelight.

The musicians stopped, the games players held their dice, and everyone turned their attention to Étain.

'I have an announcement,' she proclaimed. 'At Beltane, Tonn, our beloved youngest son, shall be wed to Tegen, *fáith* of the Winter Seas in Britain.' Everyone applauded, hooted and stamped, while the musicians struck up a lively jig. Étain patted Tegen's cheek and added a little more quietly, 'And by Lughnasadh, you will be carrying Tonn's child, the Hope that will unite Ériu's tribes against the Roman threat. I have seen it.'

Tonn glanced at Tegen who was now shaking and pale. '*Mother*! How *could* you?' Then he turned to Tegen, 'I'm sorry,' he said. 'I really thought you knew…'

Too ill to rage, Tegen's chest burned as a coughing fit racked her whole body. Tonn helped her to a chair and pulled a thick shawl around her shoulders as her shivering worsened.

'You are cruel, mother,' he snapped. 'She's too ill for a shock like this, can't you *see*?'

Étain pouted, 'But she had to be told.'

'But not now, and not like this!'

A servant brought hot mead for Tegen to sip. 'I'd like to go back to bed, if I may,' she wheezed.

'Certainly, my dear,' Étain replied. 'It's time Feradach left as well, the sun is setting. Your man will escort you, won't you dear?'

Tonn bowed his head. 'Of course mother,' he said through gritted teeth. Then he slipped his arm around Tegen's waist and helped her back to Grainne's Ráth.

*

When Tegen awoke, Tonn was seated on a chair next to her, quietly plucking at a small harp, a rippling melody that reminded her of a stream in springtime. She closed her eyes again and let the music flow over her. Despite her shock and weakness, she felt wrapped in a warm glow. She watched Tonn from under her lashes.

She could do worse than be handfasted with someone like him. He was strong, tall, good-looking and kind. But at the back of her mind, she knew she shouldn't even be thinking of such things. She had to find the prophesied Wave that would heal the Land. Most importantly of all, she was needed in Mona...

Soon the comfort of the bed and the soothing music lulled her back into her vision of running over the waves – and happiness. In her dream she saw again the man she was running towards.

And this time she knew who he was.

*

As the days went by, Tegen and Tonn became good friends as they spent long hours walking in the woods beyond Tara. She told him of her childhood, her early spells learned from Gilda, her handfasting with Griff, his death, and her longing to be trained for wearing a white robe.

Tonn told her of his youth and his decision to study druidry, but his struggle to be different from his mother.

Each time they talked, Tegen became more intrigued as to why she had dreamed of him? What was his significance for her destiny?

She forced herself to shy from even holding his hand for he was everything she could wish for in a man. He always kind and gentle and his touch made her spirit light and bright. She longed to stay by his side.

One day soon, she would have to leave Tara. She daren't risk fondness – or love. But while she was too ill to travel, she allowed herself to enjoy his company.

'Healing and music are what intrigue me most,' he told her as they sat under spring foliage one sunny morning. 'I don't enjoy magic so I'll never be more than a *file*, which annoys mother. My eldest three brothers and sisters are warriors, one brother is a farmer, and the other two are both druids. They already have their white robes: one has the gift of the sight like mother, he's an excellent lawyer as well, and the other is an historian.'

He touched the tattoo of the Watching Woman constellation on her cheek. 'Will you tell me what this means?'

'It's just my clan mark,' Tegen replied, ashamed of lying. But what would the title of 'Star Dancer' mean in Tara? She trusted Tonn, but wasn't sure whether the people of Ériu would support the British against the Romans. Their shores were still free, although Tegen guessed that the armed giant of her vision on Cadair Idris hinted at a threatened invasion.

Changing the subject she asked, 'Tell me about Mona. I've heard that you and your brothers were on your way home from there when you rescued me?'

'That's true, but you've never told me what on earth you were doing at sea in weather like that.'

She pulled a blade of young grass and chewed it. 'I was trying to get to the island of the druids. I've always wanted go there to complete my training. I was told the best way was by boat.'

'What was the captain thinking of, putting to sea in weather like that?'

Tegen twisted the blade of grass tightly around her finger. Should she explain about Brigid? Better not! 'There was no captain,' she said. 'I left in a hurry because I had a friend who turned against me – an evil spirit convinced her I meant harm – so I fled. I was given the currach.'

Tonn looked at her sideways. 'I don't believe it! You weren't trying to sail by *magic*, were you? You're mad!'

'No,' she replied, then remembered Brigid's fire. 'Well, yes, but it wasn't *my* magic…'

Tonn considered Tegen for a few moments, but sensing she had said more than she intended, he did not question her further.

An awkward silence hung in the air as Tegen wondered whether Tonn had heard about the Great Spell when he was on Mona, or whether he'd met any of her old friends there. But still wary, she said nothing.

At last she asked, 'Have your family always ruled Tara?'

'Our bloodline goes back to the Dagda himself, but we haven't always been kings. Mother and father are getting old now,' Tonn replied. 'My eldest brother hopes to be elected high king of Ériu when father goes to the Otherworld. There will probably be bloodshed over the succession, for my third brother and my cousin also have enough wealthy backers to press their cases. I hate these petty wars, but that's the way it's done.' Then he sighed, picked up his harp and began to play a mournful tune in a minor chord. 'It won't be long now. Father's wound has never healed despite mother's herbs and spells.'

'Queen Étain has very powerful magic, doesn't she?' Tegen asked.

'Yes, but she's a wise woman, not a druid. She has a good heart, but doesn't stop to listen to how the wind blows or the birds sing before she casts a spell.' He stopped playing as a wren dived into a bush. 'Most of the druids in Tara think she's a shadow-witch and they won't speak to her or come to the King's Hall. That makes my studies difficult, of course. My other brothers left long ago.'

Tonn re-tuned and struck up a lighter melody. 'Mother's problem is she's convinced she knows best and is determined to make everything happen *her* way. But she can't see that good intentions don't always equate goodness.' He sighed. 'I never speak to her about magic.'

'How do you feel about her decision we should handfast?' Tegen asked. The issue worried her deeply. Brigid's words convinced her she had to come to this country, but it was to find the healing Wave, not to wed.

This was just one of Étain's wild ideas... Wasn't it?

Taking her question as encouragement, Tonn put down his harp and took her hand.

Tegen sighed. She didn't have the energy to move away from him yet again. And a new idea was tickling at the back of her mind: maybe, when the Great Spell was made and the Romans were gone, her life might change. Why *shouldn't* she have her own hearth and children? And why not here, with Tonn? He was handsome and wise, and she loved the way he sat contentedly playing music by her side. Most importantly of all, he understood the web of magic.

If Tonn was prepared to wait, marriage would be wonderful. But she had to free Britain first.

Deep inside, the happiness she had felt in her dream on Cadair Idris was daring to open like pure white blackthorn blossom, spilling into the wintry realities of her life. But she had to be careful. The dream had warned of grief hovering behind the joy.

Tonn watched as her worries tightened into tiny lines on her face. He drew her closer. 'Do you mind marrying me so very much?'

'No.' She took a deep breath. 'I'm sort of hoping it might be possible…' *Stupid* girl! She scolded herself – why did I say that?

Tonn put his arm around her waist and held her tightly. Tegen's heart thudded. 'Then, let's *make* it happen, shall we?' he said, kissing her gently.

She didn't want him to stop, but at the same time, she was scared of letting him into her soul. She had to leave, *soon*! If only he could understand. Dare she trust him with the truth? She held her breath, but that made her have another coughing fit. 'I'm sorry,' she spluttered, pulling away.

Tonn rubbed her back gently and waited for her to breathe again. 'Let's walk back, then you can rest.' He kissed her fingertips and pulled her to her feet.

'One thing…?'

'Yes?'

'When I arrived here, I felt it was almost as if your mother had been expecting me. What sort of divination does she do? Fortune-telling makes me uneasy, especially when it's *my* future that's being read.'

Then she added silently, by someone I don't altogether trust.

Tonn shrugged. 'I suppose she looked into her dark mirror. She does it all the time.'

Tegen was intrigued. A divining mirror? She had never used one. Perhaps if I could look into it, she thought, I might be able to see why she thinks we should marry. It might help me understand why I'm here, and where to find the Wave.'

She took Tonn's hand urgently. 'Would your mother show me her mirror?'

'I'll see what I can do. Now go inside and get some sleep.' Then he blew her a kiss and left.

37 * ÉTAIN'S MIRROR *

Tonn climbed the Ráth of Grainne at dawn. The guesthouse now held several other visitors snoring behind their wicker screens. Tonn found Tegen's bed and shook her gently, whispering 'Don't say a word,' in her ear.

Tegen pulled on her shoes and overdress, found her cloak and followed him outside into the grey morning rain. Tonn led her down the slope towards the woods. 'Where are we going?' she asked, struggling not to slip on last year's wet leaves.

'Careful now.' Tonn took her hand. 'We're going to see if we can glance in Mother's dark mirror.'

'Did she say we could?'

He laughed. 'Mother woke early this morning and went to meet with her sister. They'll have gone to take a sacred bath in the river in preparation for the full moon tonight. She won't be back for ages.'

'So she didn't say yes?'

The rain dripped from the tiny leaves of an oak into Tonn's hair and down his face. 'She almost never says yes, so I haven't asked her.'

'Shouldn't we at least try?' Tegen asked.

Tonn shook his head. 'She always hoped we children would follow her ways, but we haven't, so she's become... *protective* of her lore. It can't be easy to be called a witch.' He turned to walk on. 'She's not a bad woman, but sometimes she does the wrong things for the right motives, if you know what I mean?'

Tegen didn't, but she nodded anyway. 'Where's the mirror kept?'

'I think it's in mother's sanctuary – a hut in the woods she uses for drying herbs and storing her ingredients for spells. But I'm not sure, I've never been in there. Men aren't allowed.'

'Am *I* allowed?'

'No.'

Tegen said nothing, but followed Tonn between the ash trees and soft grey pussy willows. The air was washed with the scent of rain and the path was spangled with primroses. As they walked, pale sunlight warmed the air and Tegen felt safe as Tonn's fingers entwined with hers. But her mind was whirling with thoughts.

I could simply look into fire and see Tonn's and my futures, she told herself. But unless I use Étain's mirror, I will never know what *she* saw. What I am about to do is deceitful – will that distort the images?

'Here we are!' Tonn announced, stopping by a rectangular stone shed with a thatched roof. A wooden door stood slightly ajar, and a familiar brown tabby cat sat on the threshold, licking her paws in the speckled, golden light.

Tonn looked around nervously. 'I always feel uncomfortable when I disobey mother, she always seems to know what I'm up to! Whatever happens, don't let the sun fall on the mirror, or the magic will be ruined. She mustn't know we've touched it.'

Then he stepped away between the trees.

Heart pounding, Tegen reached out her hands towards the doorway and felt for guarding spells. There seemed to be nothing.

Strange, I'd have thought she'd have been more cautious, Tegen thought as she crouched and tickled the sun-warmed cat. 'Are you Étain's familiar? Do you guard her sanctuary?' she asked. The cat flicked her black velvet ears and rubbed herself around Tegen's legs, purring in deep, rolling pleasure. 'Will your mistress mind if I come in? I'm looking for her dark mirror, she's told me things I can't understand and I need to know what they mean. So much depends on it, puss. It's not just my and Tonn's happiness that matters, it's the future of a great land called Britain, across the seas. I'm something called a Star Dancer and the whole country's destiny is in my hands…'

The cat looked up at Tegen with moon-eyes and walked sedately into the darkness of the little room.

I'm being invited in! Tegen thought as she pushed the door wider and followed. There was no wind-eye, the only light spilled in from the doorway. In the middle of the sanctuary was a small iron brazier, cold with ashy charcoal. From the ceiling hung drying racks with burdens of bunched herbs. Tegen's head knocked against one. The crisp leaves crackled, scattering fragrant fragments on the floor. Ducking, she took another step. Her head almost collided with another rack, hung with gutted fish, frogs and eels, all blackened and twisted.

By her feet the cat was purring as she rubbed her nose and face on the corner of a carved wooden box.

Holding her breath, Tegen whispered an opening spell and lifted the lid. Dust and the smell of dried yarrow filled the air. She reached inside and pulled out a heavy metal mirror.

It was round with a handle of two delicate, ruby-eyed serpents twisted into bronze loops. The back was decorated with curlicues inlaid with brass and copper. Despite its beauty, its silver face had been blackened and Tegen's hand felt mucky as she touched it. She turned the fine shape over and over in her hands. Why has Étain let it get like this? She wondered.

Tegen's father had been a fine metal worker, and she knew that silver should gleam. Without stopping to think, she rubbed at the surface with her sleeve until a smear of light shone from the murk. That's better, she thought, holding it up. The serious face that stared back at Tegen had thin, pale cheeks and wide, green eyes under a curtain of black hair.

The picture was edged with a silver circle. She had seen something like that once before. But before she could remember, she almost dropped the mirror, for behind her left shoulder there swirled an insubstantial wisp of dark shadow.

It was the demon, shifting and unformed, but definitely there and whispering disjointed, senseless words.

Tegen rubbed urgently at the silver surface. If I can make the reflection bigger, I might be able to see more clearly what it is that pursues me! I've got to know, I *need* to know…

'Go back!' a very real voice commanded from behind the door.

The vapour vanished.

In the same moment, a hand wrested the mirror from Tegen's grasp.

'*Never* do that again!' Étain said. The queen's eyes were hard and cold. 'It's too dangerous, even for druid girls.' Then with her free hand she passed her fingers over the cleaned portion of the surface and the black returned.

Tegen wanted to call out to Tonn, but dared not involve him. If Étain hadn't seen him, she might not know he was there at all.

As if Tegen had spoken aloud, Étain said, 'Your man is asleep outside. Now,' She closed her box and sat on it, 'Make yourself comfortable.' She pointed to a stool. 'Tell me why you did that? It's much better to ask than to steal, even for the finest of motives.'

Tegen swallowed hard. 'I'm sorry,' she began. 'I should have asked. I wanted to understand how you came to see that Tonn and I should wed, that's all.'

Étain raised one eyebrow. 'Why can't you just accept your fate? Let those of us who are older and wiser do the understanding. All you need to do is to marry my Tonn, have his children and be very, very happy.' Then she took Tegen's hand and kissed it.

Tegen felt soothed and lulled. She longed to submit to Étain's words, but she *had* to know more: 'How does it work? Why do you keep your mirror black?' she asked. 'Clean silver is so much more beautiful – and magical.'

Étain laughed. 'It's a *dark* mirror, my dear. It's not for looking to see how pretty you are, but for looking *beyond* all that is visible.'

'Do you mean it can see into *Tír na nÓg*?' Tegen gasped.

'That's right. There, all secrets are revealed for those who dare to look. Do you wish to have another go? I will be your guide this time, you have nothing to fear as long as I am with you.'

Tegen shook her head. The queen's words were wrapping her in a cocoon of tiredness and confusion. She needed air. 'I'd better go,' she murmured sleepily. 'And I am sorry.'

Étain stood and led Tegen to the door. 'Don't forget, just *ask* next time.'

'I will,' she replied meekly.

Not far away, Tonn was slumped under a tree. He yawned when she woke him. 'Oh dear, I don't know what came over me.'

'I'm exhausted too,' Tegen replied, then she told him what happened as they walked back to the Ráth of Grainne. 'I need some sleep,' she said. 'I'll see you later.'

Inside the roundhouse, Tegen flopped onto her bed. She had felt so well lately, why this weariness all of a sudden? Was the demon sapping her powers again? Or was the queen right and mirror magic was too weighty for her to handle? With a sigh she kicked off her boots, snuggled under her blankets and closed her eyes.

Then, with a sudden jerk she was wide awake. The cat! What had happened to it? It just *went*! Then Étain appeared so suddenly – without a footfall – without Tonn seeing! How could I have been so *stupid*? She chided herself. The cat *is* Étain! The queen is a *shape shifter*! That's why it's been following me around since I arrived here. The queen is *watching* me!

Tears streamed down Tegen's face. Being caught in the sanctuary was the least of her worries, for the two images she glimpsed in the eerie mirror were growing in her mind and taking on form and meaning.

The first was the demon: Tegen sensed that it'd also caught sight of *her*. It knew where she was. But worse than that – its whispered words had formed themselves into ideas, and she understood at last why it wanted her.

To use her magic to bring chaos to the human world and to drain it of all sense.

But the second image was too awful to be possible.

She had seen Tonn's body covered with blood. She did not recognize the place, but she knew for certain that it was in Britain. And she knew what it meant…

She must never marry Tonn or he would die.

38 * REFUSAL *

In the lengthening days that followed the mirror incident, Tegen's body was repairing fast, but her spirit weighed like lead in her chest.

She longed to run away secretly – but she needed a horse and a guide. More importantly, she could not leave Ériu until she had found the Wave that would heal the Land.

Despite trying to keep Tonn at arm's length, their friendship was blossoming into love. Tegen felt torn and trapped. Unless she could escape, in less than half a moon they would be handfasted by leaping Beltane's sacred fires, and that would either keep her from Mona – or seal Tonn's death sentence.

She could stand it no more.

She would have to risk telling Tonn the truth.

Early one morning, Tegen asked him to walk with her in the bluebell woods that lay beyond the sheep and cattle meadows of Tara. The scent of the first purple-blue flowers filled the air with delight.

Tonn was in a playful mood and picked a thick bunch of wild flowers, then sat on a log and began to weave them through a circlet of twisted willow twigs. He held up a late primrose. 'In our country, these express otherworldly beauty and they also protect from evil,' he explained, pushing several into place. 'Bluebells are for beauty too, and for binding things – we use their juices to stick the feather to the arrow shaft.' He fed the long, squeaky stalks in and out, adding their rich blue to the dancing yellow heads.

Tegen sat beside him and watched his clever fingers at work. She picked up a white starry blossom and smelled its pungent fragrance. 'And wild garlic?' she asked.

'That's for luck.'

'Don't you have a saying, *as bitter as wild garlic*?' she asked.

His fingers stumbled and the crown began to unravel. 'Everything has dark *and* light meanings. Some people think that bluebells warn of mourning. I believe if you *choose* the brighter message, then brightness will come. That's how magic works.'

Just then the twigs sprang apart scattering yellow, white and blue blossoms on the ground. Tonn laughed, then whispering a spell, he gathered them up and began the work again. This time they stayed.

'I thought you didn't like magic?' Tegen teased as she watched.

'Magic is important, but I'm more interested in healing. I have no wish to study the weighty historical spells, their meanings, permutations and possibilities like the older druids. I simply want to make people better.' Then he placed the floral circlet on Tegen's head. 'For you. This spell is to bring you beauty and luck, and to bind us together forever, my queen.' Then he kissed her.

A broken bluebell stalk dripped watery sap into her eye like a sticky tear. Tegen wiped it away. Tonn made her long to be happy – how could she tell him what she had seen in Étain's mirror? But if she didn't, he would never understand why he *had* to keep away from her…

'Listen,' she said, urgently taking his hands. 'I've something important to say. If you really love me, you must trust me.'

Tonn put his arms around her waist and looked her squarely in the face. 'I trust you now and I always will,' he said, his eyes serious under his dark brows. A smile played under his short beard and he pulled her close. He was warm and smelled of wood smoke. He made Tegen feel so safe she wanted to stay in his arms forever, and forget all about dreams and visions and demons.

But these were real. Brigid had warned her to listen and to act on them. This was her duty – this was why the stars had danced the night she was born. She had no choice.

However tightly Tonn wrapped her in happiness, her destiny would grip her even more tightly.

She pulled away and sat astride the log. 'Sit here – please.' Her heart was thudding and her mouth was dry, how was she going to do this?

He picked another bluebell and wove it into the long black plait that flowed over her shoulder.

'Have I ever told you I love you?' he asked.

'At least a thousand times since breakfast,' she smiled. She wished he *didn't* love her. She wished she didn't love him. She held his hands tightly and took a deep breath.

'Tonn, I won't marry you.'

He rubbed her nose with his thumb and laughed. 'Stop teasing me, you look so serious, I almost believed you for a moment!'

'But you *must* believe me, it's true!'

Three, maybe four heartbeats of silence followed. Tonn's face went white. 'Why?' He managed to breathe at last.

'I saw something awful in your mother's mirror…'

'W… what was it?'

Tegen looked him full in the face. 'I asked you to trust me, now I am going to trust you – with the whole truth. Listen. There is a fate hanging over me – I think you would call it a *geis* – a sacred duty I have to fulfill. I must go back to my own land. I am something called the Star Dancer. I was born to avert a great evil, and the worst evil Britain has ever known is the invasion of the Romans. You've been to Mona, you'll have heard what people are saying…?'

He nodded.

'It is worse than you could imagine. All the tribes have been forced to bow to the invaders. Old oaths and allegiances have been forsworn and the gods are being insulted. Even the remotest areas of west Cymru will fall soon and then the Romans will be looking this way. I need to go back to save Ériu as much as my own country.'

He closed his eyes and pulled her close to his chest.

Tegen felt as if she were drowning in the scent of his skin. Despite herself, she wrapped her arms around him as she prayed silently: Lady, why do I love Tonn? Why can't I just flee? Tonight?

But the only answer was morning birdsong and Tonn kissing her hair.

Tegen went on. 'I had a vision on Cader Idris – the seat of prophecy. I saw I would find you, but that evil would follow me here. The Goddess gave me the task of looking for something… A special Wave. I don't know what it means.' She looked urgently into Tonn's sea-green eyes, but could not read their expression.

'Then,' she continued, 'I must help the druids of Mona to raise a Great Spell to repel the invaders forever. That's where I was going when I was shipwrecked and brought here. I'm deeply grateful for your family's love and healing, but if I stay...' Tegen paused and swallowed hard. 'If I stay I will become a curse – for a demon pursues me. It's close by. It was in your mother's mirror.

'It will... bring the Romans.'

Tonn squeezed her hands. 'Then we'll defeat your demon together, and both our countries will be safe.'

Tegen shook her head. 'You don't understand. There's no time. Spring is here. When the planting is done it will be the season for war. I must hurry.'

Tonn kissed her fingers. 'Then I will go with you! I'm too old to be at home. It's time I had a purpose in life. Sitting by my mother's side stifles me, my father is dying, and my brothers and sisters don't need me... But you do! Your destiny shall become mine!'

He tried to lift Tegen's chin with his finger so he could kiss her mouth, but she wriggled aside. 'Listen, Tonn. I saw your future in your mother's mirror, too.'

'And?'

She stared at a broken bluebell that had slipped to her lap. 'I saw that if you marry me and follow me to Britain... You will die.'

He wrapped his arms around her and pulled her close once more. 'I'll die if I *don't* marry you,' he whispered.

Hot tears trickled from Tegen's eyes. I love him, she told herself. I cannot let this happen. What would his death achieve? I shouldn't have said anything. He'll never let me go now. He'll be watching every moment in case I run away.

*

That night, before dinner, Tegen pushed aside her mistrust of Étain and sought her out in the royal hall. She found the queen standing in a corner arguing with two elderly druids.

'Madam, your husband is dying and you are dividing the land, not healing it. You must call the law-making feast. Unless the old ways are adhered to, then when the Romans come, which they surely will, then Ériu will fall.'

Étain drew herself up to her full height. 'I know what I'm doing!' Then she caught sight of Tegen hovering nearby. 'Go, Finnegas, I will summon the gathering when the time is right and not before.' And she dismissed them with a wave.

Then beckoning to Tegen, Étain put an arm around her. 'Daughter, I am pleased to see you.'

'Were those druids?' Tegen asked, peering over her shoulder at the men who were still glowering angrily at the queen. 'I thought they weren't welcome in your house?'

She laughed. 'A good druid like yourself is always welcome, but those are fussy old fools.' Then she drew Tegen towards the merrily dancing flames of the central hearth.

What was that all about? Tegen wondered. I can feel spirits of anger and dissent in this house, and Étain is drawing them around her like a cloak.

Tegen stood watching the fire for some hint of what she should do, but the messages she read there were confusing.

At last she took a deep breath. 'Étain, I need to speak with you, when you have time… I need to tell you about something I saw in your blackened mirror.'

The queen raised an eyebrow. 'Look, meat is being brought to table. Sit with me.' Taking Tegen's elbow, Étain guided her to the high table. 'Tell me everything. You look pale – you've been worrying. This is my fault – I should have spoken to you more carefully at the time. It'll be nothing to fret over. You aren't used to mirror magic. Tell me all.'

Tegen sighed as servants put a bowl of boiled pork on the table. She picked up a flesh fork and half-heartedly jabbed at the lumps of meat bobbing in the steaming broth as she told her story.

When she finished, the queen smiled with her lips, but not her eyes. 'Just as I thought,' she said quietly. 'Any sort of scrying may tell you what will happen if a certain course of events is followed, but that's not what will *inevitably* come to pass. For example, if you see a dead man, it doesn't mean he *will* die. It could mean someone is planning his death, or he will die if he doesn't change direction quickly. Sometimes you might be witnessing something that happened a long time ago or years in the future. There may be a hundred different interpretations. Only someone like me who is deeply skilled can read the messages of the sacred mirror truly.'

Tegen rolled her eyes irritably. 'That's exactly why Tonn must not marry me. His death *can* and *must* be averted…! I am well now. It is time I left Tara – *alone*.'

The queen touched Tegen's forehead and tutted. 'I think you've a fever again. You could have been hallucinating rather than having real visions… Go and lie down as soon as you've eaten. I will send Arlene with a drink to help you sleep.'

As Étain spoke, Tegen felt weariness spread through her limbs and her neck ached, so she did as she was told. But as she stumbled back to the Ráth of Grainne, her be-numbed mind struggled with something Étain had said that had been *wrong*…

But what was it?

*

Arlene came with the promised draught. Tegen sat up in bed and sipped at the honeyed warmth, but as she succumbed to the swirling in her head, she understood what was bothering her.

Étain is scared! Tegen realised. She knows what I told her about Tonn is true – but she doesn't want *me* to know – so she's trying to convince me I was feverish when I looked into the mirror…

I may be feverish tonight, but the day I looked was *two moons* ago – and I was quite well that day!

*

In her chamber, the queen spent a restless night. Tegen was more powerful than she could possibly have imagined.

It was impossible for a novice to see so much in one glance in the dark mirror, and one that had been partly cleaned at that! Tegen must have been guessing, but how could she be so *accurate*? She didn't even know what a dark mirror was, yet she used it like a mage! The queen knew she would have to take control or the girl would flee back to her land of lost causes.

Then Tonn would follow, then…

I shall keep the girl in Ériu, Étain resolved, at least until Beltane. Once she's married, she'll get pregnant, then she'll stay.

Even *she* won't travel with a child in her belly.'

At dawn, the queen was in her sanctuary selecting herbs. The spell she had put on Tegen to make her feel ill would be wearing off soon. She needed to brew a draught to make the girl feel unwell *all* the time. 'A very little pinch of foxglove for nausea, and hops and vervain to bring weariness,' Étain muttered to herself as she selected rattling bundles of dry leaves from her racks. 'Not enough to do harm – just not well enough for her to go anywhere. We love her and we need her to give birth to a strong child.'

Étain opened a small sack of wrinkled red berries. 'And rose hips to add colour and pleasantness to the tisane.'

*

The following day, the queen sent for Tegen. 'It is time, my dear, that I taught you to understand the use of the dark mirror. Come, sit here.' The queen made space beside her, wrapped a rich weaving of dark blue and green around Tegen's shoulders, then handed her a beaker filled with an aromatic liquor.

Bleary and dazed, Tegen obeyed and tried to focus as the queen talked. But little went in as she stared blankly at the beautiful bronze mirror with its handle of twisted serpents and ruby enamel eyes.

The looking surface was black, dull and flat.

Tegen could hear the queen's voice as if in the distance. 'My name, Étain, means silvery brightness. However, I learned long ago, when I was about your age, that reflections tell one remarkably little about any situation. For real insights, one has to look *beyond* the obvious. So I left my name behind and explored the mysteries of the world more deeply through this great and ancient art.'

Tegen sighed and fought sleepiness. Étain smiled. The girl would be compliant and teachable in this state: she wouldn't bring her own wild magic to the lesson. She must train the girl to see things *her* way. Feradach couldn't be kept alive much longer, the law-makers would assemble and choose a new king. Without Tonn wearing the crown, and Tegen's magic, Ériu would become divided, opening their land to the Romans. What was worse, the child whose marriage would one day unite the peoples would never be born.

Étain stroked the mirror's twisted serpents. 'Clear your mind, child,' Étain said softly. 'Try not to think about what you expect or hope to see, or you'll create a vision of what you *desire*, not what is *there*. When that happens, the real future will be locked from you. Concentrate on the blackness. Nothing else exists.'

Tegen rubbed her eyes and stared, she didn't want this lesson. It reminded her too much of Admidios, the soft compelling voice, being forced to look where she did not wish, using powers she did not trust. And even worse, knowing she wasn't in control of her own mind!

She was susceptible to all the spirits in this state – both good and bad. She struggled to create a spirit shield, but Étain wiped the spell aside. 'No child, let my magic protect us both,' she whispered. 'Finish your tisane.'

Tegen fought a dizzy wave of nausea and obeyed. She was too weak to fight.

'Now,' Étain continued, 'Out of the blackness, allow images to appear. Can you see them?' She didn't wait for a reply and Tegen was relieved, for there was nothing except the mirror's dull, flat surface.

'What are the spirits showing you?' Étain continued, 'Take your time, look, but don't think, simply allow the shapes to become what they will.'

'I can't see anything,' Tegen managed to say, 'but I smell blood – blood and trees. Water and leaves.'

The queen stopped and stared at Tegen. 'No dear, concentrate. Don't be distracted by your own imagination. What you *see* is what matters. Can you see yourself with Tonn and your first baby? It's a girl! Isn't she lovely?'

'No,' Tegen whispered, 'That isn't it at all… I hear a blow – no, many blows and a cry…' A whole scene, fully formed, bloody and horrific sprang into Tegen's mind. She screamed as she sent the mirror clanging to the ground and spinning across the floor.

'You must *not* make Tonn marry me, don't you understand?' she yelled. 'You are sending him to his *death*…! And now I remember where I saw you before – you summoned me here with your mirror, just after last Samhain. I hate you, you've kept me from my destiny, and I'm leaving, as soon as… As soon as I feel well enough.'

And she stumbled out of the door, sobbing and gasping for breath.

39 * THE WIGHT-MOUND *

The days passed and Tonn was worried by Tegen's new illness. She no longer danced or laughed. Her rituals and learning were forgotten and she ignored the path of the moon and stars. All her fire and sparkle seeped away, like a hearth left to go cold.

When Tonn asked what was wrong she could only reply that she felt numb inside and out – as if she were drowning in goose feathers.

Beltane was close. Soon she and Tonn were to be handfasted before all the people of Tara and the gods and goddesses of the Danaan, yet Tegen could hardly stand, let alone leap a fire!

Étain sent her the very best food and musicians to play for her. Tonn laid his healing hands on her forehead, then held her in his arms, stroked her hair and told her how much he loved her.

But to no avail.

Only one tiny glimmer of clarity managed to form in Tegen's mind: slowly she realised that before food or some healing draught from the queen arrived, her head cleared a little. Even more so if the serving-girl was late.

*

That evening, saying she was tired, Tegen went to bed early, and only pretended to eat and drink the supper that was brought to her.

As darkness fell, so Tegen's strength returned. At midnight, she and Wolf slipped out of the door and down the steep eastern slope of the Hill of Tara, through the fields and into the woods beyond. She was able to think for the first time in many days.

Wrapped in her cloak she sat by a stream and stroked Wolf as she listened to the water, but the river-song only spoke of its journey through the undulating countryside and the coming of spring. Tegen needed a deeper magic, so she knelt and drank, and then she started to walk. She had no idea where she was going. The three-quarters moon was high and the stony farm track unrolled like a pale ribbon under her feet.

As she made her way, the world seemed brighter, clearer and more real than it had done for a long time. Now and then, Wolf dived into the undergrowth to chase small night creatures, while Tegen pulled wild garlic bulbs from the banks. 'If I'm right,' she confided in Wolf as she peeled and chewed the pungent corms, 'then these are what will cure me of my "ailment". They cleanse the blood, you see.' The huge dog rubbed his wet nose against her hand and she scratched his heavy pelt.

'Why did I ever trust Étain?' She held Wolf's long face between her hands. 'I didn't sense what she was doing because I was looking for *evil*. Étain is a good person, but she's just determined she's right. Perhaps she thinks once I'm married and pregnant I'll give up being the Star Dancer and stay? Well, I *can't* and I *won't*! The goddess gave me a destiny and I cannot betray her trust.'

Wolf gave her chin a sympathetic lick and dived off after another rustle in a nearby hedge.

For a moment, Tegen looked across the silvery moon-washed landscape of neat fields and homesteads, woodlands and streams. She could love this place, but she daren't. She had to go to the sea to hunt for the Wave that would heal the Land, then leave for Mona as soon as she could.

Maybe, when it was all over, she could come back…?

Meanwhile, her stomach was growling for a real meal, but her head was clearing rapidly, absolute proof she'd been drugged. Stretching her head back she examined the stars for the Watching Woman constellation. It was still there – of course it was. Whatever name the Goddess was given, she was everywhere. She *was* the Land and the Skies.

Throwing off her cloak and shoes, Tegen spread her arms, sought for the rhythm of the little drummer-boy in her head, and danced. 'Lady, help me find the Wave and show me how to get to Mona. But most of all, please save Tonn!'

*

Tonn had been unable to sleep and had slipped to the Ráth of Grainne to see if Tegen was awake enough to talk, or maybe even walk a little. Horrified at finding her bed empty and her supper scraped into the ashes of the fire, he ran to find Étain, who was sitting by her hearth twining wool.

'Mother, Tegen has run away. She's been unwell for at least a quarter moon and I *know* you are behind it.'

The queen smiled, dimpling her cheeks. 'If I hadn't made her just a *little* ill, she'd have left before she'd fallen in love with you properly. She's an impulsive child, but she'll make you a good wife. I have seen it.'

Hands on hips, Tonn glowered. 'You *see* too much and you don't *think* about the consequences! Now she's gone – and why? Because you frightened her off! What have you done with her? Sent spirits to pinch her in the night like you did to me when I was a child? Or have you turned her into a newt and hidden her in a stagnant pond until Beltane?'

'Neither,' Étain put her spindles down and reached for her mirror, like any woman wishing to adjust her hair. 'She's quite safe, dancing in the fields with that huge dog of hers. They're by the lower stream that grows the bitter cresses, if you must know.'

Tonn stormed out of the hall, leaving the wooden door swinging and squeaking in the wind.

*

Tegen was exactly where Étain had said, her long black hair swaying over her shoulders. Tonn crept up behind her, sensed her rhythm and joined in her dance, following her steps then swinging her around to face him.

'Is *nowhere* safe?' Tegen raged. 'I suppose your mother told you where I was?'

'I'd have found you anyway. Don't forget I have magic too.' Tonn smiled and touched her nose playfully. 'It's good to see you up and dancing once more. Why did you run away?'

Tegen looked at him squarely. His face was deathly pale in the moonlight. 'Because your mother was drugging me so I couldn't think.' She paused. 'I have to find a way back to Britain as soon as possible. *Alone.*'

Tonn stroked her ears. 'Listen, and listen well, this is the truth!

Britain has fallen. There is nothing you – or the good druids of Mona – can do. Mother has seen in her mirror that if we wed, our child will be the Hope of Ériu, uniting the five provinces so we may defend our shores from the scourge that has afflicted your people. You can do nothing more for your homeland, but you *can* help us.'

Tegen stared at him in silence, her mind a turmoil of longings and fears. At last she said, 'I thought you understood.'

Tonn sighed. 'From what you've told me, you've battled hard all your life. Don't you think that the Goddess wants you to have *some* peace and happiness? Here you've a new home and family. We all love you and want you. Stay with us Tegen; stop running. Let love and happiness catch up with you. Let them enfold you.' He put his arms around her and held her close. 'If you insist on going back I will do all I can to help, for your fight is my fight. I will go everywhere with you. But first, think carefully. Are you sure Britain holds your *real* destiny?'

Tegen's back shook and tears streaked down her cheeks. She could not speak.

'Come with me.' Tonn picked up her cloak and shoes, then led her to a sheltered spot by the river where they curled up together, watching the movement of the stars.

But the silent, silver light of the Watching Woman did not comfort Tegen. She knew that her vision from the Goddess could not be evaded.

I can't run away, she told herself. The queen's mirror will always betray me. But I can't stay either. Tonn's warmth and strength hold me in a wrap-around hug I can't escape from.

Angry and frustrated, she reached out, ripped up a handful of grass, and then threw it as far as she could.

*

In the first light of dawn, Tegen opened her eyes, wriggled free from Tonn's arms and went down to the river to wash. The cold water revived her. Her head was completely clear once more, and now she had a plan.

There was one place she could go where Étain would be blind to her. The wight mound, the *Lios* in the centre of Tara. Such a sacred place would keep Tegen beyond the dark mirror's magic. She could sleep with the ancestors and gain *real* wisdom.

Shivering in the early morning chill, she left Tonn asleep and strode back to Tara, Wolf trotting at her heels. 'There's always an answer, it's just a matter of finding it,' she told herself between chattering teeth. Back at the guesthouse, she pulled a box from under her bed. Inside were her precious stores of incense, charcoal, a beeswax candle and a tiny silver bowl. She packed everything into her bag and told Wolf to stay. Stealthily she crept between the Ráths, eerie in the half-light, then along the village street until she came to the hillside well. She filled her water skin, then made her way back to Tara's ancient heart.

All was silent except for a couple of blackbirds and a dog barking. Tegen took a deep breath of the rich air and poured a little of the water over the *Lia Fail*. 'A blessing on the Spirits of Stone in this place,' she whispered. 'May I enter your *Lios*-chamber and meet with your ancestors? I seek their wisdom for the good of Tara, and I mean no harm.'

Then, wary of any guarding spells that still might block her way, she walked carefully towards the entrance. Nothing prevented her. She put her things down and tugged at the covering stone, but as she had suspected, it was too heavy to move. There was no one she dared to ask for help. Dropping to her knees she discovered a gap at the bottom. Carefully she pushed her cloak and bag through, then lay on the ground and wriggled under the great slab into the still darkness of the chamber beyond.

She let her eyes adjust to the gloom and squatted on the floor. First she found the candle and touched the wick. 'Burn,' she commanded. A small golden light budded into a flame, flickered and steadied. Tegen set it down on the southern side of the tiny chamber, then unpacked her incense, which she placed in the east and her bowl and water bottle in the west. She had already made her offering to the spirits of the north, so she simply touched a stone and bowed her head.

Next Tegen wove a shield of protection and invisibility to protect her, in case Étain or anyone else felt her magical presence, then sitting cross-legged, she looked around. The place was damp, but not wet, constructed of large slabs of rock that made floor, walls and ceiling. She'd expected to find bones stacked or strewn around, but the place was swept clean. At home, in Britain, the wight-barrows were forgotten and unused, but not here, in Ériu.

Tonn had said Brigid loved this place, and Brigid was Tegen's friend.

'Lady,' she prayed aloud, 'Are you here now? I need your help. I'm sorry I doubted you at sea.'

Reverently, she lit the charcoal and shook out a few grains of incense to bless the spirits of the east, 'Give me your inspiration,' she prayed, then poured water into the silver bowl and blessed the spirits of the west. 'Lead me to the Wave that will heal the Land,' she asked. Then, sitting in silence, she inhaled the scents of juniper and amber as she watched the candle flame brighten the stone walls.

It was then she noticed the carvings by her right shoulder; circles, dots and cup shapes. She could tell immediately they were made by the Old Ones in ancient times and were a moon calendar. They were very similar to the one incised into the wall of Gronw's hut. But she also knew that these shapes had many layers of meaning and many uses. A novice could follow the nineteen-year lunar dance across Ériu's landscape.

But to a *druid*, it was so much more.

The central pattern was a set of ever-widening rings, with a deep, navel-shaped hollow in the middle. That symbolized the mound she was in, but it also showed that this was a gateway between the worlds. If the spirits had accepted her offering, they might help her to find that inner point, beyond the threshold of Tir na nÓg, where she would understand the truth without darkened mirrors! She had been to the Otherworld before, when she had walked the fire spiral on Sinodun. She was not afraid; the spirits were good to those who honoured them.

'Speak to me,' Tegen whispered. 'Please.' Then she breathed deeply and cleared her mind.

*

Tegen woke a long time later, stiff and aching. The candle was a pool of wax on the floor with the pale bluish remnant of a flame struggling to keep alight. From the cracks around the door-stone, she could tell the sun was high. She yawned and stretched as she tried to put her dream into some sort of order.

Then an awful thought struck her: how could she get out of the chamber without being seen? It was in the very centre of Tara! She'd have to wait until nightfall, but her stomach was in knots with hunger.

She commanded the candle to keep burning, then froze, for she could hear people talking close by. One of the voices was Étain's. Tegen listened hard. The other speakers were men, but she didn't recognize them. They sounded older and pompous.

'It is time,' the first voice demanded. 'You have refused the law-making feast so many times because the king is ill. This offends the gods and makes the people angry. It is six moons to Samhain, messengers must be sent throughout our land to summon the druids and the chieftains so all may prepare. The Dagda himself ordered that the High Seat of Tara hosts the great law-giving gathering every three years. You have ignored our sacred tradition. If Ériu is destroyed by invaders and petty wrangles between the kings, it will be *your* fault!'

Étain's smooth voice laughed, 'Oh Finnegas, you druids are so stuck in your ways! Go and eat the sacred salmon you are so fond of and let well alone. We will have the gathering when my husband goes to Tir na nÓg. For now, King Feradach is too ill. The chieftains won't forget their lineages just because they've had no *file* reciting it to them recently. Disputes can still be settled, have you no good *brehons* serving your chieftains? Anyway, the gods and the spirits are still here to guide us with common sense. You druids don't have a monopoly on wisdom!'

Another man's voice spoke, sharper and colder than the first. 'And you, madam, have no right to take matters into your own hands. You aren't even a druid, yet you take it on yourself to be *file, fáith* and *brehon* for all of Ériu! I ask the *Lia Fail* here to witness: I accuse you of putting yourself above the law. You will bring destruction about all our ears unless you obey us!'

Tegen leaned against the blocking stone and held her breath. Now she understood what had been going on in Étain's hall. No wonder the druids hated her!

Finnegas spoke again. 'Feradach won't last until Samhain, lady. Let the gathering be a bull feast to choose and celebrate the new High King. With the Romans on our doorstep we can't risk forgoing the gathering again. The gods must be appeased and we need unity if we're to fight.'

Étain laughed once more.

'If you do not listen, we will declare you outlaw!' Finnegas declared, thumping his staff on the ground. 'Furthermore I will ensure that the High Kingship passes from your family!'

Étain was silent for a heartbeat or two. When she spoke again, her voice was low and strong. 'Gentlemen, you are wrong about me. I have not taken any of these roles on myself. There is at Tara a new druid whose magic is stronger than any of yours. She truly is *file, fáith* and *brehon* in one.

'She alone has the power to bring peace to our warring tribes.

Her daughter's marriage will seal our peace for a thousand years.'

Tegen's heart sank – Étain is talking about *me*! I should have sought out the druids out and talked to them long ago. Why didn't I?

Outside the row was still going on.

'*Impossible!*' Finnegas snorted.

'You know nothing about druidry, you're only a second-rate shadow-witch!' the other voice added.

'Very well,' Étain replied, 'Call your bull-feast gathering for Samhain, then I will present her to you. Then you will see who understands the magic that guards our country best – you or me!'

Tegen heard someone spit, then boots stamping away. She sighed and leaned back against the cool stone wall. She could see Étain's feet close to the gap below door-stone. Did she know she was in there? Could her mirror see inside the sacred chamber after all? How long would she wait outside?

Go away! Leave me alone! Tegen shouted inside her head, jumping up and ripping all her protective spells aside. I have to leave Tara today! I don't even care if I go in the wrong direction!

Just then there was an angry shout and the men's footsteps returned. 'Woman!' roared Finnegas, 'We can feel a change – you've disturbed the warding spells on the *Lios*! What have you been up to in there?'

Étain shifted from the door. 'Me?' she asked sweetly, 'I've done nothing. You know I would never dare to touch a *druid's* spell…'

'Out of my way,' the other man roared. There was scuffling, and stone grating against stone. 'Let's see what meddling games you've been playing!'

Tegen held her breath. She longed to curl up into a tiny ball and hide, but she was the Star Dancer. Brigid herself had sent her. She had come to Ériu on a sacred mission.

As the men tugged and heaved at the stone, she gathered her things and readied herself.

Suddenly the stone fell back with a dusty thud and daylight streamed in.

Tegen blinked, stepped forward and stood tall and straight.

'Is *that* your famous druid?' sneered an old man with a straggly beard and a grimy white robe. He prodded Tegen's stomach with his staff. 'A *girl* that invades sacred places to skulk and hide?' The second man, a weaselly creature with a narrow face, drew himself up to his full height, looked Tegen up and down, then burst into derisive laughter.

Smiling, Tegen raised her hands, then brought them down. As she did, the dismayed men crumpled to their knees. There they stayed, helplessly writhing and struggling, spitting and swearing.

With a small gesture from her right hand, Tegen silenced them. She had no wish to insult her elders, but she had to get away from there.

Unable to move, the men stared up at her with bulging eyes and mouths like landed fish. Tegen rubbed her finger over her lips, *blah blah blah!*

Finnegas and his companion could not help but copy her, pronouncing *blah blah blah!* very loudly to the amazed crowd that was gathering around the fairy mound.

Then as gathering onlookers started to laugh, several tall

warriors with coloured cloaks, stepped forward and tried to grab Tegen by her arms.

Sweeping her hands high, she summoned fire to burn the grass around her feet, sending the men staggering backwards. Without fear of the flames, Tegen walked away.

On all sides, the people of Tara bowed and let her go.

As she passed the *Lia Fail*, Tegen saw Étain, standing in the stone's shadow, smiling triumphantly, her arms folded over her breasts.

Don't look so smug, High Queen, Tegen thought. I've thought of a way to defeat you too – just wait!

Then without saying a word, she strode back to the Ráth of Grainne with her head held high. The spirits had told her to marry Tonn and she would obey.

But now she knew how to keep him safe. She would steal Étain's mirror to make her blind – then flee Tara and make for the sea.

Alone.

And thanks to the map in the stone, she now knew which way to go.

40 * BELTANE *

Tegen was up before daylight. She put on an embroidered linen dress the queen had given her, and over her hips she tied her coin-shawl. Arlene combed her hair into a black waterfall down her back. Lastly, she clasped Tonn's wedding gift around her neck: a string of blue glass and golden beads.

Dawn was coming, the sky was still indigo and the birds were just beginning to sing. The stars had almost faded but as she walked towards the woods, Tegen could still make out the nine points of the Watching Woman. The air was heavy with the rich scent of early hawthorn blossom. It had such a heady perfume she wanted to breathe it in and in, until it filled her completely.

She wished she could allow herself to be happy. What she was about to do would bring grief, but it was better than allowing the man she loved to die.

It was almost day by the time Tegen reached the sacred grove to the west of Tara. In the centre burned two fires of the nine sacred trees. Around them, the druids of Ériu who had gathered for the ceremony stood silently in their white, blue and green gowns. All the girls and women wore circlets of hawthorn that glowed in their hair and the men had sprigs tied to their staffs. Beyond their circle, an excited crowd from surrounding villages waited, all carrying or wearing the creamy white blossom.

King Feradach lay on his cloak nearby with a wreath of tiny

yellow oak leaves on his head and a branch of dark holly in his hand. By his side, Étain sat on a stool with May flowers woven into her wheaten plaits. Her neck, ears and wrists were heavy with ancient gold. She smiled and bowed her head as Tegen waited outside the circle.

Finnegas and his red-haired companion guarded the gate of Beltane on the southeast where Tegen had to enter. She ignored them as she stepped to her place, but in the light of the fires she couldn't help noticing their tight, angry faces.

Then, as the first rays of golden sun pierced the leafy canopy, a ram's horn sang one long, solemn note. This was answered by more horns, and into the centre of the circle jumped a man dressed in green with leaves and bells sewn to his clothes. On his head he wore a mask and stags' antlers wreathed in white flowers.

Drummers began a heartbeat rhythm and the dance of the Green Man began. At first he moved warily, sniffing the air like a deer, then more swiftly round and round until he sprang with thistledown lightness between and over the fires. The crowd roared and cheered. He leaped back, the drumbeat followed his steps as he pranced and turned, sometimes stopping and letting out a deep-throated bellow like a roebuck.

Then his dance slowed and he began to explore the circle, his head lowered, and his movements feral.

At last he was standing before Tegen. In his right hand he offered a frothy crown of May. 'Come and dance,' he growled in a low voice. 'Be my hand-fasted Queen. Leap the Beltane Fires with me!'

Tegen drew back, looking around urgently for Tonn.

The Green Man chuckled. In his own voice, her beloved said, 'It's me, you goose!'

Before she could speak, he had crowned her, and his strong hands brought her into the circle. The crowd roared and applauded. The drum beat quickened and his steps kept pace. Tegen began to skip and sway, linking her movements with his, exhilarated with the pace and the earthy rhythms that swelled through her veins and made her want to whirl and throw back her head, laughing with the glee of being alive. Faster and faster the music span, Tonn's stag-like movements softened and became more human, more warm and enfolding, his arms encircled Tegen and drew her closer until they were moving and spinning as one.

The drumbeat swelled as whistle and harp joined in. The birds' songs and the fires' crackling melded with the scent of the hawthorn blossom and the salty smell of the man holding Tegen in his arms. The earth's pulse had become their own.

Holding her tightly, Tonn whispered '*Now!*' and turned her to face the smaller fire. Together they ran towards the glowing logs. The drum grew louder and more insistent, their feet did not miss a beat as they launched themselves up and over the flames, their robes dusted with flying sparks.

'*I'm alive!*' Tegen laughed as she became one with the glorious moment of fire and breath and blood and knowledge. *This is what it felt like to be the Goddess when the world was new!* The drumbeat slowed and she looked back to see the circle breaking, as druids, warriors and villagers also leaping the flames in pairs. Some slow, and scared, others rushing, most clutching their garments tightly.

Tonn was panting, still holding Tegen around her waist. He pulled off his horned headdress and smiled at her. 'My Queen of the May, you are beautiful and I love you!'

Tegen kissed him. She was hand-fasted once more, and just for today, she would close her mind to what it meant. 'And I love you, my beloved Green Man!' she exclaimed.

I will have at least one day of real happiness in my life, she told herself, so I can remember it when times grow dark again. Then she held him tightly.

It was a perfect morning for happiness. Above, the sky was warming to a celandine-blue. The golden oak leaves were unfurling, and beyond the music, dancing and fires, the quiet of the forest beckoned.

'Let's go for a walk,' Tonn whispered. 'I know a perfect place, quiet, by a pool where no one goes.'

Tegen nodded, still too out of breath to speak. The thought of a stroll amongst the trees sounded wonderful. Tonn picked up a satchel, then taking her hand, he led her out of the clearing. Soon, all was mossy-quiet. Together they walked to a copse of hazel and young oak edged with shiny-leafed holly. They sat on a drift of dried leaves and Tegen took off her crown and lay down, looking up through the gauzy green canopy.

I am glad the spirits in the wight-barrow told me to marry, she thought. I wish I could stay here... But when all the fighting is over, I will return! I believe that Ériu holds my final destiny!

Just then, the black shape of a raven rustled high amongst the greenwood boughs and called *pruk pruk* down at her.

She sat up. 'No!' She shook her head. 'It can't be Derowen

come back to haunt me. Not again! Not today!'

Tonn took her hand. 'What's the matter? Derowen is dead,' he reminded her gently.

Tegen stroked his worried face. 'Sorry,' she said. 'I just don't like ravens. They always seem to portend grief.'

'It's just a bird, ignore it!' Tonn opened his bag and drew out a lump of soft white cheese wrapped in bog myrtle, honey cakes, mead in a leather bottle and a bag of nuts. 'Breakfast!' he announced, then unstoppering the honey drink he poured a few drops on the ground and crumbled a cake. 'An offering to Maeve, goddess-queen and my ancestress. It's also for your first husband, Griff, a good man who cared deeply for you. I vow to his spirit I will do the same. You'll be safe with me.'

But will you be safe with me? Tegen wondered as she ate. If my plan fails, you'll be dead before Samhain.

She pushed all dark thoughts aside as the sun warmed the branches above and the intoxicating scent of blossom worked with the mead to make her close her eyes.

Then she lay down next to her man.

41 * CUTTING THE SPELLS *

Between Beltane and the longest day, Tegen tried to please Étain, said no more about leaving and talked of children. She wanted her new family to think she'd been won over.

Nothing must go wrong, for with or without the sacred Wave, the time had come to leave Tara. She knew her escape would be difficult: her mother in law could see anything she wished in her mirror, but her main problem was Tonn who rarely strayed from her side. The thought of leaving him hurt terribly, but it would only be for a while.

'I vow by all the stars in the sky, I will come back to be with you,' she whispered every night to his sleeping form. She could not face life without him.

One morning, Tonn said he had to visit a man who was going blind. 'Will you come with me?' he asked. 'I'd value your opinion.'

Tegen knew this was her chance, Swallowing hard, she lied. 'Not today. Wolf needs a good walk. He's getting fat sitting in the kitchen swallowing scraps all day.'

'Do come,' Tonn pleaded. 'We could walk together later.'

'We'll have as many walks as you like!' she promised with a kiss, then silently added, *one day…*

'I love you!' She turned to go, biting her lip and trying not to cry as she made her way towards the kitchens. Then with Wolf at her side and food in her pouch, Tegen went to their roundhouse and packed her clothes. She left her embroidered gown. It isn't practical, she told herself, but she tied on her blue glass necklace. This won't get in the way and it'll remind me of love and happiness.

Then, shouldering her bag, she and Wolf set off for Étain's sanctuary. Tegen was nervous as she walked along the woodland path that she and Tonn had so often taken together. The first time she had done this she'd been greeted by Étain in the form of a cat. Would the queen have guessed her plan and be waiting for her again? Might she have put guarding spells across the doorway? Would the mirror even be in there? They came down the slope where the path twisted around a spring, sheltered by an overhanging hazel tree. Just beyond was the little stone hut. Tegen took a deep breath. 'Sit Wolf,' she said, 'and don't move.'

The dog rolled over on his back with his ridiculously long legs in the air, and blinked up at Tegen.

'This is no time for getting comfy,' she laughed, rubbing his belly. 'You must bark if you hear anyone coming.' Then she stepped forward, raised her arms and spread her palms, searching for the tell-tale tingle in the air that meant Étain had left spells in place. Tegen soon found an invisible web. She knew she would have to work fast in case she triggered something that warned the queen. With the lightest of touches, she followed the magical threads as they wove and wound themselves in a protective cocoon around the sanctuary.

She stood quite still as she listened to the clever and

complicated words the queen had whispered to summon the guardian spirits to their duty.

Tegen closed her eyes to see the pattern more clearly in her mind. She had to be like a fly creeping along a deadly web to steal from under the spider's eyes...

Suddenly Wolf's ears pricked and he barked softly.

Tegen dropped to the ground and held her breath. Had she been seen?

Was that a rustle in the undergrowth? Then Wolf lay down and rested his nose on his paws once more. Whatever it was had gone.

Every nerve on edge, Tegen drew a golden knife from her pouch. It was so pure and clean, not even Gwynn ap Nudd, the Lord of the Otherworld would feel its cut. Tegen raised a spirit shield around herself, then, biting her tongue, she inserted the gleaming blade between the spells, paring them away one by one.

A slight movement to her right made her turn. It was a hare sitting on its hind legs, watching her quizzically. That must have been what disturbed Wolf, she thought as she returned to her work. The animal hopped closer, his ears tall and erect, his dark eyes bright. Tegen tried to ignore the audience as she pushed gently at the door. It creaked.

Startled, the hare darted away. Tegen was mildly surprised that Wolf didn't jump after it, but she was glad he stayed.

The room was almost dark. Dare she go in? Had she removed enough of the warding spells? Her heart pounded. She didn't have time to follow every thread to its source. Maybe the queen had her mirror with her and was already watching her every move? Tegen straightened her back and stepped over the sanctuary's threshold, spreading her hands before her. She wished she hadn't lost Goban's ring in the sea, that would have warned her of unseen danger – but she couldn't help that.

Another step, then Tegen was inside. She pushed the door wider. The musty smell of herbs and magic drifted towards her. Urgency tickled at the nape of her neck. She peered around. Everything was just as before, with heavy racks of herbs and creatures drying in the dark, and beyond them – *the box.*

As she stepped inside her foot momentarily caught on something. She glanced down. It was just a spider's web hung with a few droplets of mist. It felt unpleasant and made her skin crawl. It was not one of Étain's spells, and it was very faint.

Tegen's instincts screamed danger, but she was too close to give up.

She stopped and listened.

Nothing.

Her heart thumped harder and her hands became sticky.

Just beyond the crack that led to Tir na nÓg, the demon drew closer and smelled its prey moving softly in the shadowy hut. It laughed silently as it prepared its magic.

The prey was alone. And this time, there was no witch-cat to protect her.

42 * POLISHED SILVER *

Crouching down, Tegen opened the box lid. Inside, her fingers touched cool, curved metal. She eased it out. Immediately, vivid shapes and images sprang from its blackened surface. She averted her eyes. She didn't want to know! She *dared* not know! She just had to take the mirror and run.

Tegen pushed it into her bag and crept towards the door. Finding the gap she had cut in the spells, she stepped through. But the scenes she had glimpsed in the mirror shouted at her to look again, just one more time.

She dared not expose the surface to daylight. She remembered Tonn's warning that the change in the magic might alert Étain. Not far away a hazel tree hung over the spring, casting a deep shade. She could take just one peek… There might be an important warning waiting for her. Then she must run eastwards to the sea for the healing Wave, then take a boat to Mona.

Tegen knelt in the shade and pulled out the mirror. She looked into the blacked depths, but as she did so, she caught sight of something evil and hideous.

Something reaching out behind her left shoulder…

She screamed and dropped the mirror into the spring. It slid through the water and settled on the stony bottom.

Wolf was immediately by her side, licking her ears, and Tegen buried her face into the back of his neck.

The grass rustled nearby. She looked up. It was the hare, staring at her, wide-eyed and motionless.

Then it shook itself, spread its whiskers and stood tall, growing bigger and bigger…

'It's all right,' came Tonn's voice, 'It's only me!'

Tegen couldn't believe her eyes, for there was her man, crouching behind a bush and pulling on his shirt and breeches. 'I'm sorry,' he laughed. 'I always lose my clothes when I shape-shift!'

'You were the *hare*?'

Tonn nodded. 'You didn't seem yourself this morning. I was worried so I followed you – don't be angry.' He sat beside her at the pool's edge and put his arm around her. 'You're shaking, what happened? When I shape-shift I can't hold human thoughts in my head – I'm all hare!'

There was no point lying. Trembling, Tegen pointed to the mirror at the bottom of the pool. 'Remember I told you that a demon follows me and I was worried I'd lead it to Tara? Last time I used the mirror I sensed the spirit was close – but this time it was really here. Reaching out for me through *that*!'

Tonn lay flat on the ground and grabbed the handle of twisted serpents, but as he lifted it, he sneaked a quick, edgeways glimpse. He too went very pale, but said nothing as he shook off the water in the shade of the hazel tree. 'Why were you trying to use it again?' he asked quietly.

'I've stolen it so your Mother won't be able to scry where I am.'

She looked him squarely in the face. 'Tonn, I love you deeply, but I have to leave you. *Today…* '

His face became very solemn. 'I understand. You are the Star Dancer and you have a *geis* on your life – a sacred obligation that will not go away.' He stroked his beard. 'What are you going to do with the mirror?'

She shook off the drops and slid it into her bag. 'I'm going to throw it away – but not near Tara. I daren't risk your mother finding it.'

'Let me gather a few things, I'll come with you.'

'*No!*' Tegen was vehement. 'This is why I was trying to leave without you knowing. You *mustn't* come. I couldn't bear to see you die.' She took his hand and looked into his eyes. 'This is the truth: I'm not going forever. I'll be back as soon as my work is done. I *swear.*'

Tears welled in Tonn's eyes and she struggled to hold back her own.

'If you want to help, go back home and cover for my absence. Buy me time to reach the sea. There's something I have to find there – then I *must* get to Mona.'

Tonn got to his feet and held her tightly. 'Very well,' he replied. 'I'll go back with Wolf. If anyone asks, I'll say you're at a birthing.' He kissed her hair. 'I've treasured every moment with you.'

'I must go,' she said, holding onto him fiercely, her voice muffled in his chest.

Sighing, he opened his arms and stepped away. 'In one hand span of the sun, I will have the chestnut mare at the gravel ford. Will you at least allow me to escort you to the sea? You'll be there tonight if you have a guide. Walking on your own could take days.'

'Thank you,' Tegen replied softly. 'I'll be there.' Then, holding her head high, she turned away. But inside, she was bleeding and torn as she struggled between sorrow that he had found her, and relief that she would have him by her side just a little longer.

*

Étain was no fool. While the day was still young, she had known something was wrong and had gone to her private chamber. There she drew her dark mirror from its box under her bed and looked into it with sorrow. She watched as Tegen broke into the sanctuary.

She is very skilled in magic if she can work her way through *those* spells and guardians, Étain thought. She'll be stronger than me by the time I've finished with her, then I can go to Tir na nÓg in peace, knowing I've left Ériu in the hands of one who is both powerful and good. Tonn will be High King, and Tegen will be his *fili, fáith* and *brehon*: the greatest druid ever to stand beside a monarch. Together they will love truth and their child will unite all five kingdoms.

But Étain was so full of her dreams she did not pay attention to what was happening in her sanctuary.

She glimpsed a flash of evil. She gasped as she saw the demon's hungry eyes searching from out of the darkened surface in Tegen's hand.

'That shouldn't be possible!' Étain groaned. '*That* mirror's just a copy, a piece of smoked silver in case Tegen ever went snooping again. It has no magic in it at all!'

The queen tapped the real dark mirror and whispered 'again,' and once more, the spirits brought the events of the morning before her eyes.

At last Étain saw Tegen had missed one tiny, misty spell that had been triggered as she crossed the threshold.

'I didn't put that there!' the queen whispered. 'And I would never have summoned something evil to follow my newest and best loved daughter…' But what could she do? Send warriors to bring Tegen back to be safely imprisoned once more at Tara? It was too late for that. Now the evil was loose in the land and the fate Étain had always dreaded was beginning to unfurl.

The queen closed her eyes and summoned every friendly spirit she had ever worked with in all her long life. Alone she wasn't powerful enough to save both Tegen and Ériu. Now was the moment for the most daring spell Étain would ever make – and maybe her last, for it would drain all her powers.

The preparations did not take long. Standing by the *Lios*, the queen filled a silver bowl with water from the sacred spring, then she set it down next to the *Lia Fail*, the tall stone of destiny. By her feet was her cloak, wrapped around her beloved mirror. Since the first time she had held the finely crafted handle, Étain had never once let daylight fall on its blackened surface – for in that moment, all its power would vanish.

But now was the time to give up much to save all. As long as the high seat of the kings stood firm, then Tara and the Land would be safe. But this demon from the darkest pits was strong enough to destroy the sacred hill.

By her art, Étain knew that Tegen was still not pregnant and she *must* be carrying by Lughnasadh to give birth to the Child of Hope – that much was certain.

There was only one way…

She would have to send the demon back to its pit and buy a little time for her son and her new daughter to leave together, and with her blessing. The queen wiped beads of sweat from her brow. She prayed to the Dagda, the Good God, to save them, then she looked up at the blue summer's sky. 'Lugh, may your spears burn bright and true,' she said as she lifted the silver bowl so the sun's dazzling rays shimmered on the surface.

She sprinkled the Stone of Destiny and blessed it. 'Make us safe, defend us,' she prayed. Deep down she had always known her mirror images of Tegen marrying Tonn were full and strong, as was the picture of their child. But everything else, Tegen as chief druid in the island, Tonn reigning in peace and happiness: those were flat, stiff and unreal. She had pinned too much on her own wishes, and not enough on the truth.

These things would never come to pass.

It was time to face the other fate that Tegen brought with her – as Étain had always known she would.

The spell was dangerous, for any who held the image of the demon in their thoughts would become one with it, unless they were very strong.

'Tegen,' the queen whispered, 'think of the birds, the trees, my Tonn, think of anything but what you saw this morning…'

With difficulty, she balanced the bowl on the stone pillar and shook her mirror free of its woolly folds. Summoning the demon to look out from the blackened surface, the queen waited until she felt the swelling of the evil spirit's presence.

Then she held the mirror above the water-filled bowl, gleaming with sunlight.

*

In the depths of the Otherworld, the demon was compelled to look. It saw its own image reflected in the water.

Unimaginable horror twisted its foul soul in self-loathing.

But there was worse to come.

For the first time in all eternity, the shimmering rays of the midday sun flooded infinite nothing with blinding brilliance.

The demon threw back its head and howled in agony sending shock waves of hatred across the land.

In that moment it forgot its prey, and let go.

In that moment, Tegen and Tonn leaped onto the horses by the river's gravel ford and kicked their flanks as they headed for the sea.

In that moment, Wolf bared his teeth and howled as a scolding raven flew up from the corpse of a hare.

'Leave it!' Tegen yelled, 'Come!'

But Wolf would not.

'I'm going back!' Tegen yelled and tried to turn, but her man grabbed the bridle and forced the horse onwards.

'We have this one chance, and only one, to get away. For the sake of Britain and everything you love, you must take it! Wolf will follow.'

Tegen sensed the shadow of the demon closing in. Wolf was protecting them! She sent a blessing after him as she fought back tears, lowered her head and let her horse canter along the eastward road.

*

By midnight, their horses stood exhausted by the moonlit sea.

A man was launching a boat on the black, surging waters.

Tegen clutched Tonn's hand, knowing the moment had come when she must let go.

She was leaving for Mona.

*

LOSING

43 * WAR DRUMS *

The journey back was much easier on Tegen's stomach than her first voyage. The fisherman had been glad to exchange two royal horses for a trip to Mona. The boat was well built with a strong leather sail that cupped the wind. It sped through the dark towards Britain, the waves slap-slapping under the hull.

Tegen huddled silently under her cloak. When they were well out to sea, she closed her eyes and opened her bag. With one swift motion, she pulled out Étain's mirror. It scarcely made a sound as it slid into the black depths. Tonn put his arm around her. 'All will be well. We're beyond Étain's power now,' he whispered.

'But you shouldn't have come.' She looked at him in the starlight. 'You *must* go back with the boat or you will die in Britain. And that would break my heart.'

'I understand,' Tonn replied, and he held her tightly.

Tegen leaned against her man, needing his warmth despite her fears. In the dark, she listened to the waves as they nudged and sucked at the boat's wooden stern. Which Wave am I meant to find? She wondered. And how do I hunt it? But exhaustion claimed her before she could think of an answer.

They sailed all the next day, until at last the boatman called out, 'The druids' island is ahead!' He pointed to a misty silhouette of a shoreline. 'Where do you want to land?

'Take us south,' said Tonn. 'There are plenty of safe places to beach the boat along that coast.'

The man pushed the tiller across and re-set the sail. Slowly, dark rocks loomed high on their left and beyond them, smudges of green pastures glowed in the evening sunlight.

Tegen leaned against the mast, watching the hills of Mona become more definite with each rise and fall of the boat. Her heart skipped, she longed to jump overboard and run across the waves as she had in her dream. Faster! Faster! she urged the sail. She couldn't wait. The moment for which she had been born had come. It was almost dark when the keel of the boat ground against the fine white sand of a small, rock-framed bay. 'This place is as good as any,' the boatman said. 'Help me beach her!'

Together, the three of them hauled the craft above the line of dry seaweed that crackled under their feet. 'Safe enough here, I reckon,' he said. 'It's too dark to go further tonight. You two find driftwood for a fire. I'll look for food, then we can have supper.'

Tegen kicked off her shoes and danced across the warm sand. 'I'm here! I'm here!' She squealed with delight, then kneeling by a freshwater stream that trickled across the rocks, she drank and washed.

The summer night was hot and still as the three of them lay by a blue-sparking fire, drinking mead and eating mussels roasted in the embers. Tegen felt almost happy. She had come to meet her destiny at long last. Perhaps all would be well, and she would be back with Ériu in her beloved's arms before winter.

She snuggled down to sleep, her head on Tonn's chest. 'Perhaps what I saw in the mirror was what *might* come to pass, not what *will* – like your mother said?'

Tonn stroked her hair. 'Perhaps,' he said quietly.

*

Tegen woke from her dreams, screaming.

The night was still dark, there was not a sound, except for the soft hushing of the wavelets on the beach and the occasional call of a night bird.

The boatman swore in his sleep and turned over.

Tonn sat up. 'What's the matter?'

Tegen stared wide-eyed into the remnants of the fire, then with a shaking hand she pointed at the glowing, charcoal remains. 'There... there, *look*!' she said in a strangled voice. 'We have to go, *now*!'

Tonn stared where she pointed. 'I'm not much good at scrying.' He passed her a water skin. 'Here, have something to drink, then tell me exactly what you see.'

Tegen gulped urgently and slowed her breathing. 'I see a place where the sea becomes narrow and very fast, like a wide river. The land is high on both sides. There are druids, lots of them. And ships, not like ours – strange ones – long, flat bottomed and with many men on board. Warriors.'

She paused, then whispered, 'They're *Romans*! It's not far away and it's happening *now*. Please, we have to go.'

With much swearing and complaining, the fisherman was roused and persuaded with silver to set sail again. The tide was out, they had further to drag the currach, but Tegen's urgency was unquenchable. The boatman raised the sail and caught the fresh breeze that heralds dawn.

'A place where the sea is narrow, between hills and mountains? I know it.' Using the starlight and the low moon, he negotiated rocks and bays, currents and headlands, until as the first streaks of light appeared in the northeast, they could just about make out a narrow passage of water. 'There you are,' he grunted. 'They call it "the Straight Sea." It divides Mona from the rest of Cymru. Now the tide is out it'll be too shallow to navigate. I'm not going no further, not until morning anyway.'

'Then put me ashore,' Tegen yelled, grabbing his leather jerkin. 'I have to get closer, I have to be *there*! Tonn, make him understand, *please!*'

Just then, the rolling sound of thunder rumbled across the skies, but no hint of lightening flickered. Tegen held her breath. It came again, and again, a low rhythmic rumble, echoing around and around. In the pale light, she could see that although the island of Mona was made of gentle hills, to her right, on the far side of the water were mountains that disappeared into the sky.

In the semi-darkness, the boatman chose a small promontory that appeared out of the shadowy haze in the swiftly flowing narrows. He pulled the currach alongside a tangle of rocks, dark trees and muddy undergrowth.

'Get out, both of you!' the boatman roared. 'That's the sound of war drums, that is. I'm going home!'

*

The demon did not cower in the depths of darkness for long.

The witch's blinding sunlight had done no permanent damage, but its prey had escaped once more. With furious curses, it struggled back through the hollow loathing of its own particular hell towards the bright, painful world of humans.

Then it heard a sound it loved.

War drums.

The demon turned its ghastly thoughts to the mountains of Cymru, where new slaves were calling on him as they gathered. They were begging for the demon's power to stir the cauldron of hatred into a boiling, murderous chaos and bloody victory.

A prayer the demon was pleased to grant.

The one that led the army was a particular favourite. Not only did he hate with an energy and skill that even the demon admired, but he also had a personal loathing for the druid girl with black hair.

Emerging from the Otherworld, the demon cloaked itself in fog once more and sniffed the sea breeze. Despite the witch's blinding spell, not all was lost. Its prey was just where it needed her – heading straight towards the sword arm of the man who sought her.

The demon breathed its poison into the early morning air, infecting all who waited on the banks of the Straight Sea. But the humans only noticed a slight, foetid-smelling mist that hovered between the waters and the shore.

*

The dawn world was silver-grey with dark blue shadows and ghostly tendrils of fog. On the mainland, the mountains rose slate-black above the whiteness, towering above the Straight Sea and Mona's low, wooded hills. As the sound of rhythmic thunder rolled back and forth across the sea, the stale smell thickened.

Standing on a slippery rock above the swirling waters, Tegen shuddered as she shouldered her bag. 'Maybe we aren't too late... Do you know which way is best, Tonn?'

'I'm not sure exactly where we are,' he replied as he clambered up behind her. 'Can you remember any more detail from your vision in the fire?' Then he stopped and pointed. 'Oh no! *Look!*' Just a little way ahead was the sea once more.

Tegen stamped and swore. 'This is an *island*! That man's *marooned* us! I'll send sea monsters after him... I'll...' She began to weave a curse.

'Calm down.' Tonn laid a gentle hand on her arm. 'Let him go, he's just frightened. It's not far to shore. We'll find a way across,' he promised.

'You're right.' Tegen stood still and closed her eyes. 'But I smell the demon's breath in the air. There will be untold horror before nightfall,' she added.

Then she stopped and stared up at her man. '*You're* still here.' Anger and grief flared in her heart. 'You must find a boat back... *Please* Tonn... *Go!*' She shoved at his chest.

Tonn wrapped her in his arms so she couldn't fight. 'I'm not leaving you, Tegen.'

'But you mustn't die, you mustn't!'

'I'll be careful,' he promised. 'Perhaps it's the Goddess's will?'

'It can't be.'

Just then, the thundery echoes began again. *Brrrm-ba-brrrm, brrrm-ba-brrrm brrrm-ba-brrrm.* The drums were getting clearer as evil tightened in around them.

Tegen wriggled free from Tonn and stretched her arms

towards the land. 'At least let's *see* what's happening,' she said, blowing long and hard into the mist. The whiteness parted. The mountains of Cymru seemed to be closing in – capturing warriors and soldiers alike at the bottom of a raging pit of rock, water, wind and darkness. Tegen's heart thudded in tempo with the echoing drums and the shouts of men. Then she saw the boats moored on the far shore, just as she had seen in her fire-dream – long, low craft, packed with men. Alongside them, horses were lined up ready to be swum across.

Waiting. Shouting. Watching.

Then a different drumbeat began, just to her left, below the soft, low hills of Mona.

The hair on Tegen's neck rose and her skin prickled. Not with fear, but with magic.

Slowly she turned. There, on the open slopes that swept down to the shore, hundreds of flickering torches twinkled in the grey-blue of dawn.

A steady stamping of feet brought the torches towards the sea. As they came closer, Tegen could see figures in white walking in a long line, in time to the steady rhythm. *Druids!* They stopped on the higher ground above the shore. Then, from the shifting shadows between them, stepped wailing, black-robed torchbearers.

The drums of Mona stopped. The throbbing silence clutched at the receding night. Then, raising their arms, the druids began chanting in low, steady voices.

From all around, hundreds more shadowy shapes swept down

the hill, darting to and fro. By the flickering flames, Tegen could just make out an army of warriors. Most of them were naked; the torchlight caught the angry, swirling patterns painted on their pale skins. Their hair had been limed stiffly back from their faces like white explosions in the darkness. With one motion, they raised their shields and held their glinting swords aloft.

Then it began.

Across the rippling, sliding water, came long, black shapes – Roman boats rowed in near-silence towards the shores of Mona.

Tegen could just make out the wan, taut, faces of the soldiers. Tongues of druid-fire gleamed blood-red on the men's helmets and breastplates. Tugging at Tonn's sleeve, she whispered breathlessly, 'I've *got* to get ashore! You *must* help me! This is the moment I was born for!'

'I don't know how,' he confessed as he reached to comfort her with a shaking hand.

On Mona, the drumbeat began afresh, this time joined by the throaty clattering of carnyxes. The warriors swaggered down towards the shore in time to the rhythms. On and on they came, stamping, waving swords and thumping spears against their shields. As they reached the water's edge, some even tossed their weapons aside and turned somersaults, leaping over each other and mock-sparring. Others danced and sang defiantly.

Closer and closer came the Romans.

Closer and closer came the clattering, clapping, chanting and drumming.

The boats thudded into the sandy shore, some cracked against rocks and spilled their men into the water. Others caught the smooth sand and the soldiers leaped out almost dry-shod. Then dark, dripping shapes of horses rose out of the sea, shivering as they staggered to gain their footing on land. On their backs, their riders held their swords drawn ready.

A centurion bellowed a few curt words. The invaders tightened into shield wall formations. Above them, bronze eagles stood proud and standards fluttered in the early morning breeze.

No one moved in the semi-dark. Then with a single shout from a thousand throats, the warriors of Cymru leveled their spears and ran full-pelt towards the enemy. Behind them came the swordsmen, hacking and sweeping like summer scythes through overripe grain.

A whistling shower of light Roman javelins caught shields and flesh alike, tangling and snagging. Warriors stumbled and fell. Screams echoed between hill and sea and mountain.

Tegen struggled to find spells to help, but the dark chaos was too much for her. She hid her face in her hands, ashamed that she, the Star Dancer, could do nothing. Admidios had told her she would arrive too late, and he had been right. 'I wish Sabrina was here,' Tegen whispered. 'She'd know what to do!'

Tonn squeezed her shoulder.

Shaking herself free from his grasp, she rushed to the shore, lifted her skirts and stepped into the icy water. She screamed as the waters closed over her shoulders and she was swept away.

'*Tegen!*' Tonn yelled, jumping after her and seizing her wrist.

'Come back! You won't make it!' And he dragged her back.

From the shelter of the trees, Tegen shivered and wept as she watched the far shore. From behind the warriors, a chorus of higher voices screeched. Black-robed druid women ran forward with wildly disheveled hair and red-rimmed eyes, weaving between the warriors and waving burning torches.

One by one they took up an awful lament as flickering orange flames scattered inky shadows, jagged and erratic, weaving to and fro, in and out, in and out.

The druids chanting became deeper, slower, and the women wailed a descant.

Together, they began to weave the Great Spell.

Tegen watched open-mouthed as shimmering strands of magic settled into patterns that hung high in the air. She held her breath for she had never seen anything like it before.

Every colour she knew and a thousand she had never imagined, became entwined with the singing. The breeze played the dancing threads of magic harp strings, adding music of hope and courage to the weave.

As Tegen watched, the colours ignited, burning with flames of deep blue, purple, turquoise, orange, red, yellow and white: glowing, crackling and spitting. Then the drops of fire turned into petals that grew and spread across the valley.

Deep down she recognized every line and curve as they folded and twisted, repeated themselves, then shifted slightly, like music changing key, again and again.

This was the web of magic. These were the patterns of every living thing.

But something was wrong. Was it an incantation that was missing? Or a spiral badly formed? Or maybe a word was spoken that shouldn't have been, worming its way between the druids' meanings?

At the back of her mind, Tegen heard demonic laughter.

It mingled with the screaming and howling as it rose to a crescendo. Keening, cursing, knotting *all* the fury of *all* the gods into one, hideous, screech.

Tegen examined the web that still hung like a glorious curtain from the sky to the sea. Her mouth went dry, for sliding insidiously within the weave were bitterness and hatred. She recognized the work of the demon that had pursued her so long. Its threads were alive, spitting and slithering, strangling and devouring the wholesome living magic that the druids had made. How long would good spells hold against it?

Tegen stared at the Great Spell in horror. How could she strengthen it against the new threads? She had never worked with magic like this before.

Tonn touched her arm. 'Tegen,' he whispered, 'are you awake? Look!'

She rubbed her eyes, realising she had slumped against a tree in a trance. She turned to where her man pointed.

Across the narrow stretch of water, more and more Roman boats were landing, but the soldiers were hesitating, refusing to disembark. On shore, no one moved.

From the Roman ranks, an order was shouted.

A few javelins were raised, one or two swords scraped from

scabbards. Firelight reflected in bloody gules along the short, cruel blades.

For a long moment, there was silence. Everyone froze as the web of magic shimmered in the air.

The whole world held its breath.

Then with a sudden cry of terror, the enemy soldiers turned and fled back to their boats.

Some made signs against the evil eye, others knelt and prayed to their gods. Men leaped fully armed into the water, only to be swept away in the current, their voices gurgling into stillness.

Their iron discipline was broken.

On the shore, the people of Cymru cheered and carnyxes resounded.

Angry Roman officers shouted more orders, trying to regain control. The wild-haired women rushed forward and jabbed torches into horses' eyes, making them shy, flinging their riders onto rocks or into the sea.

The druids raised their voices and quickened their incantations. From behind their lines, the drummers changed their marching rhythms to proclamations of victory.

Exultant warriors levelled their spears, pressing their advantage, driving the heavily laden boats back into the current, where one or two twisted away, out of control, knocking and banging the others, toppling them into the flood.

Horses and men screamed.

Once more the Roman officers tried to rally their men, ordering them to disembark and form ranks.

Behind them on the shore, the frenzied women wailed and

swung their firebrands. Warriors thrust their spears into necks and thighs, and the druids chanted on and on.

Tegen held her breath. The malice the demon had woven into the spells was becoming more dangerous, unraveling the weft and the warp of the druids' weave faster than they could make it.

The spell was falling apart.

She had to *help*, but *how*?

Which spirits will serve me best? Earth, water, fire or air? Think! *Think*! My mind's gone numb. Gronw was right – I must listen to the Goddess, and not just react to the fear and hatred. Tegen told herself.

Just then, a tall man on a black stallion rode to the centre of the fray and spoke clearly and loudly in Latin, then for the benefit of any mercenaries amongst the troops, he added in British, 'Call yourselves *men*? Are you prepared to go home and tell your sons that today, when the future of your homeland was at stake, you were scared off by old men and jabbering witches? Go on then, run away! But are you sure you can live with your shame?'

As he spoke, a naked warrior ran forward, screeching and waving his spear at the Roman, who calmly turned his horse and with one swipe, impaled the man's throat on the end of his sword. Blood squirted up his arm, and drenched his tunic.

And the Great Spell started to unravel.

Furious and ashamed, the Roman soldiers rallied and with a shout, they raised their javelins and the assault began afresh. Fear melted with the spreading daylight.

The tide was rising now and along the shoreline bodies were

swept away, hair loose, robes swirling, blood mixed with weed. The Roman dead were dragged under by their armour, but as Tegen watched, hands and feet drifted by the island, betraying corpses below the surface.

Tegen took a breath. 'I've got to focus,' she said. With her fingertips, she tried to re-work the pattern of spells. She had to bring order to the weave, but she'd been no part of its making, so had no authority to work with it. The few threads she touched slipped from her fingers as if they were oiled.

Raising her arms she tried to summon rolling waves to turn the boats over. 'Help me!' she called to Tonn, 'We have to stop them or *Ériu will be next!*'

Standing side by side, they called on the servants of Lir, lord of the sea, but the noise and confusion of the battlefield drowned out their words, and the god did not hear.

Tegen stamped and swore. To have come so far and to be so close… Tonn held her hand and tried to calm her.

Now the sun had risen from between the mountains. The first rays poured blood on the distant mountaintops and washed the Romans' polished armour with fire.

Brilliant spears of light stabbed the eyes of the defenders of Mona. The few torches that still burned were pale and weak. Exhausted warriors, weary druids, and bleary-eyed women re-grouped on the bloody beach to face yet another new wave of Romans stepping fresh from their boats.

44 * PROMISES *

The final slaughter was over quickly, then the conquerors rode inland, putting all they met to the sword and leaving fire and desolation everywhere.

Borne along by human bitterness and rage, the demon slithered between the injured, whispering failure into dying ears. With delight it fed on their horror and sent their spirits spinning to Tir na nÓg in despair.

Suetonius had done well. The demon swore he would be rewarded with more of the destruction he craved. Here was a human who knew how to hate – a worthy slave.

As the Governor rode across the hills, the demon whispered into his ears. *I am your servant, a spirit from the gods sent to bring you victory, but to prove your worth, you must do one small thing. You must capture the girl druid with long, black hair. I have searched your memories – you know whom I mean – she dances with stones, she threw the fire in your face.*

She is here.

Bring her to her knees with terror, make her serve me, and all of the Britannic Isles will be yours. I will even give you all of Cymru, Alba in the far north, and Ériu in the west. You will be the Lord of it all, the Emperor of the North.

As it spoke, the demon filled the man's mind with images of victory parades, laurel wreaths, honour and gold.

She isn't far away, it went on. *I can feel her… Somewhere amongst hills of sand. Find her. Bring her to me – unharmed.*

Suetonius's scar-twisted lips spread into a bitter smile. 'I promise,' he said.

And so do I, swore the demon.

'And then,' Suetonius said to none but himself, 'with the help of my new servant from the gods, I shall become Emperor of *Rome…*!'

45 * 'I HAVE SEEN IT' *

The tide was rising. Using a branch, Tonn captured an empty boat as it swept past on the current. It was long, with a shallow draught. He had never handled one like it, but rowing hard with Tegen they soon grounded ashore.

Slowly Tegen led the way inland, creeping through the dense hazel and ash woodlands that fringed that part of the shore. The going was hard, not just because of brambles, but also the dead and dying of both sides.

Here and there, Tonn helped a man or a woman to the Otherworld with one swift cut of his knife. Tegen gave them a reassuring blessing to ease their passing, but she could not make herself slit their throats the way Tonn did. Even for mercy's sake.

All day they walked inland. Soon the trees gave out to wild sand dunes that slid under their weary feet as they trudged.

For the first time since they set off, Tonn voice unease. 'Why are we here? What are we looking for?' he asked. 'We must go Tegen – this is madness. It's too late!'

'I don't know… I just can't leave yet.' She paused and scanned the sandy hillocks and distant forests. In the north, smoke rose into the blue sky. 'What's on fire?' she asked.

Tonn shook his head. 'Farms, sacred groves, anything that matters to us,' he said quietly. 'It's over, Tegen. Without the druids Britain has died. There is nothing left for you to fight for.

Let's find a boat. Come back to Ériu with me. Help me defend the Land of the Danaan. Please Tegen… I love you, I don't want to die. I want to live – with you.'

Tegen bit into her lip until it bled. The longing to just give up, and do as Tonn asked wrenched at her soul.

Just then she tripped over another body that groaned. Once more Tonn drew his knife, although it was getting too dull to do its work kindly. He gritted his teeth as he pressed the blade under the dying man's beard.

'No!' Tegen grabbed his arm.

She knelt and stroked the man's hair. It was wet with blood and the whites of his eyes glistened between his half-opened lids. His life force was all but drained into the sand.

'There's no hope for him,' Tonn said. 'Let me help him towards his rebirth quickly.'

'Wait! I know him.' Tegen touched the dying man's hand. 'Huval?'

He struggled to sit. Fresh red blossoms swelled on his filthy white robe. She slipped her arm behind his back. 'Huval, it's me, Tegen. I tried to come before, I really did.'

At the back of her mind, Admidios's prophecy that she would come too late still tormented her.

Her throat was tight. 'I'm so sorry. I let you all down. I was born to help you fight this evil and I failed. Can you forgive me?'

Huval tried to speak, but blood trickled from the corners of his mouth and his ears. Tegen put her head closer to catch his words.

'I… saw we'd… meet again…' he managed to wheeze.

Tegen squeezed his hand and fought burning tears.

'You didn't fail...' he took a deep, rattling breath. 'Not final... battle. Not yet.' Then dragging in one more breath, Huval opened his eyes and tried to smile. 'You *will*... turn evil aside,' he wheezed. 'It's not what... you think. Romans not... real enemy.'

His chest heaved and he coughed, splattering Tegen with blood. 'I have seen it.'

Then he was gone.

Tegen closed his eyes. 'May you be reborn again soon,' she whispered. Then taking two large handfuls of warm sand, she sprinkled his corpse in token burial.

Her man did the same. 'Who was he?'

Tegen could not speak. Collapsing in a heap she hid her head between her knees and wept.

Tonn sat next to her, silent and nervous. Tegen's grief was heart-wrenching. He could not ask her to move, not yet.

*

All too soon, the inevitable thudding of horse hooves came their way. Tonn tried to make Tegen lie flat, but she wriggled free and stood.

'This is part of my fate,' she said. 'I will not die today.' She watched the men approach. There were five or six, and riding a black stallion at their head was a tall commanding officer. The man's heavy plumed helmet nodded and his armour shone. Down the right side of his face was a dark, crinkled burn scar. He raised his hand for the others to stop, then urged his horse forward a little. Fine sand rose and fell in the warm air.

'Suetonius Paulinus,' Tegen whispered. Images of fire and

cruelty flashed through her memory.

'So, we meet again,' Suetonius sneered in British. 'The druid girl who dances with stones and pretends she's a slave!'

He raised his hand to order their deaths, when the voice inside his head spoke *Stop! This is the one I want alive. Bind her. We will make her suffer.*

Suetonius looked down his long hooked nose at his captives.

'Bring them both to camp! This British bitch knows more than she ever lets on! I will question her personally.' He wheeled his mount around, leaving his companions to tie them and drag them to camp.

*

A garrison had been hurriedly built not far from the sea. A square ditch and palisade surrounded hundreds of leather tents, all pitched in exact rows. The smell of cooking made Tegen's stomach rumble, although she knew from experience not to expect food from Suetonius.

They were thrown into a pit edged with sharpened wooden stakes. As they landed, something squealed, shifted and swore.

Tegen wriggled away and tried to adjust her eyes to the semi-dark. 'Sorry,' she mumbled, as Tonn and she tried to help each other free of their bonds.

The other figure sat up, stared at Tegen and exclaimed, 'I don't believe it!'

'It can't be…?' Tegen's spirits soared as she hugged their fellow prisoner. 'Sabrina! It's really wonderful to see you! This is Tonn, my man, and this is Sabrina, Queen of the Dobunni tribe.'

'Shussh! Don't say that aloud! They'd send me to Rome as a

"prize" if they knew who I was. I've more chance of getting free to fight again if they believe I'm a nobody.' She reached across and helped Tonn with the last knots at his wrists.

He bowed his head. 'Madam,' he whispered in his lilting accent, 'I am honoured to meet you, Tonn, youngest son of the High King of Tara in the blessed Land of Ériu, at your service.'

'Shut up, down there!' a surly voice bellowed from above, 'No one gave you permission to speak!'

'Go and piss in your dinner!' Sabrina yelled back, then in a low whisper, she smiled as she said, 'You know, with *three* of us here, there's a chance we might actually escape!'

46 * PULLARIUS *

They waited until dark. The sentries marched to and fro at regular intervals. Sabrina counted the heartbeats between patrols, but there was no pattern to them. They were keeping the prisoners uncertain.

'This pit isn't that deep,' she said. 'They dug it in a hurry. I'm injured and can't haul myself up like I used to. If one of you stands on my shoulders, you'll be able to look over the top and see where the men are and what they're doing.'

'If you're hurt,' Tonn, suggested, 'then why doesn't Tegen stand on my shoulders? She's the smallest and I'm the strongest.'

'Just be careful,' Sabrina replied.

Tegen climbed onto her man's back from where she could easily see where the men huddled around a brazier. 'They're playing dice!' she whispered. She watched a little longer, then jumped down. 'One man looks up occasionally, but they aren't keeping very good watch.'

'They're probably cross because they aren't drinking and celebrating victory with the rest. They'll be the cohort's dregs. Is anyone guarding the main gate? It's to your left.'

Tonn shuffled around the pit, as Tegen peered over the rim in every direction. 'No, everyone's in the game.'

Sabrina chewed her finger. 'Have either of you still got your knives?'

'No, they disarmed us,' Tegen said miserably.

'Never mind, there're a couple of good sharp stones down here. First, we scrape away just below the top lip of the pit, that'll loosen the wooden stakes. A good, hard pull and a couple should come free. 'But to escape, we'll need a diversion. Any ideas? Something magical maybe?'

'I could use fire,' Tegen suggested.

'No, that would bring every soldier in the camp. We only need a small distraction for the men close by, the less fuss the better,' Sabrina replied.

'How about I shape shift into something?' said Tonn. 'I just need a pattern to copy...' He jumped and gripped the edging spikes. 'I can see a cage of birds – I don't know what they are – large red doves? Or a sort of a duck...?'

'They're called chickens,' Sabrina replied. 'They use them for divining.'

'Can you look like them?' Tegen asked.

Tonn dropped down again. 'In this light, no one will notice if I get it a bit wrong. What do you want me to do when I'm out? Once I've taken animal form I forget I'm human. I can move in a general direction, but there's no guarantee I'll follow an exact plan.'

Sabrina leaned against the damp earth walls of the prison. 'Any sort of diversion will do. Just flap around on the other side of the courtyard. While they try and catch you we'll get out. Then we all run like the wind for the gate. Can you do it?'

But Tonn didn't answer. There was simply a flurry of feathers, a raucous squawking and his clothes scattered around the pit.

'The Goddess go with you!' Tegen whispered as a feathered tail disappeared between the stakes.

In the courtyard above, the soldiers were miserable, bemoaning their sentry duty while their companions at arms were celebrating the day's victory. One man accused another of cheating at the game and slammed a fist into a jaw. Dice were tossed aside and the men squared up for a good fight.

Suddenly a chicken landed flapping in their midst. 'Get that bloody bird back in its coop!' someone yelled.

'Where's the chicken-man? He's the one who should be catching it!'

'*Oi! Pullarius! Chicken-man!*' another guard hollered. 'Where are you?'

'Probably pissed by now,' the first voice said. 'Why can't he keep his birds safe? It's all very well bringing them with us, they're great for eggs and foretelling the future, but they're a pain in the arse when they get out, then who gets the blame?'

'We do!' the men chorused.

'Exactly! *Pullarius!*'

There was the sound of belching and running feet. 'What's the matter? Can't you say boo to a fox without getting scared?'

Sabrina translated quickly for Tegen who held her breath as she prayed, 'Please let Tonn be all right.'

One of the men swore and dived at Tonn's shape-shift, making him squawk. 'Here you are mate!'

The *pullarius* grabbed the stray and looked at it. 'Never seen it before. Damn ugly looking creature, where d'you get it?'

'The sky! Where d'you bloody think?'

'Perhaps Jupiter sent it! Don't ask us, you're the chicken-man.'

The pullarius was worried. His job was to look after the sacred chickens and to augur the future by they way they behaved. He held the wriggling shape-shift firmly under his arm and strolled over to his coop. The man counted his birds. All there. 'Definitely not one of mine,' he said, taking the bird back to the light of the brazier. 'Looks more like a duck that's had it off with a cuckoo on a bad day. Must be a local.'

'These pagans don't have chickens – never seen 'em before!'

The pullarius put the newcomer in with the others and threw in a bit of bird-cake. Tonn backed away, clucking nervously. Worried, for that was a very bad omen, the man offered food to his own birds, but the stranger scared them, so they flapped and squawked as well.

'I'm getting the captain,' the pullarius announced, slamming the coop door and striding away.

At that moment, a hen nibbled the new bird's wing feathers. In pain and surprise, Tonn jumped, yelped and sprang back to his human form. His strong spine and shoulders burst all the ties that held the coop's framework together.

Tonn stood amazed and stark naked in the middle of a smashed cage. On all sides, terrified birds flapped wildly, scattering feathers.

Beyond them, the flickering firelight danced on the soldiers' disbelieving faces as they stared up at him out of the darkness.

Tonn grabbed a handful of straw to keep himself decent as he kicked at the chickens, sending them clucking and crowing into the shadows with a flurry of claws and feathers.

Sabrina squeezed Tegen's arm. 'Quickly! Climb on my back, wriggle the bars loose, then pull me up.'

'But what about Tonn? We can't just leave him!'

Sabrina was exasperated. 'He'll get out somehow! Now's our chance – *Move*!'

Tegen did as she was told, using the covering mayhem to hack with a stone at the base of the first bar. 'Keep going, Tonn,' she whispered between gritted teeth.

And Tonn did. At that moment, he chose to throw back his head and bellow like an angry bull.

The men stood, staring, wide-eyed and open mouthed.

Tonn grabbed a dropped cloak and tucked it around his waist, then squaring his shoulders, he charged: first the pullarius, then the one cowering behind him. Both men dropped their daggers, tripped over their swords and fled.

Chickens squawked and fluttered.

Tonn seemed to grow and swell, taking on bovine proportions.

Trembling, the pullarius pointed at Tonn with a shaking finger. 'Let the prisoners go,' he gasped. 'Look, look, it's Mithras come to stand among us. Magnus, open the prison pits! Put down ladders! Help the captives up! Justus, tell the guards to open the gate, and for all that is sacred, the rest of you bow down. If you so much as look at the Lord's face something dreadful will happen to you!'

Tonn did not understand a word of what was being said, but, as the men prostrated themselves, he realised that maybe, just *maybe*, the soldiers were afraid of him.

Beginning to enjoy himself, he rolled his eyes, raised his free hand and shook his fist.

Then from behind an upturned stool, one young man stammered, 'But... but the Governor... he'll have our heads...'

Shielding his eyes from 'Mithras', the pullarius glared at the young auxiliary. 'Don't be *stupid* boy, what's it to do with the Governor?'

He looked around the terrified men.

'We must obey. *The chickens have spoken!*'

47 * SABRINA'S STORY *

A ladder was dropped into the pit. Sabrina threw Tonn's clothes at Tegen and pushed her hard from behind. 'Quick!' she said. 'Before they change their minds!'

They were not the only prisoners. From here and there, more figures in druid's robes or chieftain's cloaks scurried from holes and huts into the night. Tegen found Tonn in the melee and helped him dress. 'Follow them,' she whispered, pointing towards the shadowy shapes slipping between the garrison gates.

A tall figure led the way through the midnight woods and down to a stream. There he stopped. 'I am Moryn, chief druid of the Ordovices tribe,' he announced in a deep voice. He looked askance at Sabrina. 'You weren't in the battle! Who are you?'

Sabrina drew herself to her full height. 'I am Sabrina, daughter of Eiser, King of the Dobunni, rightful heir to that kingdom. I am also the betrothed of Owein, last son of King Cara, also known as Caractacus.' She glanced around at her listeners, all exhausted and skeptical. 'I didn't fight because I was imprisoned. Take me with you and I will slit the belly of every Roman who dares breathe our air.'

Moryn looked her up and down in the moonlight. 'You may come. And you two?' he glowered at Tonn and Tegen.

Tonn gave their names. 'We arrived from Ériu as the battle raged. We were too late to help.'

Moryn grunted. 'Very well. Hurry!' he urged. 'There's a boat hidden nearby. Come.' He led the refugees along the stream to a stony beach at the northern end of the Straight Sea. In a little starlit cove the obsidian water lapped a currach.

Some refused to leave the island, but three men and two women jumped aboard. Sabrina followed. Tonn steadied the craft with his foot and helped Tegen across. She looked up at her man. 'Please don't come,' she begged.

'Only if you return with me!' he whispered urgently.

'I *can't*…'

'*Hurry!*' Moryn shouted.

Tonn judged the rise and fall of the sea and sprang to Tegen's side.

'Casting off!' a voice called from the shore. 'May Lir's spirits of water guide you, may Manaan keep you, and may the Lady Goddess bring you home.'

'And may we meet again merrily,' a voice replied as the boat took to the waves and the leather sail flapped and filled.

*

The Roman garrison was in uproar. The centurion stared in disgust at a smashed chicken coop, ladders in opened prison pits, and the camp gates wide open. The guards swore that Mithras himself had appeared and commanded the release of the captives.

The men were tied and dragged before the Governor of all Britain as he picked at a dish of figs, reclining on his dining couch in the main tent. Suetonius Paulinus did not believe that the gods appeared to scum such as these, and dawn saw a dozen crucifixions on a hill, in plain sight of all.

Around the neck of the pullarius was a taut piece of twine. From it flapped a chicken, slowly strangling itself as it struggled.

The voice in Suetonius's head was conciliatory although it barely concealed a raging fury. *That was unfortunate*, the demon said. *Not your fault at all, it was the imbeciles under you. The gods have ordained, master, that very soon you will travel east, and there will be more chances for you to capture the girl and to show your skill at war. I will be with you to guide you.*

Suetonius took his dagger and pricked his thumb. Warm blood trickled down the blade. 'I will find the druid girl and deliver her to you!' he vowed as he licked it clean.

The demon smiled as it flowed away towards Britain's most easterly edge on a wind that blew no good. There, in Iceni lands, there had been an important death. Amusing injustices had followed, and now the newly-widowed queen was filled with rage. To make things even better – this flame-haired woman had as much intellect and venom as the Roman.

She was ripe and well matched for the battle to come.

Face to face, these two would be like deadly vipers, each mortally pitched against the other.

The demon did not care which of its pets won the fight – or even if they both died. It never permitted human winners, but the game was certain to attract its prey.

And that was what mattered.

*

The night wind was bitter. The mountains had long been left to starboard. The druids in their boat still traced the northern curve of the coast of Cymru. Daylight showed crags giving way to a few low hills where muddy inlets met the sea. Bread was passed around, but there was no fresh water, so it was difficult to swallow.

The mast, the yardarm, the sheets and the cleats intrigued Sabrina, who had never sailed in a full sized boat before. Soon she had taken a turn at the tiller and was talking of having her own currach. 'When you druids have crowned me queen of the Dobunni and Britain is at peace again,' She laughed.

Moryn pointed out a river mouth ahead. 'Steer for there, my lady,' he said quietly, 'If Britain can still be saved, that is where it will happen.'

Tegen sat silently as the boat tacked across the silted estuary. 'Where are we going?' she asked at last.

Moryn looked her up and down. 'Tell *your* story first, we don't know for certain who you are. I can see you're both druids, and I can feel your power, but where are you from?'

Tegen blushed, deeply ashamed of her failure to help at the battle for Mona. 'I'm Tegen of the Winter Seas.' She swallowed hard and hesitated.

'She's your Star Dancer,' Sabrina added cheerfully.

Everyone in the boat fell silent, turned, and stared.

'I...' Tegen tried to say something useful, but couldn't find any words.

Tonn leaned forward. 'It's my fault she didn't come earlier,' he said, his eyes earnest. 'I am Tonn, the druid son of Feradach and Étain, High King and Queen of Tara in Ériu. I kept her against her will. But now we are both here to do what we can to save Britain.'

The only sound was the water slapping and sucking at the bottom of the boat. At last, Moryn let out a slow sigh. 'Thank the Lady you *weren't* here any earlier,' he said. 'Because you were late, you are still alive and Britain has hope.'

Tonn squeezed Tegen's hand. 'And so will Ériu when you conceive our child,' he whispered.

Tegen closed her eyes. The thought of bringing a baby into such a world made her heart-sore. She tried to change the subject. 'How did you get here, Sabrina? You were the last person in the world I expected to meet, even though I often wished you were with us.'

The queen of the Dobunni steered the prow away from the treacherous banks that were closing in on each side as the river narrowed. 'Let me think – last time we met I'd just killed that slave who couldn't keep his hands off me.' Her eyes gleamed. 'That was a magnificent moment! I'm glad you were there! Anyway, Suetonius Paulinus was the guest of honour at the arena that day. He liked the way I fought, so I was purchased for troop entertainment during his campaign across Cymru.'

She spat in derision. 'Sometimes I fought other girls in a makeshift arena, the men seemed to like watching that. Then I was put against the army's prize wrestlers, one to one, but it didn't go down well – Roman men don't like losing to a woman!'

Tegen laughed, then stopped, remembering Suetonius's taunts on the shores of Mona. An awful thought struck her. 'Did they make you fight as part of their army?'

Sabrina shook her head. 'I'd have died first. Anyway, I was too important to them as a gladiatrix. Military morale had to be kept up! How much of their campaign do you know? Since midwinter, the Romans have subdued all the lands to the west of the Rearing River. The Silures and the Ordivices gave them a run for their money, they are as fierce as rabid dogs, but the Ceangli are more gentle and had a hard time of it.

Of course, the tribes had met the Romans before and treaties had been drawn up, but Suetonius decided that those weren't good enough and wanted the people terrorised. I've never seen a man so possessed by bitterness. He wasn't happy until he had war-hardened kings grovelling at his feet, begging for their lives.'

'And he got his way,' Moryn added quietly as he stared over his shoulder at the low, green hills of Britain.

Tegen shuddered, remembering the devastation of Y Fenni.

Sabrina leaned across and whispered, 'I've heard it was *you* who burned Suetonius's face…?'

Tegen smiled. 'After you left and your father was murdered, Owein and I searched Admidios's room for evidence of his guilt. We managed to get into the camp with Owein shaved and dressed in a toga. I pretended to be a slave he was presenting to his uncle. We found what we were looking for, but Suetonius caught us. There was a fight,' she hesitated and examined her fingernails – ashamed and proud of herself at the same time. 'I… got a bit carried away with my fire magic.'

Sabrina threw back her head and roared with laughter, then she slapped Tegen on the back. 'Oh well done!' she exclaimed. 'We'll make a battle druid of you yet!'

'Watch out for those eddies,' an old man called out, 'there's mud banks here.'

Sabrina adjusted the tiller. 'The river's getting very narrow,' she said.

The man craned his neck and looked around. 'The tide's not in our favour. To our right is Dewa – it's swarming with Romans. If we land on the left bank, it's a long way before we can cross this river, we need to go as far upstream as we can.'

'Why don't you take over from here, Fynbar?' Moryn asked. 'You're used to this stretch of water.'

Sabrina moved aside and the elderly druid took his place at the helm.

Moryn looked around the weary passengers in varying states of despondency. 'Listen,' he said, 'all is not lost. We still have the Star Dancer, so I wish to propose a few things.'

Everyone turned to him. 'Firstly, we must take off our jewellery and cut down our robes, or alter them so they look more like peasant's garb.'

There was a murmur of discontent at that, but Moryn was adamant. 'The Romans attacked Ynys Môn because our sacred company gave hope to the peoples of Britain and Cymru. It's said the Romans plan to wipe out the druids completely.'

'I've heard that too,' Sabrina added.

'So, we must look like ordinary people about our business, farmers, wives, healers, whatever we choose. But without our regalia.'

The group nodded reluctantly. A woman produced a small pair of shears from her pouch and began to cut the embroidered insignia from the hem of her gown. She passed the cutters around, and one by one, lengths of cloth were dropped into the swirling waters, then headbands, bracelets and torcs were put away.

Tonn untied Tegen's blue glass beads from her neck and she wrapped them in her dancing shawl at the bottom of her bag.

Moryn went on, 'We must travel in ones or twos, not as a whole group, and I propose we meet in the place where silver and gold, iron and copper, lead and tin all bleed from the great rock in the marshlands.'

Tonn looked at Tegen. She shrugged. 'I've never heard of it.'

Moryn pointed due east. 'Three days' walk. Anyone in these parts will tell you how to find it.'

'It'll be heavily guarded by Romans,' Fynbar said. 'They came here to steal our minerals.'

Moryn smiled broadly. 'Yes, but these mines are also swarming with the Old Ones. They are the forced labour in the mines, and understand the hidden labyrinths like no one else. We haven't always seen eye to eye with these lovers of stone and earth, but for once, we're on the same side.'

Fynbar nodded, then leaned on the tiller and steered the boat towards a small jetty. 'I can't go any further on this tide,' he said. 'It's just mudflats. Best get ashore while we can.'

He lashed a rope to the ladder, slimy with bright green weed. Tegen winced as she grasped the rungs. She wished with all her heart she was in Ériu, but she knew she must climb up and face whatever came next.

48 * TEGEN'S FUNERAL *

Under the cover of tall bulrushes, the druids formed a circle and blessed the spirits with a few precious grains of incense, then they went their separate ways. Sabrina led Tegen and Tonn due east across the marshes and low hills for three days, turning south on the morning of the fourth.

At last they saw a great rock towering proudly above the undulating landscape. As they drew close they could see that except for the top and the steepest side, it was almost bare of trees – and bustling with busy-ness.

Around the base, Romans supervised the loading of mineral-laden rocks onto carts. Black smoke from furnaces and forge fires billowed into the summer skies.

It was almost Lughnasadh and, beyond the industry, the people of the villages were preparing to gather in their harvests and set aside their grain taxes for their new overlords.

No one noticed two grimy women and a man walking towards the main settlement. Sabrina found lodging for herself and her 'brother and sister' at an inn. Tegen paid with coins from her dancing shawl, which was now a great deal lighter than when she had first worn it.

The building was Roman style, oblong, with a large downstairs hall for drinking and eating, and two upstairs rooms, one for guests, and another for the landlord and his family. Straw mattresses and brightly coloured woven rugs made the place look cheerful, but at night they were kept awake by the fleas. Worst of all were the drinkers who sat up late guzzling ale and wine under the waning moon.

For two days they waited for Moryn and the others. All that time, Tegen struggled with a bindweed of fear that strangled anything that resembled hope. In the still hours of darkness she lay awake, holding onto Tonn and he to her. He was careful not to speak in public in case his strong accent betrayed him as a foreigner.

On the third day, just half a moon before the festival, more druids arrived, Moryn, Fynbar and people from another boat. Tegen spotted them while she was in the market. At first they looked like ordinary travellers, the three men in short, undyed smocks and breeches and the two women wearing dirty garments with badly cut hems and uncombed hair. But it was their bearing that gave them away. They walked with exhausted dignity.

Tegen contrived to drop a parsnip and ran in front of them to retrieve it.

At first Moryn just moved aside and made to walk on, but Tegen pushed her hair back from her face, showing the dark marks of the tattoo on her right cheek. 'Want to buy fresh food Mister?' she whined. 'Nice and crispy…'

Moryn scowled, hesitated, then said, 'I'll buy your parsnip, girl. Do you have any more?'

'Back at the inn. Want to come and look?'

Moryn beckoned to his companions and they followed Tegen past the market stalls and away to the whitewashed building where the others were waiting. The druids ordered wine and sat on benches in the yard, eating bread and cheese.

Tegen ran to their room to tell the others. Sabrina watched the group below from the wind-eye. 'I can see Moryn and Fynbar, and there's Meredith and the others we sailed with, but I don't know everyone. Can we trust them?'

'What else can we do?' Tegen asked. 'We can't stay here forever, we're almost out of money.'

'You're right,' Sabrina replied, and led the way downstairs and into the garden where the druids sat drinking in the shade of a rowan tree.

Tegen touched the heavy red berries and remembered Brigid and her smithy fire. 'Shield us now,' she prayed, as she slid onto a bench beside her new companions.

Moryn was talking quietly and quickly. 'More of our order are already with the Old Ones,' he said. 'I think about twelve of us escaped, and three warriors including yourself, my lady.' He gave Sabrina a tiny bow.

She leaned forward urgently. '*Warriors*? Do you know where they are?'

Fynbar nodded. 'They have gone east – to the Iceni.'

'Traitors!' Sabrina spat and made a curse with her fingers. 'What have they gone to those Rome-lovers for?'

The old man raised a thin hand. 'Haven't you heard? The Iceni king is dead and the Romans have so misused the queen and her daughters, there is rebellion. Queen Boudica herself is mustering the troops from every tribe. She has become the eye of the storm.

There is to be war at last!'

Sabrina's eyes sparkled. Leaping to her feet, she slapped the table and gulped her wine. Then putting her cup upside down on the ground, she smashed it with the heel of her boot and crushed it to red powder. 'I swear on my father's life-blood, I will do this and more to our oppressors!' she snarled. 'Now, excuse me, good people, I must be away. I must stand by the side of my sister Boudica. She will need someone who knows how the Romans think!' And with that, she marched inside.

A few heartbeats later, she reappeared, dressed for travel, her bag over her shoulder. Ignoring the others, she went to the stable and re-emerged with a fine piebald mare, which she mounted bareback and rode out of the yard without a backward glance.

Tonn watched, wide eyed in amazement. 'When did she get *that*?' he whispered.

Tegen leaned across and mouthed very softly, 'I expect she *requisitioned* it, a little like your father got his prize bull. Sabrina won't hesitate to take what she needs to fight this war.'

Tonn nodded and sipped his wine.

At the other end of the table, Moryn was sitting quietly, watching everything and stroking his greying beard. When Sabrina had gone, he looked around and beckoned the company to move closer. Leaning forward he spoke quickly and quietly. 'We will enter the caves of the Old Ones tonight,' he said.

*

It was pitch black. Heavy clouds stole the fingernail moon. They met in a wood behind the village. On the ground was a bier woven out of willow. Meredith and the other women stood on one side, veiled Roman style and holding small terracotta lamps with wavering lights.

Moryn turned to Tegen. 'You're the lightest of us all, lie on that and don't dare move a muscle, whatever happens.'

Tegen did as she was told, then the women draped her with a white sheet. Tonn and the other three men took the corners, lifted the bier and started to walk. The women went ahead wailing a dirge while Old Fynbar shuffled behind, head bowed and silent.

Tegen's heart thumped. She could hear Tonn's breathing by her right shoulder. She wanted to sneak a hand under the cover and touch him, just for a moment. But she dared not. The women's tiny lights flickered and made pale patterns through the white pall. A leaden presentiment weighed on Tegen's chest. What if she sneezed? What if she were *really* buried alive? What if? *What if?*

I mustn't be afraid, she told herself. This is the only way past the Roman guards. Pretending to be dead just *feels* unnerving. That's all. There's nothing wrong. Nothing to be afraid of. When I get to the rock, I'll become a part of the magic that'll drive these demons from our land at last! Keep breathing, keep breathing…

The women stopped their wailing and the procession walked on in eerie silence. Tegen tried not to panic as she was carried along by the tramp, tramp of their feet in steady rhythm. They sounded like soldiers marching. Someone coughed and that made Tegen long to do the same. Phlegm caught in her throat and she tried to swallow, but it would not go away.

Think of something else… she told herself.

But she could not.

The bier was uncomfortable and an awkward piece of woven willow stuck painfully into her back, scratching and digging at every step.

If only she could jump down, grab Tonn's hand and flee...

That would mean betraying her destiny. But where should she be? Was there hope for Britain, or should she flee to Éiru?

The procession stopped.

A gruff voice in poor British demanded who they were and where they were going.

Fynbar spoke. The Romans didn't listen to women. 'My daughter's died. A lovely girl, about to be wed too...' On cue, the women sobbed and wailed.

'So what are you doing out here?' demanded the sentry. 'You passed the cemetery way back.'

Fynbar spoke again, 'We're taking her to the top of the hill so her spirit can fly to her ancestors in the sky. We'll watch until dawn and she'll be cremated. It's an ancient ritual, everyone does it around here.'

The soldier hesitated, 'I've not seen it before...'

Fynbar groaned. 'And it's terribly bad luck to halt a funeral procession, didn't you know?'

That flustered the soldier. 'Pass then, but I'm watching you!' Fear tightened his voice.

Tegen's hurdle was tipped and joggled as the path wound up hill. She felt as if she were about to slide off. Gripping the poles she held on until her aching fingers could take no more. Then the procession stopped.

At last, the bier was lowered and the sheet folded back. 'Quick!' Moryn whispered. 'Follow the light.'

All the funeral lamps had been extinguished bar one little flame that flickered to Tegen's right. Stiff and painful, she rolled herself upright and ran almost blind across a rocky surface.

In the dark, hands grabbed her. She wanted to scream, but remembered to be silent. She held her breath while small, vice-like fingers tugged at hers.

'This way!' a voice whispered. 'You come, yes?'

The strange manner of speech told her it was one of the Old Ones. Tegen felt a surge of hope and breathed again.

The light came closer. Soon she could see a wide crack in the rocks at her feet. 'Down!' the voice commanded. Tegen put one hand on each side and slipped into the crevice below.

She was pushed forward and guided to the left. She passed another tiny lamp that burned on a boulder. Yellow rock was above, beneath, and on every side. The shadows were too deep and dark for Tegen to guess the shape of the space, but the air was close.

'Sit now, slide bottom!' warned the voice again.

Beneath Tegen's feet the floor sloped steeply away, so she lay back and slithered into complete darkness.

49 * INSIDE THE ROCK *

The demon roamed the blackness, seeing and knowing all. As the druids found safe places to sit and wait, it crept between them, listening, whispering, suggesting, hinting.

As Tegen slept, it pressed in on her like earth over her corpse. I've got to get out, she thought. I'll die if I stay here, this place is filled with despair.

Tonn sensed her fear, held her close and stroked her hair. He gave her all his warmth. She hated herself for being glad he had come. She needed him desperately, but all was far from well. She had brought the man she loved into a stone-jawed trap.

At first, everyone slept. The slaughter at Mona swaddled the sleepers in nightmares. They had rest, but little healing, for the demon was very much at home in the cool, damp, discomfort.

An unbearable smell drifted up from the corner that everyone used as a privy. Time did not exist. Tegen had no sense of the waxing moon or days passing. They lived in an eternity of musty stone and unwashed bodies. Every sound was magnified – the drip of water, the scrape of a foot, and far, far away, the knocking of the miners searching the hill's secret inner-self for precious minerals.

When they could, the Old Ones brought bread, water, cheese and once, some plums.

Sometimes there was oil for a lamp, sometimes not.

Tegen preferred the darkness; she did not have to look at the worried faces of those around her. She could not bear to see Tonn so gaunt and haggard.

The Old Ones came and went, whispering news that the Romans were scouring the countryside for fleeing druids.

In the empty hours, the refugees told their stories. They were much the same – of how the invaders destroyed their homes, their families and their lives.

Tegen said little as she lay in the dark and listened. She had too many memories of what she had seen the Romans do – and even worse, of caves and the demons they held. Heartbeat by heartbeat she fought the dread that was slowly suffocating her.

At last, the others wanted to know more of her history. She could not ignore the request. She began with her birth and told of how she had struggled to be proclaimed and recognized as the Star Dancer. 'I longed to come to Mona to be trained. I believed my destiny was to become part of the Great Spell to drive the Romans away,' she said. 'It breaks my heart to know I failed.'

'But you are *alive*,' Moryn's deep voice put in. 'That means we still have hope.'

'I slept on Cadair Idris,' Tegen told the darkness. 'I dreamed I should go west and find happiness and "hunt for the Wave that would heal the Land".'

She felt Tonn shift slightly beside her. 'Why did you chose to hunt for that Wave in Ériu?' he asked.

'I didn't come on purpose. The lady Brigid put me into a boat and said it would take me where I needed to go. The boat sank and you and the men of Tara rescued me.'

'And did you find the Wave that would heal the Land?' someone asked.

'No,' Tegen replied. 'I have sailed for days and nights and stared at each wave as it came, but I never did find what that meant.'

At the thought of the rise and fall of a sea-going boat, Tegen fought a rush of nausea that swept over her. She excused herself and shuffled across to the other side of the cave. When she returned, she made herself as comfortable as the hard sloping floor would allow and slept.

When she awoke, her stomach was churning once more. Her vomit filled the cave with a sour stench. 'I *have* to go outside,' she whispered to Tonn. 'I think I'm going to be sick again!' She started to scramble up the slope. A faint intimation of grey at the top hinted that it might be day.

'Stop! It's dangerous!' Tonn tried to grab her, but she was too nimble for him.

'If I don't see daylight, my soul will go to Tir na nÓg and never return,' she called back. Her feet scuffed and slipped, but she found good handholds and was soon standing upright in the crevice above. Early morning light and song-birds made Tegen want to dance, but her empty stomach had tied itself in painful knots. Her mouth felt terrible, she needed fresh water. Nothing, *nothing* would make her go back into that hole.

She leaned forwards over the rocky crevice-lip and rested her head on her arms. Her eyes hurt after so long in the dark. Above, the sky was grey and heavy with impending rain. The sandstone rocks around her were layered with red, gold and yellow. Below her, a tree-edged escarpment fell away into a steep drop. Beyond that, the whole world was laid out before her: a gold and green patchwork of fields, farms and woods.

But there was no peace. The air was filled with hammering and the sour smell of burning – and, searing across the landscape like a sword blow – was a Roman road.

This is it, something told her, *this is almost the moment you've been dreading.*

No! she screamed inside her head. There must be another way!

There was a touch on her elbow and she realised Tonn was standing quietly by her side. He wrapped his arms around her and nuzzled the back of her neck.

'Let's run away,' she whispered. 'You were right and I was wrong, there *is* nothing I can do, it's too late. Let's go back to Tara. Right *now*. I feel as if I'm dying here. I'm sick of hiding from the Romans. I hate war… I loathe this cave. I don't feel well. I just want to rest, I am so tired.'

Tonn was about to speak, but the sound of the others coming out into the open air made them pull apart.

Moryn came first, pale and wide-eyed. The others followed, ten in all, twelve including Tegen and Tonn. 'This way,' Moryn said, and led the little group under the cover of the trees where they would not be easily seen.

'I think we are safe for the moment.' Moryn glanced nervously over his shoulder. 'The Old Ones say the only soldiers around are overseeing the mining and smelting. They seem to have given up the search for refugees from Ynys Môn.

'The Old Ones are working on the southern slopes. Tomorrow is the full moon of Lughnasadh.'

Moryn looked around at the group. 'We may be the only druids left in the whole of Britain. This may be the last Lughnasadh ever celebrated so we must honour the gods with our very best.'

Tegen's heart sank as she remembered the festival a year before when Goban the smith had been sacrificed as the *Mabon* – a harvest offering whose blood gave life to the Land for another year.

Suddenly she grasped Moryn's meaning. Shaking, she reached out for Tonn's hand. 'But not like *that!*' she whispered urgently.

The tall druid turned to Tegen and looked down at her through narrowed eyes. His expression was as hard as the rock they sat on. 'Things must be as they must be, child. You of all people should know that!'

Fynbar patted Tegen's free hand. 'It is the way. The Land has fed us, we must feed the Land!'

'*No!*' Tegen got to her feet. Her stomach churned. She forced the bile back. 'You aren't going to go out and find some poor, innocent person and slit their throats. The Goddess *wouldn't want it*! It's *wrong*! It achieves *nothing*!'

The old man spread his hands. 'If a farmer does not fertilize the soil, it becomes barren. Maybe the Land has become weak against invasion because we've not honoured the Old Ways as we ought? Is this why the Romans have marched across our world and managed to destroy it? Because we've failed to keep our trust with all the ancient laws and rituals?' He bowed his head, grabbed a handful of dirt and rubbed it into his thin hair. Then, through the dust, Fynbar looked up at Tegen, his eyes red-rimmed and rheumy.

Then Moryn spread his hands towards the endless rolling hills, richly draped in harvest colours. 'Here is the Goddess in her most regal robes. She is crowned and glorious!' He turned to face Tegen. 'You are right, child; we can't just sacrifice some innocent passer by. It would not be seemly. It would not be *sufficient*.'

Tegen stared up at Moryn. At that moment, she disliked him intensely. Who'd appointed him? Who'd given him the right to make these decisions?

She was the Star Dancer, *she* was the one destined to save the Land, *she* was the one for whom the Lady's stars had danced the night she was born. Surely *she* should…

Then the realisation hit her.

Tegen took a deep breath. 'It's me, isn't it? Because I'm the Star Dancer *I'm* the one who must die…? Enid was right, I really *have* become the Mabon.

'This is how I am destined to avert the evil!'

50 * BAKING THE BREAD *

'Sit down!' Tonn urged, jumping up and taking her hand. 'You've gone quite white.'

Tegen's legs gave way as she slipped onto the warm rock.

So, this was it.

She remembered the calm way Goban had died and how he had comforted her, promising he would be born again: like the grain that has to die and be buried in the earth, so it can sprout the following year.

'But it has to be a gift of love,' he'd said. And he was a god.

So, this was her great test. Did she love the people and the Land enough to die for them all? She swallowed hard. 'Has anyone got water?' she asked, her voice cracked.

Merdith passed a leather bottle. The liquid tasted foul, but not as bad as sour bile.

'We aren't *certain* it's you.' Moryn patted her hand awkwardly. 'I will ask the Old Ones to bring us what we need, then we will see how the gods decide.'

Tegen looked around at the group of whey-faced druids. All had their eyes cast down to the ground. 'When?' she croaked.

'Tomorrow,' Fynbar replied. 'Meanwhile, we'd all better go inside and wait, it's too dangerous out here.' He nodded to Tegen. 'You look ill, you need to rest.'

'I *won't* go back in that hole!' she said, getting up. 'I need light and air and trees and wind.' Especially if they are to be my last, she added to herself. And she ran down the slope into the woods below.

Tonn followed, but made no attempt to catch up. He understood her need to be alone. He sat under the whispering birch leaves and sang softly as he waited.

At last, she came back and squatted by his side, angrily ripping leaflets from a fern. After a while, she looked up, her green eyes wide with fear. 'My destiny has caught up with me,' she said. 'I have my duty to perform. This may be the last chance we have to turn aside the evil of the Romans. If I give myself as a sacrifice with love, then maybe all shall be well… Who knows?'

Tonn did not move.

She scrunched the remnants of the fern into a damp ball, threw it as far as she could, then began to tear another one to pieces. Then she stood and hauled him to his feet.

'*Go AWAY!*' she yelled, shoving him hard in the middle of his chest.

But he did not move. 'Do you really want me to?' he asked quietly.

'*Yes.*'

'You're lying.'

'I am not,' she retorted. 'I saw what I saw in your mother's mirror. If you stay, we'll both be dead and it'll be because you followed me. My fate is mine, not yours, get away from me and you'll live. Can't you *understand*?' She threw the limp, leafy remains into his face. 'I love you!'

'Maybe I too have a fate I must fulfil?' he answered.

'*Ignore it! Go* back to Ériu!' She stamped, turned her back and stormed off through the trees.

Tonn watched her carefully from a distance all day. As night fell and the full Lughnasadh moon rose, he followed her to the crevice they called home.

In the entrance, Moryn was working at a small saddle-quern. On the ground was a cloth catching rough barley flour. Backwards and forwards he moved the stone, muttering incantations under his breath as he worked.

One by one, the others took turns. Each ground several handfuls of grain into the growing pile of flour. The chant grew louder as they worked.

Grind the barley, bake the bread,
One to die, that we be fed.
From every stalk one seed must fall
To the earth to feed us all.

At last Moryn beckoned to Tegen. 'Your turn,' he said quietly. 'Then Tonn. As druids we are all privileged with position and power, but we also have to stand in the place of sacrifice if we're to truly serve.'

Tegen took the stone, warm from so many hands and scooped golden grain from the basket by her knee. '*Grind the barley, bake the bread…*' she began. But she was not listening to her own words. Round and round in her head went the thought that dying couldn't be that terrible. It would only hurt for a short while, then would come the journey to Tir na nÓg and rebirth.

She stopped grinding and sat back on her heels. A couple of tiny lamps flickered a weak light across her work. In her mind a new thought began to grow.

This is all wrong! Goban died and he will come back. He's a god. That's what gods *do*. They bring the seasons round each year.

Our job is to keep living and to make the world as good a place as we can. *That* is the strongest way to fight evil! Human sacrifice, however willing, achieves nothing – except there's one less good person alive to bring blessings to those in pain.

Tegen stared at the half-ground barley in the saddle-quern and touched its pale softness. This isn't about death, she realised. It's about *life*. We should be saving grain for planting, not grinding the very last of it.

Whether the Romans are driven out or not, there'll always be work for us druids to do. There'll be battle wounds and bitterness that will need healing, old stories and songs that need to be sung to strengthen our spirits and to teach children wisdom. And we'll need to make up new tales to honour these terrible days.

Her thoughts spun on: the tribes of Britain need to be united – her old friend Owein was right about that. *Every* healer, lawyer and teacher would be needed, maybe all working in secret for many years. Then they must train new druids…

Her mind ached with the enormity of the task.

But I have pledged myself to be the Lughnasadh sacrifice, she reminded herself. I cannot revoke my word. Then she prayed to the Goddess: please change Moryn's mind, show him evil must be fought with life. Not death…

Now she understood that staying alive to heal Britain in the years to come would be more difficult than dying.

Her thoughts were broken by Tonn gently nudging her aside. He took the stone, then began to grind his portion of the meal.

When he finished, one of the other women lifted the flour-filled cloth and shook the contents into a bowl. Ale was added to moisten and leaven the dough, and, one by one, all present took turns to stir the mix, chanting as they worked, '*Grind the barley, bake the bread…*'

Then the mixture was covered with the cloth and left on a boulder at the end of the crevice. 'We'll bake it in the morning,' said Moryn. 'Get some sleep everyone.'

Tegen lay with her head on Tonn's chest, listening to his steady heart beat. She had to wake him and persuade him to run, but he would not go without her – and *her* duty was to stay and argue against Moryn. When Tegen slept, she fought dreams of the demon that pursued her. She must not allow it to feed on her dread. She *would* destroy it one day, however long it took.

At last, the movement of the others roused her. She smelled wood smoke drifting down from above. Once more she felt sick and rushed outside to vomit. Her stomach rumbled. She was so ill and so hungry, all at once!

One by one the druids crawled into the daylight and seated themselves around a fire in the cave entrance. It burned with blood-red flames that crackled spitefully. A griddle sat black and impassive over the heat. On it a lump of lard swayed and sizzled as it melted.

Chanting under his breath, Moryn laid the bannock dough reverently into the pan and cooked their ceremonial breakfast. With utmost care, he flipped the bread, then slid a red-hot knife back between the dough and the pan.

The smell was good, but the moment was filled with dread.

Tegen's palms were cold and sweaty. Fear choked her. Was I right last night? she wondered. Is living more difficult and important than dying? She forced herself to take another breath. Whether I live or die, what happens this morning was what I was born for.

Run away, now, before the bread is baked, screamed a voice inside her head. Was it the Goddess that spoke? Or her own fear? What should she do? She almost rose to her feet, then she glanced at Tonn who was kneeling next to her, his eyes half closed as he chanted a prayer.

Get up! Take Tonn! Go, now!

Her legs would not obey her. I *can't*! she screamed back silently. He won't leave without me and this is my destiny!

Tegen counted the heartbeats until the bannock became a rich golden brown on both sides. Her ears pounded with noise.

At last, Moryn drew the griddle from the flame. 'Let it cool as we have no platters,' he said, and nodded to Meredith to pass a jar of mead around. 'Now drink,' he smiled, 'for today is Lughnasadh, the celebration of harvest. We thank Lugh for his golden spears of sunlight that bring life to the corn and honey to the hive. Mother Bera brings her son, the child whom she also calls the Mabon, and offers him to the people that they may eat for another year.'

'Today, one of us must become the Mabon. A druid is the highest possible sacrifice, and there are so few of us left the gods will honour the generosity of our gift and bless all of Britain in return.' He touched the bannock to see if it was cool enough to handle.

'Where this knife was, there will be a burn mark. I will break the bread and put it in a basket. We will all take a piece. Whoever has the burned portion is the one the gods have asked us to give so the Land may be healed. He or she will be our Mabon, turning aside the evil that is destroying everything we hold dear.'

He looked around, his grey eyes examining every face. 'Do you all understand?'

One by one, the company nodded.

'Are you all willing to take part?'

Tegen held her breath. She had been at such a ceremony before. She had said 'yes,' that time. She had been the chosen one, but chosen to live, not to die. On that day the druids of the Winter Seas had proclaimed her as the Star Dancer.

Now, she knew she must scream 'NO!' and drag Tonn away, to live, to fight for what was right, to take the path of life. She started to get up, tugging at his hand…

But Tonn was speaking in his lovely, lilting voice.

'Yes.'

It was too late.

51 * THE BURNED PIECE *

Moryn tore the bread and piled the basket, taking care to rearrange the slices several times, so even he did not know where the burned piece lay.

Then he stood, raised the broken bannock to the sky and called out to the gods. 'Lady mother, Bera, guide us. Tyrannis, Lord of Thunder, speak to us. Esus, who hung on a tree to spill blood on the soil, accept our blood, and Bran, giver of rebirth, catch the soul who is coming to you.'

And Dagda, the Good God, put a stop to this, Tegen found herself praying as tears streamed down her face.

The bread-basket was put in the centre of the circle and one by one all present reached out and took their portion.

Tegen closed her eyes and allowed her fingers to grasp a piece. The smell took her back to her childhood when she had baked for Griff, and he had laughed as he smeared butter and honey on the bread, stuffing it into his mouth before it fell apart. Perhaps she would see Griff again before the day was out. She almost smiled.

Best to get this over with quickly. Tegen took a breath and opened her eyes.

The piece in her hands was golden brown and evenly cooked. She turned it over.

The other side was the same.

One by one, the druids proffered their pieces, showing each

other what they had taken. Faces that had been white and drawn were now flushed with life once more. A few words were spoken...

But then there was silence. The basket was empty. Who had taken the burned piece?

Tegen reached out to hold Tonn's hand, to reassure him, but from his loose fingers fell a piece of bread with a black sear mark straight across it.

Tegen snatched up his bannock. 'It's mine!' she said, 'I took the wrong piece. I knew I had! I didn't listen to the Goddess! I wasn't doing it right... I...'

She felt faint as she panted for air.

Tonn looked at her, a thin smile on his ashen face. Carefully he uncurled her fingers and retrieved his portion. Then before she could stop him, he solemnly ate it.

'It is mine, beloved, see?'

'But it's *not*!' she screamed, '*I* am the Star Dancer, *I* am the one who was born to die. It's me, can't you *see*? Can't *any* of you *see*?'

Tonn wrapped his arms around her as she burst into tears and howled like a child. As the sobs subsided, he spoke quietly. 'Listen, when you were in my land you learned that we have many words that are different from yours, is that not right?'

Tegen nodded and sniffed, wiping her nose on the sleeve of her dress.

'My name, Tonn, means "Strong Wave," in our old speech. You were the Wave Hunter, you came to my island to hunt for the Wave that would bring healing to the Land. I am he. Let me go. Don't fight my destiny, for Bran will put me into his cauldron and bring me to birth again.'

Tegen shook her head in disbelief. Now she understood her visions of his death on the mountain and in the mirror. 'I *can't* have hunted *you*, my love!'

'But you've also given me life,' Tonn went on quietly. 'You were handfasted with me. I have known joy because of you. And there is something else…' He laid his hand on her belly. 'You have been very sick these last few mornings. It is Lughnasadh and as my mother predicted, you are carrying our little girl.'

Wide-eyed, Tegen slid her hand under Tonn's. There was nothing to feel, but she knew he was right. Somewhere deep down, she had guessed she was pregnant, but had been too frightened to admit it to herself. In the spring there would be another life to treasure.

'But, this sacrifice – it's all wrong! It shouldn't be like this at all! We need every druid alive to restore hope. The sacrifice that is needed is about working for *life*, not death. You see…'

He closed her mouth with his cool fingers. 'That will be your task, my sweet. You must teach our child the same.'

Jumping to her feet, Tegen stamped petulantly. 'You don't *understand!*'

Moryn came and stood quietly behind Tonn. He touched him on the shoulder. 'Time to go.'

Tegen rounded on him. 'I've hunted your Wave that will heal the Land – but now you've got to set him free to do his work. Kill him, and we'll all be ruined. Britain will fall.'

Moryn shook his head. 'The old ways are always right. You of all people should understand.'

'No. You're wrong!' Tegen moaned through blanched lips.

Tonn reached into his pouch and pulled out a smooth, rounded piece of quartz. It was white, but streaked with blood red. 'Keep this to remember me. It's my druid's egg. You might need it one day. No one can gainsay you while you hold it.'

He folded her shaking fingers around the stone, then he fell silent as the other druids gathered around him. 'I'm ready,' he said quietly, and turned away.

But Tegen would not release him. Holding the egg high, she yelled, 'Then listen to me now!'

Tonn shook his head. 'Not this time. I must go.'

'Then I'm coming too,' she said. 'I'll not let you go to the gates of Tir na nÓg alone!'

Through his tears, Tonn smiled and kissed her.

Together they scrambled down the far slopes of the great rock, then weaving their way through the woodlands, watching every moment for military patrols.

As the sun rose, the day warmed, the sky was blue and the birds sang in the leafy canopy. On level ground, they turned west and made their way along a farm track. Tegen and Tonn gripped each other's sweaty palms with white knuckles. Where the lane turned, a wooden pole barred the path. At either end stood two armed soldiers.

One said something in Latin, then nodded to a terrified little man who sat on a stool at the edge of the road. 'Th… th… they want to kn… know who you are and wh… where you're going,' he stammered.

'Migrant harvesters,' Moryn called out. 'We're reapers and threshers. We travel from farm to farm at this time of year.'

The man translated, then the soldier spoke again. The little man glanced nervously at the druids. 'Th… they s… say you've got no s… sickles w… with you, how can you be har… harvesters?'

A tall druid just in front of Tonn drew a very sharp looking knife from a sheath at his waist. 'This is all we need,' he said quietly.

The first soldier nodded and the others pulled the pole aside.

At the sight of the blade, Tonn dug his fingernails deeper into Tegen's palm. She winced, but remained silent.

'Oh Lady, why didn't you make them stop us?' Tegen longed to turn back and yell, 'We're the druids! You're looking for us!' But that would get them all killed.

On and on they walked. The ditches at the roadside were filled with late spikes of meadowsweet, filling the air with the soft scent of summer. Tegen's soul writhed. Will Tonn's death preserve this? Won't the flowers still bloom anyway? Today is Lughnasadh, the fields are almost harvested, we should be dancing and drinking tonight.

Tegen knew she had to try one last time to make Tonn flee. She would take his place. She pulled her man's arm so he leaned towards her, then she whispered, 'I came to Ériu, I found the Wave I was seeking, but how will your *death* heal anything? How can I live knowing I brought you to this?'

'Because this is my one chance to be of use to Ériu… and to Britain.' Tonn stood still for a moment and glanced up at the clear blue sky. 'Today, for the first time in my life, I feel as if my life matters.'

Tegen was furious. She grabbed Tonn by his shirt, screeching as she shook him. 'Your destiny is to live with me, to be a father to your child and to be a leader to your people.'

Moryn grabbed Tegen's shoulders and pulled her back. His eyes were narrow and his mouth was tight under his grey moustache. 'You and your man both agreed to take part in the choosing. This is the way things have always been done. There is no turning aside now. Stop these hysterics or I'll send you back!'

Tegen flushed and fought her welling nausea. They walked on in silence.

Tonn reached for her hand. 'Talk to me. Tell me a story.'

Tegen realised how precious it was to walk with her man for this last time. 'I will tell you the tale of Bran's cauldron. Bran had one sister, Brangwen, whom he loved,' she began, and told of the girl's disastrous marriage – the mischief of one brother, and the healing from the other. The arguments, the fighting, and Bran with his gift of the cauldron of rebirth.

As the story unfolded, the lovers picked their way between tangled hazels and oaks. When the ground became marshy and difficult, Tonn scooped Tegen up and carried her in his arms. All the time, she continued her tale. When she came to the part when Bran's head was cut off but he was still cheerful company for his fellows, Tegen swallowed hard. She had meant to hearten her beloved with hope of rebirth, but now she regretted her choice of tale. Something merry and light would have been better.

But it was too late now, for the party had stopped in a small clearing with an almost empty pool in the middle. There they sat.

Tegen finished her story. 'But Bran said, "And on that day, you must take my head and bury it under the white stronghold on the white hill by the Tamesis to protect Britain forever".'

'Thank you,' Tonn whispered. 'That was a good story, and one I believe to be true.' Then he kissed her. 'Now, I want you to do something for me. I want you to dance, like you did on our wedding day, then go away. It would break my heart to think you had to witness… *this*.'

'But… I need to be with you to the end.'

Once more, Tonn put his fingers on her lips and shook his head. His eyes were spilling tears. 'Please, for my sake. And for our baby's, I've heard it said that the unborn can hear what their mothers hear. I don't want our child's first memory to be this.'

Tegen nodded. She slid her arms around Tonn's neck and held him. And he held her.

Then, very slowly and gently, Tonn let her go.

She stood, then closed her eyes and tried to think of Bran's cauldron of re-birth. Slowly she moved, but her steps were angry. She would have vengeance on Moryn and the others for Tonn's murder!

In her fury, she stumbled over a root. She opened her eyes and glimpsed Tonn kneeling by the muddy hollow, watching her. The other druids stood behind him.

'If you hate,' Tonn said quietly, 'my death will have been in vain.'

Tears burned Tegen's eyes. 'But what you're doing won't bring healing. It's not what the Goddess meant for the Strong Wave. I'm certain of it.'

*

Hovering close by, the demon gloated. This was a glorious moment. *But you will learn to hate.* It told Tegen. *You must have vengeance. You cannot let them get away with this…*

*

'Tonn's right.' Tegen whispered back. 'Vengeance will only make things worse.'

Softening her steps, Tegen breathed more slowly and calmly, then danced as if their child was already in her arms and she was showing the little one to her father.

Tonn mimed a kiss, then looked up at Moryn and nodded. The others closed in a circle around him.

Then Tegen turned and ran.

She did not need to go far. Bright sunshine poured between the hazel trees and muddled the world into a confusion of dancing green and deep shadows.

Tegen sat on a rotting trunk and held her breath.

There was a heavy thud. An involuntary cry. Another thud.

Then silence.

And nothing happened.

53 * SPIRITS OF WATER *

The day went on being sunny, the birds kept singing, the leaves went on being green. It was just the same. What difference had it all made?

After a while, Tegen stood and found her way back to the clearing. It was empty. Perhaps they'd changed their minds and had gone away? Why hadn't Tonn come to find her, to tell her everything was all right?

A fly buzzed near her feet. Tegen glanced down. In the pool lay Tonn, half curled, like a sleeping child. His face was turned away and his hair slicked with dark red gore that glistened in the dappled sunlight.

The air smelled of salt-sweet blood.

Tegen vomited, then falling to her knees, she screamed and screamed until there was no more breath in her body. Trembling uncontrollably, she hugged his still-warm back, but could not bring herself to look at his dear, kind, bloodied face.

At last she stood, panting. 'They didn't even bother to bury you!'

Furious at the insult, she scratched the ground for loamy twigs and leaves, piling them over her man's body. She worked until her own fingernails broke, but she was getting nowhere, just a sprinkling of sticks and rotting leaves soaking up the dark blood.

Taking her knife, Tegen hacked at her own hair until she was almost bald, then strand by strand, she covered Tonn in a pall of silky black.

But it was still not enough.

Her legs and arms shook and threatened to give way.

*

Hovering close, the exultant demon wound tendrils of hatred and fear into Tegen's mind.

She did not fight him. Her passionate words about hope and healing crumbled as the fiend slithered into her heart and embraced her grief.

It had won. Finally, it had entered its new host, the one who would now be so angry she would wed her magic to its foul will. Murder and chaos would reign for thousands of years, tearing not only this damp, feeble country to shreds but infecting all the peoples on this miserable rock they called the world.

The demon roared with triumph.

*

Tegen felt that triumph swell as an idea grew in her mind. Standing tall, she breathed calmly and raised her hands to the sky.

Then she began to dance.

Throwing her head back, Tegen cried an ululation until her throat was sore, then twirling and stamping with anger, she called on Tyrannis.

And Tyrannis came.

The god's voice rolled across the summer-blue skies.

Tegen danced until heavy clouds gathered into sky-mountains and day became night. Lightning flashed. Thunder cracked.

Cheered on by the demon, Tegen swung her arms and the trees

bowed in rhythm with her. The sky was her drum. The earth shook with the dread of it.

And the *rain* began.

At the back of her mind Tegen could hear Gronw's voice scolding, 'This is a very unkind spell child, think of the harvest, think of the people!'

'I don't *care!*' she shouted. 'The people *deserve* this! Look what's been done to a good man in their name! *Druids* have destroyed the Land, not me!'

And the rain kept coming. The heavy splashes smoothed the thick blood into reddish smears that dribbled down Tonn's back and arms. Tegen knew it would take a very long time before her beloved was submerged. He deserved better.

Wiping angry tears aside, Tegen stretched her hands over her man's body and commanded the spirits of Water to rise.

Laughing, the demon obliged.

From the bottom of the muddy pond, a spring began to bubble. Tegen clawed at the air. 'Water, *come!*' she demanded. Slowly, the hollow filled, lifting leaves and twigs, trickling between the tree roots and floating Tonn's shirt.

Gritting her teeth, Tegen's dance raged on until she splashed ankle deep in the spreading pool. Her own hair mingled with her beloved's as they drifted together in the dark, bloodied water.

Then Tonn's arm floated free, his hand reaching towards her.

*

All afternoon, Tegen staggered mad, blind and exhausted through the torrential rain.

At last, Meredith found her and threw a cloak around her shoulders. 'Come dear. There's a friendly farm nearby,' she said gently, steering her away from the woods, up a slight slope and into a roundhouse. She saw nothing and heard nothing, but was vaguely aware of Meredith washing and dressing her like a child.

The new clothes smelled of lavender and thyme.

In the morning, Tegen awoke. The well-built house had kept off the rain, but puddles outside the door reflected the light. On the hearth, bread was cooking and there was a bowl of whortleberries near her face.

The smells were overwhelming. She retched.

'When is the child due?' asked Meredith, squatting beside her.

'After the spring equinox,' Tegen mumbled back.

Several voices muttered with great concern. 'No, no, dear, you can't have a baby, not now!'

'Give her a tisane of pennyroyal,' insisted Fynbar. 'That'll get rid of it.'

Tegen was livid. 'How *dare* you?' she roared, sitting up. 'You've killed my man, now you want to murder my child even before it's born!'

Leaping across the room, she lashed out at everyone she could reach. A man jumped forward and held her arms tightly so she could not move. 'Calm down,' he breathed gently in her ear.

Tegen lifted her right foot and stamped down hard, then kicked at his ankle, making him yell, and let go.

Moryn grabbed Tegen's wrist, twisted it and pulled her down to the ground. 'Stop. Listen.' he demanded. 'Let me explain why you must not carry this baby.'

'Why *should* I listen? I hate you! I wish you'd died on Mona!' Tegen spat in his eye. 'You have killed all hope. Tonn was a healer. His skills were a thousand times more use than his death could ever be. How can his smashed skull and spilled blood help an orphaned child – or appease a god come to that?'

The man she had kicked crouched next to her. 'My woman was killed by the Romans,' he said quietly. 'They didn't let her die straight away, they made me watch…'

Tegen stared at him. He was not old, but his face was haggard with loss and grief. He held her gaze. 'One way or another, this hate and killing have to stop.'

Tegen writhed. 'So murdering my Tonn brings your wife back?' she sneered.

'None of us understands,' Meredith tried to explain. 'But it is the way of the Mabon. Every druid knows that he or she may be called upon to play that part one day.'

'The old ways are lies and stories! By the way, the Romans pray too – did you know that? The gods don't raise a finger to help either side. If they exist, they are sitting around cynically playing a board game with us. They don't care who wins.'

Tegen wrenched herself free and paced the room. 'I am going back to Ériu to have my child and to teach her to work for goodness and kindness.'

'Sit down,' Fynbar pulled up a stool and Tegen flopped onto it, head in hands. 'Have something to eat.' He offered her bread and wine. Despite her fury, Tegen was famished. She snatched the food and ate.

Moryn crouched next to her. 'You've heard of queen Boudica of the Iceni? You know she's leading a revolt?'

'Of course, Sabrina is there too. So what?'

'Boudica's druid died of a fever. She needs someone at her side, someone who can be an advisor to kings and queens.'

With a shudder of horror, Tegen realised what they were saying and she leaped to her feet. '*No!*' she screamed, 'I've told you – I'm going back to Tara to have my baby.'

'Won't you go for my wife's sake?' asked the man.

'Or for my son?' asked another.

'My daughter.'

'My mother.'

'Your man…?'

Or vengeance? The demon whispered.

Tegen looked from face to face. It made no sense – none of it did. Is that what old Gwen meant? She wondered. That *I* must make sense out of chaos? I can't. That's too much to ask.

She tried to shut her eyes to close out the pain… But all she could see was Tonn's body lying in a pool of blood and water, with one small, green leaf floating in his hair.

Tegen ran outside. The air was clear, but smelled of rain. The landscape glistened with well-watered earth-jewels of gold and green and blue. How *dare* the day be beautiful when Tonn was so cruelly dead? She threw back her head and keened.

Exhausted, she leaned against a tree and calmed herself. It was then she noticed her new dress was long and plain white. A druid's robe.

'Why did you put me in this?' she asked Meredith and Moryn who had followed her outside.

Moryn solemnly offered her a tiny golden knife like the one she had used in Tara. 'You cannot escape your destiny. You're a full druid now. Your calling is clear to us all, and in the end, it comes down the strength of your magic, not how many stories and poems you can recite by rote, or how well you understand obscure laws.'

Tegen glared at the knife. Without Tonn her future was blank and empty, even with his child to care for. 'I don't want it,' she said, pushing the blade aside. 'I don't want to be a druid either.'

A snuffling noise and a heavy tread behind her, made her turn. There stood a white horse, about fifteen hands with a long, well-combed mane flowing in the summer breeze.

'Epona?' Tegen gasped, stroking the mare's neck. 'How did you get here?'

Moryn stood behind her. 'Goban sent her – to help you in your quest to make sense of everything that is happening. It's your destiny to try and change the future so all shall be well. You must go.' He offered the ceremonial knife once more.

'*Please*?' chorused several voices at once. The other druids gathered around her, their weary eyes begging.

Meredith took Tegen's hand. 'Tell me, what do you want most of all in the world, my dear?'

Tegen shook her head. 'I have told you. I want to have my baby somewhere safe.'

'Then free Britain. Tara may be safe now, but for how long? What will happen when the Romans get there?'

For a few moments, Tegen fought back the vision of the Roman giant on Ériu's shores. She shivered then narrowed her eyes. 'If you all vow to protect my child with your spells and blessings, I will work with Boudica, but only until the little one is due.'

Moryn and the others exchanged nervous glances. 'That doesn't leave long…'

'What if you miscarry on the way?'

'It's too dangerous…'

'That is my final word,' Tegen said firmly. 'This child also has a destiny – to unite the tribes of Ériu.'

Epona shifted a couple of steps and whinnied. She was keen to be away. Tegen clenched the reins in her fist and looked from face to face.

Oh, Tara! She sobbed inside her head, if only I could walk on your green slopes again, but it won't be home without Tonn.

Then in her mind she heard Sabrina's promise as she had dreamed it on Cadair Idris: 'We will fight together.' If Sabrina were at her side, maybe she could face one more battle, if it really would make the world safe… *Things don't always happen the way we think they should, Star Dancer,* Gronw had said.

Tegen leaned her hot head against Epona's neck and breathed in her musty scent. The horse nickered and rubbed Tegen's hair with her velvet nose.

If Epona is here, then Goban is with me too, Tegen decided. I can't just ride away from these people's grief, or even my own. Unless I at least *try*, I'll never live at peace – not in Tara or anywhere.

Faces and voices flooded Tegen's mind: Gilda, Griff, Huval, Owein, Sabrina… Tonn. She had to at least try to make sense of their lives – and deaths.

But one thing's for certain, she told herself, despite all of dear Huval's wisdom, he was wrong about the Romans not being the enemy: they are the essence of the evil I was born to avert.

Tegen drew herself tall and took the knife. 'Very well,' she said aloud. 'I am the Star Dancer. That is who I am, although I have never had a choice. I will go. But I will advise the queen as *I* see fit. If there is a Goddess, she will have to prove herself true.'

Moryn sighed and bowed his head. 'Then keep the child, but hurry – evil is rising and spreading like yeast.'

Tegen climbed into Epona's saddle. Fynbar handed her bag bulging with provisions.

All around her, the weary faces broke into smiles.

Fynbar raised his hands towards Tegen. 'May the Lady smooth your path. Go east by southeast for half a moon, keeping the great marshes on your left. When the land becomes dry again, turn due east. Someone there will guide you to Boudica's camp.' Then the old man stepped back to let Tegen pass.

Meredith pushed a soft piece of cloth into Tegen's hand. 'Your hair makes you look a little conspicuous at the moment, dear. Use this to keep your head covered like the Roman women.'

'Thank you,' Tegen said, then out of habit, she raised her hand and wove a blessing in the air.

As she did, the scarf she had been given fluttered free.

It was of leaf green silk, just like the one she'd loved as a child.

Joy and grief caught in Tegen's throat as she wrapped it around her head and wiped away fresh tears.

Then with a gentle nudge to Epona's flanks, she turned eastwards, and a grey morning mist swirled behind her.

*

The demon was not worried that its prey had rejected its insinuations once more. For a brief moment she had let it in.

The death of her mate had crushed her spirit.

All it needed now was to introduce her to another woman who grieved with equal fury.

*

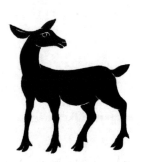

*

WHO'S WHO IN TEGEN'S WORLD

*

Druids in Book 1 – Star Dancer

Tegen: A British girl born during a meteorite shower that seemed to come from Cassiopeia in about 43AD, just as the Romans were invading. These 'Dancing Stars' are seen as a sign that a great druid has been born who can save the British people.

Witton: The elderly chief druid of the Winter Seas, (the Somerset Levels). He recognizes Tegen's powers and begins to mentor her.

Huval: A kindly druid who takes over Tegen's mentoring when Witton dies.

Gorgans: An albino who longs to be a warrior but can't bear sunlight. Addicted to power, he becomes a druid. He wants to be the Star Dancer, and sets out to destroy Tegen with Derowen's help.

Druids in Book 2 – Fire Dreamer

Owein: An ovate (second stage druid), a little older than Tegen. He is secretly the son of Cara (Caractacus) the British warlord who almost defeated the Romans. He was raised in Rome by his uncle Admidios, to become a puppet king acceptable to both sides. An accident left him disabled, excluding him from kingship by British law. He is a natural diplomat who can see that if the Romans can't be got rid of, then a humane co-existence must be worked out.

Druids in Book 3 – Wave Hunter

Gronw: the Chief Druid of the people of Bera. He is very wise and he mentors Tegen by teaching her to question everything.

Enid: Gronw's apprentice. At first she is Tegen's friend, but when she has to undergo a grueling winter ritual, she learns to hate.

Witches and 'Wise Ones' in Book 1 – Star Dancer

Derowen: A failed druid, who resorts to black magic to control and destroy. She raises the cave demon, and is killed by it, but even after her death, she still hunts Tegen. In Fire Dreamer, she takes the form of a raven.

Gilda: She gave up her druid training for love, but was cheated by Derowen. She is a 'wise woman', a white witch who uses herbalism and kindly magic. She was Tegen's midwife and always believed in her. Derowen tricked Tegen into killing Gilda.

Griff: He is a 'Gifted One', who has psychic power and wise insights. He is Derowen's secret son whom she abandoned because he had Downs Syndrome. A foundling, he became Tegen's foster brother, and for political reasons, Griff and Tegen are handfasted. They care deeply for each other, and Tegen is devastated when Griff dies in the floods caused by the cave demon.

Witches and Shadow Walkers in Book 2 – Fire Dreamer

Admidios: A minor British king who sided with the Romans very early on. He betrayed his brother Cara, and stole baby Owein as a 'gift' for the Emperor Caligula, hoping to buy favour. When Caligula died, Admidios was ignored by his successor, Claudius. Admidios's lust for power turned him into a 'Shadow Walker,' a black magician in league with the demon. Derowen the Raven is his familiar.

The Demon – all four books

A creature from the Otherworld, the essence of evil, serving only itself. When Derowen's spells open the way between the worlds, the Demon seizes the chance to wreck havoc. He rages through all the books, becoming more powerful and desperate.

Gods and Goddesses in all books -

The Watching Woman: The Celts didn't have a clear pantheon of deities as the Greeks and Romans did. Tegen worships a benevolent earth goddess with many aspects and incarnations. Her star sign we now call Cassiopeia.

Gods and Goddesses in Book 2 – Fire Dreamer

Bera: Another aspect of the Watching Woman, the goddess of cereals and growth, the mother of Goban and Brigid.

Goban: A smith god who gives Tegen an iron ring of protection. He becomes the Samhain sacrifice to bring fruitfulness to the land for the following year. His belief in re-birth is absolute, and his loving determination to ensure that life goes on, moves Tegen deeply.

Gods and Goddesses in Book 3 – Wave Hunter

Brigid: Another form of the Watching Woman, and Goban's sister, with special care for blacksmiths, poets and midwives.

Kings, Queens and Commoners

Princess Sabrina: The only surviving child of Eiser, King of the Catuvellauni tribe. A warrior at heart, Sabrina had no wish to be queen. Impulsive and passionately anti-Roman, she leads her people into a Roman trap and is sold as a gladiatrix (female gladiator). She and Owein were betrothed as a political match, but neither wanted it.

King Eiser: King of the Catuvellauni. He is spearheading the campaign to destroy the Romans, so Admidios and Derowen murder him with black magic. This murder brings Tegen into a new level of magic and precipitates the events of Wave Hunter.

Kieran: A son of a salt-trader and a minor warrior. Brought up by his abusive aunt and a weak mother, he is resentful, wary and bitter. He becomes Admidios' slave in lieu of unpaid taxes. Tegen befriends him and he helps her defeat the Shadow Walker.

Romans – Book 2, Fire Dreamer and Book 3, Wave Hunter

Suetonius Paulinus: He became Governor of Roman Briton in AD 59, and quickly gained a reputation for unnecessary cruelty and savagery. Tegen tricked him and burned him with magical flames in Fire Dreamer, exacerbating his hatred of the British, and of druids in particular.

★

HISTORICAL AND MADE-UP NAMES
USED FOR REAL PLACES

The Winter Seas – the Somerset Levels
The funeral caves – Wookey Hole in Somerset
Sul's Land – Bath
The Hill of the King – Silbury Hill
The Stone Forest – Avebury Stones
The first Wight-Barrow – West Kennet Long Barrow
Bara's stronghold – Barbury Castle, on the Ridgeway
The ruined stronghold – Liddington Castle, on the Ridgeway
The second Wight-Barrow – Wayland's Smithy, Uffington Castle
The White Horse – the White Horse of Uffington on the Ridgeway
Tamesis – the Thames (Tegen and Owein join it at Streatley)
Sinodun – Wittenham Clumps
Dorcic – Dorchester on Thames
Corinium – Cirencester
Bagendun – Bagendon
The Rearing River – the River Severn at Frampton on Severn
Y Fenni – Abergavenny
The House of Bera – Castell y Bere in Gwynedd
Cadair Idris – part of the Snowdonia range in north Wales
Tal y Llyn – a lake at the top of Cadair Idris
Brigid's smithy – the village of Tywyn, Gwynedd
Tara – Tara in Meath, Ireland
Mona/Ynys Môn – Anglesey, Wales
Diva – Chester
The Hill of Gold, Silver and Tin – Alderly Edge

ANCIENT NAMES FOR SEASONS
AND FESTIVALS

*

(Pronunciation varies. Guides can be found on the internet)

Imbolg – Feb 2nd. Now St Brigid's day, previously the first day of spring, a festival of the goddess Brigid, and Tegen's birthday.

Beltane – Early May (usually the 1st). A fire festival to celebrate the coming fertility of the summer. Marriages are often contracted and blossom of the hawthorn or May tree is highly prized.

Lughnasadh – Early August, the beginning of harvest, and dedicated to the god Lugh (strength and sunlight).

Samhain – Oct 31st – Nov 1st. We now call this Hallowe'en / All Saint's Day. It marks the last of the harvest, and is the festival of death, when the spirits of the departed visit the world to make sure they are remembered. Cakes and drinks are left out for the ancestors. It's also the end of the ancient year and diseased and unwanted things are burned to start the New Year clean and fresh – we now have 'bonfires'!

Equinoxes – When the days and nights are of equal length (March 21st and September 21st)

Solstices – Midsummer and midwinter's day (Dec 21st and June 21st)

*

STONE KEEPER:
THE BOOK OF EARTH

Book 4 concludes the Star Dancer quartet.

★

Stone Keeper tells of Tegen's last chance to save Britain
and fulfill her destiny.

Following the ghastly sacrifice of her beloved Tonn, and with a
baby on the way, Tegen has grown to hate the druids and to lose
faith in the Goddess. Yet she has been ordered to stand at the side
of Boudica as her battle druid against the Romans.

The Iceni queen and Tegen neither like nor trust each other,
and the pursuing demon is growing stronger and closer, bringing
horrific battles and reprisals in its wake.

With new and daunting magic, Tegen struggles to master the
demon as Boudica loses control of her troops, and of herself.

In betrayal, blood and disaster, Boudica falls.

The Star Dancer has failed her destiny – or has she?

★

Stone Keeper is due out 2012

★

To read the opening chapter of Stone Keeper, log onto:

www.stardancerbooks.com

* BETH WEBB *

Lives in Somerset, on the edge of Tegen's 'Winter Seas' and is a collector of daydreams and stories. You can find out more about Beth and her books on **www.bethwebb.co.uk**

* TOM RALLS *

Designed the cover and the Celtic animals. He can be contacted through March Hamilton Media.

* MARCH HAMILTON MEDIA *

Is a new publishing company specialising in books for teenagers and adults. **www.marchhamilton.com**

M H M
March Hamilton Media